DEADLY ENEMIES

DEADLY ENEMIES

DEADLY DANGERS ON THE ZAMBEZI RIVER

WILLIAM W. BENNETT

Auctorem House
276 5th Ave, Ste 704-2591
New York, NY 10001
www.auctoremhouse.com
Phone: 1 888-332-7718

Published by Auctorem House: 09/12/2025

ISBN: 978-1-968059-16-3(sc)
ISBN: 978-1-968059-17-0(e)

Library of Congress Control Number: 2025920937

To my children: Jeremy, Jeff, and Serena

Special thanks to my beloved wife, Cathy.

²"I know that You can do all things, and that no purpose of Yours can be thwarted. 'Who is this that hides counsel without knowledge? 'Therefore I have declared that which I did not understand, things too wonderful for me, which I did not know." 'Hear, now, and I will speak;
I will ask You, and You instruct me. '"I have heard of You by the hearing of the ear; but now my eye sees You; therefore I retract, and I repent in dust and ashes.

–Job 42:2-6 NASB

CHAPTER 1

*A*msterdam–Martin Marius Wikffels slammed his phone down hard enough to break it. His face was suffused with anger, redder than his secretary had ever seen it, making the blotches on his skin appear even darker. Wikffels had an egg-shaped head with soft tufts of blonde hair parted in the middle, a ridiculous goatee, and lamb-chop sideburns. He was wearing that day, a golden suit that was most unsuitable to his skin and hair color. He gathered the pieces of the phone angrily and threw them at the wall, causing more damage to both the wall and the phone.

"Wire the funds to Maximiliano and tell him to get moving!" he spat.

Without showing any of her thoughts she turned to her computer and made the transfer of funds. Wikffels had another cell phone out, his third this week, and was calling one of his many contacts. It turned out to be the chairman of the board of Randstad Corporation.

"I'm collecting that favor!" Wikffels said without preamble or pleasantries. "I want a court order to cease and desist on salvage of *Wilhelmina's Song* by *Bring It Up* in the Arctic Ocean," there was a pause followed by an explosive answer to the comment on the other end. "I don't care what it costs! I'll pay it! Do it! Now!" his cell phone snapped shut and followed the phone to the wall, shattering on impact against the brick façade of the inside office wall. He used a most unsavory word, threw himself back in his office chair, and brooded for the rest of the morning, saying nothing. Too enraged to even think rationally he allowed his thoughts to wander, his face remaining suffused with red, his heart rate accelerated.

Madagascar–Massoona Maximiliano was a mercenary soldier with a very bad reputation. He didn't care about his reputation. What he did care about was his mansion and estate on the mountaintop overlooking Mahajanga. He noted the transfer of funds and the order to get moving and made several calls. Doing only a cursory study of weather in Alaska he made a critical error. Unaware that the temperatures in the Artic Circle were sixty or more degrees colder than central and southern Alaska, he ordered cold weather gear for his team, knowing the sizes. Zeke, following the money, noted the order for cold weather gear and wondered if Massoona was really that foolish. Apparently, he was!

Zeke caught the incoming cease order from a court in Amsterdam and immediately forwarded it to Ken Worthington, the company attorney. Within two hours Ken had the cease order squashed. Maritime law was specific when it came to rights of salvage and *Bring It Up* made a legal and binding claim on that ship. Having prepared carefully, every legal channel was checked and rechecked to be sure they missed nothing. That was why it took only two hours to squash the order.

At his computer Zeke connected all the dots. He found the record of the call from Martin Marius Wikffels to the president of the Board of Directors of Randstad Corporation. From there he traced the money transfer to Massoona Maximiliano. It didn't take him long to discover Maximiliano's calls, and what gear he'd ordered for the attack on the ship.

Tete Mozambique–Gilles Ramanantsoa looked over the huge open pit mining operation and studied the trucks of coal leaving in one long convoy of specially designed dump trucks. The huge eighteen-wheelers belched black smoke from diesel exhaust pipes, pushing the flaps open with explosive power, each time a trucker changed gear.

Coal dust was everywhere, and he had been careful to choose a spot where the wind blew the dust away from him. He saw some villages further away but gave them no thought.

Wikffels, his partner in this mining operation, was well on his way to becoming the one and only distributor of type IIb blue diamonds. When he had gathered them all Ramanantsoa would take them away from him. He smiled at the thought of the rage Wikffels would exhibit. With the blue diamonds, and his new acquisition, a titanium laser with the power and capabilities to target and destroy communication satellites, he would become the richest man in the world, because anyone that didn't buy one of his satellite services would have theirs blown out of the sky!

All of those evil thoughts were hidden behind a boyish expressive face that looked quite pleasant. His wide set brown eyes always looked slightly surprised, and the way he lifted his eyebrows wrinkled his forehead, and when he smiled that way, he looked completely harmless. It was only in observing the way those that worked close to him acted that gave anyone any indication that things were different. Body language spoke of fear and caution in every person who knew him even a little. Ramanantsoa was unaware of this. His cell phone beeped.

"Wikffels is going after the gold," It was the voice of Massoona on the other end. Ramanantsoa smiled. Wikffels did not know that Massoona was loyal to Ramanantsoa. There were many things Wikffels didn't know, and Ramanantsoa planned to use them to destroy the angry man.

"Good. Help him," Ramanantsoa replied and clicked the phone off. Both men found a waste canister and disposed of the phones.

CHAPTER 2

Jim put down his Bible with a sigh. He'd been reading through the Bible chronologically once again, fascinated as always, deeply convinced that this book held everything he needed to be a servant of his God, a good husband, father, and leader to his men.   It was the final words of Solomon's book *Ecclesiastes* that caught his attention this time. Solomon had written from the perspective of being the richest and most powerful man in the world in his day, concluding correctly that in comparison to God's riches and glory, might and power, his was simply useless. Yet his concluding words dug at Jim's heart, reaching into his very soul with truth that he knew through empirical evidence was absolutely necessary to life. All through his military career he had seen the truth of those words exhibited time and again.

"The conclusion, when all has been heard, *is*: fear God and keep His commandments, because this *applies* to every person. For God will bring every act to judgment, everything which is hidden, whether it is good or evil." Those were the last two verses of the last chapter. He lifted his Bible and turned back to Numbers 32:23 because he'd underlined it three days before as a reminder to tell his son over and over this truth.

"But if you will not do so, behold, you have sinned against the LORD, and be sure your sin will find you out".

People didn't really talk about sin anymore. In a culture where everyone did that which was right in his or her own eyes sin was a subject that couldn't exist. The old excuse was always there: "If it doesn't hurt anyone else who cares?" That was the real problem, because sin of any kind had far reaching effects on everyone and everything. There was no such thing as a victimless crime, or a victimless sin. Sin was like yeast in bread, it spread through everything and everyone. And it corrupted and destroyed everything it touched.

In his own heart Jim knew there were sins he kept secret, or at least he thought he did. But God knew. He had seen in his career the truth of those words that sin would find you out! Most of the people he dealt with ultimately believed that they were above the laws of God and man, and that they could do whatever they wished. But the punishment for sin was always the same, and God had a way of revealing it, and punishing it.

Jim bowed his head and prayed quietly. Sitting next to him on the bed, holding Robert John in her arms while he suckled at her breast, Cecilia listened to her husband's prayer with a deep sense of appreciation. Her husband was good man, a moral man, and a true follower of Jesus. He didn't put on airs or insist that others believe as he believed, but he *followed* Christ diligently. His prayers always told her that. She listened to his words.

"Your holiness, Father, is unquestionable. Only You can see into my heart, and all the hidden things there are before You. I so easily forget that I can hide nothing from You. When I came to You, I had nothing to offer other than acceptance of Your offered salvation. As I sit here before You, I have nothing to offer other than the willingness to let You use me as You see fit. Keep me from thinking I can hide things from anybody. Help me be honest, especially with Cecilia and RJ. I want to face today clean before You. So, search my heart. If there's anything there You need to talk to me about, let me know. I know I screw up all the time, so give me the courage to admit that to myself and to You, and to ask Your forgiveness. Don't You ever tire of forgiving us? I would! Anyway, I love You. Thanks for reminding me that You see it all, even the things I think I'm hiding from everyone. Amen."

Cecilia smiled, her eyes shiny with unshed tears of joy and Jim looked at her for a moment and then leaned over and kissed her. RJ giggled and Jim turned his lips to RJ's tummy and blew a raspberry, listening to the squeal of joy from his son.

"Ouch! Sandpaper face on my tender breast, dear!" Cecilia scolded, laughing at him. Jim rubbed his face against her again and she playfully hit the back of his head. "Stop that! Now go and shave!"

Grinning at her he got out of bed, and she looked at his rock-hard body with appreciation. He had a lot of scars on that torso, visible under the hair, and she appreciated again just how physically powerful her husband was as she watched his muscles ripple under the flesh. As he walked into the bathroom, she studied him, aware that he stalked like a tiger, every motion smooth and filled with menace. She smiled, knowing there was no menace for her.

Shivering as he got out of the two-minute shower, the last thirty seconds under cold water, Jim grabbed a towel and toweled himself dry. Padding back into the cabin naked he caught his wife looking at him and he grinned. His clothing was ready, he'd laid it all out the night before as he always did, and he dressed quickly, going from being chilly to hot almost immediately. Necessary clothing for this part of the world insured the sudden change.

Thermal underwear, the old-fashioned union suit, made of a special material designed to whisk any moisture from the body away was the first item to go on. His work uniform was next, followed by his insulated waterproof boots made of sealskin because that held up best in the icy Arctic waters. Uniforms were tan, made of tough material, with double-knee pants and elbow pads and showed only the company logo on the sleeve, no rank insignia.

Sea Venture lay at anchor over the wreck of *Wilhelmina's Song,* the steamer full of gold they'd found the year before. On his desk the paperwork giving his company salvage rights was signed and stamped by the appropriate authorities and ready to be filed. There had been the expected cease and desist order that had to be squashed in court, but it had been routine to do so.

"I've been thinking about that ship," he said, the thoughts of the papers reminding him of his earlier reading. Tying the laces of his boots he looked up at his wife. "I just read that your sins will find you out. I have a feeling that the ugliness of past sins is about to be brought to light, and that certain people will not be happy about that, putting us in danger once again. Since I watched you give birth to our son, I no longer worry about you in battle. You're a lot tougher than anyone I know!" he grinned at her.

RJ picked that moment to burp, spitting up on his mother. She grimaced and held him away from her. "You little monster!" Cecilia grinned at her son who was smiling at her. "I agree," looking over at Jim as she wiped away the mess from her shoulder and her sons face, she smiled again, her dimples tugging at his heart as they always did.

"Judging from the reaction of Randstad Corporation, and how quickly it came, I'd say there's something down there nobody wants brought to light, and not just the gold!" she covered her breast and sighed. "You're just about done nursing, little one!" she said, kissing RJ. "When it comes to my breasts, he's as bad as you!" Cecilia added, laughing when her husband blushed a deep crimson. Nature had blessed her with an astonishing figure her husband had always appreciated.

RJ was almost asleep, and she changed him, put him in the crib, and moved into the shower. As Jim left the stateroom she sighed with pleasure. RJ would sleep through most of breakfast, giving her an hour of peace to enjoy with her husband and family. Her shower went longer but Jim was heading up to the bow with Andrea, Wade, and John and would not tease her about it as he often did. Today they would not greet the dawn, but instead marvel at the constant light of this season in the Arctic. Even in the half-light of the early morning he could see the northern lights waving in the distance, a constant reminder that he lived in a remarkable world.

Jim Shepherd met every morning with his brother John, their best friend Wade Adams, and Jim and John's uncle, Andrea Orvieto.

Although Wade was not technically family, he considered Jim and John his brothers, family, and happily accepted Andrea's inclusion of him as "nephew" whenever he addressed the three. The three boys grew up together, worked together on the Shepherd boats, and now lived together on *Sea Venture*, leading a crew of great people.

"How's JAS?" Jim inquired, the last to arrive. He certainly wasn't hot anymore. Huddling in his arctic gear he sipped at his iced tea mug and looked around the ship. Carefully, each time he sipped from his insulated mug, he let the moisture from his tongue melt the ice that formed where he sipped each time. The arctic was a challenge.

"Hungry this morning. How about RJ?" John asked his brother with a smile.

"The same. At least he'll sleep for an hour so Cecilia can have breakfast," Jim replied. "And how's the newlywed in our midst?" Jim asked Wade, turning to look up at his tall friend.

"Hungry!" Wade replied, rubbing his stomach.

Wade and Dr. Angela Rysdale were now married, and now Mr. and Mrs. Adams. Angela, barely five feet tall, looked tiny next to her six-foot five-inch husband. Wade had incredibly wide shoulders and a powerful physique, dwarfing her even more. Truth be told, his biceps were actually bigger around than her thighs! But she was able to wrap him around her little finger, a fact that earned him a lot of teasing. Wade had never done well with teasing, but he was thawing and accepting it, even enjoying some of it.

Jim didn't miss the opening. "Oh! Were you busy last night working up an appetite?" Wade turned crimson and his three friends laughed at him. "Jeeze, Wade! You're making my tea warm!" Jim added as he sipped from his insulated mug. The four men laughed together at the quip and sipped from their mugs, huddling in their heavy clothing against the cold, holding the cups in heavy Gripper Gloves. Andrea, John, and Wade drank coffee and wisps of heat could be seen escaping from the narrow holes in the covers of their mugs.

"Today has an odd feel about it," Andrea said softly, looking around.

"Yes. Things will happen today to set in motion many other things, some of which will not be pleasant," Jim replied. He felt it too.

They always greeted the morning this way, and often came away with a very accurate feeling for what the day might offer.

"How are you getting along with the plans to raise the ship?" Jim asked Wade.

"I'll have a completed plan for you later this morning," he replied. Jim nodded, expecting nothing less. Wade was a genius when it came to this sort of thing. Finally, they sighed and headed together down to the dining room where a sumptuous breakfast was already on the buffet tables. Breakfast in this cold environment included scrambled eggs, bacon, sausage, oatmeal, fresh fruit, fried fish, toast, muffins, bagels, and everything to accompany those dishes. In the cold the men burned calories faster than ever.

Cecilia joined Jim in the line, and without thinking about it he leaned down and kissed her. She smiled at him and the two of them continued down the line taking the items they wanted. Cecilia had RJ in a carrier that cuddled him close to her breasts and he was sound asleep. For good measure Jim kissed him too. The little tike did not move, his sleep deep and peaceful.

Cecilia ate oatmeal with blueberries, a bagel with cream cheese, a cup of coffee and drank some orange juice. Jim heaped his plate with eggs, fish, bacon, sausage, an English muffin toasted and buttered, and several cartons of milk. Since most of his day would be spent out on the ice, he was stocking up on much-needed calories to keep him going.

They sat, as they always did at breakfast, with their family. Alistair and Gwyneth, John and Penelope, Wade and Angela and Andrea filled their table. Dr. Alistair Gregg married their mother Gwyneth just two years earlier, and the two were obviously enjoying each other's company. Jim, John, and Wade were glad to see Gwyneth so happy. Her years of widowhood were ended in a joyous relationship, and all three knew that Jim and John's father would approve of Alistair.

Breakfast on board *Sea Venture* was at 05:00 hours, continuing until 07:00. Jim was not surprised to see everyone in the dining room promptly at 05:00. His crew was dedicated and disciplined. From 07:00 to 07:45 a Bible study would take place in the library, taught by Abe and Sturdy, and Jim knew that everyone on the crew would be present for that event. They all loved those morning studies and prayer.

RJ woke up and Jim picked him up and held him while Cecilia finished her breakfast. He saw that John was holding JAS and the two men smiled at one another across the table. Their sons would grow up together, almost as brothers, and that felt right to both fathers. Alistair turned to Jim and held out his arms.

"May I?" he asked. Jim smiled and passed his son to his stepfather with pleasure. Gwyneth took JAS and the two infant boys looked at one another and smiled. They played together regularly and being less than a full two days apart in age Jim knew the two boys would grow up appreciating the company of each other, especially on the ship. Most of their lives would be lived on the oceans of the world.

At Bible study the boys sat in a playpen off to one side and played with toys, tasting everything, happy to be where they were. Jim liked the fact that the library could seat ninety people easily. Abe was teaching, his voice easily penetrating the far reaches of the room. After about fifteen minutes of interesting lecture, he began to ask questions, and for the next fifteen minutes animated conversations went on. The last fifteen minutes was spent in prayer, with two or three people leading.

Sturdy closed in prayer, and Jim remembered that it was the quiet giant he was praying with who taught him about prayer. None of the team prayed rote prayers or made inane requests. Each knew that God was always watching over them and constantly in attendance, so no one asked for Him to be with them or watch over them. Instead, they thanked Him for never being out of His sight. Jim noted that no one asked for protection. Rather the prayers were focused on living as we ought to live, and being witnesses to the world, and trusting, no matter what happened.

Abe was a nickname for Charles Lincoln, the head cook on the ship, and Sturdy, the nickname for his second in command, Tom

Sturdevant. Charles and Tom were body builders, their bodies sculpted and huge with muscle. Lincoln was an inch over the six-foot mark, and Sturdy was an inch shy of seven feet tall. Both men seemed as wide as they were tall, impossibly huge, and like many strong men, they were quite gentle and quiet.

When eight bells sounded everyone was already heading about the day's business. The kitchen crew headed back down to finish cleaning up and get ready for lunch. Goody, or Zeke Good, head mechanic, led the mechanical crew down into the bowels of the ship to check that everything was operating properly before heading out to the work on the ice. Sparks, or Bill Kline, one of the Kline twins and lead electrician on the ship led the electricians to the electrical shop to look at the job list for the day and get started. Other crewmembers went about cleaning the ship from stem to stern, while the administrators went to their offices and the science crew to the labs.

In his office Jim sat down and signed the reports from the previous day, reading them carefully, and making notes on his iPad. Ives came into the office and sat down across from his desk. Jim looked up from his reading the last report, looked down and signed it, and put it aside, focusing on his administrative aid.

Tom Ives was his administrative secretary, a competent man, the same height as Jim but slimmer in build. Marvin Finn, or Sharky as the crew nicknamed him, had been difficult, but with the addition of Ives had mellowed a great deal and become a better team player. Jim liked Ives for many reasons, the latter most of all.

"The courts squashed Randstad's cease salvage request. According to Maritime Law our company has full rights to the salvage and all contents of the ship. The judges of the court were adamant on that point," Ives waited, following his report. He knew that Jim would always think before he spoke, unlike his brother John, who often spoke before he was finished thinking. Jim nodded, tapped his fingers on the salvage claim file, and then looked at Ives.

"Do we know who was behind the challenge?" he asked, going right to the heart of the matter. "Randstad Corporation never had any holdings or interest in the mine or the ship. At least, there is no record of that anywhere in our discovery process."

"A man with the unlikely moniker of Martin Marius Wikffels. According to our research *Wilhelmina's Song* was owned and operated by a maritime freight company in Holland controlled by Wilhelmina Wikffels. Zeke will brief you on that bit of information later this morning. He would like you to stop by the CIC on your way to visit the bridge," Ives got up, took the salvage file, and left to file it.

Jim signed the rest of the reports, finished his notes, and brought the pile of signed reports to Ives desk before heading out of the office. John was leaving at the same time, and Jim noted that Finn no longer stood when a superior officer was present. He looked down at Ives who raised an eyebrow and shook his head slightly. They shared a smile. Finn was a stickler for protocol but unbending nicely.

"Good morning, Lieutenant," Jim addressed Finn, getting a salute, which he returned.

Walking together up toward the bridge the two men rustled strangely in the steel corridors, their arctic gear thicker than their usual clothing. Used to making almost no noise at all when they walked both men noticed it at the same time. It was unusual enough to comment upon, and it was John who spoke.

"Hope we don't have to sneak up on anybody in this stuff!" he said.

"With the wind out there, as long as we're downwind we're okay!" Jim commented. Both men shivered at the thought of going out in the icy cold arctic air, and John nodded, remembering the raging roar of the polar winds.

In the Command Intelligence Center, or CIC, Jim leaned down and kissed his wife. Zeke Kline, always a joker, raised his face and puckered his lips. When Jim didn't move away from Cecilia he sighed and threw up his arms.

"That's right! Leave me hanging! I won't forget that!" he laughed.

"What do you have for us?" Jim asked.

"Our friend Wikffels transferred a huge amount of money to a bank in Madagascar. The account belongs to one Giles Ramanantsoa, son of Major General Gabriel Ramanantsoa. Remember him?" Zeke looked up at Jim and John and got a nod from both. "Giles has transferred seventy-five percent of that money to one Massoona Maximiliano! I've been following the money. Maximiliano has hired 20 mercenaries, and outfitted them with cold-weather gear, but not arctic gear. He seems to think that it's summer up here! That mistake could very well cost him the lives of his men."

"Wikffels went all the way to Madagascar? Why? Does he have holdings anywhere near there?" Jim asked after a few moments of thought.

"I'm so glad you asked those questions, because once again I get to demonstrate just how valuable I am to this outfit! My importance to this venture is noteworthy! You will see that I have anticipated each question you might raise. How am I doing toward that promotion?" Zeke said grandiosely.

"Yes! Of course, PO3 Kline," John joked with a grin at his friend. Zeke raised his eyebrows.

"That's Lieutenant Kline, sir!" he replied sarcastically.

"Not if you drag this out any further!" John replied with a straight face. His eyes were dancing with laughter though.

"Just dazzle us with your INTEL," Jim said with a grin at his brother.

"You guys are no fair!" Zeke said, sticking out his lower lip. "However! As I was saying!" Quickly he went back to his report.

"Wikffels is a communications industry tycoon but he's also a member of the World Foundation of Diamond Bourses (SFDB) and a sightholder. It appears that he is actively attempting to purchase every type IIb blue diamond available, as well as blue diamond chips, to control a portion of the communications industry that uses blue diamonds as conductors. From what I've seen of his dealings he's well on his way. Within a year he may own the major portion, if not all, of the blue diamonds in the world.

"He's also in bed with Ramanantsoa in a coal mine on the Zambezi near Tete in Mozambique. I've sent the information to Sir Edward Marsh. Do you suppose he goes by "M" at MI6?" Zeke laughed at his own joke. Sir Edward Marsh was Director of Operations at MI6, and a member of *Bring It Up's* founding group. "I also sent a copy to Ira in Israel, and one to Duck Ashley." Ira was Ira Lehman, Director of Operations (DO) of Israel's Mossad, and Duck Ashley, was Admiral Donald Ashley, DO NCIS in Washington, DC.

"Send a copy to General March too, and don't forget to include our retired hounds in Greece," Jim instructed after a moment of consideration. General Marsh was head of Australia's SAS and the retired hounds in Greece included Admiral L. Charles Runion, retired, Admiral William Dawes, former director of NCIS in Chicago, and Sir Angus Bidwell, Rear-Admiral of Her Majesty's Navy, retired. Jim saw them in his mind as he gave the order and continued. "Cold-weather gear, but not arctic gear?" he went to a question he had from an earlier part of their conversation. "That demonstrates a carelessness in planning and ignorance."

"Yes! Apparently, Maximiliano thinks the weather in Alaska is the same as that in the Arctic region and he only needs cold-weather gear," Zeke replied, getting serious. "Their sleeping bags are good for ten below, but on the ice, they'll freeze to death!" Zeke shook his head. "Those mercs are in for a bad time!"

"And you think Maximiliano and his mercenaries are coming here. Why?" Jim asked quickly.

"Because Wikffels was behind Randstad's attempt to stop us from salvaging *Wilhelmina's Song*." Zeke replied. "He's on the board and it was his insistence that led to the legal attempt. Wilhelmina Wikffels, who was quite a dragon in her own right, is his great-great grandmother, if you can imagine someone like that finding a husband.

"Maximiliano twice took over treasure ships on the Indian Ocean with a force of twenty mercenaries, so he obviously thinks twenty is the magic number. Also, he purchased twenty-one tickets to fly from Antananarivo International Airport all the way to Fairbanks, Alaska. In Fairbanks he's rented some trucks and in Prudhoe Bay he's rented two fishing trawlers." Zeke leaned back in his chair, put his hands behind his head, and his feet on his computer desk.

"The sins of the fathers are visited on the third and fourth generation." Jim said quietly.

"What?" John asked, catching that cryptic comment.

"I was reading about our sins being brought into the light this morning. Wikffels grandmother's influence is evident in the family!" Jim replied.

"Let's get cracking on Wikffels and this Ramanantsoa character. Keep us in the loop, and well done!" Jim said, clapping Zeke on the shoulder.

"Uncle Zeke is watching!" Zeke chanted his mantra.

"Watch the money," John replied. "It's too bad that past sins don't stay in the past, and they just compound with present and future sins," he added, shaking his head.

"Oh! I plan to tell JAS all about your past sins!" Jim laughed, clapping John on the shoulder.

"I'm sure John has already told him everything!" Penelope laughed, looking over her divider at her husband. "Was he really that bad in school?" She asked.

"You have no idea!" Jim and Wade said in chorus. Wade had entered behind them at that moment. All three laughed.

"I recall having two partners in crime most of the time," John said loftily.

"The three Musketeers!" Cecilia laughed.

"They would look dashing in tights and waving long swords about, wouldn't they?" Penelope burst out laughing at the picture.

"Tight tights?" Wade asked in a high voice.

"I'm sorry, men, I can't wear tight tights," John said, shaking his head as though saddened by the thought. "The women would never recover," he added.

"It's cold up here, darling. No one will notice anything!" Penelope had tears in her eyes she laughed so hard, and Cecilia had the grace to blush deeply even while she roared with laughter.

CHAPTER 3

"**I**f I could pull you away from comparing your, uh, manhood, I've got a plan for our salvage job," Wade said, his own face deep red. Shaking his head Jim patted him on the shoulder and motioned that they should leave the CIC.

"Let's go down to the computer lab and see how brilliant you are!" Jim said. "I heard there was a biologist down there who needed a kiss," he added, and chuckled when Wade looked at him, missed his step, and hit his head on the hatch.

In the computer lab Wade did not kiss Angela, his new bride, but complained that Jim made him hit his head on the hatch. She kissed his head and glared at Jim. Jim shrugged his shoulders and made a motion to show that Wade was too tall, and it wasn't his fault. Everyone laughed.

"We can get this ship to the surface in about nine-hour's-time," Wade claimed, switching on the smart board and firing up his laptop. In seconds they were seeing the plan drawn out on the computer. "See these holes here and here?" Wade pointed with a laser pointer. "We can seal those with the submersible equipment and weld a plate on the outside of this big breach here," again, he pointed with the laser pointer.

"Once we get those sealed, we can use every air bag and pump enough air in the hull of the ship to lift her, using the winches up here to bring her up to the surface. If we cut channels in the ice here and here, we can literally tow that thing out of the water and onto the ice. That will give us time to see what's inside, while making final repairs so we can tow her back to Barrow shipyards. They bought the contract for the scrap," he looked up to be sure Jim and John followed him.

"How will we get it off the bottom if it's stuck in silt?" John asked.

"We'll rock it out," Wade said confidently.

"Rock it out?" Jim narrowed his eyes and looked at his friend.

"We set directional charges on tripods on each side that push the boat in the opposite direction," Wade explained.

"They call those big ones, ships," John corrected, grinning at his friend. "A focused blast underwater would certainly move the ship, but will it damage it?" Everyone turned to look at Wade. After a moment of thought Wade answered.

"Not if we aim them in the right place. If we do this right, we should be able to rock it back and forth two or three times each direction and break it free," Wade stood up, nearly hitting his head on the pipes just half an inch from his scalp.

He took them to another spot in the lab and showed them a model of the arched braces he would use to lift the ship to the surface. The model was carefully constructed and was indeed an exact tiny replica of what he was planning to build. Explaining each section carefully he finished and looked at his two best friends.

"Let's get everyone started!" Jim said with enthusiasm.

Surprisingly, *Sea Venture* was devoid of ice, thanks to Dr. Putnam's nanobots. Putnam, who the men called Dr. Dundee, was a biologist on the science team. There were none of his nanobots on the gangplank, and it was covered with about two inches of ice formed overnight. John planted his feet and slid down the first part of the ramp, catching the chain railing, turned, and slid down the rest of the way as if surfing. With a grin Jim did the same, but instead of staying on his feet as John did, and falling face first in the snow, he sat down on the final few feet of the ramp and stood up as his feet hit the snow.

"Show off!" John said, grinning at his brother. He was still brushing snow from his clothing.

They made their way along the channel behind the ship and joined the machinists and deckhands erecting an arched bridge of steel that would help raise *Wilhelmina's Song*. It was Wade's design and Jim saw immediately that it was indeed a brilliant plan. Using the cranes and a series of block and tackle sites they would raise the ship, keeping it level, and then literally tow it up onto the ice with *Sea Venture*. Once on the ice the ship could be repaired enough to be towed to shore where it would be taken over by the company who bought the steel.

While the hull was repaired a team could unload the gold and any other treasures from the ship. Jim was confident they would find some in excellent condition, because the colder the water, the less deterioration occurred. Zeke Good handed Jim a four-foot-long pipe wrench and had him attaching couplings to eight-inch pipe that would be used for bracing. When they were finished the entire structure would be torn down so that parts of all of it could be used for other projects. Jim was proud that his crew wasted nothing.

Working steadily until lunch attaching couplings to pipes, Jim handed them off to the welders, who attached them in place. No one complained about the pain from the cold. Jim's eyes hurt, painfully, from the extreme cold, even covered by goggles. His lips needed constant doses of chapstick to keep them from cracking painfully. Even his teeth hurt from the cold! In fact, if he was honest, just about everything hurt from the extreme temperatures.

Handing off the last length of pipe he watched the welders for a moment, perched high up on the rig, welding the braces in place. Wade wanted to make sure that the weight of the ship would not crack the ice anywhere, so he spread the load with the braces. Although he had never formally studied engineering on a college campus, Wade had a natural aptitude for it, and made up for his lack of education through voraciously reading everything he could on the subject, taking on-line courses, and devouring every bit of information he could find.

At present his idea on paper was taking shape and Jim looked at it with the experience of five years of salvage work on the ocean and nodded with appreciation. According to Zeke's computer simulation of the job confidence was high, and Jim understood why. He made a mental note to praise Wade for his brilliant idea. People began climbing down to the ice, carefully making their way to avoid injury, and Jim stood in line to turn in his pipe wrench.

Earlier, men with sledgehammers cleared the ice from the gangplank, but climbing up to the ship was still a precarious effort. Shoes slick with frozen snow didn't give the best purchase on metal. At the bottom of the gangplank FM solved that problem as he sat on a 5-gallon can with an acetylene torch, warming the bottom of everyone's boots.

FM, short for Frank Miller, was a former Navy Seal, and a former Marine, like Jim. On the ship he was a Master Chief Petty Officer (MCPO), serving on the military team, and as a deck machinist. Frank was one of the men who could bring the house down with laughter at just the right moment. He joked about melting soles and giving everyone a hotfoot as he cleared the snow from each shoe.

Jim was grateful for the service and said so, then made his way up the ramp onto the ship without mishap. In the locker room men were removing their Arctic gear and hanging it in the lockers, or on a line to dry. The room felt hot after being in the icy cold, but Jim knew that was just his body getting used to the temperature change, and nothing more. He listened to the small talk around him, knowing that it would give him a sense of the mood of his crew. Light bantering among the men meant that the crew was in a good place psychologically and emotionally. Complaints and sharp responses meant that things weren't going well. His crew once again proved their worthiness as they joked and laughed, despite frozen lips, eyelids, and fingers.

Cowboy and Gearhead appeared and began to check the men to make sure no one had the beginnings of frostbite. They were better known as Dr. Will Penny, and Dr. Leo Axlerod. Because of his name it was inevitable that the men would nickname Dr. Penny cowboy, and he dressed the part, arriving today in jeans and a western style shirt. Although approaching his fifty-seventh birthday he was still in great physical condition, ran every day, and kept in shape. Jim knew he had a gem in the good doctor.

Leo, the newest acquisition to the crew, was the physician the company hired to take the place of Dr. Wozniac who finally retired with his wife Millie. Leo was a trim six-feet three-inches tall and weighed 185-pounds. At Harvard medical school he'd played basketball and was on the swim and dive team. With his dark brown hair and pale skin, he looked like a young physician, and not at all like a Gearhead. It wasn't just his name that led the men to nickname him Gearhead. An avid fan of the BBC hit television show Top Gear he recently purchased a 2016 BMW Z-3 and talked knowledgably about the car and other BMW models he appreciated. Like many of the men on the ship he loved exotic sports cars and powerful engines.

At thirty years of age, he was already at the top of his field, and, in his case, the medical field lost great physician to *Bring It Up*. He brought with him his lovely wife René, two years younger, and an outstanding nurse. The men nicknamed her R&R, the acronym for rest and relaxation. Jim suspected it had to do with the first initial of her name and the letters RN on her pin.

She followed the two doctors, taking notes, smiling at the men in the way nurses had of putting people at ease. Her pockets bulged with chapstick, which she handed out to those who were running low. His doctors took care of the smallest details of medical care. Both doctors insisted on treating the lips constantly in the cold and the men appreciated it. Jim was pleased that he had such a caring medical team on board.

Wade and John came over, and when Will Penny arrived in front of Wade, he looked at his lips and shook his head. "When did you run out of chapstick?" he asked.

"About half an hour before we came in," Wade admitted.

"Well, this looks bad!" Doc Penny said, keeping his features calm. "No kissing that pretty little bride of yours tonight, young man!" he added. Wade, thinking he was serious, looked crestfallen and everyone burst out laughing. Wade didn't always react well to being the butt of a joke, but today he was in a fine mood and broke into a red-faced grin. Cowboy smiled at him and patted his shoulder in a friendly way. Jim appreciated the moment of humor from his medical team. They often surprised the crew with unexpected hilarity. René handed several tubes of chapstick to a red-faced Wade.

Soon everyone was cleared and passed into the corridors of the ship that would take them down into one of the two rooms that would hold everyone on the crew. The library and the dining room were the only rooms large enough to hold all 80 crewmembers. Getting to those areas in this ship did not require going outside, for which everyone was thankful.

There had been the usual negative reactions to a library that size on a ship, but Jim had insisted with the shipyard, and the library even had wooden floors, carpets, and ladders on rails to reach the higher shelves. It looked like a real college library, and did, in fact, rival the premier college libraries in the world. It should! His library crew had purchased books from four colleges closing their doors.

The dining room was set for lunch, which meant no tablecloths. Placemats, and plastic plates and glasses were used. For dinner every night the tables were covered with white, black, and gold tablecloths, runners, and napkins, all fine linen, and each place was set with a Corelle Ware Cherry Blossom set of plates, bowls, and fancy silverware.

Beef stew was the fare for the day, with rolls, honey, jam, butter, hot tea, hot chocolate, and coffee, plus the usual cold drinks the men liked. Judging from the silence during the first twenty minutes of lunch, everyone was hungry, and the food was excellent. No one was surprised that the men working outside ate as if they'd had nothing for days.

Jim found the beef stew thick and hearty, with tender slices of real roast beef in a dark thick sauce with potatoes, onions, sugar-snap peas, water crests, broccoli, and carrots. He would gladly have polished off a third bowl, but discipline won the day. A second roll was allowed with a sweet cactus, honey, and peach jam made by

Frenchie earlier that year. Waiting until Frenchie came to his table Jim made sure to thank him for the excellent jam.

Frenchie was the nickname given to Petty Officer Second Class (PO2) Frank Lafayette of the kitchen crew. Although one of the cooks on board the ship, he was an avid martial artist, and kept his body in excellent shape. With his sandy hair and rugged good looks he was popular, often spending his free time in the science labs helping and learning everything possible about marine biology.

After lunch Jim went down to his office to take care of the necessary paperwork and business of being Captain of this vessel. John would be overseeing the crews outside with Wade. Beneath his feet the rumble of the huge hydraulic engines could be felt as the ship prepared to reverse for a hundred yards, and plough through the ice again, keeping it broken and open for passage. For a moment he longed to run up to the bridge and take the wheel, but knew he had work to do, so he sighed and entered his spacious office. Ives, as usual, had everything neatly organized so that he was able to leaf through his work quickly.

Ives joined him in the office a moment later and the two went over the reports that needed signing and filing, ordering supplies, and other details that every Captain had to deal with. When he was a young boy Jim believed that all a sea Captain did was drive the boat and order the crew about. Once he got on his father's boat and learned the ropes, he discovered there was much more to it, and though he hated some of the tedious jobs, he loved the life as a whole.

His phone rang in the middle of the afternoon, and he picked it up. Zeke was on the other end.

"Maximiliano and his thugs are due to arrive in Fairbanks later tonight. I imagine in an hour or so after arrival, a group of trucks will leave the airport headed for Prudhoe Bay and the two fishing boats," Zeke always had a smile in his voice, as though the world was full of jokes and fun. Jim blew through his nose.

"Let's get the team together in the conference room tomorrow night at 21:00 hours. Get me the INTEL we need for this one so we can make a plan. I want to know everything we can about this character who thinks he can play pirate in the Arctic Ocean! I don't want that force anywhere near my wife and son!"

Zeke hung up the phone without answering, which would have infuriated Finn, had he known. Zeke had served with Jim long enough to know that Jim believed they were equals, and though he had a higher rank, he never used that rank to his advantage. That was one thing about working for Jim that Zeke loved. He'd served long enough in the Navy to hate officers who thought rank equaled privilege.

Looking across the room at Cecilia Zeke caught her eye. "Your husband has become very protective of you since you've added a son to the mix!" he said with a broad smile. "My guess is that just because this clown Maximiliano targeted this boat, Jim is taking it very personally, and plans to make a statement no one will miss!"

Cecilia smiled at him. "*Sine poena nulla lex!*" she said. "Without punishment there is no law!" she translated. "Benefits of a classical education. I think Cicero said that, and he was right. My Jim will punish him appropriately for this foolishness!"

"Ooh! Bloodshed!" Penelope said, standing up with expectation on her face. The two women shared a knowing grin of expectation. Penelope had once served Sir Edward Marsh, DO MI6 as his top agent. Married to John, she was now on permanent loan to *Bring It Up* as a representative of Her Majesty's Secret Service.

Jim had changed, and on one hand she loved the difference, but on the other worried that he might strike back too brutally at anyone that threatened his wife and son. She decided she would talk to him later. Her husband had, heretofore, never waded in blood, even when given every opportunity and reason to do so. She didn't want him starting now!

"You're always ready to go into battle Pippi!" Zeke grinned, picking up the phone. Pippi was the nickname the men had tagged on Penelope when she first joined the crew. He made a call down to the kitchen and asked for Windy. Some things had changed recently, and Windy was one of those things. He was now a certified pilot, checked out and a natural at flying the PBY Catalina Flying Boat they'd purchased. He and Loony were the pilots for the PBY now, because Jim wanted all his soldiers with boots on the ground for the next part of their mission. Wrench and Inchworm were checked out for the AH-1W Super Cobra helicopter the company owned, and with Ives were flying the CH53-D Sea Stallion. Zeke needed Windy to fly him to Prudhoe Bay tomorrow so he could get eyes on Maximiliano and his thugs, as he called the mercenaries the man hired.

After talking to Windy he called Loony and early the next morning the PBY glided across the ice that had been cleared for a runway and took off with Windy as pilot, and Loony as co-pilot. Zeke, FM and Smitty were along for the ride and to help with the gathering of intelligence. Loony had the most difficult assignment. Having arranged beforehand to land outside of town where the plane would not be spotted, they arrived an hour before the trucks.

Loony was Petty Officer First Class (P01) Leo Johnson, a tall black man who served on the ship as an electrician. Windy was Wendall March, a former lawyer who lost everything due to alcohol abuse, recovered through the work of Abe and Sturdy, and was now a respected and loved member of the crew. He was also a certified pilot, as was Loony. Smitty was Lieutenant Junior Grade John Smith, the ship's Navigation Officer.

Windy took out his fishing pole, license, and some bait, and set up on the pier close to the two boats that had been rented by the mercs. Hidden on the side of his hat, beneath a patch sewn onto the leather, he had a small but very clear camera that Zeke could use to get shots of every face coming along the pier. The lens was hidden in the center of an "o" in a word. The tag read: "Fish the World".

Loony, acting the part of an electrician out of work, had actually bribed a boat owner to let him upgrade his equipment. The owner, smiling because he was actually making money, left the boat as requested and headed into town for some early dinner. Nor did he notice Loony engaging the captains of the fishing boats and looking at their electronics as a quick check, no charge. He planted tracking devices where they wouldn't be noticed. Nor did the owner notice the other three men taking positions on rooftops or balconies for reconnaissance.

For the next hour the pier was quiet and normal. Then the trucks arrived. Zeke shook his head. Twenty-one black men, obviously from a foreign country, dressed in military uniforms with red berets on their heads were so out of place that everyone in town would know about them before the end of the day. Maximiliano apparently didn't care about being subtle.

Massoona was a big man, nearly six-feet three-inches tall but getting heavy around the middle. He was still a formidable enemy and strutted with that arrogance that comes from taking lives and liking it. His skin was the darkest of all the men he led and they, Zeke was quick to note, were in great physical shape. Civilians who saw them up close stepped away from them, instinctively aware that they were dangerous men.

On top of one of the winter warehouses where boats were stored, FM used his field glasses to study the men and the crates they carried to the fishing boats. One of them was opened on the boat and radios were distributed to all the men. Beneath the radios FM could see the weapons.

"AK-47's, brand spanking new! Were they on the manifest from the airport?" FM spoke into his COMLINK.

"According to the manifest the crates contain sensitive barometric testing devices. Customs officials usually check at least one crate, or if paid well, none. There may be a crate of testing equipment. If there is it will remain with the trucks for future use," Smitty replied, "I'll check," he sauntered past the trucks.

"One crate in the last truck," he reported. He continued walking around until he could duck into an alley and return to his vantage point.

"Windy, were they talking?" Zeke asked.

"Yes. It sounded like Shona," he replied.

"That's right! You've been studying the languages of Mozambique and Zimbabwe!" Zeke commended. "Could you decipher any of it?"

"I was able to pick out the words 'night raid,' and 'tonight,'" Windy chuckled. "Apparently they don't know about the daylight up here!"

"We'll make a super spy out of you yet, Windy!" FM chortled.

"I'll stick to the kitchen. I have six really nice salmon in my net already!" Windy replied.

"I noticed that Massoona checked to see if you had fish," Zeke chuckled.

"I'm getting the once over at the moment," Loony reported calmly as he worked at the control center of the yacht.

Loony had stopped work to stare at the men as they got on the boat, as anyone would do, and gone back to work. They were now watching him carefully. He was dressed in insulated coveralls and his tools lay about him, obvious to any looking on. What he was doing was complicated, something only a trained electrician could do. He looked over at the men staring at him.

"You want something, bud?" he asked arrogantly.

"What are you doing?" Massoona demanded.

"What does it look like?" Loony berated, shaking his head. "I'm updating this boat's electronics. These old contacts rust out on the ocean, so they need to be replaced from time to time. This is a new style of male and female connector that won't rust." Loony went back to work as if the encounter meant nothing.

Massoona watched him for a while longer, decided he was what he said he was, and turned away. It never occurred to him that Loony could be both an electrician and someone gathering INTEL. Loony finished the job, put everything back in place, and carefully cleaned his workspace, leaving the yacht spotless. He could have described every one of Massoona's men, what weapons they carried in the open, and other things which many would consider useless or superfluous details. To a trained operative nothing was useless. When he was done, he gathered his tools, picked up his box, and sticking his rag in his back pocket to complete the picture stepped to the dock away from the fishing boats.

He stopped by, looked at Windy's Salmon, and then sauntered to the crew-cab pick-up truck they'd borrowed for the day, and drove around the corner and out of sight to wait for the others. Smitty joined him first, followed by FM and Zeke who came together, and finally Windy with his tackle box, pole, and Salmon.

Soon they were airborne in the PBY flying back to the ship. Windy had to land with a crosswind but managed it smoothly, setting the plane down on the ice with only one little bump. He taxied carefully to the spot where the winch would lift the plane from the ice to the hold, where it would be protected from the ice and snow. From a short distance an ice storm was building, and the men knew that Massoona's men were going to be in trouble when it hit.

CHAPTER 4

As the men climbed the ramp to the ship, they saw that lifting *Wilhelmina's Song* was already in progress. All three of the winches on board *Sea Venture* were straining against the tremendous weight, and the structures on the ice groaned but stood strong. It was too cold to stand out and watch so the men hurried into the ship to change and get back to work.

Jim, back outside with John and Wade, watched while the cables slowly drew the ship toward the surface. *Sea Bullet* was watching the progress from below and constant updates were coming over the COMLINK. Those were new too. Gone were the cumbersome black headpieces with an ear link and voice link on the throat. In its place was a lightweight earpiece that was virtually invisible, and a small patch on the neck, also coated to match the skin color of the wearer and virtually invisible. Conversations were much clearer than before, and the men liked them.

"She's coming up level now, no more movement from side to side. Whatever was moving around in there has stabilized," that was the voice of Driver in *Sea Bullet*. "Let's increase the lift speed a little at a time to see what happens." Driver was Jack Boswell, a former Navy Seal, one of two submersible pilots on the ship and a member of the military team.

Jim missed the diesel revving of the engines when they picked up speed. With the hydraulic system the cranes were almost silent. What did change was the sound of the cable passing through the block and tackle winches they'd set up.

"Roger on speed increase. Everything is going well down here. Take her up another notch," Sparks voice sounded in Jim's ear.

Again, the winches whirred faster as the cable drew the ship from it's watery grave. Wade moved over to one of the braces on his structure and put his heavily gloved hand on it, nodding as if satisfied. He returned to watch the cables.

"Twenty fathoms!" Sparks sounded. "Eighteen, sixteen, fourteen, twelve." When he said twelve the outline of the ship beneath the surface could be seen. "Ten, eight, six, four, two, all stop!" Sparks sounded.

The cables slowed and stopped, and in the silence, they looked at the superstructure of the steamer. Everything above the deck that could be was crushed and Jim knew what that meant. An ice storm had hit the ship, covering it in ice, and crushing things as the ice expanded. A group of men now moved out in rigid raiders to attach the bollard pull to the bow of the ship. Moving slowly, to avoid freezing water washing over the sides of the raiders, they took their places where they could attach the pull.

Once this was completed, they traveled around the winches, to a place behind the sunken ship, through the channels that had been cut and back to their ship where they were winched up to the deck and quickly cleaned and stowed their boats. Jim looked at Wade and shook his hand.

"I'm going up to the bridge. This was a great plan!" he commended his friend.

John stayed below with Wade and Jim made his way quickly up the slippery ramp to the deck of the ship. He stopped in the locker room to remove his arctic gear and hang what was damp up to dry, and what was dry in his locker. This completed he made his way through the corridors up to the bridge.

"Captain on the bridge," Dorf said, when Jim appeared. Jim

knew he was letting the people in the submersible know he was there. They'd waited for him, for which he was grateful. Dorf was short for Lieutenant Commander Waldorf Bernard, the tallest of the soldiers at six feet nine inches, a powerful man and graceful. Jim grinned at him as he made the announcement.

"Roger that, bridge," Driver drawled. "Winches, are you ready to coordinate?"

"Ready!" Three voices said in unison. Jim recognized them as Goody, Hammer and Wrench. Hammer was PO1 Sam Hammer, another electrician, and Wrench was Mike Romentowski, a deck machinist and mechanic.

This was the tricky part of the maneuver. As *Sea Venture* moved forward slowly the winches had to let out cable to allow *Wilhelmina's Song* to follow, and once she was started up on the ice the winches would be released and reattached to the rear of the ship, one at a time, to make sure it stayed near the surface.

Dorf was at the wheel, because he was the best they had when it came to towing anything. He had a natural affinity for the job, a feel, a touch that set him apart. He eased the throttles forward and slowly *Wilhelmina's Song* inched forward, her bow hitting the ice ramp that had been cut, and with horrendous screeching moved up the ramp for a total of twelve feet before forward motion stopped. Now the men sprang into motion unhooking the cables, threading them through the block and tackle, and hooking them back up at the rear of the ship.

This required men in the water, and at those temperatures the men in the water were using the NEWT suits rather than dry suits, or thermal wetsuits that would give them only a limited time in the icy grip of the ocean. NEWT suits were slower, but also stronger. Still, the job took a full hour to complete. Finally, however, strain was taken up on the cranes and the back end of the ship came up to water level.

Behind the ship the NEWT suits were winched out of the water using one of Wade's arched towers, and then pulled to the ice where the men could be released. A Hilleberg Salvo 3-person tent had been erected and heated so the men could move from the suits into relative warmth.

Once again *Sea Venture* began to inch forward, Dorf easing the throttles forward slowly until they were moving at a steady two knots. Behind them the screeching of the hull against the ice filled the air. Even with the trench dug and the snow cleared the sound was horrendous. Jim noticed that the hull was not crumpling as it slid over the harsh surface outside. Wade had predicted it would not.

Finally, the entire ship was out of the water and on the ice, and still Dorf inched forward until the all-stop was called from the ground. Wade made the final call. Water poured from burst seams that would have to be welded before the boat was put back in the water. Even then some of them would leak, but they would have pumps on board keeping up with the seepage.

Wade had considered the leakage and had trenches dug on either side of the ship to siphon the water back into the sea. Dorf finally powered down, reversing a little to slacken the lines so they could be removed. As he brought the ship to a full stop, he looked at Jim.

"That ship is way heavier than it should be," he said softly. "The manifest said she was carrying 30-tons of gold bars."

"We'll know tomorrow," Jim said, looking back at the ancient steamer sitting on the ice. "I suspect we'll know everything tomorrow," he added.

At dinner that evening, held late because of bringing the ship up onto the ice, Jim stood just after the prayer and the room grew silent when he raised his hands. He looked around the room making sure everyone was present before he spoke.

"I want to commend the crew for a job well done!" he announced. "Give yourselves a round of applause!" There was a crescendo of clapping that faded away when he raised his hand again. "Let's see if we can get Angela to give Wade a congratulatory kiss while we applaud his contribution to getting the ship up on the ice!" Jim grinned at his blushing friend. Angela, not at all shy, crawled into his lap and kissed him soundly while the catcalls and applause went on.

"We made a plan, and we made the plan work! That's teamwork

at its best, and you are second to none!" Jim proposed, and applause broke out again. When it faded, he looked around, then pumped his fist in the air and said loudly, *"nulli secundum!"*

Nulli secundum roared from the lips of the crew as they pumped their fists into the air. It was Latin for 'second to none' and something new added to their vocabulary. Coming from the Omega Force teams it spread through the crew quickly. Jim smiled as he sat down.

After dinner the crew gathered in the library for the most part, dividing up to play board games, put together puzzles, or sit and read. RJ and JAS played in a playpen near where their mothers sat working on a puzzle and talking together.

Jim sat in a comfortable leather reading chair near the playpen reading a book when he wasn't watching the boys at play. John sat at the puzzle table with the girls but was also reading. Both men were reading about the gold rush in Alaska and subsequent events, hoping to have a better understanding of what they found in the ship the following day. It was one of Jim's favorite hobbies and he enjoyed the moments of reading with his family nearby.

At 20:00 hours Cecilia and Penelope got up, kissed their husbands, and took the babies up to bed. Jim and John remained, reading, until it was time to go to the conference room for the scheduled meeting at 21:00 hours. Putting their books back on the shelf where they found them the two men walked side by side to the conference room.

Jim noted that the men all stood at attention when he and John entered the room, a habit they kept up despite knowing they didn't have to. It touched him deeply that his men respected him like that. He nodded to them and took his seat, and they sat down. Zeke took his cue to get started, and he cleared his throat.

"Maximiliano is on his way here, thinking he will arrive tonight, unaware that he will have to travel three full days before he gets to this location!" Zeke said smiling at the humor of the situation. "His men were planning a night raid tonight, but they have since realized that isn't going to happen. Loony planted bugs on both fishing boats and they are working well.

"So far, the men are cold, complaining about being cold, and the captains of both vessels are now being held hostage at gunpoint and pushing their vessels at full speed despite the danger to their hulls. When we were flying back, we noticed that the channel is frozen over five miles behind us and snow has drifted to a height of about twelve feet over the channel. That's where they're going to be stopped.

"I've included photos of all the mercenaries and Massoona for you to study. They are wearing Russell Outdoors APX Gale Jackets and insulated snow bibs. Their boots are military grade, probably waterproof, but definitely not insulated. No tents were ordered as part of their gear, so they have no shelter outside of the boats," Zeke stopped and looked at the men.

"If I remember correctly, that was a portion where the ice was really thrust up in a few places, and the snow settled in high mounds," Sparks said, looking at the map. "We had a bear of a time getting the A&R railroad through that!"

"It's a good place for an ambush," John said, looking at the photos taken from the plane earlier that day.

"What if they use the pilots of the boats as hostages against us?" Jim asked.

"Snipers from the front, and both sides, and one at the rear," John said after a moment of thought.

"I'm hoping we don't have to take any lives," Jim said sadly.

"Let them all get off the boats, with their weapons, before we hit them," FM suggested, looking at the photos once more. "They'll have to move forward, and about a hundred yards up is another good ambush spot. Let's keep one sniper back, just in case they leave guards on the boats. I don't think they will. They're gonna know they have to hit us hard and fast."

"That makes sense," Jim agreed, writing it down on his notepad. "We wear full body armor and snow cammies!" he added. "Snow doesn't stop bullets! How do you see it going down once we have them on the ice?"

"We'll have to hit a few of them to make our point," Dorf prophesied quietly.

"Aim for the legs. If they get lethal, we will respond in like kind."

The men looked at John quietly and nodded. None of them liked the bloodshed, but they knew what battle situations were like. Every situation was fluid, and things changed from moment to moment, and one had to adapt.

"Air support would quickly subdue any resistance," Wade said suddenly.

Jim and John looked at each other and nodded. He picked up his phone and asked Inchworm and Wrench to step into the conference room. They appeared five minutes later, in their uniforms. Jim smiled at that. Inchworm was PO1 Walt Rule, another mechanic on the ship.

"We're going to need air support," Jim said when they sat down. "Our ambush is planned for here, and we need you to appear from behind here when we make our presence known, as soon as I call for you." Jim looked at the two men expectantly as he pointed out the points on the map and was not disappointed. Walt and Mike looked at the terrain and both pointed to the same spot.

"This is good cover," they said together, and then smiled.

"Very good gentlemen," John grinned. "Very good!"

"If they decide to fight their way out you are the factor that will dissuade them," Jim added.

"Don't worry Jim! Wrench can shoot the wings off of flies with that system!" Inchworm exclaimed.

Jim nodded. He and Chief held the top score with the AH-1W, and Inchworm and Wrench were less than a tenth of a second less. They were good. But this was their first time in actual combat. He'd drilled them and practiced with them, but he knew that combat was different.

"You've proved that," Jim agreed. "Just remember everything we've practiced, and you'll be okay."

Discussion followed on how they would deploy, who would have what responsibilities, and finally the plan was satisfactory to everyone. Jim looked at his watch and realized it was near midnight! He pushed his chair back and stood, and the rest of the men shot to their feet.

"Let's all come back in one piece from this one," he said.

Cecilia and RJ were sound asleep when he entered their stateroom.

For a long moment he stood by the door and looked at them. He was a soldier, strong, virile, and experienced. But in that moment, he knew that there was nothing he could do to protect the two he loved most from the dangers of the natural or spiritual world. Only God could do that. He was their refuge and strength, not Jim.

Smiling at that thought he made sure the door was closed properly and padded silently into the room. He paused by JR's crib, put a hand gently on the boys back and felt him breathing under the soft blanket, marveling at this tiny life that had been such an amazing gift from God. When he'd laid out his clothes for the next day and disposed of his dirty clothes in the hamper, he crawled beneath the covers and gathered Cecilia in his arms. She moaned softly in her sleep, came halfway to wakefulness, and smiled as he kissed her. Snuggling into him, she fell into sleep once more.

Jim's inner alarm woke him at 04:00, just as RJ began to fuss in his crib. Getting out of bed he picked the toddler up, took him to the changing table, and removed three very wet and messy diapers. On the ship they used cloth diapers exclusively. After cleaning his son carefully Jim slid two clean diapers under his bottom, pinned them in place, and found a pair of baby pants to go over them.

This finished he delivered his son to Cecilia, who was sitting up and getting ready for his morning feeding, and Jim took the messy diapers in to rinse them out in the toilet before depositing them in the diaper pail. Four minutes later he stepped out of the shower, toweled himself dry, and dressed for the day. Although this was routine behavior, he loved it, for his wife and son were there with him. Cecilia blew him a kiss on his way out.

Up on the bow of the ship he discovered he was first, but Andrea appeared half a minute later, with John and Wade following very quickly. Beneath the helipad above them they stood in the shade, despite the early hour, and gazed northeast at the approaching storm. Jim looked over the bow and noted that the water around the ship had frozen to a depth of one inch over night.

"That is going to make Massoona's life miserable!" Wade predicted, pointing his chin at the storm.

"Ours as well if we have to deploy in the middle of it," Jim grunted.

"I think they will be ready to give up by the time you spring your ambush," Andrea said, laughing quietly. "Last night it was forty-eight degrees below zero!"

"It doesn't feel much warmer!" John said, shivering in his heavy clothing.

"No. It doesn't!" Andrea laughed. "I thought winter at the vineyard was cold!" he chuckled at that.

"How does the grape harvest look for this year?" Jim asked.

"My Rosa says it will be our best yet! Two of our wines won awards last year! Already our sales are up, and the winter games resort was full this year, and half the rooms are already reserved for the next season. Your attorney friend was correct. The prices are just right to draw the right crowds, and the activities appealing to the crowds we want to draw."

"How do the townspeople feel about the resort?" John asked.

"They have learned that tourists visit their shops and spend money. Of course, they complain about all the automobiles and buses. But they are content to have more money in their pockets this year than they had last year. So, it is all good," Andrea said philosophically. No one liked change, he knew, His three relatives accepted the philosophy of his statement.

"And today we learn what's inside *Wilhelmina's Song*," Wade cited. He was looking back at the ship now covered by about an inch of ice and a light coating of snow. "She's got some tales to tell, I guarantee that!" he challenged.

"What's our tonnage for cargo?" Jim asked, knowing Wade would already have considered that question.

"We can hold 32.8 tons per square foot on the deck itself, and we have over nine thousand square feet of deck space. In the cargo holds we max out at sixty tons. We'll be full when we head back to shore, but we'll be able to hold it all," he answered quickly. "Actually, this ship is far better designed for hauling cargo than our last two ships!"

"Geek," John said hitting his friend on the shoulder.

"I'm Wade, not Zeke!" Wade admonished. "Can we go down

to breakfast now. I haven't seen Angela in twenty minutes and I'm beginning to forget what she looks like!" he whined the last sentence and got all three of his friends to laugh.

Breakfast was a merry meal, and though everyone wanted desperately to know what was on the ship they'd pulled from the bottom of the ocean, no one hurried. Everyone attended the Bible study and Jim decided it was a good thing. Sturdy talked for fifteen minutes on Romans 7 and 8:1, bringing them all down to the realities of life.

"How does God bear it?" Jim asked during the question and discussion time. "How can He stand to have those He saved continue in sin as if helpless?"

"Why do you think we needed Jesus in the first place?" Abe asked with a smile at his friend. He could remember a time when Jim didn't know his Savior. Now he was one of the most-godly men he'd ever known. "Jesus came because you and I were incapable of saving ourselves. And our sinfulness reminds us of that need every day! One sin, or a hundred sins, its all the same in His eyes. That's why we present our bodies daily as living sacrifices!"

"Well, I for one am grateful that He has infinite patience!" Jim replied with a smile.

After prayer that morning the daily chores on board ship had to be seen to before they went out and explored *Wilhelmina's Song*. Jim moved among the men and women working on his ship and saw that they were giving their usual best, complimented them on their work, and pitched in where help was needed. After his tour of the ship, he stepped into his office to find that Ives had everything ready for him.

When ten bells sounded, the signal that it was time, Jim put the last report in the out box and sighed with pleasure. His desk was clean and his paperwork for that part of the day was done. Gathering the reports, he dropped them off at Ives desk and thanked him for his meticulous work.

Ives watched the captain leave the office and thought that he was very fortunate to have this position on this ship. Jim Shepherd noticed things, and when a job was done well, he noticed and said so, and when a mistake was made, he didn't come unglued like some Captains. He often corrected the mistake without comment, or if something needed to be done again simply asked. He always asked.

Zeke had taken the diagram of the ship and divided it so that every portion could be investigated quickly, assigning various team's areas to examine. In the CIC Zeke, News, and Neff kept a watch on the radar and sonar to detect if any vessels or aircraft were close and to warn the crew if they were. Everyone else was part of a team exploring *Wilhelmina's Song*. News was PO2 Ned Vintner, one of the intelligence officers on the ship, and Neff was Ensign Bob Neff, the ship's science team geologist.

CHAPTER 5

Flamethrowers were used to melt the ice and open the hatches and doorways. Everyone wore a filter mask over his or her mouth and nose as a precaution. This helped some with the smell, and it protected them from any elements that might cause respiratory problems or health issues. The mask also protected the nose and lips from the icy cold.

It turned out that three 120 mm DeBange Cannon, modified in 1878 had been loose in one of the holds, rolling back and forth and causing the ship to roll. The cannons were in amazing condition, and they would probably be cleaned up and sold or donated to museums. Thirty tons of gold on the manifest was present, along with an extra fifteen tons of zinc and copper. That had not been on the manifest, and Jim wondered why. In another spot they found five tons of gold ingots that also did not appear on the manifest.

Crates holding the gold had long since rotted away, and the ingots had settled to the floor in a heap. Jim hoped that those searching the cabins and offices would find something to indicate these strange discrepancies. Wade radioed that he was already working on the most practical way to transfer the gold, zinc, and copper to *Sea Venture*.

Goody, who with the engine room staff had penetrated the very bottom of the ship radioed that he thought the burst seams could be repaired in about three days of work. It would deplete their supply of welding materials substantially. Jim considered the value of the gold and told Goody to go ahead, and to order more materials to be picked up at Barrow.

Jim knew that he was looking at over two billion dollars of gold at today's prices. What the copper and zinc would bring he didn't know, but he thought it might be significant. The gold he would sell to the U.S. Mint for about seventy-five percent of its value, yet even then with the zinc and copper he would score close to 2 billion.

His company once more achieved a major find that would make headlines across the globe. And, he thought with pleasure, the cost of the new ship had been covered and that debt could be wiped out completely. *Bring It Up*, with this find, had just become debt free again, and solidly in the black as far as assets were concerned. What Ken Worthington would do with the money was impossible to imagine. Silently he breathed a prayer of thanks to God.

He spotted a tar-covered box in one corner of the room where he found the extra five tons of gold. For a moment he felt a strange premonition that this box would be important to unfolding the mystery surrounding this ship. Photographing the box several times from different angles he finally allowed his team to lift the box and put it with the other items that were going back to their lab.

On the way back to *Sea Venture* he listened to the elated conversations about what had been discovered on board the ship. Like him, most of the people thought the historical discoveries as valuable as the treasure on the ship. There had been many of those. Jewelry, pocket-watches, and trinkets like those were not important. What was important included things like eyeglasses, photographs that were still viable, dishes, bowls, silverware, and period-piece furnishings that could be saved. Some of the clothing was still viable and would eventually be displayed in a museum. Abe and Sturdy were very excited about adding the fancy porcelain plates and amazing silverware and cutlery to their supplies.

Maps, maritime instruments, mining instruments and tools were also valuable finds. Those three DeBange cannon would make wonderful museum pieces. The documentation inside the tar-smeared box, as it turned out, would be of tremendous value, both historically, and in solving the mystery of why *Wilhelmina's Song* was so far off course.

After lunch on *Sea Venture* the crew set to work stacking the gold bricks on metal pallets created from the scrap from Wade's arched towers and other steel they had on board the ship, and steel they found on *Wilhelmina's Song*. Once a pallet was loaded with gold, stacked four-deep, it was winched out of the hold and ferried to *Sea Venture* with the CH53-D Sea Stallion helicopter.

It took that afternoon and the remainder of the next day to transfer the gold, copper, and zinc to the ship. While that work went on the archaeology department in the lab worked over the other finds and discovered the fate of *Wilhelmina's Song*. Mutiny had indeed taken place and as the captain and his crew that were loyal to him rowed away an unexpected and unforeseen ice storm hit.

It buried the ship in two feet of ice, and the storm sank the lifeboats with the captain and his loyal crewmembers. Another storm hit shortly after that adding more ice to the ship and driving it under the water. Off course and lost they'd run into ice, broken some, but been stuck now for days. Knowing that they would not survive if the ship went under the mutineers decided to leave and take their chances in the storm. They knew they had no chance, but they went anyway. Sometimes that happened, because even a very remote chance was better than none at all.

This was all contained in a note, written to a sweetheart in Holland by one of the mutineers. He left it behind, in the tar-covered box, hoping against hope that she would one day receive the message. In his note he mentioned that the new Captain had sealed orders that he carried with him.

"How far do you think they got?" John Dinsmore asked Alistair Gregg. He was thinking of trying to move about in this type of storm. It was brutal, even with proper equipment and clothing. They probably had not had the proper equipment and clothing.

"Hundreds of yards at best," Alistair surmised with a sigh. "We need to find them, and to find those sealed orders."

"We'll need metal detectors," Heidi VanHaaten said.

"Also, a grid pattern for searching," Lisle Mirelle said.

Jim arrived in the lab shortly after these discoveries and approved the science team looking for the bodies. He suggested taking the A&R Railroad so that when they found the bodies, they could uncover them, and have safe habitation while that work went on. Having a warm place to rest would help the team accomplish their task.

"You're not going to send a military team with us?" Alice asked with a surprised expression.

"No. You're quite capable. Make sure you're armed against polar bears," Jim cautioned.

"That's a change!" Alice said when Jim left.

"He needs all his men for the ambush on the mercenaries coming to steal our gold," her husband replied, his thoughts with the captain as he left. "That he trusts us with this is indeed honoring," he added softly.

Windy and Loony had been flying over the channel and watching the progress of the fishing boats. Zeke was monitoring the tracking device and listening in on the conversations close to where it lay hidden beneath the dashboard. Jim, as a result, knew about the hour they would reach the stopping point, and so he had his men in place and ready at the appointed time.

Fifteen minutes after his men were in place the fishing boats appeared. When it was obvious they could go no further, Maximiliano swore. He knew he was within five miles of his objective, and now he would have to walk. Unwilling to even leave a guard to guard the boats he had his lieutenant disable the engines and left the boats to trudge toward his objective, not caring if the captains of the boats died in the extreme cold.

Sending a scout ahead was useless. Their radios didn't work in this cold, and they could see only a few yards ahead. Taking the lead Massoona stalked through the deep snow feeling the cold in his toes first, shivering in the wind, and miserable. Only the thought of the gold kept him going.

Less than a hundred yards into the first mile the men began to complain, and Massoona began to have second thoughts. He was shivering almost uncontrollably and wondered how anyone could stand this infernal cold. Angry because he hadn't done his homework properly, and afraid this mission might fail, he spun and pointed his pistol at the face of his lieutenant.

"Anyone else who complains dies immediately!" The pistol spat fire and the Lieutenant screamed as the bullet tore through the lobe of his right ear. "Is that clear?" Massoona screamed in a rage.

A shot rang out, and he fell, thinking at first that he'd tripped. But he saw the red spreading in the snow and looked at a broken leg, the bullet having gone straight through the bone. His men immediately raised their rifles, but an ominous sound stopped them. Before them the AH-1W rose from behind the snow mound where it had been waiting.

"Throw down your weapons and put your hands on top of your heads." The voice came from the chopper, and with it a short burst of the machine gun, spraying snow in their eyes as the bullets thumped into the ice. "This gun can put a 20-mm. bullet in every square inch of a football field in less than ten seconds. Do as you are commanded!"

Wrench watched as the men slowly threw their weapons aside. Some pulled outside arms and threw them away as well, but many didn't. They did, however, put their hands above their heads. Jim and his team stood up at that point, and they were so close they touched some of the mercenaries with the barrels of their assault rifles. That, Wrench saw with a satisfied grin, took the fight out of them. None of them even knew how close to death they were!

Ghostly figures rose out of the snow, and hard eyes glared from behind goggles, protecting them from the cold. Thirty-six men who had crept so close none had even known they were there frightened the men badly. Wrench smiled as he watched it all unfold, and spoke to Inchworm over the COM. He was just speaking to his gunner, not to everyone, but he was enjoying the moment.

"I'd bloody be pissing myself if those blokes rose up that close to me!" he laughed. "I'll bet some of them will have frostbite in a bad place!" Inchworm laughed with him, both men grimacing at the thought.

Zip restraint ties were used to secure hands and feet, and all weapons were then removed. Massoona did not resist, because the pain of his wound had finally hit him. Jim sent Zeke to the boats with the engine parts and allowed the captains of those boats to head back to Prudhoe Bay. Zeke told them that the coastguard was sending transport for the prisoners. They were so relieved to be rid of the pirates that they complied without asking the questions that crowded their thoughts.

Sean splinted Massoona's leg, gave him a shot of morphine to take away the pain, while others were setting up the six Hilleberg Salvo tents. Once the heaters were working properly, they moved the prisoners inside. With that done Jim assigned six men to stand guard with hunting rifles until the Coast Guard arrived, and he ordered that anyone that tried to exit the tent was to be shot. Inside the tents the men remained still.

Since they were in the good graces of the Alaska Coast Guard response was swift. Two hours after the rest of the team disappeared into the storm the Coast Guard arrived. The storm blew itself out just as they arrived, but the six men standing guard did not relax their guard until armed men were ready. That told the coast guard what they were working with. Captain Holmes watched the men relax a little when his armed men appeared.

"There are twenty-one mercenaries in those tents, hired by Martin Marius Wikffels to steal the contents of the ship we raised. Massoona Maximiliano is the leader. He has a bullet wound and broken leg. We collected their weapons in a pile over there," FM pointed to the pile. "Those are new, recently purchased, and flown into our country illegally. They were involved in two acts of piracy over the last two years in the Indian Ocean. They're all yours!" FM grinned, waved to the other five guards, and moved off.

Massoona was furious. *How had they known?* And he'd heard

one of the guards give Wikffels name. Now he was going to end up sitting in a holding cell until Ramanantsoa could arrange to have them extradited to Madagascar. Ramanantsoa was not going to be happy he missed the opportunity at the gold either. Maximiliano admitted to himself that he feared Ramanantsoa.

He knew he had not prepared thoroughly for this mission, and that was his fault. If Ramanantsoa let him live he would have to earn back everything he'd worked so hard to achieve in the last five years. He cursed *Bring It Up*. He also knew he was dealing with dangerous men. When they rose up out of the snow he'd known. No one had prepared him for that kind of a covert military response. Maybe Ramanantsoa would let him live. He could shift most of the blame to Wikffels, he knew, but would it be enough?

Maximiliano also knew that he owed his life to the men of *Bring It Up* and that frustrated and infuriated him. They had provided the tents and warmth to a group of men close to freezing to death. That meant they knew he had been unprepared for this mission. He swore that one day he would bring them to his own country, where he would have the advantage.

His men were subdued and quiet on the journey back to Barrow. Some were relieved to be captured, for they had indeed been close to freezing to death, and they knew it. Others were angry with Massoona for not planning a better mission, though they did not express this. Massoona tended to be brutal when it came to discipline. Massoona quelled the anger with one statement.

"If they ever come near our country, I will call all of you to even the score," he spoke in Shona, their native language.

Unrelenting freezing temperatures and a hostile environment could be blamed for this failure. Massoona was sure they would have the advantage in their own country. Somehow, he knew, he would find a way to bring them to Africa, and then he would have his revenge. Sealing his men to him Massoona finished.

"I was wrong to take a job here in this place. You will be paid."

Three more days passed as material traveled from *Wilhelmina's Song* to *Sea Venture*. Jim arranged for the men working to have only one shift of ferrying things across the ice, to minimize the effects of working in arctic conditions. He took one of the shifts, not because he had to, but because he wanted his men to know that he thought of himself as part of the workforce.

About three hundred yards southwest of their position the science team discovered the mutineers, huddled together and frozen in the ice. Jim sent two teams of men out to help them break the ten feet of ice covering the bodies and recover what they could. It would turn out to be a considerable amount of information and all the outer clothing on the bodies. So quickly had the ice formed that those garments were still in good condition.

The bodies were thawed enough to lay them out, placed in body bags, and turned over to the Alaskan government. Once scanned, the sealed orders, carried by the captain of the mutineers, were also released to the authorities. It would be those documents that would finally bring closure to the mystery behind the lost ship.

His name was Richard Verick. He had been the agent that spirited the extra minerals on board the ship without them going on the official manifest. It had been his plan, coupled with a bribe, that kept the captain from complaining, and the promise of further riches once they reached Holland, and something even more sinister.

The ship, once in Verick's hands, was to travel through McClure Straight, Viscount Melville Sound, and finally Lancaster Sound, traveling down through Baffin Bay into the Labrador Sea, and finally across the Atlantic to Holland. Once the ship was far enough north the captain and those loyal to him were to be released in one or two lifeboats.

Jim knew the orders were cruel punishment, and sure death for the men put into those boats. Verick had just enough hands to keep the ship going, but he had not figured on the early ice storms that had stopped his plot. The ship had been scheduled to stop first at Scheveningen to unload the materials showing on the false manifest in the sealed packet. After that it would make port in Amsterdam where the gold was supposed to be turned over to Queen Wilhelmina, sold to her government for sixty percent of its value at that time.

Wilhelmina Wikffels would have, in that one act, made herself indispensable to the throne, and been able to manipulate Dutch treaties and law to the favor of her company. Jim was sure that *Wilhelmina's Song* was just one drop in the bucket regarding this woman's plots to gain power. That she had was evident. Martin Wikffels was one of the twenty richest men in the world.

It had been he who hired the fishing trawlers to drag the bottom in hopes of finding the ship. He knew what it held, and his attempt to steal the gold from *Bring It Up* was evidence of that. The gold would have very quickly enabled him to solidify the plan to corner the market on blue diamonds and chips.

Further study of the history of the family bore out that they were intelligent, ruthless, and always on the cutting edge of industries that exploded in value. What they didn't control they manipulated. And now the family owned a communications company that had three satellites in space. The story of how they acquired that company said volumes.

Jim studied the picture of Wikffels. Egg-shaped head, egg-shaped body, close-set pale blue eyes, wispy blonde hair, and a tendency to wear a yellow-gold suit made him look outlandish and even a little foolish. He probably did that on purpose, so that people would underestimate him. One thing that came out in the photo was an almost savage rage, radiating outward from those eyes.

Megalomaniacs came in all shapes and sizes. Jim watched a short video with Wikffels in it, not about him but about Randstad Corporation, and decided that Wikffels had all the earmarks of a megalomaniac. Men like that were dangerous, even deadly enemies. Once thwarted men like Wikffels never let go, never forgot, never forgave.

Jim sighed as he signed off his computer and gathered his notes together. It was time for a conference with the whole crew, in the library. He walked through the corridors and felt immediately better when he saw his wife and son waiting for him at the door. RJ jumped and wiggled and held out his arms for his daddy to take him, and

Jim swept him high in the air, swirled him around, and bent to kiss Cecilia.

Taking her hand, he walked into the library. Everyone wasn't there quite yet, but half the crew arrived early, or were still there from the evening games. Zeke, of course, was already there, setting up the smartboard so that everyone could see what was on his computer. People began to move to the tables, plug in laptops, or just open them up if they were well charged, as others came in. The science team was last to arrive, probably because they had a presentation to make.

At eight bells signifying it was 20:00 hours, the room grew silent. Jim stood and looked around at everyone for a moment. His heart swelled with pride as he observed his crew.

"Let me begin by saying that this crew is second to none!" Cheers erupted and the room became silent again. "We're probably all curious to hear what Uncle Zeke has to say about how clever and amazing he is," Jim began, smiling at Zeke, who winked back. People chuckled because Zeke was like that. "So, let's just turn the meeting over to him for the present," Jim finished.

"And well you should!" Zeke began and glared down a few who gave out catcalls and quips. "Uncle Zeke sees all!" he said turning to the smartboard. Tiffany, put the gum back in your mouth," he added without turning around. Tiffany Millstein had indeed taken part of her gum and stretched it out in front of her, a habit she had. She wrinkled her nose at him and made a cute face.

"I saw that!" Zeke said, again without turning around. "As you can see by this most excellent graph, Wikffels has managed to secure about half the Type IIb blue diamond and diamond chips available. I used color in the graph so that people like FM would at least look at it. It probably would have been better to put it in comic book form, but I didn't have time," Zeke grinned at FM.

"Pretty!" FM quipped. "What color are blue diamonds?" he added.

"Type IIb diamonds make up approximately 0.1% of all natural diamonds, which makes them very valuable because they are so rare. Low levels of nitrogen impurities, compared to Type IIa diamonds, Type IIb diamonds contain significant boron impurities. If one examines the absorption spectrum, boron causes these gems to absorb red, orange, and yellow light, therefore lending Type IIb diamonds a light blue or gray color, though examples with low levels of boron impurities can also be colorless," Zeke replied.

"Huh? Could you give that to us in English?" FM quipped, bringing a laugh from most of the people listening.

"What makes these diamonds interesting," Zeke continued, ignoring FM, "is that they are also p-type semiconductors, unlike other diamond types, due to uncompensated electron holes. That's what makes blue diamonds interesting as a semiconductor, and valuable to satellite and laser technologies.

"We can analyze the electrical properties of blue diamonds by looking at their band structure. Energy bands form as a quantum mechanical consequence (as in Pauli's exclusion principle) when isolated atoms are brought together forming a crystal. At that point we distinguish between the *valence band*, which consists of the electrons forming the chemical bonds, and the *conduction band*, which consists of electrons of higher energies, which can move freely across the crystal. Electronic conduction only takes place within these bands when one band is partially populated by electrons. Everybody got that so far?"

Zeke turned to look at his audience and together they opened their mouths and said "huh?"

"Yes!" Zeke continued, shaking his head. Jim knew that most of the people in the room were indeed following him. This was the kind of information that shouted the proof of intelligent design. He was reading his own notes from Zeke with interest.

"A blue diamond is an intrinsic semiconductor. It contains relatively small amounts of impurities compared to the thermally generated electrons and holes. In order to obtain the electron density (the number of electrons per unit volume) in an intrinsic semiconductor, one needs to integrate the electron density $n(E)$ in an incremental energy range dE from the bottom to the top of the conduction band. The density $n(E)$ is the product of the Fermi-Dirac distribution $F(E)$ and the density of allowed energy states per energy range per unit volume $N(E)$. The Fermi-Dirac distribution gives the probability at the absolute temperature T that an electron occupies an electronic state with energy E. The Fermi level E_F is by definition the energy at which the probability is one half and k is the Boltzmann constant.

"Evaluating the integral returns, the electron density in the conduction band where N_C is the effective density-of-states in the conduction band. And for diamond it is given by the expression: with m_e being the density-of-states effective electron mass and h the Planck constant. According to the experts, the hole density p in the valence band can be obtained in a similar way: where N_v is the effective density-of-state in the valence band. For diamond it reads: with m_n being the density-of-states effective hole mass.

"In an intrinsic semiconductor, the number of electrons per unit volume in the conduction band equals the number of holes per unit volume in the valence band and the intrinsic carrier concentration n_i can be calculated from the mass action law which reads $np = n_i^2$. By using the second and third equations I showed it follows

"Now what's really interesting is this! Looking back at the intrinsic carrier concentration for diamond as a function of temperature it can be clearly concluded that because of the wide bandgap, the intrinsic charge carrier concentration is very low and becomes only significant for temperatures exceeding 1000°C. That indicates the use of the concentrated beam of a laser.

"On the smart board you can see a photograph of Gilles Ramanantsoa, who just happens to be in possession of the latest technology titanium prototype laser. Here's a picture of the schematics of the laser. Using titanium means he can focus incredible amounts of heat without damaging the laser unit. What would destroy many lasers doesn't phase titanium.

"So, we have Wikffels attempting to buy up all the blue diamonds, in bed with Ramanantsoa who has a new type of laser capable of targeting things in space, and a world dependent on satellite communications. As if this soup is not already thick enough, enter the Zhanzhu Triad.

"Ke Yi Zhanzhu and his sister Mae Hao Zhanzhu along with their uncle Tao Ling Zhanzhu have already attempted to purchase the prototype. Ramanantsoa refused their offer, so my guess is they are going to attempt to steal it. If they know about Wikffels, they may also be attempting to steal all the blue diamonds as well. That would be a good move on their part.

"Why?" Loony asked in the small silence that followed Zeke's presentation.

"If you had a laser capable of targeting and destroying satellites in the sky, and you made and sold satellites, you could literally own the satellite market. Anybody who didn't buy your product got their satellite blasted out of the sky." Mark Drumheiser answered the question, putting the pieces together and not liking what he was seeing.

"They would have every communication company by the . . . uh, I mean over a barrel!" John said, glancing evasively at his mother.

Alice Dinsmore caught the look and snorted. "By the balls was just as descriptive!" she said with a short laugh.

"John Robert Shepherd!" Gwyneth snapped. Jim smiled as his brother blushed a deep crimson.

"She used your middle name, mate. You're in barney now!" Sean warned. Sean Oxton was one of the medical officers, and a member of the military team, a former SAS operative and Lieutenant on Jim's team. The men called him Ox.

They all needed to laugh at that moment. This was serious stuff. Worse, it was happening in a place in the world where few governments dared to interfere. Africa was in an uproar, and the mines in South America were not much better! Wikffels had agents at work there too.

"Will our getting the gold from *Wilhelmina's Song* cramp Wikffels plan?" Sparks asked as the laughter died down.

"It will slow him down, but he's already got a head start and his efforts will gain momentum with time," Zeke replied. "I think we should hear from our science team about the Wikffels legacy."

CHAPTER 6

Alistair came forward and using a laser pointer outlined the history of the family and what they had learned of their nefarious and legal activities. His witty report took the better part of fifteen minutes until he came to *Wilhelmina's Song*.

"Verick was an enforcer for great-great-grandmamma Wikffels. It seems he was a good-looking chap, and therefore he could charm women easily. He used this ability to steal industrial secrets and other secrets. His reputation was that of a ruthless man that would do anything to get what he wanted. He was certainly successful until *Wilhelmina's Song*. She proved to be his Nemesis.

"You can see from the report we've provided that there are at least a dozen murders attributed to Verick, two that he was officially charged with, but when witnesses and family members of the deceased disappeared mysteriously the charges were dropped. In this one particular case the prosecuting attorney's daughter was kidnapped, but later returned unharmed once all charges were dropped. To the Wikffels family literally dozens of corpses litter their legacy.

"In the case of Captain Malik van der Steur, his daughter Tamara disappeared two hours before the first "unauthorized" cargo was loaded. We've been able to decipher some of the captain's log. To ensure his cooperation, he was promised that his daughter would be on the next ship to Amsterdam, and that she would be well cared for and arrive safe and sound.

"Verick's diary indicates that the girl was taken out to sea, weighted, and dropped overboard. She was thirteen, and I don't want to think what that poor child's last hours might have been like. It is as if God became enraged at Verick at that point and took a personal hand in stopping him. It would not surprise me. Job talks about the storehouses of snow saved up for times of war! Amen?"

There was a huge chorus of "Amen" from the crowd in the library. Alistair continued.

"Wikffels was branching into electricity, and I think the copper and zinc were earmarked for that endeavor. We did find a record of a company that made arc lamps that had agreed to sell to Wikffels, and then backed out of the deal in 1878. By 1882 Wikffels owned the company, and the board of directors, and company president of that 1878 institution all mysteriously died over that same period of time. According to my research, no investigation turned up any useful evidence.

"Now we get to something interesting. That extra five tons of gold was a gift, according to the false manifest provided, to the Wikffels family from the directors of the mine from which it was taken. One ton of gold was to remain with the Wikffels family, and the other four returned to the directors of the mine. That was the deal brokered by Great-Great Grandmamma Wikffels.

"That suggests to me that the directors of the mine fell into line with her suggestion that they gift her five tons of gold, and she return four that never showed up on the director's records, thus making them quite rich. The gift was for supplying over ten million dollars worth of rail, cars, and mining equipment that history indicates she stole.

"Everybody lost on that deal!" Alistair stopped and looked around to be sure he still had his audience, which he did, because he was a dynamic and energetic speaker. "Truly, God is not mocked!"

"After the loss of *Wilhelmina's Song*, the Wikffels family continued their nefarious dealings until the present, when we see yet another

Wikffels attempting to corner the market in a very popular commodity today.

"Martin Wikffels has a very bad reputation and is said to be succumbing to a venereal disease that is slowly driving him insane. His rages are often newsworthy and have cost the company a good bit of money to hush them up. I cannot think of anything more frightening than a madman who has the capability to think rationally.

"Now let's turn our attention to Gilles Ramanantsoa of Madagascar. He is not, I regret to report, a cute and cuddly zoo animal of cartoon fame." Several people laughed and he smiled at the room.

"If he was, he'd be a bloody crocodile!" Sean remarked, getting a laugh. "The one that eats all the cute and cuddly animals!"

"His father, Gabriel, became a friend to the Soviet Union in 1972, but never achieved much. Gilles is very bitter about what happened to his father, and how he was literally forgotten during the second Republic and by the third Republic his name meant little except in the circles of those with wealth.

"Gilles has decided, it appears, to embrace crime as a way of life, though he has taken a page out of history and is doing it like the Mafia leaders in America before the Second World War. Hiding behind that boyish exterior is a ruthless killer. He holds two martial arts titles in his country, and one in France. In Germany he became enraged when an American champion was defeating him and tried to cripple his opponent. Our American champion countered the blow and put Gilles in the hospital for three weeks. He has not competed since. His reputation in that world was badly damaged by his fury during the match.

"Rumors in Madagascar among those who work for him are frightening. If half of what we've discovered is true we are up against a very evil man with almost limitless financial resources and many Communist connections. He is, however, very prejudiced against China. It took some digging, but we found an incident where a Chinese woman put him in the hospital. That would probably be Xun, who is no longer among us.

"A few years ago, Ramanantsoa hooked up with our friend Martin

Wikffels and they bankrolled a coal mining operation near Tete in Mozambique. A few have dared to oppose the mining operation, but so far, all who dared have disappeared. Officials seem to be satisfied with bribes to allow the operation to go on, and truth be told, it is generating a lot of income for the country. It's the old story, I'm afraid, of graft, greed, and murder." Alistair went to his seat while the room applauded.

"Nobody applauded my work on blue diamonds!" Zeke said, sticking out his lower lip.

"That's because only the geeks in the room understood it, and they're too afraid to applaud until everyone else does!" PU said.

"Hey! I understood Zeke's equations!" Dr. Lowe said from the next table.

"Point made." PU replied without hesitation.

After the laughter died down Jim stood up. Everyone grew quiet and waited for him to arrange his thoughts and speak.

"We're going to get all this information out to our friends in the intelligence community. Tomorrow we drag that beautiful old steamer back into the water and take her back to Barrow. I want the PBY in the air, and I want Wrench and Inchworm ready to take the AH-1W up at a moment's notice! We don't know what assets Wikffels has here, or what he'll attempt, so I want this crew on high alert. We repel all borders with extreme prejudice!" Jim finished.

"Ooh rah!" Bulldog, Firefox, and Zulu shouted the Marine agreement loudly in the room.

"Jarheads!" Hobbs said when the echo died out.

"Limeys!" Dodge replied.

"Men!" That shout came from the Millstein sisters, Elizabeth Minor, and Lynn Ross. A roar of laughter followed.

Jim stood smiling and when everyone got quiet, he dismissed the room. Walking amongst the crew he thanked Zeke and Alistair for their reports and the rest of the crew for their hard work.

With the bollard cable attached and the ice broken right up to the bow of *Wilhelmina's Song*, water was pumped onto the ice beneath the derelict until it was dragged into the water. On board a small crew patrolled the hull of the ship from inside, checking for leaks. What leaks there were the pumps could handle.

Wilhelmina's Song began her long journey to the scrap yards of Barrow. Jim stood in the bridge and Andrea had the wheel. Dorf was at the wheel of *Wilhelmina's Song* and progress was steady, if slow. Satisfied that all was going well Jim left the bridge and returned to his office to get some work done.

As fate would have it, Wikffels had no assets in Canada, Alaska, or Russia. Ramanantsoa was insisting he pay for the extradition of his mercenaries and Wikffels, after a fit of rage and another broken phone along with a chipped brick in his wall agreed. Stewing about his defeat did not help and his secretary soon fled the office and did not return for three days. He fired her on the spot.

She reminded him that her contract included a clause that allowed her three years severance pay if she was fired, and he relented. She refused, left, and later mailed him a copy of a tape she'd made of his firing her. Her attorneys appeared an hour later and insisted he pay her severance package to them. Stoically they endured his rage until he signed the proper papers.

Three days later her body was pulled out of one of the canals running through Amsterdam and her bank account was mysteriously empty. Both of her attorneys also disappeared without a trace. Wikffels, wisely, left the country the day he paid out the severance package, but not before leaving explicit instructions on how his former secretary was to die, and where her money was to be sent. Lacking the necessary evidence, and an apparent overdose of heroine evident in the victim, Wikffels was never brought to trial. Yet he knew it was just a matter of time because he was being watched constantly.

He left for the coalmine in Mozambique, planning to stay in that country for some time. There, at least, he had protection. Wikffels was confident that no one could touch him in Mozambique. Even the government left him alone there. At the airport a British agent watched him board the first flight that would take him to Spain, where he had reservations on another flight to Luanda, and from Luanda to Harare in Mozambique. At that airport he would climb aboard a small plane that would take him to Tete where his car would meet him.

Because he was in Mozambique when his secretary's body was discovered the Amsterdam police department filed the case in a special drawer, reserved for any who dared return after committing a crime. The case would remain unsolved and open until Wikffels returned, when a warrant for his arrest would be issued and he would be brought to trial.

After the sale of the ship to the scrap yard *Sea Venture* departed for Baltimore. Jim kept in the shipping lanes as close to the west coast as he was permitted, putting in at San Francisco for supplies and fuel. Because they had so much gold on the ship no one was permitted shore leave. Supplies had been ordered and were loaded onto the ship as the diesel tanks were topped off. With the hydraulics moving the ship Jim noted that they used less fuel to travel from England to Alaska, and then down to San Francisco, than they used in the *Pearl* sailing from Panama to Baltimore the year before.

He made a special trip down to the engine room to share that bit of information with his mechanics and to praise their engineering. Jim also called Calvin Beardsley to thank him. This propulsion system would save them thousands of dollars every year in fuel costs.

Because Jim was selling the gold to the United States, the escort he requested joined them in the trip through the Panama Canal. Twenty Marines lined the rails of the ship in full battle gear, armed to the teeth. The ominous presence of two flat-black AH-1W Super Cobra helicopters escorting the ship offered further protection and dissuaded any interference.

In the Caribbean Jim greeted Captain Cummings who arrived to ferry the Marines back to their base. He was given a tour of the ship and a five-star dinner before he returned to his own ship. If anything, Jim's team was in even better condition than before, and he said so as he waited for his launch to come alongside *Sea Venture*.

"Why the Marines? Your team looks more deadly than ever!" he commented quietly as the two men stood together.

"They are. I didn't want anyone to see guns in the hands of my men. Our secret is still somewhat safe, though in time it will come out that we are a private anti-terrorist unit. When that happens, we'll have to see what the results will be. So far, our scientific work has kept us clandestine," Jim replied.

"That makes sense. There's a Senator in Miami who will ask to come aboard your vessel. Duck says you should grant that permission and determine how to respond to his request. It's genuine, not a trap, and the American Government is in a desperate position," Captain Cummings shared when the launch was close enough to mask his words from anyone close by.

"Thanks for the tip. Keep your feet dry." Jim said, shaking hands. "And thanks for the loan of the Marines and helicopters."

"Any time. Just ask," He replied, smiling and stepping onto the gangplank that would lead him down to the launch.

"You honor me," Jim said quietly.

"It's mutual," Captain Cummings replied with a nod.

As the launch pulled away Dorf blew three blasts on the air horn. Captain Cummings destroyer answered with the same sign and the two crews waved at each other as the ships parted. Jim went up to the CIC and stepped into the Navigation portion.

"Smitty, would you be so kind as to set a course for our Island retreat and make sure we arrive after midnight?"

Ensign John Smith waved his hand to indicate he would comply. Jim grinned at him and went into the CIC kiss Cecilia. RJ and JAS were in a playpen in the middle of the center. Jim picked each boy up and kissed him, played with the two boys for a few minutes, and headed to the bridge. Dorf was at the wheel.

"Captain Daddy on deck!" Mark said facetiously.

"Who's your daddy?" Jim asked automatically with a grin.

"He was much shorter than you," Mark laughed. "What's up?"

"How do you feel about a little night probe?" Jim asked casually.

"What ever gave you the idea of putting a vault in a pool inside a cave?" Mark asked, shaking his head. "Do you have any idea how hard it was to put that thing in?"

"Some," Jim admitted. He had, after all, helped.

"Actually, it's quite clever. A walk-in safe, complete with airlock, buried beneath the ocean! Even if curious divers enter that cave, they'll never know it's there! We built it, in secret, and we're the only ones who know about it," Dorf nodded his approval.

"Somebody searched the island for the safe a month ago," Jim admitted casually. "They're now convinced that we have the safe in England."

"Cheeky pelicans!" Sean said, coming into the bridge. "Who was it?"

"Two professional thieves that work for a drug cartel that has a reason to retaliate against us. What they no longer have is a large enough organization or the funds to carry out such an attempt. Unfortunately, the two thieves fell into a pit and were captured on the island. Now who would dig a trap on an island?" Zeke said, coming in as Sean asked the question.

"Maybe there were tigers on the island," Ox replied with a grin.

"None of us were there," Jim said quietly. For a moment his men looked at him, all wearing a very feral grin. Pippi came in at that moment with John and paused.

"Mercy me!" she exclaimed. "The testosterone in here is thick enough to walk on!"

"We were discussing tigers," Ox replied. "I came up to make sure you all had a good reaction to the shots. Anybody feeling queasy or ill?"

"Are you kidding?" Pen asked, taking her husband's hand. "Every time a mosquito came close to one of us it died of fright!"

"It was the Marines standing guard," John said. "Ooh rah!"

"Semper fi!" Rang out on the Bridge and Ox shook his head.

"Aussie! Aussie! Aussie!" he pumped his fist in the air. A moment later he noticed the baleful stares he was receiving. Hunching his shoulders, he tried to look chagrinned, almost pulling it off. "I'll just leave, then," he joked, pretending to sneak out of the bridge. Everyone laughed, and again Jim marveled at the ability of his men to take the edge of difficult situations.

On the following night *Sea Venture* dropped anchor off the island.

On the observation deck, using night vision glasses, Steve Coleman spotted the small yacht that dropped anchor on the north end of the island. It had approached without lights.

Down in the depths of the ship six men in wetsuits loaded the gold ingots that the company was keeping onto 4 sea sleds. The only light in the water was the compass on the sleds. When all the gold was on the sleds the six divers entered the water, two grabbing onto a sled, while the other four piloted, following Mark. Using only the compass and depth gauge on the sled Mark took them directly into the underwater cave that would lead them to the pool in which the safe had been set.

Once inside the cave he turned on the sled's lights after rounding a curve. He had judged correctly and was still near the middle of the passage. When they reached the pool, Jim removed a waterproof remote-control device from his dive bag, punched in the code, and a group of rocks, indistinguishable from the other rocks on the bottom, rose almost eight feet.

The airlock was large enough to receive the gold and the divers. Once inside Jim punched in another code and the stones settled back to the bottom. In minutes the airlock was clear of water. The men removed their tanks and fins and while Jim opened the hatch that would lead them to the safe, they prepared to transport the gold. Once the safe was open Jim joined them, and in teams of two they carried heavy trays of gold into the room, stacking them neatly on the shelves. In here the temperature was controlled and the air pure.

That done the safe was locked, the hatch to the corridor closed and locked, the airlock filled with water, and the door opened to allow them to leave. All six men remained at the bottom of the pool for a few seconds while Mark set up the program to return the sleds to the ship. It was designed to exactly duplicate its inbound trip, reversing it, and taking them automatically to the ship's moon pool.

When all the lights across the instrument panel turned green the men grabbed hold of the sleds and set off, letting the autopilot take them out. No lights were used. Anyone on the island, looking at the water would see no bubbles, because their tanks didn't release air like normal scuba tanks. It was the sound of the propellers slowing that alerted the divers on the sleds they were under the ship.

Looking up they could see a dim light above the moon pool. Hooking the sleds one by one to the four cables dangling there they crowded on the final sled and a winch pulled them straight up and to the surface. On the island, unaware that he was being watched, a man studied the water with binoculars, probably with night vision technology, looking for telltale bubbles. Steve Coleman watched him from the observation deck knowing he would not find what he was looking for or suspected. He wondered if the man knew he was being observed and doubted it.

At ten the following morning a rigid raider took the Shepherds to the dock on the island. Both women were wearing one-piece bathing suits, and both dads were holding a baby. All the boys were dressed for swimming. It was obvious to those watching that no gold was being carried to the island.

They opened the beach house and spent the morning swimming in the ocean. Two men watched them hoping against hope that they would give some indication that gold was being transferred to the island. Around noon the party prepared to leave the house, called the main office and said goodbye to the staff who worked there and cared for the property, and returned to the ship.

At fourteen hundred hours the ship anchor rose, and *Sea Venture* continued north to Miami. All the next day the two men searched the caves beneath the island but found nothing changed. Frustrated they gave up at sunset, returned to their yacht, and headed north after the ship. Zeke caught their call to the contact in Miami and smiled as he listened. When the call was disconnected, he logged the numbers in his computer, set up a program to monitor both, and went down to eat dinner.

CHAPTER 7

Senator Knight stood at the bottom of the gangplank and asked the solid-looking Petty Officer First Class for permission to board, and he stated his name and office. FM smiled, changing his whole demeanor, stepped aside, and saluted the Senator. Bemused the Senator returned the salute and walked up the ramp to step down on the deck. A short man with broad shoulders and the musculature of an active gymnast greeted him. Senator Knight noted that he was a Lieutenant.

"Welcome aboard, sir. I'm Mark. Follow me to the captain, if you please, sir," Mark said. "I'm told you will be joined by a member of her Majesty's government in a few minutes," he added.

Senator Knight, while serving in the Air Force, had been on board ships. He'd never been on board one like this. Everything gleamed, there was no sign of rust anywhere, and the crew was busy, as if still serving in the Navy. Those working at cleaning and painting wore simple coveralls with no insignia. Those like the man he followed wore full dress uniforms. He liked the insignia, ribbons, patches, and pins the men wore.

Jim Shepherd looked much like his picture from six years previous when he served in the Navy. If anything, he looked even more fit than he did then. The captain stood up, shook hands, and indicated a seat in front of his desk. Like all ships, the chair was latched to the floor, but unlike other ships, this one was very comfortable.

"Welcome aboard *Sea Venture*," Jim said, sitting down. For a moment Senator Knight studied the man before him. Admiral Ashley briefed him on what to expect. Jim still wore the jarhead haircut; his wide set green eyes were intense and his face serious. Everything about the man exuded competence and an aura of readiness. Senator Knight remembered seeing a tiger staring at its prey and thought that the two were not dissimilar.

Remembering that the man before him had been a SEAL, Force Recon, and Navy Intelligence Senator Knight nodded once, quite satisfied that Admiral Ashley had been correct. Jim Shepherd was the man who could get the job done.

"I like your uniforms," Senator Knight said. "Your ribbons are interesting. Your crew has a military bearing, even the one woman I saw as I came to your office."

"Most of my crew is ex-military. I have eighteen scientists in the crew, and a few crewmen who were not military. However, you wouldn't be able to pick them out," Jim claimed this with some pride. "My crew trains daily, including our scientists, and we drill three times a week. I think I owe much of my success to my military training, sir."

"Can we drop the sir?" Senator Knight asked. "Just call me Sam."

"Jim will do for me, Sam. Thanks," Jim smiled.

Just then Sir Edward Marsh was ushered into the office. There was no formality here, Sam noticed, as Jim shook hands, each man resting the other hand on a shoulder as close friends. For a moment neither spoke as they studied each other. Finally, the British agent let go of Jim's hand, dropped his other hand from his shoulder, and spoke.

"I'd like permission to speak to Lieutenant Calvin Weston when we're done here," Jim nodded in the affirmative, hearing the hint of ominous news, and offered a seat next to Sam Knight.

"Ah! Mr. Knight! I've heard so much about you, and I read of your exploits. It is an honor to meet you, sir," Sir Edward said, shaking hands before taking his seat. "I'm Edward Marsh, MI6. Ed will do for this meeting. May I call you Sam?"

"Sure thing, Ed," Senator Knight said with a smile. This was getting interesting.

"I'm sure you're here to talk to Jim about the same thing I'm here for. Mozambique and Zimbabwe," Sir Edward said crisply. "Duck Ashley and I had a conversation earlier yesterday," Sir Edward added to Sam's raised eyebrows. Sam nodded.

"Very well," he said, sitting back and looking at Jim. "Your intelligence on Martin Wikffels, and Giles Ramanantsoa stirred up a hornet's nest at Quantico. INTEL so far is dismal, and what's worse, as a government we can't interfere!"

"What do you know? We've been gathering INTEL for some time so we should start there," Jim suggested, his face now seriously intent.

"Dutch industrialist Martin Marius Wikffels owns a company that builds and designs communication satellites. They're very good. However, Wikffels is also a member of the World Foundation of Diamond Bourses (WFDB) and a sightholder. Our intelligence indicates that he is actively attempting to buy every blue diamond available, as well as blue diamond chips. We think he's trying to gain control of that portion of the communications industry that uses blue diamonds as conductors.

"At present we know he's holding the diamonds in what he believes is a secret facility along the Zambezi River in Mozambique where he owns a portion of land near the Sassa dam near Cabora. I have to say, I'm not impressed by the number of people who know that supposed secret! Wikffels also owns the mineral rights to his land, and part of a coalmine near Tete. In that he's a silent partner and Gilles Ramanantsoa is the public face of the company.

"Gilles is the son of Major General Gabriel Ramanantsoa who was, in the short period he held the office of Prime Minister, very useful to our Russian friends and the Communist party. What bothers us is that Ramanantsoa owns a company that built a titanium laser prototype that is capable of targeting communication satellites in space and destroying them."

"Quite James Bond!" Sir Edward muttered with a grunt.

"Yes. But his plan may work. If he and Wikffels are in this together they may be attempting to take over the satellite communications of the world," Sam sat back and slapped the arms of his chair in frustration.

"It's worse, old chap," Sir Edward said, still resting easily in his chair. He studied it for a moment. "This is actually one of the most comfortable chairs I've ever been in," he smiled at Jim.

"As I said, it gets worse. Our old friends the Zhanzhu Triad are at it again. Out of the ashes you left last year the company regrouped, now under the leadership of Ke Yi Zhanzhu, his sister Mae Hao Zhanzhu, and their uncle Tao Ling Zhanzhu. Because of what happened last year we had an agent in their company offices very near the top.

"They are watching Wikffels and Ramanantsoa with the ultimate plan including taking their organization down, seizing the blue diamonds and the laser, and literally owning the communication satellite industry for the next decade at least. I've shared my information with the CIA, NSA, FBI, and Homeland Security.

"Unfortunately, after uncovering this information my agent, a relative of Calvin Weston of your crew, was discovered and killed. He was very much like Calvin, so I'm quite certain he didn't talk. However, they have assets we don't know about yet and they know that MI6 is watching them. We've pulled all our agents," he looked at Sam and then at Jim, his face bleak.

"Neither of you can act in Mozambique or Zimbabwe for political reasons," Jim said simply. "Who knows you're speaking to me?" Jim asked quietly.

"At the moment Admiral Ashley, NSA Director Runner, and FBI Director Cornell," Sam answered. Also, Senator Brass of Wyoming, because his influence will help provide the grant you need for your cover," Sam said quietly.

"How did you get to the docks this morning?" Jim asked.

"I left my hotel early for a conference, checked in, left by a side door, caught a cab, had it drop me at the train station, and took several buses to a car rental agency, picked up a car rented by a friend and drove here," Sam sat back as if exhausted.

"That's clever," Sir Edward said.

"And you, Sir Edward?" Jim asked.

"I am currently in a closed-door meeting with some Intelligence chaps in a major hotel on the beach. Disguised as a waiter removing the room service tray, I took the freight elevator down to the garage, borrowed a Mini Cooper parked there by an associate, and drove here."

"Also, clever! Good. Tell me about the cover story," Jim turned back to Senator Knight.

"There's been an outbreak of red algae in the Mozambique Channel. Scientists believe it is coming from pollutants flowing down the Zambezi River. At the same time another epizootic ulcerative syndrome (EUS) has killed hundreds of fish in the river, and their sore-covered bodies have been found the length of the river below the second dam.

"Mozambique's government has requested a scientific study to determine if the disease can be passed on to humans, since so many eat the fish out of the river in that country. Several governments along the coast of the Indian Ocean are also deeply concerned about the red algae. You have Doctor Michael Putnam on your science team, and the Dinsmores. No group is better equipped to tackle both these problems than yours.

"General ecology of the river has suffered serious reductions in many areas causing the governments to take a serious look at what they should do. Sewage Effluent, construction of dams that have had serious effects on wildlife, and there's been a massive reduction in emplacement of silt and associate nutrients. Animal preservation groups are seriously worried about the reduction of wetland ecosystems and want to get on board to provide a grant for a study to determine if a cross-border conservation park would work. Also, another group wants a hypertrophication paleolimnology study," Senator Knight watched Jim carefully.

"It has to be a legitimate grant," Jim said after a few moments of silence. "And we need time to dock in Plymouth and pick up our river boats. Have the request sent through the usual channels to John and Alice and Michael. We'll apply for all the correct papers and make sure everything is legitimate. In four month's-time we'll be anchored off Quelimane and heading up the river.

"Make sure we get constant updates on INTEL through Sir Edward and Admiral Ashley. Both know how to contact me personally and both have an encrypted satellite phone to use. Copy me on agents in place so no mistakes are made and brief them. Sir Edward, bring Mr. Runner, Brass, and Cornell into the picture, as far as you are able. I'll give each of you a uniform and a hat so you can leave the ship looking like one of the crew. You'll each leave with a group of people and then go your separate ways. That should fool anyone keeping an eye on the ship. Now that the gold is gone, I doubt if anyone is, but we should be safe.

"Gentlemen, we have work to do," Jim picked up his phone. "Ives, would you step in my office, please," Jim requested.

Ives came into the office, stood at attention, and saluted. Jim returned the salute.

"Would you please escort Senator Knight to our dining room for some lunch and then provide a uniform for him. He'll return it when he's safely away from us." Ives nodded and waited for Senator Knight to rise.

"Jim, I feel quite relieved there are men like you serving our country," Sam said, shaking hands with the captain.

"Thanks, sir," Jim replied. Senator Knight was moved to hear the humility in Jim's voice and see it in his eyes. He smiled and left with Ives. Jim pressed a button of his uniform activating the COMLINK all of them now wore almost all the time they were awake.

"Calvin, would you please drop whatever you're doing and come to my office?" Jim asked politely.

"On my way, Shep," Calvin answered immediately.

"Nice!" Sir Edward said when Jim sat down. "I never would have picked up on the COMLINK. Where's the voice link?" he asked. Jim pointed at a spot on his throat. "Very clever!" he said. For a moment he studied the spot on Jim's neck and looked in his ear as well to see the tiny transceiver. "What's the cost per unit?"

"A little over nine thousand dollars!" Jim replied.

"Who makes them?" Sir Edward asked.

"We do," Jim supplied the answer with a grin. "Zeke and Bill designed the prototype, built it, and then started a company. Our cost is about half that for putting it all together."

"Your company public yet?" Sir Edward asked, as Calvin entered the room.

"Yes," Jim replied, nodding at Calvin who drew to attention and saluted. Jim returned the salute from his seated position and nodded to the chair Senator Knight occupied only moments before.

"Calvin, I'm very sorry to have to tell you that your cousin Austin was killed in action," Sir Edward put a hand on Calvin's shoulder. Jim watched his friend as he absorbed the information. There was a slight hardening of his features.

"Can you tell me what happened, sir?" Calvin asked quietly.

"He was under cover in the offices of the Zhanzhu Corporation, very high up in the chain. After passing on some vital information to us he was discovered somehow and eliminated by the Triad. I'm so sorry. He was truly a first-rate soldier," Sir Edward replied.

"What is his status, sir?" Calvin asked. Jim knew what he was asking. Would his cousin be honored for his sacrifice?

"No worries there!" Sir Edward said quickly. "Because of his distinguished career and exemplary service to his country he will be remembered with honor. He is the recipient of the Victoria Cross," Sir Edward replied. Calvin breathed out and Jim noted a sheen of unshed tears in his friend's eyes. Jim knew that Austin and Calvin constantly competed against each other, though in different fields of service.

"Thank you, sir," Calvin said. "Austin's father will be proud."

Calvin wiped his eyes without shame and with him Jim mourned a soldier lost. All three men spent several minutes talking about Austin and his distinguished service, wiping away the tears, and giving honor to a fallen comrade. At last Calvin stood up.

"With your permission, Captain, Sir Edward?" Both nodded and he left.

"He's as good as his cousin," Sir Edward said. "Maybe better."

"He is that," Jim agreed. "May I invite you to lunch?"

Down in the dining room most of the crew had already arrived, and Jim and Sir Edward were two of the last four to come in. FM, who had been standing guard at the gangplank was last. The gangplank was up and secured for the moment.

Lunch consisted of a salad bar, and cold cut meats and cheese bar, with various breads for making sandwiches. Sliced tomatoes, onions, lettuce, mayonnaise, various mustards, and sandwich spread were complimented by pickle slices, whole pickles, and olives. Fresh fruits lined another portion of the buffet.

Sir Edward made a sandwich of turkey, rye bread, mayonnaise, honey mustard, tomato, and lettuce. Jim stacked rare roast beef slices on his plate, took some cheese, a dollop of mustard to dip the beef in, an apple, orange, and bunch of grapes. At the salad bar he dished out a small side salad with blue cheese dressing.

Jim purposely sat with Calvin and his team, saving a seat for Cecilia. Bond, Bear, and D.C. were sober faced for a change, and since the word had spread so were most of the others. At the appropriate time Jim stood up and raised his glass of iced tea.

"Here's to Austin Weston, soldier, servant, and hero," Jim offered, lifting his glass.

"To Austin!" Echoed through the room as men and women drank to his memory.

Jim led the group in grace. Jim remembered the loss of Bob Stankus and sat quietly through the meal. Cecilia too was quiet, while RJ, in his highchair, smeared his meal all over his tray and clothing, face, and hair, as babies do. Having a toddler at the table seemed to help the men. Jim loved his son to distraction and realized that he now knew what it would feel like to lose a son in service to his country.

After lunch groups of crewmen left the boat to visit Miami. Among them Senator Knight and Sir Edward slipped away unnoticed by those watching the activities on the docks. Earlier that morning the gold had been loaded into armored trucks with a military escort, and with the work on the ship done the crew had free time to enjoy the afternoon. Jim and Cecilia left with RJ in a stroller along with John, Pen, JAS, Gwyneth, Alistair, Andrea, Wade, and Angela.

Jim rented a Mercedes conversion van and with his family he traveled into Miami to shop, eat out for a change, and return to the ship before midnight. He was immediately aware of a tail but paid no mind. Today they were merely enjoying the time away from the ship. He did tell John and Wade, putting them on alert in case anyone tried anything. He doubted they would.

Whoever was following them didn't have a lot of assets, because they didn't switch cars on a regular basis. That meant they were amateurs. Unfortunately, amateurs often made dangerous mistakes. Knowing this Jim and his men were on full alert as they walked through the shopping mall, ultra-aware of the two men following them.

Both were Hispanic, bearing prison tattoos, one with two tears on his cheek indicating he'd killed two people in prison. Jim guessed correctly that both would be armed. He also guessed they were there to try to take a child, or one of the women. On the way to the mall, he'd called Team Raider. Calvin, he knew, needed to get some aggression out after the news about Austin. He felt no remorse for choosing Calvin.

Jim and John were carrying RJ and JAS, giving the two men the women as their only targets. Both of the would-be attackers moved into position and pulled their guns; or tried to pull them. Before they could get them all the way out from behind their backs and under their jackets rough hands grabbed their wrists, easily taking the weapons away. When the two men tried to resist Bear and Hobbs put them in sleeper holds until they were unconscious.

Security arrived, appalled to find two thugs carrying guns unconscious on the floor. Bear, towering over the guards looked over their heads and winked at the girls.

"We saw these pelicans go for their guns, so we decided to step in and stop whatever they were trying to do," Calvin answered the questions. Police arrived soon after and when they saw the faces of the two captives they smiled.

"We've been looking for this pair for two days!" one officer said. "Good thing for these ladies you happened to be here," he looked at the four British men and raised an eyebrow. "Dress Barn isn't exactly a place I'd expect to find four men."

"Gotta buy something for the bit at home, don't we?" D.C. asked innocently. The officer asking the questions noticed the uniforms, the physical prowess of the men and nodded, unconvinced.

"Indeed." The officer said, not believing it for a moment. He was sure the four men were military, so he didn't press the issue. His men finished frisking the still unconscious prisoners, removing a number of weapons from both. "Well, thanks," he added lamely.

"These blokes weren't a problem," Matthew said, looking down at them. "Always glad to oblige. Cheerio!" he finished, and the four men turned and left.

"Did you see what happened?" the detective asked Jim, John, and Wade. He noticed that their uniforms were the same as the men he'd just questioned. If anything, these men looked even more fierce than the last group. But these men were Americans. "They were with you?"

"Yes. We're off the *Sea Venture*," John watched the connection take place in the detective's mind.

"Right. They were after one of yours to get at the money," he concluded, nodding his head slowly.

"That would be my guess," Wade said.

"Marines?" the Detective asked.

"Used to be," all three said together. "Civilians now," Jim added.

"Ah!" the Detective nodded. "Well, we'll take these two downtown and you can go about your shopping," he turned away and the groggy attackers were half dragged, half walked out of the mall and into police custody.

"That was interesting," John said.

"Imagine! A South American drug cartel with connections in Miami! Who would have believed it?" Jim stated sarcastically. "What is our country coming to?" he grinned wolfishly at John and the two gave each other a high-five handclap.

"It's a bad old world we live in!" Wade said, shaking his head.

"Are you boys done playing yet?" Angela asked, taking Wade's hand in hers. "I want you to look at a dress."

"Sorry, boys. Duty calls, and this man is ready for duty!" Wade said, emphasizing the word 'man'. Jim and John snorted.

"Some tough guy!" John quipped. "Let's a little girl order him around."

"Yeah, but the perks are worth it!" Wade admitted, leaning down and kissing Angela.

"Get a room!" John teased.

CHAPTER 8

Jim called a meeting for the library to take place after the Bible study in the morning. Outlining the mission, and their scientific work, he brought everyone up to date on what they were going to be doing over the next months.

"Jeeze boss!" FM said at the end of the meeting. "I don't think my arctic gear is going to work in the jungle!"

"I've had loin cloths made for everyone," Zeke said with a laugh.

"Did you remember coconuts?" Cecilia asked with a straight face. Jim smiled as the room broke up in laughter. Once the noise died down, he raised his hand.

"Our esteemed medical staff is going to figure out what inoculations we need, and our INTEL staff is going to figure out what else we might need," he broke off as a series of groans sounded in the room. "In the meantime, I want you all to study the maps of the river, all histories, and remember to pay special attention to the political situation in Zimbabwe. Now, let's see if we can be ready to leave for England by high tide tonight. Dorf, would you lead us in prayer, please?" Jim sat down with a sigh.

After the prayer, activity on deck, and below decks indicated the ship was preparing to depart. Crewmembers went about their duties with a purpose and by mid-afternoon, two and a half hours before high tide, the ship was ready to depart. Jim looked at his spotless ship with pride from the observation deck and waved and gave a thumbs up sign to crewmembers that looked up his way to thank them.

Dorf stood beside him and heaved a heavy sigh. Jim looked up at his tall friend.

"Such a big sigh. What's up?" he asked.

"I really like Dr. Lowe," Dorf said, his neck growing red. "I can't stop thinking about her. It's like she singles me out sometimes, you know? She's always at my table in the dining room. It scares me."

"So, ask her for a dance, and when we get to England ask her out. While we're on the way invite her to play a game or watch a movie with you," Jim smiled at his big friend. Dorf was a giant, standing six feet nine inches tall in his stocking feet, and built like a gymnast, fast and strong. That he would be afraid of talking to a girl seemed somehow odd. Yet Jim understood. Training for a soldier didn't include talking to women.

"What's she going to see in a lump of muscle like me?" Dorf asked quietly. "She's a doctor!"

"She's also a woman. Maybe she's putting herself in your way because she likes you too," Jim responded. "Come on, big guy. Suck it up and invite her to sit with you at dinner tonight. I've noticed that she sits at your table often," Jim smiled.

"You think she might actually like me?" Dorf asked, hope coming into his eyes suddenly.

"You won't know until you ask. Just sidle up to her at dinner and ask her if she'll dine with you tonight," Jim replied.

Dorf squared his massive shoulders and flexed his upper torso, as if preparing for battle. He raised his head.

"I'll do it!" he said emphatically.

At dinner that night Jim smiled when he saw Dorf escorting Carol Lowe to his table. Zeke and Bill Kline seemed to have paired up with the Millstein twins and he realized he'd seen them together at just about every meal for the last couple of weeks. Shaking his head, he took Cecilia's hand as they stood in line at the buffet and kissed her neck.

"Is there romance in the air?" Cecilia asked, her blue eyes twinkling mysteriously.

"Perhaps," Jim replied. "With us it's way past just romance. It's love, and romance!" he said, kissing her again.

Cecilia smiled and blushed. Sometimes her husband surprised her with his passion and unexpected compliments. She caught him looking at her cleavage and grabbed his chin.

"My eyes are up here!" she said quietly but sternly.

"They're pretty too!" Jim said making her giggle.

In the morning Jim met his three friends on the bow of the ship to greet the dawn. First to arrive he sipped his iced tea and watched the first ribbon of light appear on the horizon. Andrea came, followed quickly by John and Wade. For a few moments they silently watched as light pushed away the blanket of darkness.

"It's nice to have morning and evening again," John sighed. "Having it light 24/7 messes with the mind!"

"Remember, they have it dark for months at a time too," Jim said. "I've heard that's even worse."

"It will be nice to see my Rosa," Andrea said. "I have missed her."

"She's leaving the vineyard?" Jim asked.

"My Rosa says it will be our best year yet. It appears my dear wife will make us wealthier as wine growers. But she is confident everyone knows what to do. She's completed the important work and now is a good time to see how her staff does without her." Andrea smiled with pride.

"Some of your labels are world class, Uncle Andrea!" Wade said, clapping him on the shoulder. "All of it is good stuff."

"Yes. We make good wine. Our orders are growing, and we are shipping wine internationally. Each year we set aside five cases of wine in the cellar for future auctions. Who knows, nephews? Some day you may sell one of those cases for hundreds of thousands of dollars!" Andrea said.

"Probably your grand-nephews will have that pleasure," Jim chuckled. "Wine has to be at least seventy-five years old to hit that market."

"Anybody hungry?" Wade asked.

Together they walked down to the dining room. It was going to be a calm day on the ocean. Jim felt the movement of the ship beneath his feet and swelled with his own pride. *Sea Venture* was free and clear of all debt! His company was growing financially far beyond anyone's expectations.

He knew it wasn't about him. It was never about him, or his men.

"Father help me remember that any success is a gift from You, and that it belongs to You ultimately. Keep me from believing in my abilities and in myself," breathing that prayer of thanks to God he joined Cecilia in the line.

Training for the jungle began almost immediately, and with the usual intensity the crew expected. Ox talked to everyone in the library on the importance of hydration in a hot and humid climate. There were diseases in Mozambique and Zimbabwe, and all the way up to the source of the Zambezi River their bodies had never encountered before. He briefed them thoroughly on all of those, the symptoms to watch for, and the importance of the buddy system when it came to hydration.

Alistair spoke about the animal and insect threats they might face, spending a lot of time talking about the dangers of hippopotamus attacks. The huge animals were fiercely territorial, and more people died in hippo attacks than any other animal attacks in the jungle. Poisonous snakes were another danger, and everyone had to pass a test on recognizing various venomous reptiles.

In the training room Jim cranked the temperature up to a hundred degrees, and because the room was designed for that purpose, made it nearly ninety percent humidity in the room to boot. It took most of them six days to adjust to the hot and humid temperatures and the amount of water and electrolytes they needed to recharge their systems. If they weren't on duty, they were training in the Jungle Room, as they began to call it.

Upon arrival in England Jim gave his entire crew twenty-one days of vacation time. Alistair and Gwyneth went home to Live Oak Retreat because Alistair wanted to do some digging in various university libraries and museums. Barbara and Mary Ann went home to visit their respective families. Jim, John, and Wade stayed at Hill House, and Andrea went home with Rosa to Villa Orvieto near Alleghe in Italy.

Studying the maps of the Zambezi River daily gave Jim some inclination as to what his team would face. Reflecting on the practices of most underdeveloped countries he thought he would easily be able to discover the cause of the increase in red algae and the decrease in hypertrophication. A paleolimnology study would confirm his suspicions.

Underdeveloped countries, often referred to as third-world countries, which was, for Jim at least, a demeaning term, hadn't learned the benefits of sewage treatment, toxic waste treatment, or even water treatment. People dumped sewage and toxic chemicals in the water, left dead animals in the water, and bathed in the same water. No wonder diseases and epidemics so quickly spread throughout the populace.

Because much of the lower Zambezi River flooded every year the government built the Cahora Bassa dam in Mozambique, and in Zimbabwe the Kariba dam. It hadn't been long after the Kariba dam that epizootic ulcerative syndrome (EUS) killed hundreds of sore-covered fish in the river. EUS frightened both governments and tests were done to determine if the disease could pass to humans, but no tests had ever been done to determine the actual cause of the disease. That puzzled Jim.

Further, when the two countries built the dams, developers did not consider the effects that would have on wildlife, or how the massive reduction in emplacement of silt and associate nutrients would affect hypertrophication. During the recent rebellions in both countries, hunters had been allowed to go into those areas and decimate the populations of big game, elephants, and rhinoceros. Water buffalo suffered as well.

Bring It Up would complete a study on the feasibility of a cross-border conservation park, emphatically demonstrate why such a park would not work unless there were two parks, each run by its territorial government. There was just too much bad blood between groups and governments.

It didn't help that Mozambique drove out the farmers who actually knew how to farm when it embraced communism. Now the farms were failing, and they were trying to lure the farmers back, while at the same time still telling other farmers they had to leave their land. None of it made sense, but that was the nature of confused governments.

Communists brought in sugar cane farmers from Cuba, an experiment that failed miserably because of cruelty, slavery, and greed. Portugal's influence on the countries was almost feudal in nature and had done neither country any good. Nor had the British, with their prejudices, done much better, although their farming had been successful. Nationalization of the sugar cane farms had all but destroyed them. There was much to be learned from these examples. Jim thought about that.

What the British should have done was to train the people of those countries how to farm, teach them the skills, and let them decide what crops and livestock they wanted to raise. Instead, they grabbed up the land and enslaved a people meant to be free, equals among other men, simply because the color of their skin was different. He shook his head. Christian missionaries did the same sort of thing, trying to "Westernize" people, instead of simply introducing them to the Lord Jesus and allowing Him to lead them.

He allowed himself only two hours every morning to study, spending the rest of his time with Cecilia and his family. Often, they rode over the property on the Friesian horses they kept. Jim loved riding with RJ tucked in front of him, laughing as the horse moved beneath them. He and John often rode side by side, with JAS perched in front of John, the four Shepherd boys reckless, jumping obstacles and being scolded by wives.

Summer in Plymouth was a delightful time and they spent much of it swimming, picnicking, and resting. Those of the team who remained were always welcome, though they respected the privacy of their Captains and family. As a summer resort Hill House was bustling with business, almost completely full even though it was their first year of business.

In town the restaurant was doing very well and was a popular spot for many because it offered free Internet service, comfortable seating, and a friendly atmosphere. Rev. Allen Candle was a regular visitor and even held a Bible Study there on Tuesday mornings, which was equally popular. JimJim insisted that food and drink was free to those who participated in the Bible Study, and thus far that perk had not hurt profit margins. Local police were offered free coffee and other drinks at cost as a perk, and often visited the establishment, making it one of the safest in town. His manager would continue the service for both the good will of those attending the Bible Study, and the good will of those teaching it.

However, as all good things, vacation time came to an end. Summer business had come to a close only a day before the crew returned, but the staff had the houses and main house in order and ready for them. Two of the houses were rented out for two weeks at the very tail end of the summer season, but the main house was empty and ready. Jim was glad to greet the crewmembers as they arrived at the house, and he realized he'd missed all of them.

Writing the grants for their journey on the Zambezi River took the better part of that next week, with everyone contributing to the effort. Some of the crew worked on outfitting the exploration properly, while the science staff worked on writing the grants. Once that task was completed Jim began training the team, getting them back to riding the crest of the wave of perfection.

Everyone on the team stayed in contact with the Wozniacs, now working with Doctors without Borders and stationed in Mozambique. No one considered that assignment good luck or fate. Every member of the crew believed that God put him or her there at this time because He wanted *Bring It Up* there for a purpose. Because of that contact they knew a great deal about the health of the people, medical and spiritual needs, and what medicines the hospital needed most.

The Wozniacs also kept them informed of the political situations and criminal activities there and Jim knew his team would be in danger the moment they set foot on foreign soil. As a result, he expanded the company paradigm to cover air support without taking men from the 36-member military unit. Five of his crew took the challenge and ran with it.

Wrench, Ives, Inchworm, Loony, and Windy accepted the invitation to become certified members of the *Bring It Up* Aviation Operations Team. Of that group, Windy surprised everyone by rising to the top of the class when it came to flying the PBY. It was as if he'd been born with the controls of that plane in his hands. Although never trained in the military, and especially in piloting military aircraft, he learned evasive maneuvers and attack maneuvers with the reserved recklessness of the true military pilot.

Wrench and Inchworm proved to be the best combination in the AH-1W Super Cobra, second in scoring only to Penelope and D.C., and Shep and Chief. Wrench, Ives, and Loony worked best together as a team to fly the CH-53D Sea Stallion. Lessons from Dorf and Mark allowed them all to become licensed pilots of fixed wing prop driven planes, and helicopter pilots.

At the beginning of October Jim and John presided over the promotion ceremonies for the crew. This was held in the library of Hill House. Because of their efforts in learning to fly as a military team, and their success, Jim and John presented Inchworm, Ives, Loony, Windy, and Wrench their Aviation Operations pins in formal ceremony. Windy was promoted to PO2, and Loony and Wrench were promoted to PO1.

Abe, Chief, Counselor, Driver, and Izzy received their promotion to WO3 status. Sharky and Sparks were promoted to Lieutenant. As Jim pinned the lieutenant bar on Finn's collar, he thought about how much the man had changed. Thanks to the influence of Ives, Finn learned to lighten up. Although still irritated occasionally by his perfectionism, most of the crew have come to like Finn, and for him that changed everything. He shared later with Jim that he felt part of something special, and he viewed himself as an equal partner in *Bring It Up* for the first time ever.

As part of the formal ceremony *Bring It Up* gave a 200£ bonus to all the employees at Hill House and the Restaurant, and a substantial raise in pay, based on the earnings of the resort for their first summer. Mr. and Mrs. Tuggle, and Mrs. Jennings were complimented on choosing the new livery for those in service, Mr. Osborne complimented on his keeping of the grounds, and Mr. Nigel Cossgrove received commendations for running the restaurant at a healthy profit margin. Less than a year before Nigel had been homeless and in need. Today he and his wife and children occupied a small house they rented in town, and he was serving at the shelter where he once resided. Jim and John both told him how proud of his progress they were.

Nigel was still going to school to get his degree in business management. He received his accolades with humility and tears and hugged Jim and John fiercely. Then he turned to JimJim, who had worked closest with him, and the two embraced.

"I see now why your company is so successful," Rev. Candle said, watching JimJim and Nigel wipe tears from their faces. "You expect the most from your team, but you also give the most personally to that effort. Did you know that every family you helped this past Christmas is back on their feet, in their own residence, and working?"

"I've kept tabs." Jim replied.

"We do like to make sure we follow through," John added.

"Every day you are gone I pray for each of you by name," Rev. Candle confessed quietly. "I pray for every person in my parish by name every day. What that has done has made me love them all the more. What will you do next?" he asked.

"We've been given an amazing grant to study conditions on the Zambezi River. We'll be leaving for Mozambique at the beginning of next month," John replied.

"That will put you on the Zambezi River at the beginning of the rainy season!" Allen exclaimed.

"We will go up the river during the rainy season, returning at the beginning of the dry season," Jim explained, nodding. "We actually have some friends in Mozambique working with Doctors without Borders. It will be fun to bring them some much needed supplies."

"Dealing good wherever you go!" Allen said with a smile. The smile disappeared as Jim looked at him.

"Not always, Vicar," he said softly. "Sometimes we deal in death too. We will be in harms way the entire time we are on the river. Men are always our deadliest enemies. Sometimes they're men with good intentions, but most often they are men bent on evil. A few years ago, in South America, we were forced to kill hundreds of such men. So, keep praying for us.

"A few years ago, we lost one of our own, one of Abe's rehabilitated alcoholics and drug addicts. His name was Bob Stankus, and he became a man, and then a man of God, and last, a hero who gave his life for a friend. A pirate shot him," Jim finished.

"Heavens! What happened to the pirate?" he asked.

"I told him I would personally kill him for shooting Bob. It wasn't a threat. He's dead," Jim's face was so grim that Allen realized something about the man he'd never known before. Jim Shepherd was a soldier, and sometimes he had to kill. But he hated killing. That made him one of the good soldiers. Jim was a man of honor and duty. Having never really thought about it before he decided that he liked this young soldier, much more than he had realized. It surprised him to realize how much he valued this friendship.

"Having to do what you did takes a lot out of a man. If you ever need to talk, stop by my office. My door is always open," Allen said, putting a hand on Jim's shoulder.

"Thanks, Vicar," Jim replied, moved by the offer.

"I served in Her Majesties forces in the early eighties," The Vicar said. "Having seen action, I can talk about it with you, my friend. I mean that."

"Only someone who's been there can really understand. I'm glad to know that. Again, thanks," Jim replied.

CHAPTER 9

On the eve of October 31, *Sea Venture* left the dock and headed through the English Channel toward the Atlantic Ocean. Jim stood at the wheel, his eyes looking off the bow, at the instruments, and left and right to be sure no boats came dangerously close. He'd been hounded by reporters regarding the grant and was glad to be past that part of his job.

Green Peace and other organizations had tried to piggyback on his grant, but the grantors kept them all at bay. They made it clear that they wanted *Bring it Up* alone for this study. His science team helped as well. Jim didn't dislike organizations that wanted to help the people of the world, but many of them were so entrenched in their own dogma that they did more harm than good.

Finally, it was just his crew, his ship, and the water, and he breathed a sigh of satisfaction. He listened to the chatter on the COMLINK with pleasure and concentrated on his piloting the ship safely to the ocean. Too soon he would have to relinquish the wheel to another.

In his mind he reviewed the journey to Mozambique. Their first official stop would be to test the waters off the port of Casablanca. Two hundred miles off the coast of Africa they would put in at Las Palmas de Gran Canaria and test the water there. After that Dakar, Conakry, Freetown, Monrovia, Abidjan, Accra, Lagos, Luanda,

Cape Town, Port Elizabeth, Durban, Maputo, Beira, Chinde, and Quelimane. The last four were all in the Mozambique Channel and in Mozambique.

"Captain, we are ready to switch to hydraulic propulsion," Goody's voice sounded in his ear. Jim pressed his shirt button that activated the COMLINK.

"Roger that, Goody. On my mark! Three! Two! One! Mark!" Jim commanded. As he said the word "mark", he cut the diesel engines and eased the throttles forward for the hydraulic system, making the change so smoothly the boat barely slowed one knot before picking up speed to 12 knots.

"All hydraulic systems nominal," Goody said over the COMLINK a few minutes later.

Four hours later, with the Atlantic in sight, Jim reluctantly gave up the wheel to Dorf. Dorf pressed his uniform button. "Lieutenant Commander Bernard has the bridge," he said.

"Are we there yet?" FM whined over the COMLINK.

"Don't make me pull this boat over!" Dorf shot back. Jim grinned. There were comments like "I have to go to the bathroom!" "I'm hungry!" Somehow in the tedium of daily routine his men could always find humor and crack jokes. Carol Lowe came over the COMLINK next and caused a lot of laughter.

"I feel like I'm baby sitting and not getting paid!" she said.

It was almost ten o'clock, but everyone was still up. Jim found most of them in the library as he passed that way, waved, and went on to his stateroom. Cecilia and RJ were sound asleep, and he undressed quietly, laid out his clothes for tomorrow, and crawled into bed next to his wife.

Cecilia was pregnant again. So was Penelope, this time about a week apart, and Angela was a week ahead of them. None were showing yet. Jim smiled at the thought of another baby in the family, sighed with pleasure, and closed his eyes. He was asleep in minutes.

On November 4th they reached Casablanca at dawn. Three container ships were being loaded at the docks when the tugs nudged *Sea Venture* in place. Shortly after that the Rigid Raider davit released and the Rigid Raider dropped slowly to the water. In the raider Dr. Alice and John Dinsmore, and Dr. Michael Putnam, Dr. Iris Copeland, and the Millstein twins sat quietly. Jack Boswell was at the helm, and Frank Miller at the bow.

Once FM and Driver released the stable hooks Driver started the outboard motors and eased the throttles forward. At a steady twenty knots they moved toward their first test site, where runoff from the city flowed into the ocean. Garbage, dead fish, and other unsavory things covered the surface of the water near the runoff, and everyone wrinkled their noses in disgust.

Water samples were taken in glass jars, marked, and put carefully in carrying cases designed to keep them safe on a moving boat. After that they went to where the sewage ran out into the ocean, again offended by the horrible smells, and took more samples. The Rigid Raider took them a full nautical mile each direction from those two points for more samples, and then headed out to about a hundred yards from the entrance of the harbor to take yet more samples. This time they took samples from various depths, and by the time they returned to the ship they had two cases of samples to test.

Driver and FM locked the stable hooks in place and signaled Wrench to activate the winch. Slowly the raider rose out of the water, remaining level, until it was locked into place and the davit rocked back so that the passengers could exit safely. As soon as the Rigid Raider was locked in place the ship moved out of the harbor to drop anchor two miles south, where the smell of the harbor was lost.

No sooner had they dropped anchor than a police boat appeared asking permission to board. Having prepared for just such a reception Mark walked slowly to Jim's office to relay the request, and slowly back. When he returned John accompanied him, with Dorf, Wade, Santa, Bear, Hayseed, and Sturdy. Goody manipulated the controls to bring the gangplank down to the boat and John walked down with Mark.

"What is your reason for asking to board my ship?" John asked bluntly when they reached the patrol boat. The officer in charge was taken aback. His eyes narrowed as he measured Captain John

Shepherd, and the Lieutenant standing beside him. These men looked like and acted like soldiers. Their uniforms were unique, and it was obvious they were not in the United States Military. Yet they carried themselves with the confidence of men who knew how to handle themselves. Opting for diplomacy the officer responded.

"I wish to examine your paperwork for two reasons: first, to establish that everyone on board is indeed part of your crew, and second to ascertain if you have permission to test the waters of Casablanca. It is merely a formality," he added, spreading his hands.

"The Moroccan government issued permits to this company through the grantors to test the waters of Casablanca. You already know this. State your true purpose for coming on board my ship!" John replied, his voice flat, his eyes hard.

"I have been ordered by my superiors to search your vessel!" the officer answered angrily.

"Then why didn't you say so in the first place?" Mark asked quietly. His muscular arms were crossed over his chest, and he hadn't moved since he stopped, despite the slow roll of the ship.

"I do not have to ask permission to board your ship!" the man spat. "If I want to board your ship I will do so. Do you understand this? My men bear arms."

"We are in international waters, and you cannot board this ship without my permission!" John snapped. "You might want to take a look up at the rail of my ship," he added.

The officer looked up and saw the railing lined with a dozen men pointing shotguns down at his boat. Merely the way they stood, calm, but coiled, ready for battle, warned him. He looked at John for a long moment before dropping his arms and shrugging his shoulders.

"You have my permission to board this vessel but understand that in international waters the authority here is mine, not yours. If any of your men step out of line, I will personally throw them over the side of my ship. Am I understood?" John held the eye of the officer in command.

"You will find that diplomacy is a wiser course than bravado," the officer retorted.

"Am I understood?" John asked again, and this time the officer understood this was not bravado. He swallowed hard and nodded.

"We offer no aggression here," he said, once more lifting his hands as if in supplication.

Leaving the pilot with the boat the officer stepped onto the gangplank with two of his men and followed John up to the deck. Mark followed the party. On deck the officer found himself surrounded by very tall, very powerful, men in uniform. Looking at them with a policeman's experienced eye, he realized that he and his men were in no position to make demands or take control of the situation. He didn't like that.

"You and your men have access to the entire ship. You will be accompanied by one of my men at all times. Any lockers or crates you want opened will be opened for you. When you are finished with your search you will be brought to my office. I will have all the paperwork there for you to examine. Now get on with your search!" John commanded.

Wade and Dorf escorted the officer in charge through the ship, and he carefully looked at everything. He'd been on a lot of ships, but none like this one. Everything was in place, and everything was well cared for. He saw no signs of rust, and everywhere crewmembers were busy, glancing his way with curiosity, and without fear. He knew before he went below decks that *Bring It Up* had nothing to hide.

In the laboratories he was amazed at the equipment and capabilities of the science team. Later, he looked at the AH-1W helicopter, looking closely at the equipment mounted, noting that it was scientific, and that the front gun was capped. He looked in a few lockers and saw that even here things were carefully stowed. At last, he motioned for Dorf and Wade to return him to John's office.

Seated at a desk in the same office he saw Jim Shepherd, brother to John, also a Captain, busy with paperwork. Jim didn't even look up! As promised, John had all the paperwork ready for the officer to inspect, which he did merely because he'd been told to do so. Seeing it was all in order he asked to see the visas of the crew.

"Lieutenant Finn!" John commanded. The quintessential

administrative officer appeared in the doorway and saluted the captain.

"Sir?" he said differentially.

"Show this man our crew visas and passports, please," John ordered.

"If you'll come with me," Finn invited after saluting John once more.

Finn opened a locked file drawer and took out all the visas and passports, organized so that the officer could look through them alphabetically. He took random passports and noted with surprise that many of the crew were from the United Kingdom and some even from Australia. One of the scientists was from Holland.

"This is an international crew?" he asked, his eyebrows knitted together in a frown. Finn, he felt, he could intimidate. He was wrong.

"Sir. With all due respect, you already know the exact make-up of this crew, and if you don't you didn't do your homework very well. This is a scientific research ship, and a Search and Rescue and Salvage ship, all wrapped into one. We are well known in the maritime community as a successful venture. Our crew is the best on the ocean, bar none. *Nulli secundum*, which is second to none in Latin. Everything you are looking at is legitimate and straightforward. There are no criminals on this crew, and we have nothing to hide," Finn picked up the information and returned it carefully, relocking the drawer.

"We will see," the officer said officiously.

"You have seen. Stop wasting my time and get out of my office. I have work to do," Finn demanded. His whole manner was one of dismissal and the officer didn't like that at all.

"You will do well to cooperate with local law enforcement!" he said.

"I have cooperated. My Captain commands me, not you. If you have a problem with that, I suggest you take it up with him," Finn answered without fear.

Angrily the officer returned to John's office. John looked at his watch and at the officer. "You have now wasted one hour and fifteen minutes of my personal work time on a fool's errand. Get off my ship," John said the last as a direct command. Before the officer could respond John spoke.

"Escort these men back to their boat. If they ask for permission to board this ship again deny it," John walked around his desk, sat down, and began to work through a report of how much fuel they'd used so far in the journey. He did not look up.

"This way, sir," Dorf said, motioning with his hand. The officer sighed and followed. With his two fellow officers he was escorted to the police launch. Balefully those men watched them board their boat and depart. Not until the launch was away, did they walk back up the plank and the plank raised and stored properly.

At his headquarters he gave his report to his superior. Major General Marcus grunted at the conclusion. "You saw no weapons other than a dozen shotguns?" he asked gruffly. He suspected there must be other weapons on board the ship.

"No sir. I saw no other weapons. And I made sure I saw every part of the ship," he added.

"That is all," the Major General said, dismissing him. Sergeant Octavius was surprised, saluted, and spun on his heels and marched out. He decided he would keep an eye on that ship and its crew, and if they stepped on land, it would be he who was in charge this time.

As high tide began to eb the Rigid Raider reappeared, took more samples, and headed back out to sea to the anchored ship. To Sergeant Octavius' dismay, no one from the crew set foot in Casablanca.

The following morning Jim and John walked together to the labs. Those in the biology lab were all busy at something. One of the lab techs was using pipets to fill tubes for the centrifuge. Others were at microscopes and the Dinsmores were working on a gel electrophoresis. Countertops had dozens of slides already labeled and placed in special holders so they wouldn't move as the ship rolled gently. Beakers and test tubes were also in holders.

As the two Captains walked into the lab heads looked up, and then the scientists went back to studying whatever they were looking at. John stood up while Alice continued working at the electrophoresis.

He joined the two men as they walked around. It would be his report they would hear today as he summarized what they knew so far.

"Two years ago, Professor J. Anderson of Sweden took the same samples we took, so we have something to measure against. Did you notice the oil slick on top of the water in the harbor?" he asked. Jim and John nodded.

"Well, that's worse. Not only are they still dumping raw sewage into the ocean, but it is also mixed with low levels of toxic waste, insecticides, and even some interesting proteins. Even a hundred yards outside the harbor the water is filled with pollutants. Anyone who eats fish from that part of the ocean is in danger.

"It gets worse. There's a higher density of red algae and plankton is almost completely depleted. I'll have to ask the whale watchers of this part of the world if the whales have come here less than in the past. Even where we're anchored the plankton concentration is about half of what it should be! Oxygen levels in the water are lower than two years ago, which is a bad sign." He sighed.

"When will you have a full report?" Jim asked quietly. It made him sad that countries treated the ocean like a giant sewer, a place to get rid of their garbage and toxic waste.

"Tomorrow morning," John Dinsmore replied.

"I'll send a security detail with you," Jim replied.

"A security detail?" John asked.

"We're going to send all of our biologists to talk to the university in Casablanca, and to the government. It's a dangerous time for Americans to be anywhere without an escort. When we go, we go in uniform, if you don't mind. I want to give the impression that we are bona fide." Jim added.

"The government is sending representatives to meet us on the dock tomorrow morning at nine," JR added.

"Okay!" Dr. Dinsmore said with shrug. "We'll be ready."

"May I ask one more favor?" Jim asked.

"Sure, Shep. What do you need?" John replied.

"Include some economical solutions and safety precautions the government can take," he said simply.

"We never do a report without including that," John shared with a grin. "Most scientists leave that part out," he added.

"Thanks," Jim nodded. "I knew I could count on you."

Later that evening the copy machines were running at full speed making copies of the 208-page report prepared by the marine biologists on board. Every finding had been documented with concrete evidence, but it did not read like many scientific reports. Iris wrote the report, and she wrote it so that the average layman with an eighth-grade education could follow the formulas and decipher the terms. It was one of the reasons she was such a popular teacher before *Bring It Up* stole her away from her university job. Thinking like a scientist didn't mean she had to write like one.

Firefox and Bulldog had the security detail. Eight Marines, even unarmed, were a formidable force to reckon with. R.C. drove the HSB, knowing the suspicious looks he was going to get as the flat gray craft pulled into the Marina. It was a military HSB when they needed it. Today it was a Civilian HSB, without weapons of any kind.

Bulldog was first out of the boat. Hayseed, Neil, and MP formed a semi-circle of protection around Chief, who was helping the scientists out. They watched as two groups moved toward them, one the government contingent, the other Sergeant Octavius and three of his squad. Octavius arrived first.

"Your papers please!" he demanded belligerently.

"What do you think you are doing?" a deep voice said as the government contingent arrived. "These are world famous scientists, noteworthy men and women who have come to help us! Are you out of your mind?"

Octavius turned to the government official, spotted one of his superiors in that back of the group, and swallowed. He cleared his throat and tried to appear compliant. The soldiers watching him didn't think he did a very good job.

"The boat is a military boat. I was suspicious, so I asked for their papers," he said in a conciliatory tone.

"They were invited here by our government! Who cares what type of boat they came on?" the official in charge sputtered.

"My man was simply doing his job, sir," Octavius looked gratefully at his superior.

"The boat used to be military. It's a civilian boat. Nobody's on board so you can look if you want to," Chief said. "Let's get everyone off the docks please, for security reasons," he added.

Octavius swore under his breath and was about to board the boat when Dodge stepped up to him.

"Touch anything on this boat, put anything on it, or in it, and you get to deal with me. I'm not like John Shepherd. I have zero tolerance for fools!" Octavius looked into the eyes of the man known as Viper and suddenly he had no desire to search the boat, or to plant the evidence he had on his person. He backed away and his superior took his arm, shaking his head, and led him apart.

"I have heard of these men. Do not cross them. Leave the boat alone," he warned tersely. "They have been welcomed as guests and the Minister of the Interior is in charge of this party!"

Octavius nodded, cursing in his mind, and spun away, waving for his men to follow. He remembered those eyes and decided his best option for now was to be patient and watch. On the way off the dock, he pulled the drugs he'd put in his pocket to plant on the boat and threw them in a burning trashcan. Dodge watched him, though he was unaware his clandestine movement had been noted by anyone. Shaking his head, he decided Octavius would need watching.

Reception at the university was warm and cordial, colleagues gathering to discuss a real problem with a chance to rub shoulders with some renown scientists. Alice and John passed out copies of the report and summarized the contents, focusing on the economic solutions Morocco could take to reduce the danger.

City Hall in Morocco proved to be a very different proposition. The politicians were wary, expecting to be chastised by the scientists for their failures, and unwilling to spend funds to fix the problem. Some of that eased as they realized that the scientists were merely going to report and offer solutions. Even then, there was an invisible wall of separation between scientists and politicians. Doctor Copeland

and Doctor Lowe were able to thaw the politicians a little because of their beauty, a fact that amused both of them.

After a formal luncheon and further questions and answers the scientists returned to their boat, boarded, and left. Mike Putnam knew that they would be depressed after the chilly reception from the political side, so he entertained all of them about nearly killing his chemistry teacher in high school. By the time they got back to the ship everyone was in a better frame of mind.

In the library the crew welcomed the scientists back, eager to hear the results of their visit. After half an hour of sharing the scientists drew to a close. Jim looked at them and smiled.

"What's your assessment of the chances for change?" he asked.

"There's a slim chance. Some of the politicians know that diseased fish are a problem. Their own university has been pleading with them to clean up the harbor. We shared your idea of using low-risk prisoners in small rowboats to clean the harbor waters. That got some interest because it was a low budget fix. As far as sewage treatment and proper toxic waste disposal I think it will be years before we see any of that. Unless an epidemic breaks out that is directly connected to the sewage or toxic waste problem the government will ignore it.

"The university is barely holding on, keeping its doors open, so they have no real influence. I think the deadliest enemy those people who live in Casablanca have is the people that run their government." Alice sighed unhappily.

"We did our best. Let's pray about it, and then move on to the next test site," JR suggested.

"You know, for a Captain he's pretty smart," Penelope commented in the moment of silence that followed. That got a chuckle from those who heard it.

CHAPTER 10

Las Palmas proved to be a very different port of call. *Bring It Up* was welcomed officially and every effort was made by the government to aid the scientists in their study. Though only two hundred odd miles from the African shoreline the water at Las Palmas was much cleaner. Sewage Effluent was still a concern, but much less than that of Casablanca. Crew enjoyed going ashore and visiting the historic city and were welcomed everywhere.

Government officials and university professors met the crew at the city of Dakar in Senegal. In recent years they were making Herculean efforts to clean the port waters and keep the ocean waters free of chemicals that might harm fishing, one of the major industries of the area. *Bring It Up* researchers were able to show them that their efforts were paying off, and pollutants in the water measured far less than they had just two years prior.

Conakry's reception was not warm, but neither was it hostile. Officials knew that the pollutants would be a problem and that international pressure would be placed upon them to do something toward cleaning up the situation. They were quite bitter that none of the international groups would offer financial help. Prepared for that reaction *Bring It Up* grant writers worked with local officials to write some grants to ask for funds to help with the problem. Because of language and interpretation constraints, they spent three days in port, rather than one, but no one begrudged the extra time. When they left their efforts had proved that they were not only serious about the problem, but also willing to help governments find plausible solutions. Word spread fast.

Freetown, Monrovia, and Abidjan welcomed them with open arms and begged for the same help they'd offered Conakry's government. More than happy to oblige the tests were carried out and help provided. International news teams arrived in Accra to witness this new phenomenon of cooperation between scientists and governments.

Jim knew better than to trust reporters, as did his team, so those individuals were forced to turn to government officials for information and quotes. Ghana's government took full advantage of the international press to beg for help in many areas. Later, alone with the leaders of Accra Jim commended them on that ploy and wished them every success.

Lagos proved to be a different and difficult assignment. It was a city torn by difficulties and political pitfalls. With over twenty million people the city was the largest in Africa, and people, yellow busses and taxis clogged the streets. Getting anywhere in the city took hours! Only in the district of Yabba, at the University of Lagos, were they welcome, and even that welcome was cool.

Sensing the political tension *Bring It Up* kept the crew on board the ship with the exception of the trip to the university. For that they flew the scientists in on the CH-53D Sea Stallion. Because the INTEL group on the ship was monitoring communications within the city, they learned of a plot to take the scientists hostage.

Thanks to quick action the group was hustled out to the waiting chopper, which lifted off just moments before the would-be-kidnappers arrived on campus in force. Government troops moved in immediately and fortunately, no blood was shed that day. After that Jim allowed only university personnel to visit the ship.

To do so they had to provide their own transportation from the city to the ship, anchored now in international waters, and only those invited were permitted to leave the boats and step on the deck of *Sea Venture*. By the end of the day the city leaders declared that all scientific studies cease. Officials from the city demanded the samples taken by the scientists.

Jim had several containers filled with seawater from one of the moon pools and handed them over. When a military officer ordered that the ship be searched Jim refused. The attempt to board the ship was repelled with non-lethal ammunition and a humiliated and demoralized group of soldiers retreated to the city. International pressure caused the government to back off, but Jim knew the nature of such governments.

Under the cover of darkness, he left Lagos.

Luanda, Cape Town, Port Elizabeth, and Durban all received *Sea Venture* and the *Bring It Up* researchers with open arms. Major efforts were already under way in all of those ports to reduce sewage effluent and pollutants. Jim suspected that some international pressure was exerted for their benefit, though he kept those thoughts to himself because the communities were working toward solving the problem.

His team decided to release the results of their studies while in Durban, before arriving in the Mozambique Channel. Because it was science news of interest to most developed countries almost every news agency picked up the story and ran the results. Two days later Jim smiled as he opened an official document from the government of Lagos, apologizing for the incidents. Lagos had been making efforts to clean up their harbor, and the study showed that their efforts were among those most successful.

Jim knew that Lagos government officials did not expect to be favored fairly in the report and was glad for the apology. He dictated a letter responding in a friendly fashion to the agency that sent the letter and complimented them on their efforts toward cleaning up their waters. Rick Nelson smiled as he typed the letter for Jim.

After war, trade with the enemy. It was an old axiom and it worked often. In his letter Jim mentioned nothing of the incidents or danger to his team, concentrating on Lagos, Nigeria, and the efforts made to clean the water. It was diplomatically worded and carefully phrased to indicate willingness for future endeavors together.

Once in the Mozambique Channel of the Indian Ocean *Sea Venture* hugged the African shoreline taking numerous samples at various depths. At Maputo the ship put into the docks, and Jim paid for a week's dockage. To improve relations the ship resupplied at Maputo, filling the diesel tanks, and buying necessary staples and supplies. Jim encouraged the crew to spend money shopping in the city, and they did, purchasing unique items to commemorate their visit to Mozambique.

No one went alone. Everyone on the crew knew the danger of Americans alone. The women went in pairs or threes, always accompanied by at least eight men. Men usually went in groups of six or eight. Since the crew was polite and genuinely curious most of the locals were willing to look past the unusual numbers.

Scientists in Maputo met with the researchers and scientists of *Bring It Up* and the scientists of *Sea Venture* soon discovered that the local scientists were at the point of defeat when it came to cleaning the water of the harbor and Channel. At every front they met resistance. People refused to stop using the rivers and streams as urinals and bathrooms, as a place to dump their garbage and other waste, and the government refused to spend money. Most of them had reached the point of losing hope in ever gaining success.

Instead of chastising them for giving up, the scientists of *Bring It Up* promised to give what aid they could, and to increase the international pressure for change. Water samples were dismal and the red algae concentration truly frightening. Fishing, a major industry for the coastal communities, had fallen off dramatically. With the oxygen depleted water fish were staying away or dying. In some places the stench of dead fish was almost unbearable.

Worse, carrion birds that fed on the fish often died of chemical poisoning. An entire flock of ravens littered the grounds near the docks, adding to the stench of death and decay. Jim wondered how the government could see such things and ignore the implications. Rats scurried among the dead bodies of the birds, some as large as a small cat. It was truly horrifying.

Since the government was located in Maputo Jim accompanied

the scientists, serving as interpreter since he spoke fluent Portuguese. In Mozambique over forty different languages were spoken, but Portuguese was the official language of the nation. The body language of the officials when they entered the chambers where the meeting would take place told Jim this meeting would not go well.

There were, according to the dignitaries, more pressing issues to concern the government than the condition of the waters of the Indian Ocean. After the initial presentation, which lasted only fifteen minutes, about thirty minutes of questions, discussion, and answers followed. Near the end of that time Jim signaled the scientists it was time to end the debate. They were getting nowhere. It was Jim who delivered the final remarks.

"We do not minimize the multitude of difficulties your government faces. Nor do we propose that we know better than you what priorities you choose. Our scientists are here to help, not hinder your government, and we will do everything within our power to help you. I'm sure that in time international pressure from nations affected by the rising red algae count will force you to face this issue.

"My only hope is that you respond quickly enough. Once the red algae population reaches exponential growth everything in the Channel will die. What we have given you is a gift, proof that the problem exists and is growing. You must decide how to respond to that. You have both our respect and our willingness to work with you toward ending the problem. Thank you." He bowed, politely, spun on his heel and walked out of the room.

Inwardly he was seething. Turning a blind eye to the red algae problem in the Channel was stupid. Convincing these officials of that was the difficult thing. They just didn't understand the nature or destructiveness of red algae. He hoped that someone would study the problem and realize that it was real, and the potential for disaster high.

Bring It Up had one major advantage. The fishing industry was vastly affected by the red algae problem, and the loss of revenue from taxes might wake some of the officials up. His science team had shown in their presentation the fiscal effects of the problem in the last two years. That one thing had gone home to the officials. So often with governments it would be loss of revenue or loss of face that would turn the tide, rather than loss of people, jobs, and natural resources.

Beira's waters proved to be much the same, as did those of Chinde and Quelimane. It was at Quelimane that they would anchor the ship, launch the river craft, and begin their journey up the Zambezi River. Documentation was checked by both Finn and Nelson, secured, and put on board *River Venture 1*.

Jim had six specially designed river exploration craft that bore the company logo, paint scheme and were named *River Venture* and numbered 1-6. He would command *River Venture 1*. Andrea had command of *River Venture 2*, Sean Oxton had command of *River Venture 3*, Jack Boswell had command of *River Venture 4*, Dorf Bernard had command of *River Venture 5*, and JR had command of *River Venture 6*.

Each vessel had two enclosed decks, and an open observation deck on top, displaced only three inches of water when fully loaded, and operated on the hydraulic system designed by TRT and Goody. *River Venture 4* was unique in that it contained a galley. Each boat had a dining table capable of seating fourteen people in the main lounge.

Cabins were small but comfortable. Every boat had a science and computer lab. *Sea Venture 1* carried a Cray supercomputer and Zeke's Computer Intelligence Center, or CIC. Computers on all the other boats were connected to his computers and transmitters giving them the ability to communicate via satellite.

Each boat also had very cleverly designed lockers for military weapons and supplies. Searches by professionals were always negative when it came to discovering weapons. Jungle gear and normal hunting rifles and pistols were out in the open for anyone to see. Jim was very aware that some of the mining companies would certainly try to slow or even stop their research, by legal and lethal methods if the legal methods did not work. In this case legal methods were probably not going to work, so Jim prepared for the worst-case scenario.

Trusting God for their protection he covered the mission in prayer and prepared to do the work and let God decide what happened.

His team was in top physical condition for this endeavor. Mentally and emotionally, they were in a good place, and spiritually they were trusting God. Even if they had to face death, they would trust God. Jim knew that. He felt like his men rivaled Hananiah, Mishael, and Azariah, who when faced with the fiery furnace, told the king that even if God did not rescue them, they would still bow only to Him. The faith of his men inspired him often and he was glad that all of them studied God's word together and prayed together.

Counting RJ, Jim had thirteen bodies on *River Venture 1*. He looked down at the roster that listed them in order of rank. Zeke Kline, Calvin Weston, Cecilia, Bill Kline, Richard Nelson, John Smith, Zeke Good, Frank Miller, Matthew Banks, David Carr, and Paul Donnelly filled the list. That gave Omega 1 and Raider point on the journey.

Everybody called Weston "Hobbs". Calvin was SAS trained and held the rank of Lieutenant on the team. He was the team leader for Team Raider, that included three other SAS trained soldiers, Matthew Banks, David Carr, and Paul Donnelly. Banks had been dubbed "Bond" because of his choice of sidearm, the Walther PPK. Carr had been dubbed DC because of his initials, and Paul Donnelly was affectionately known as Bear, towering over his teammates at six feet six inches tall. Richard Nelson hated being called Ricky, so he was dubbed Rock & Roll after the famous Ricky Nelson.

Andrea had thirteen on his boat as well. Bob Neff, Norm Geissler, Terrance Red Claw, Lee Ainsworth, Lloyd Brookstone, Earl Duncan, Gene Hardesty, Neil Meyers, Mel Pierson, Iris Copeland, and Alice and John Dinsmore made up his roster. That put Sniper and Bulldog as backup. *River Venture 2* was his charge, and Andrea took his position seriously. He was also humbled to have command of two of the military teams.

Team Sniper was led by Norm Geissler, who had been dubbed by the men as "Counselor" because his father was a famous British barrister. Norm held the rank of Warrant Officer 4th Class (WO4).

His team consisted of Lee Ainsworth, dubbed "Lord Lee", Lloyd Brookstone, dubbed "Rock", and Earl Duncan, dubbed "Donut". All these worthy men were SAS trained.

Team Bulldog was a team of U.S. Marines led by Terrance Red Claw whom the team had dubbed "Chief" because he was a full-blooded Blackfoot Indian. Gene Hardesty, dubbed "Hayseed", a Pennsylvania farm boy, Neil Meyers, whom everyone simply called "Neil", and Mel Pierson, dubbed "MP".

Iris Copeland was a marine biologist, as were John and Alice Dinsmore. Iris had been dubbed "Dr. C" by the crew. John had received the unlikely moniker of "Dr. Flush" and Alice was dubbed "Dr. Wonderland" by the crew. All three were renowned in their own field.

Sean Oxton had command of *River Venture 3* with a roster of twelve. With him were the four medical team members, Leo and René Axlerod, and Will and Donna Penny. Alistair and Gwyneth Gregg were there with Carol Lowe, Lisle Mirelle, and the three men that made up his team, Knife. Lee Roy Brown, Chance Edwards, and Phil Eustus finished the roster for his craft. Sean's team would join with Omega 1 and Raider if they divided into teams of twelve men.

Team Knife was an Australian SAS trained team led by Sean Oxton, called "Ox" by the crew. Sean was a field physician, held the rank of Lieutenant, and was loved for his earthy humor. Lee Roy Brown, dubbed "Lunch Box", was an Aborigine, tall, slender, and full of fun. Chance Edwards was a sturdy black man the team had simply dubbed "Chance". Phil Eustus was dubbed "PU", pronounced pew. He was white, shaved his head, and was best mates with Lunch Box.

Carol Lowe and Lisle Mirelle were on the Science Team, Carol a marine biologist and Lisle an archaeologist. Carol was dubbed "Dr. Mermaid" and Lisle was dubbed "Dr. Devastation." Both were lovely young women and well known in their individual fields.

Jack Boswell had command of *River Venture 4*, which the team had already christened "Garbage Scow" because it housed the galley. He had team Nightfall on his boat, led by Tom Izbicki, with Steve Coleman, Bernie Finlay, and Richard Kagan. Most of the kitchen crew was on this vessel. Abe, JimJim, Sturdy, and PJ were present on his roster. He also had Mary Ann and Barbara and Dr. Putnam. Ned Vintner was the thirteenth name on his list.

Team Nightfall was led by Tom Izbicki, dubbed "Izzy", holding the rank of WO4. Steve Coleman was dubbed "Santa" because of his initials, Bernie Finlay was dubbed "Fingers" because he looked like a number's runner, and Richard Kagan was dubbed "Fagan" because he looked sinister. PJ was Paul Jennings, one of the kitchen crew, a powerful, tall black man with infinite energy and great love for his work.

Mary Ann and Barbara were dubbed "Spanky" and "Babs" and were lab technicians and assistants to Dr. Gregg. Dr. Putnam was a marine biologist from Australia, well known in his field, and dubbed "Dr. Dundee" by the crew because of his Australian accent and humor. Ned Vintner was one of the youngest on the team, a computer technician the team dubbed "News".

Dorf Bernard was in command of *River Venture 5* with thirteen on his list. Mark Drumheiser, his usual second was there. Two other members of Team Delta were on other boats. Firefox was on his boat with Bill Dodge, Sid Barrett, Roger Corrigan and Sam Colt. Hammer was a member of his crew for any electrical problems that might arise on the journey. He had two of the kitchen crew, Bull and Winky. Along for the ride were four of the lab technicians, René and Tiffany Millstein, Elizabeth Minor, and Stephanie Morris.

Team Firefox was another group of U.S. Marines. Led by Bill Dodge, nicknamed "Viper" by his men and holding the rank of Lieutenant, the team was respected by all. Sid Barrett, dubbed "Scope", Roger Corrigan, dubbed "RC", and Sam Colt, nicknamed .45 were the members of that team. Bull was Bill Franklin and Winky was Bob Hinkle, both on the kitchen crew.

René and Tiffany Millstein were twins who had been nicknamed "Hot Lips" and "Tiffer". Elisabeth Minor was dubbed "Cup Cake", and Stephanie Morris, "SOS" because of her last name. All four were actively working toward a Master's Degree in marine biology.

John Shepherd was the rear guard, commanding *River Venture*

6. The rest of his Team Zulu were with him. Wade Adams, C.G. Franklin, and Vince Hall would provide the rearguard services for the team. Penelope and JAS were with him, as well as Finn, his administrative assistant. Angela Adams and Heidi Van Haaten also occupied his boat with lab techs Rachel Hague, and Lynn Ross. Frenchie and TP from the kitchen crew completed his roster.

Ives, Johnson, Romentowski, Rule, and March were providing air support for this mission. At the moment all five were occupied. Ives, Wrench and Inchworm were flying the CH-53D to an airfield just outside of Mopeia Velha. Windy and Loony were following in the PBY to bring Wrench and Inchworm back to ferry the AH-1W Super Cobra. Because of the danger of their mission Jim had requested and received permission to have the Super Cobra fully armed to provide air support if needed.

For that matter, the CH-53D was armed, as was the PBY for emergencies as well. The cost of receiving permission for those armed aircraft was well worth the price. Finn, of course, was still furious that the Mozambique government had needed so much money in bribes to obtain the proper papers and permission. Ken Worthington set up the contract, which was signed once the money was provided. Jim didn't mind. The peace of mind of knowing that he had air support was all that mattered for this dangerous mission.

It was mid November when they began their journey up the canal that would connect with the Zambezi River. It was the beginning of the flood season and the waters had already risen a few inches. Jim chose the timing on purpose. Rainy season would make the journey more treacherous for them, but also for any enemies that attempted to waylay them along the way.

Along with that advantage, the surging waters would bring the pollutants down the river to them as they moved forward. By determining the speed of the current they could pretty much target the locations of the worst polluters before coming upon the sites. Jim was quite certain that some of those sites would shut down until his group had carried out their survey and testing and moved on.

They began the journey just before sunrise, and after traveling two miles against the current switched to the hydraulic system. Goody listened to the machinery working beneath the floor of the boat and nodded his head in satisfaction. Not only were the hydraulics nearly silent, the system produced more torque. He listened to the hum of the system and watched the dials in front of Jim carefully. Finally, he opened his COMLINK.

"All systems nominal, power at full. Turn off the diesels." The sudden silence was almost eerie in the pale dawn. Pilots had matched the hydraulics to the diesels in speed and so the switch was flawless, smooth, virtually undetectable. Smitty came up to the bridge, plugged his iPad into the system, and downloaded the information necessary for the autopilot.

"Captain Rob has the helm," he said when he'd finished, switching over to the computer system. Jim took his hands off the wheel and folded his arms over his chest, watching the boats line up and come to within three feet of each other. Captain Rob would warn them of any deviation or danger long before the boats encountered it, make automatic changes if an underwater obstruction appeared, and stop the boats completely if necessary. These boats had been tested in the Amazon region and had performed perfectly.

"Breakfast, anyone?" Jim asked with a grin.

As he stepped away from the helm a three-dimensional holographic image appeared in his place. He looked at his image and nodded. "That's a good-looking captain!" he said.

"He's the silent type, not much for conversation," Smitty smiled.

"Best kind. I hate the ones that are always yelling at their crewmembers," Jim replied.

"Tell me about it!" FM scoffed at the bottom of the stairs.

"Aargh, matey! Get yer duty done or I'll have yer guts for garters!" Smitty mimicked the Disney pirate voice.

"Must be a sailor. Needs garters!" FM quipped without missing a beat.

"Avast! The floggings will continue until morale improves, ya scurvy dogs!" Smitty shot back.

"Does somebody need a hug?" Bear piped up as he joined the fun.

Donnelly stood six inches over the six-foot mark, and weighed an impressive two hundred and sixty pounds, all of it SAS muscle. He lifted Smitty off the floor as Smitty pretended he was being crushed. It was a good start to the morning, as the men continued to joke with each other on the way back to grab breakfast, return to their boat, and sit and eat it. Leaping from boat to boat was not difficult.

"Four thirty in the morning and it's already ninety degrees!" Weston grumbled. "Are we there yet?"

"Shut up and eat your porridge!" DC snapped.

"We're having gruel for breakfast!" Weston complained, looking into the pot of porridge.

"It's porridge," Banks whispered.

Weston made a face as he moved on to the eggs and ham. Penelope shook her head and smiled at the man. She helped herself to a generous bowl of the porridge, sprinkled a little brown sugar on top, and poured milk into it. After that she sprinkled some blueberries over the top and returned to her boat to eat.

On *River Venture 1,* Bill Kline kept watch ahead, while the crew ate, and was relieved by Banks to get his own breakfast. It amazed him how quickly the scenery changed from the city of Quelimane to African tundra. He watched some giraffes striding majestically along the riverbank and smiled, pointing them out to Banks as they switched.

After breakfast things got tidied in berths and cabins, the decks were scrubbed clean, and a thorough check of all systems was done. Satisfied things were as they should be the crew began to work on their assignments. Those who had no specific duty tagged along with those who did, learning, taking notes, asking questions, watching the scientists at work in the labs, and looking into microscopes.

CHAPTER 11

Every scientist on board held teaching positions before they joined forces with *Bring It Up*. It came naturally to them to teach as they studied things. That the men of Omega Force were not only willing, but intelligent and avid students only made their jobs more enjoyable. Although they'd been together long enough to know each other well, it often surprised those teaching just how intelligent these men were.

"What might you have become if you didn't go into the military?" Dr. Alice Dinsmore asked FM after he identified a specific bacterium on a slide through the microscope. He looked at her with one eyebrow raised.

"Eventually I might have become a detective, because I like this kind of work. But I needed the discipline of the military. Before I joined the Marines, I didn't have focus and lacked the will power to gain what I needed. Perhaps it was because I was still just a kid, but I think on some level I needed the structure and discipline of military life. I wouldn't trade what I do for anything, doc!" FM shared honestly in his quiet voice.

"On this crew I can be a detective, a scientist, a hunter, and a soldier. That's a pretty exciting life. And searching for lost ships, finding treasure, discovering pieces of our past all thrill me. It is a life of adventure and also constant danger. Every single body of water is unforgiving, a force of nature that can kill you in an instant. Each day I open my eyes offers amazing challenges."

"Wow!" Stephanie exclaimed, looking at FM with a strange thoughtful expression. Most of the time when FM talked, he was making jokes, keeping everyone laughing, and seemed a footloose happy soldier. She'd never heard him talk like that. "Is that why you work so hard to keep your body in top condition?"

"My body gives me one edge, my mind gives me a second edge, and my spirit gives me a third edge. Being strong doesn't mean you can always win. Every time I spar with Jim, I learn that. I'm stronger than he is, but he takes me every time. And having a sharp mind doesn't always mean I'll be able to think fast enough to know what to do. In my inner man I know who is in control, and that gives me a peace in the midst of the toughest challenges. Put all three together and what you have is a man who can accept what is, face any challenge including death, and do his utmost to succeed."

"You rarely talk like this when we're around," Stephanie pointed out softly.

"I guess I never felt comfortable enough before to share that kind of thing," FM said a bit sheepishly.

Alice watched Stephanie as she digested that bit of information and smiled to herself. She had an inkling that Frank Miller was about to be swept off his feet by one of the prettiest girls on the ship. Keeping that bit of information to herself she went back to her work. Putting a new slide under the microscope she whistled softly.

"Take a look at this, Mr. Miller!" she said. "Do you know what those tiny rust-colored organisms are?" she watched him put his eyes to the microscope.

There were four elongated almost teardrop-shaped organisms, rust colored at the widest and top part, and green and yellow towards the part that came to a point. "Am I right in identifying this organism as red algae?" he asked, looking at Alice.

"Bang on! You go to the head of the class," she smiled. "This one is *Euglena sanguinea*, and when there are enough of them, they turn the water almost blood red. They also produce a poison similar to fire-ant venom. I read about an outbreak of these in an Ohio lake this past summer. Usually, Ohio lakes are susceptible to blue-green algae. That one is called *cyanobacteria,* and it produces liver and nerve toxins that make people sick and can kill pets. They've had to put warning signs up to keep people out of the lakes before for cyanobacteria.

"I believe that since the Ohio breakout of *Euglena sanguinea* there have been other findings in Texas, Arkansas, and Mississippi, as well as this part of the world." She watched FM carefully print the species names in his notepad, with the information she'd just given him. She was not surprised to see that he'd gotten it all down in his neat block printing.

"Don't they like warm still water best?" he asked, looking up.

"Once again you've asked the right question!" Dr. Dinsmore smiled at him. "Yes! They do! Thus, finding them in this concentration in a slow-moving muddy river is a cause for real concern."

"Teacher's pet!" Smitty muttered at his side.

At his microscope station Dr. Putnam had Nightfall listening avidly as he described the organisms on his slide. They were gathered around his laptop, looking at the display from the microscope, following his instructions as he directed them to capture some of the pictures for his report. He was looking specifically for toxic waste particles and organisms that fed off such products.

Beside him the centrifuge spun, separating particles so he could look at them and identify what he found. His face was grim and his voice low as he described what he was seeing, and how to tell which particle belonged to which material. Hazardous waste from sewage effluent, insecticides that had been banned in America and other countries, and waste from mine machinery, boats, autos, trucks, animals, and people filled his slides.

"It's a wonder the fish can find room to live with this stuff!" he growled finally, putting his hands on the counter and lowering his head. "This country is in barney, and no mistake!" he added, shaking his head. "I've got chemical waste from mines that I haven't read about before!" he looked over at John Dinsmore.

"Coal mining has picked up since the revolution ended," John replied, nodding sadly. "The concentrations will be highest at this end of the river, rather than at the sources themselves. That's probably why they're having the red algae explosion in the Channel. Bacteria must be thriving in these conditions."

"Bacteria counts suggest that the pollution has reached exponential reproduction rates," Dr. Axlerod looked up from his work as he spoke. "What worries me is a virus epidemic," He commented quietly.

"Such as?" John asked, turning to his colleague.

"A plague of some kind," Leo answered.

"That might explain the outbreak of epizootic ulcerative syndrome." John nodded. Alice stood beside her husband.

"Studies were done the last time that happened and EUS did not spread to the human populace. Most people were wise enough not to eat a diseased fish, I think," she said. "But carrion birds won't make that distinction, and that may strengthen the mechanism."

Later that day the findings were the subject matter of discussions around the table as the crew ate lunch. Crewmembers tended to travel from boat to boat during mealtimes, listening and joining in the conversations. Jim thought his crew was amazing in that everyone took a personal interest in what was happening to the Zambezi River, and by consequence, what could happen to the people of Mozambique. They cared.

In the town of Mopeia Velha their boats drew much attention, despite the heavy rains that were falling that morning. Children especially ran down to the docks to see the amazing riverboats of *Bring It Up*. Scientists waded through the muddy streets observing how run-off was affecting the river, and what might be in the waters streaming down toward the river. Several vials for further study were gathered, while the children scampered on and off the boats.

An official appeared in a new Range Rover, and under an umbrella approached the lead boat. Jim watched people react to the man approaching his boat and decided that this man was not much liked. He stopped on the dock and smiled at Jim.

"Captain Shepherd! May I come aboard on official business?"

Jim decided the man smiled like a Crocodile. He nodded in the affirmative.

"Thank you!" the man said as he lowered his umbrella once beneath the canopy of the boat. He looked around with interest. "I need to see your paperwork and visas if you please. I am Provost here for our government," he added.

"You know my name. May I have yours?" Jim asked politely.

"Ah. You may refer to me as Mr. Katanga," the man replied. "I am Mosi Katanga, Provost."

"If you'll follow me, Mr. Katanga," Jim invited, turning away, and leading the man into his office. He went to the file cabinet, unlocked it, and brought out all the paperwork, permissions, permits, and visas, as well as the copies of the identification pages of the passports of his crew. Katanga studied the paperwork carefully.

"You have an international crew?" he revealed, raising an eyebrow. "People from America, Australia, Greece, Holland, and the United Kingdom?" he made it a statement more than a question.

"Yes, sir. Our company has facilities in America, the Bahamas, and the United Kingdom," Jim answered.

"Would you permit our police department to search your vessels?" Katanga asked, returning the papers.

"Any time, sir," Jim replied with a smile. Just then three of the children from the village passed the doorway, followed by Bear, who was carrying a fourth.

Some of the people of the village also walked by, talking among themselves regarding the opulence of the boat. It was obvious, even to a casual observer, that the people visiting the boat were comfortable and unafraid. Katanga raised an eyebrow.

"You are not afraid things might be stolen?" he asked. "I know these people. You should be very careful when allowing them on your vessel. They are like rats, getting into everything," his voice showed his disdain.

"I doubt it," Jim said easily. "We brought extra food to entertain people from the villages, and to welcome them. It will give us a chance to talk to them about how to protect this water source."

"If these people find money, they will take it!" Katanga warned.

"I doubt that very much," Jim said evenly. "You, I would worry about when it came to money."

"You insult me?" Katanga asked dangerously.

"The village outside is poor, most of the people can barely feed their families. You drove up in a very expensive vehicle and you wear very expensive clothes. If you choose to see that as an insult, then yes, I insulted you. I watched the people react to your presence. They hate and fear you. That tells me all I need to know."

Katanga stood up and stared at Jim, but it was he who first looked away. There was something in those hard, green eyes that told him he was not dealing with a typical blustering tourist, but a confident and dangerous adversary.

"You are either a very brave, or very foolish man," Katanga commented softly.

"It's a fine line of distinction," Jim replied, his eyes still hard. "Why don't you make your call and get this search over with?" Jim suggested.

Katanga nodded, pulled out his cell phone, made a call, and nodded to Jim. "My men will be here shortly."

"If they step out of line with any of the ladies of my crew both they, and you will not like the consequences," Jim added just before Katanga turned away. He watched the rage flood the official. It told him what to prepare for.

As Jim suspected, it was a small military group that arrived, a total of six men, obviously used to having their own way and having people move out of the way in fear and terror. They strutted to the lead boat where Jim and Katanga waited.

"Tell them!" Jim said as they came to a stop. Katanga looked at him, and this time he shivered inside at the look in those eyes.

"Be respectful in your search. There are ladies on these boats and in the village. Show them every courtesy," Katanga said nervously.

The leader looked from him to Jim and then laughed raucously. "You do not give orders here! We are in charge!" he said.

Jim disarmed him so quickly the man only had time to open his eyes wide when the barrel of his own gun pressed under his chin, and he found himself looking into eyes so cold he could swear he smelled fresh earth from his own grave. All the swagger and aggression went out of him.

"I hear of one incident involving you or your men and you will regret it. Am I clear?" Jim said.

Some of the other men in the group raised weapons. One of them, close to his leader, extended his weapon toward Jim only to find Jim's Colt Python an inch from his right eye. Jim turned to him for a moment, including him in his glare.

"Try it," he challenged quietly. Katanga, who had been startled by how fast the American moved, saw others of the crew surrounding his men. He knew that things were going to get very bad if this went any further. He snapped angrily at his soldiers and told them to lower their weapons immediately. Jim turned his attention back to the leader and the man swallowed nervously under that cold stare.

"You can have your weapon back when you leave," Jim said, stepping back and holstering his Python. Sturdy, Abe, Dorf, Wade, and Bear appeared, and all the fight went out of the soldiers. "Sturdy, please escort Mr. Katanga wherever he wishes to go," Jim ordered. Sturdy nodded.

Cecilia came up to Jim, holding RJ, smiling at the soldiers as they filed past. Katanga studied her, a beautiful woman to be sure, holding a baby and showing the first signs of another on the way. When Jim took RJ and began to toss him up and down as the child squealed with delight Katanga realized that the child belonged to the captain.

John, Pen, and JAS appeared. It was obvious that this was the other Captain Shepherd, and that the two brothers were close. He waited, not daring to explore the boats with the giant Sturdy in attendance. Wives and children left a few minutes later and Jim invited Katanga on a tour of the boats.

It was a thorough tour, and Katanga marveled at the technology. Goody explained the hydraulic system to him, though he couldn't quite follow it. Zeke's computer center was amazing and every image on the monitors surrounding him showed data and pictures of their current assignment, as well as all the public sections of the boats they occupied.

Another thing Katanga saw was the neatness of everything. Even in the cabins everything was in its place. In the galley every surface gleamed with the exception of the dishwashing station where Frenchy, PJ, TP, Winky, and Windy worked together, joking with each other easily as the dishes were cleaned and stacked. At another station in the galley JimJim was creating a huge fruit salad.

None of the men saluted Jim, at his earlier request, and greeted him with their typical friendly fare. Greetings of "Hey Shep!" and "Hi boss!" came from the men. PJ clasped hands and bumped shoulders with Jim, and Frenchie and Jim exchanged high fives. JimJim nodded as Jim came over and offered a slice of mango to his Captain. Jim tasted it and nodded approval.

"That is good Mango!" Jim praised with appreciation. JimJim smiled and continued his work.

Mary Ann and Barbara came into the galley at that moment and rushed over to the fruit salad. They both took bits of fruit and tasted them and then on either side of JimJim leaned down and kissed his cheeks.

"Hey! I didn't get any!" two of the dishwashers complained. Suddenly the men joined ranks, arms around each other shoulders they leaned forward and sang. "We've got sunlight on the sand, we've got moonlight on the sea, we've got mangos and bananas you can pick right off the trees, we've got volleyball and baseball and a lot of dandy games; what ain't we got? We ain't got dames!"

Jim laughed and applauded with Barbara and Mary Ann, and then the two women dashed to the dishwashers and began kissing each one. Katanga watched in amazement as they kissed PJ, who was a black man. English ladies did not act this way where he was from! Obviously, they were not prejudiced, as many he had met. Barbara hugged PJ.

"I love a man who can wash dishes!" she laughed. He grinned at her.

"Get out of here and let us get to work!" he ordered.

Again, Katanga was amazed. The two women waved at everyone and left as full of energy as when they'd come. He looked at Jim who had smiled and nodded through the whole performance. Jim looked at his men and shook his head.

"Guys. When it comes to singing on Broadway, don't quit your day jobs!" he warned with a grin. Although the men had done a good job with the song, it was obvious they were not professional singers. They laughed good-naturedly.

"What! Give up a life of washing dishes for glitz and glamour?" Frenchy said comically.

"Trust me guys, most of the people I know who do get parts on Broadway are still waiting tables and washing dishes!" Windy replied with a chuckle.

"Noble professions both!" TP said, striking a pose.

Jim led Katanga out. As they walked to the next boat Katanga's men were just completing their searches. Each one took a boat and searched thoroughly, finding nothing to report. Jim had Katanga back at the lead boat when they were ready to leave, and he handed the leader his gun.

"I could arrest you for taking this!" the man snarled.

"You could," Jim agreed. "But then you would have an international incident on your hands and your job here would be over," Jim added. "You know it, and I know it. Now get off my boat!" he turned to Katanga. "My regards to Ling Yi."

Katanga's eyes widened and he hurried off the boat. *How had the captain known he had been bribed by Ling Yi to have the boats searched and check their credentials?* As he drove out of town, he passed a Mercedes Benz GI450 SUV. Gilles Ramanantsoa, behind the wheel, knew Katanga's vehicle. He turned and followed.

In Katanga's official office Gilles listened as the man ordered his secretary to get Ling Yi on the phone. Knowing that Ling Yi represented a Chinese company called the Zhanzhu Corporation that seemed to have unlimited funds interested him. He wandered around the office, looking at various pictures and awards as he listened to Katanga talking loudly enough for him to hear the entire conversation.

"The Captain of *Bring It Up* knew that you sent me to inspect his boats! He knew!" Katanga said hotly.

"Of course, I did!" he replied after a moment.

"The company is doing research on the Zambezi River and the red algae in the Channel. It is sanctioned by my government; and they are working off of three grants that have funded the whole expedition. They have respected scientists on board, and they are traveling with family. We found no military weapons in a thorough search. They do have the usual hunting weapons and it is obvious that many of them had previous military training.

"Furthermore, Captain Shepherd disarmed one of my best men like I would disarm a child of three! Authority does not intimidate him. He knows that he is on legitimate business and has nothing to hide and obviously nothing to fear. The men I saw were all quite fearless, as was he. He as much as called me a thief and a liar!"

Gilles smiled at that, and the other man must have laughed.

"Do not laugh. He knows you work for the Zhanzhu Corporation and that I accept financial donations from your corporation!" Katanga sputtered. Gilles went to a seat and sat down. He now wanted to talk to Katanga very much.

Once the proper greetings had been observed, and a thousand Euros passed to Katanga Gilles got all the information he wanted. *Bring It Up* was obviously on legitimate business, though the timing for the presence of that entity at this particular time was unfortunate. Gilles decided he would let Wikffels deal with it, using Maximiliano to even the score from the Arctic Ocean fiasco. Smiling to himself he decided that would take care of that threat.

The Zhanzhu Corporation was another matter all together. He refused their advances in purchasing his new laser earlier this year, and he was not surprised that they had people on location where he was. Warned now Gilles slipped out of town and for nearly a month did not reappear.

Back on the *River Venture 1* Cecilia sat next to her husband as they ate lunch, everyone up on the observation decks of the boats so that local villagers could join them. Instead of chairs they all sat on the deck, eating delicious fruit salad, various cheeses, and water that had been purified for drinking.

Villagers commented on how refreshing the water was and the crew had fun telling them it had been taken from their own river, purified, and made fit for drinking. Not only were they curious how this was done, but amazed that it could be done so easily. Every family in the village learned the process and was told that if they did this for all their drinking water, they would be safer, healthier, and happier. Filtering and then boiling the impurities out of the water was not difficult, but the purification tablets were difficult to get.

Later that afternoon the PBY landed in the river and taxied to the boats. Boxes of the tablets were unloaded and passed out to the people of the village. Jim knew that some of them would sell the tablets, rather than use them, but he knew of no better way to distribute them than he was employing. Life was like that.

CHAPTER 12

Gilles Ramanantsoa made two phone calls. Zeke recorded both. The first was to one of his best agents, a former soldier from his father's days. Though the man was in his late forties he still managed to get the job done when Gilles needed something ugly. This was going to be ugly. Kirabo was as vicious as they came. Ramanantsoa gave him the task of spying on Zhanzhu's agent Ling.

His second call was to Martin Wikffels. Martin was staying in a house near Tete overseeing work on the coalmine. When he learned that the crew of *Bring It Up* was on the Zambezi River, and what they were doing, and that he could employ Maximiliano, Wikffels rubbed his hands together in anticipation. They were here, on Maximiliano's turf, and he could exact his revenge.

Wikffels made two calls, both of which Zeke again recorded. One was to his bank in Zurich, the other to his old friend Maximiliano. Zeke listened to the two men talk; his usual smile gone for the moment as he knitted his brows in concentration. When the phone calls were finished, he saved the conversations and forwarded them to every member of Omega Force.

Ling was not without assets, and he was aware of Gilles interest in him immediately. He made a phone call to Tao Ling Zhanzhu. Tao reported to Ke Yi. Gregor Vasovitch ambled into the office of Ke Yi half an hour later. Everything about Vasovitch gave off an aura of death. Used to his awareness of Vasovitch Ke Yi ignored his feelings and instead explained what he needed. Vasovitch was on the next flight out of China, headed for Mozambique.

There were names that were on the watch list of most anti-terrorist agencies in the western world. Zeke didn't trust names. Instead, he'd written a program that identified salient features of known terrorists, war criminals, and criminals in general. If any of them passed a security camera he could access he knew of it almost immediately.

Vasovitch passed through three such security checkpoints on his way to Mozambique. Each time Zeke's security program flashed the picture on the monitor with a red flashing signal to catch his eye. Zeke knew Vasovitch only by name and reputation, but he was a person of interest to Omega Force. When he discovered the man's destination it was easy to connect the dots. Vasovitch worked for the Zhanzhu Corporation. Known to be a troubleshooter and problem solver, it was obvious that Vasovitch was coming to Mozambique to deal with Kirabo.

Later that evening Jim met with the team leaders in the dining area of his lead boat. Zeke joined the nine leaders at the table. He brought everyone up to speed.

"So, what is Vasovitch coming to do?" Ox asked.

"Probably give Ling Yi some much-needed backup," John said quickly. The other men nodded.

"Is it possible that Ling Yi knows about Gilles interest in him?" Jim asked.

"It's possible. That was my first guess when I saw he was coming here," Zeke responded. Several of the men nodded. "Ramanantsoa was approached by the Zhanzhu Corporation about his laser. He turned them down."

"They probably have the capability to do what Zeke did, capture his phone call to his agent, and are sending Vasovitch to deal with Kirabo," Dodge said. "Kirabo is going to end up very dead, if that's the case," he added.

"Okay. Let's deal with Maximiliano," Jim suggested, shifting in his seat. "How would you ambush us?"

"Our plane and choppers are vulnerable," Weston said. "I'd take one of them."

"There are dozens of places in the jungle along the river that would make an excellent ambush site," Counselor said, looking over his maps.

"This cat Maximiliano is going to want payback. I think he'll go for us in a remote region where no one will know what happened," Chief said slowly. "He'll want an escape route that won't be threatened by floods too. That narrows down where he can hit us."

"I'd want a spot on the river where I could use fast attack boats," Izzy provided on the heels of Chief's comment. "Failing that, I'd want a place where I could get my troops to a road and get gone." The men looked at the maps with concentration. Experts at this they soon identified likely places for such an ambush.

"Do you suppose it was Vasovitch who killed Austin?" Hobbs asked suddenly. There was an uncomfortable silence.

"If he did, he had some help," Jim mused quietly. "Do you want Vasovitch?"

"I'd like to know what happened. Vasovitch might know. So yeah, I'd like him," Weston answered. "If he's here to kill Kirabo we can use that to turn him over to local officials for trial."

Jim nodded to Weston. "Good enough. You and your team get Vasovitch. After we gather the INTEL, we'll decide what to do with him."

"I have a feeling this will be Mr. Vasovitch's last trip anywhere," Penelope surmised, her eyes hard.

Conversations continued regarding the problems they faced, not to mention the dangers from hippos and other denizens of the jungle. Maximiliano, they decided, would hit them between Kanyemba and Chirundu, or between Shsheke and Sioma just before Ngonye Falls. Both of those locations offered a hundred miles of dense jungle that would be virtually unpopulated at that time of the year. Also, both offered escape routes.

"Once we leave Mopeia Velha we are vulnerable," Jim declared at last. "But we have air support that can patrol the river, and we are forewarned. Threatened men live long," he said quietly. "Let's just be on the alert from the moment we move out."

"Roger that, Shep!" the men agreed.

"Get your teams up to speed. Good night, all," Jim stood up and left the table, going to his cabin where Cecilia was feeding RJ a bottle.

"Uh oh! Daddy looks grim!" Cecilia commented as Jim came in. "You need to cheer him up!" RJ giggled. Jim smiled. "Good job RJ!" Cecilia encouraged.

"Doesn't it worry you that it will only get more dangerous now?" Jim asked as he kissed his wife and son.

"Life is dangerous," Cecilia said. "Losing my family taught me that, more than anything else," she said, running her hand over Jim's head. "But God was there. He was there for them in their deaths, and he's here for us in whatever we face. I didn't used to think like that, but I do now. It took losing my family to realize it. Yet somehow, knowing He was there with them at their worst moment gives me peace. I want my children to know the Lord that way."

"And I tend to take more than I should on my shoulders when it comes to protecting my family and my crew," Jim offered after a few moments thought. "There's really only so much I can do, and the rest is in His hands. I wish I could remember that!" he chuckled, shaking his head. "I must be getting old and forgetful!" he joked.

"No dear. Wisdom comes with age, and there's no sign of it yet. Not to worry!" Cecilia laughed.

"That was a quick repost!" Jim laughed. But Cecilia wasn't done. She continued.

"You wouldn't be who you are if you didn't do everything you could to the very best of your ability. God wired you that way husband mine! It's one of the things I love about you!" she reached up and kissed him lightly on the lips.

Later that morning Jim saw Paul Donnelly and Sid Barrett setting up their most expensive cameras on the observation deck. Both of them looked up with anticipation when Jim appeared and went back to work.

"Hey Shep!" Bear spoke when Jim joined them. "If we see something worth photographing, could we ask the boats to stop?" Jim looked at the shore, judged their speed at five or six knots and slowly nodded his head.

"Why not? You guys take great photos. Let's use every talent we have to make a point for this study. I'll let everyone know you'll be calling out an all stop occasionally. Will you need to go ashore?" he looked up into the thoughtful eyes of his tall friend. Bear nodded finally, and Sid was already nodding in the affirmative.

"Okay," Jim agreed. "Take at least two people with you for protection. Let's be ultra cautious while we're here," he added. Turning away he went down to Smitty to see how the men could stop the boats. Smitty grinned.

"They yell all stop," he answered. "Captain Rob is programmed to actually hold the boats as still as possible when that command is given. I'll tell them. If they use their COMLINK Captain Rob will respond immediately," Smitty left his computer and ran up to the observation deck to talk to Bear and Scope. He could easily have relayed the information on his COMLINK, but Jim knew he wanted to see the camera equipment and talk to his friends.

Jim went up to the front patio of the boat that was screened in and even had a fan slowly turning on the ceiling. Most of the crew that didn't have duty was seated there, watching the shorelines with interest. He reached into the refrigerator and pulled out a Diet Coke with Lime, popped the top, and let the cool liquid run down his throat with pleasure.

At the very front Weston and Carr scanned ahead and to the sides with binoculars. Every boat had two men doing the same thing, looking for signs of danger, anything out of the ordinary, or movement in the brush. Jim knew they would alert him instantly if they spotted anything. Beside them, in special holders, two hunting rifles stood ready.

It was raining, as was typical, a steady downpour. Heading back through the boat he checked that all was going according to plan and stepped across the three-foot span to the second boat. Almost two hours passed as he stopped and visited with crew, talked to various people, and made his inspection. He was just coming back to his own boat when the "all stop" order came from the science crew.

Every three hours the boats would stop, and the science crew would venture out on the rigid raiders to take samples. While they did that a second crew would go ashore with ropes and tie off the boats. Sometimes there were trees to use, but other times they merely drove a six-foot metal pole into the ground and used that. Men who swung the sledgehammers came back soaked in sweat, for any exertion in this humidity caused heavy sweating.

Jim noted that most of the men who did the driving with the sledgehammer went ashore wearing only a T-shirt. When they were done, they removed the shirt, washed off the sweat, and put a new shirt on. It meant washing more than one T-shirt that day, but they didn't seem to mind.

Jim remembered the discussions regarding the schedule with a smile. He had insisted they only stop twice a day for testing, the first at 09:00 and the second at 14:00. They planned to run the boats for twelve hours a day at six nautical miles per hour, covering seventy-two nautical miles or 82.872 statute miles per day. The boats could go much faster, but long hours of study determined this would be the optimum speed for safety and to space the test locations equally along the river.

Dr. Dundee, Dr. Flush, and Dr. Wonderland were in the rigid raider. That was Dr. Putnam, and John and Alice Dinsmore. Jim smiled as he thought of their nicknames. His men could sometimes be whimsical, and at others just crude. They called John Dr. Flush because his name reminded them of a toilet. Fortunately, Dr. Dinsmore didn't seem to mind the nickname at all and used it often himself.

Driver was at the helm of the raider, and FM sat up front with his rifle at the ready. Rachel Hague, Elizabeth Minor, and Stephanie Morris were assisting the doctors in the boat. In a second rigid raider Dorf was at the helm with Firefox at arms to protect the scientists. Above them the PBY circled keeping watch. Looking up Jim caught a wave from Windy, guessing correctly that the man was having the time of his life, flying that beautiful old plane around for reconnaissance.

Jim stood on the observation deck of his own boat and watched as the scientists collected their samples and headed back to *River Venture 2*, and the lab there as the first stop, and then to *River Venture 5* with its lab. Number one and four were the only boats without a lab, because of the computer lab and galley. Number one had the computer lab, number four the galley.

Once the raiders were properly attached the boats moved forward. Every two hours the lookouts were exchanged for a fresh pair of eyes. Jim took his own two-hour shift toward evening, FM opposite him. Using his eyes and his binoculars he studied the south shore carefully, focused, his eyes catching movements many people would miss. A cape porcupine waddled beneath some bushes near the shore causing the branches to move slightly. Not far away a huge cane rat slithered out of the water and into the tall grass.

In the trees a family of Grant's Dwarf Galago monkeys romped through the branches voicing their odd high-pitched cry as they scolded and literally seemed to insult each other, chasing each other wildly above the forest floor. Graceful and swift they unerringly swung from branch to branch using feet, hands, and tails interchangeably.

A family of blue monkeys moved on the floor of the jungle looking for food, and as the Galago monkeys sped past them they looked up and danced and screamed as if to warn them away. Monkeys could be brutal, Jim knew, and the smaller monkeys in the trees, hearing the rebuke, moved higher as if to keep out of reach. Somewhere further from the water an elephant trumpeted.

"Hey boss! Take a gander at this crock!" FM interrupted, pointing to a monster sitting on the bank. Jim looked, noting that the reptile had to be at least twenty-five feet long! With mouth slightly open he could see the rows of teeth. Everything about a crocodile seemed menacing, even lying still and at rest. Jim sighed.

As if sensing that men were watching it the crocodile slowly turned its head and opened its huge mouth, showing its teeth and hissing as the boats slid quietly by.

"Yikes!" Jim said softly.

"I'd say about a hundred briefcases, a hundred purses, and maybe a hundred pairs of boots and shoes!" FM suggested with a feral grin.

"Take your knife and go get him!" Jim grinned back.

"We need Dr. Dundee for that," FM quipped.

"Did you guys see the size of that crocodile?" Bear was leaning over the railing of the observation deck and looking down. FM looked up and signaled a thumbs up.

As darkness fell the boats were tied fast to sturdy trees on shore, just before dinner was served. Dinner was served at 18:00 hours. Planks between the boats were fastened in place and everyone made their way back to *Sea Venture 4*, collected their plates of food, and made their way back to their own dining rooms on their own boats to eat.

Those on watch would wait until relieved before going for their own dinners. Everyone was on high alert with the threat of retaliation from Maximiliano, Wikffels, and Ramanantsoa, so the guards took their duties seriously, moving their heads from side to side as they stared through binoculars. The long wooden canoes of the local people that floated downstream disappeared when they were far enough away from civilization and villages. No other boats were to be seen.

Wildlife, however, was abundant. A heard of water buffalo came down to the river to drink. Paul Donnelly longed to take pictures, but he was on duty. Sid Barrett was using his video camera to record the herd. He'd moved to the forward boat from his when he saw them coming, and he stood close to Paul as the beasts jostled each other, lowing quietly, drinking from the river.

Suddenly Paul saw the head of a crocodile appear in the water and he trained his binoculars on it for a moment. He whispered to Sid that a crock at least twenty-five feet long had just appeared. Sid lifted a thumb to signify he'd seen it and from the way he kept the camera in one place Paul knew he was waiting for the crock to make its move. When it did it was violent and noisy.

Seeming to spring from the water with blinding speed the huge crocodile grasped a cow by the neck and immediately began to thrash and roll, dragging the bawling beast out into the deeper water until the two disappeared. For a moment the herd hung back, and then returned to drink. Sid caught it all on digital.

Later that night Zeke put the video on the screen, edited it, and estimated the size of the crocodile at a little over twenty-six feet! The entire crew watched the attack from start to finish in startled silence. Jim wondered what many were thinking. When it was over Dr. Putnam nodded a few times.

"Big feller!" he finally said. "We'll need bigger boats and bigger guns!" That brought laughter.

"Aren't you supposed to take your knife, dive off the boat, and wrestle that thing?" Dr. Copeland teased.

Mike pulled his penknife out of his pocket, looked at the tiny blade as if contemplating using it. Finally, he sighed. "I think I need a bigger knife," he said, shaking his head. "And you have me confused with someone else. I'm Dr. Dundee, not Crocodile Dundee," he added. "I wrestle things like red algae."

"My hero!" Iris joked, putting her hands to her breast.

After RJ went down for the night Jim took Cecilia up to the observation deck and they watched the sky turn various shades of red and orange as the sun set over the African lowlands. On *River Venture 5* the Millstein sisters let out a startled yelp. Someone had arranged a paper cutout in one of Dorf's uniforms, and it lay flat on the floor, as if Dorf had been deflated.

"Don't step on him!" Sam Hammer exclaimed. "Did you guys see the size of that mosquito?" Laughter followed and Cecilia looked up at Jim with a happy smile.

"We have a very interesting crew, don't we darling?" she asked, putting a hand on his face gently.

"That we do!" he chuckled. "That we do." Others came up to look at the scene on the observation deck of *Venture 5*, laughing at the imagery. Eventually Dorf arrived, wearing nothing but his bathing shorts, with a perplexed expression on his face. For a moment he stood scratching his head, as if deciding what he was looking for or going to say.

"My uniform seems to have disappeared. Did anyone see it?" he asked. More laughter broke out. Carol Lowe came up behind him, slid around him and looked up at her giant friend.

"If you walk around like that, you'll probably end up looking like that!" she indicated, pointing to the flat cutout. Dorf flexed every muscle in his body, an impressive sight, and made a horrible mean face, growling heavily.

"You want a piece of me? Come and get it bug!" he growled. "He relaxed and stood to his full height. "They wouldn't dare bite me!" he said, and then slapped his bottom and yelped. "I'd better go get some more clothes on!"

Jim was certain that Sam Hammer, Mark Drumheiser, and Dorf had worked out that little scene very carefully and chuckled as his big friend headed down below to dress more appropriately. Dorf rarely did something like that, but Carol seemed to be bringing him out of his shell. Jim was glad that Dorf had finally found the courage to approach Dr. Lowe, and he was glad that she seemed to be very interested in him.

Jim and Cecilia went down to the front deck and sat at one of the tables, drinking coke and tea, and joining in a game of hearts with Zeke and Bill. After Zeke and Bill won three games in a row Jim chuckled. He knew the two could communicate in a unique way, being identical twins, and as a team they were almost unbeatable. He suggested changing partners. After that the game became a little more even, although Zeke and Cecilia won two out of the next three hands.

They switched to Mille Bournes and after two games together decided to turn in. Soon all six boats were silent, the only noise the occasional groan of the ropes and the slap of water on the hulls. A torrential rain began after midnight. On the observation deck FM had the watch and he leaned on the rail, listening to the water patter against the surface of the river and the outer skin of the boats. Movement in the water caught his attention and he saw the crocodile surface, just its eyes and nose out of the water. From his vantage point he could see all twenty-six feet of it. As a predator it was almost perfect, silent, nearly invisible, and pure power.

FM wasn't fooled into believing the crocodile would leave the boats alone. Crocodiles were known to be crafty hunters, even brazen when it came to human habitation. On the Zambezi River several incidents of croc attacks on boats were registered each year. He raised his hunting rifle and stared down into the eyes of the predator, softly sliding the safety to the off position. Seeming to know it was threatened the crocodile submerged and swam away. FM sighed but kept his eyes on the water just in case the crock returned.

There were other noises around the shoreline near the boats as curious animals studied the strange floating houses. Lowering the rifle, after putting the safety back to the on position, FM turned his head to study the animals he could see. He was not bored at all during his two-hour watch, often feeling more than seeing a predator studying him from the shore. There were grunts from the brush that came from big cats he never saw. Africa was a dangerous place.

Each boat was equipped with a defense perimeter, an electrified mesh that delivered over a thousand volts of electric shock. That defense was against large snakes and other dangers that might come out of the water, or a nearby tree, and try to board the boat. That night nothing triggered the system and FM watched dawn arrive with a yawn. He'd had the last watch of the night and he wasn't tired, physically, just mentally from the constant listening and watching. As dawn approached, he watched the hippos return to the water, huge animals that spent the night foraging for food near the river.

Writing the time the hippos appeared, and reentered the water in his digital log, he closed the iPad and stretched. D.C. appeared at the head of the ladder and climbed onto the observation deck. He was ten minutes early, a practice the men kept, and took that time to read FM's log entries for the night. When he was finished, he handed the iPad to FM, watched him log out, and logged in.

"Jolly good, then!" D.C. stated to FM with a grin. "My turn to keep watch on the creepy crawlies!" FM grinned and headed down to breakfast. D.C., never one to take chances, broke down the rifle, checked all the parts, oiled it, and put it back together. This occupied about four minutes of his time, all the while moving his head from side to side to keep watch. Once he'd completed his task, he checked his own sidearm, a Colt Python, and picked up the binoculars.

A flock of old-world fruit bats, now known as flying foxes, fluttered overhead, heading for a cave somewhere inland, or to trees in which they sometimes roosted. D.C. watched them, marveling at God's amazing creation. These creatures used sonar to find prey, navigating using the polar magnetic forces. To suggest that a creature with such a fine-tuned system for navigation and finding prey was the product of mere chance was ludicrous. Yet many people believed completely in the theory of evolution.

Saying that bats could develop through evolution was like saying that a pile of junk in a junkyard would become a fully functional radio-controlled car in a few million years. It was just stupid. Yet his own country had led the charge toward Darwinism and evolution, casting aside the knowledge of a creative genius behind all of it for something so silly it almost defied explanation. Almost. Men wanted to be rid of God, the Creator, and to live without His laws overshadowing them and making them feel guilty.

A small herd of Nyala wandered down to the riverbank to drink. Bucks had dark brown almost black fur, but light brown legs below the knee joints. Females were striped, and from the front looked like they might be wearing a necklace. Bucks had large, curved horns and too-small heads, with the whites in the middle of their face making them look like they had close-set eyes and gave them a rather doltish expression in the early morning light. Apart from that feature, the males were delicate-looking, graceful creatures.

As he swept his eyes over the water, he saw the crocodile returning. The huge reptile gave him the willies and he watched it creep right up to one of the bucks drinking. The poor Nyala never knew it was there until it was too late. Once again, the water turned red with blood as the huge reptile thrashed and rolled, taking the buck down. Somewhere near here it had a place to store the meat, to tenderize it, and D.C. wondered what all those dead carcasses in the water did to the ecology. Having thought about it, he was glad he wasn't getting breakfast at the moment.

CHAPTER 13

Morning seemed to promise a normal day of mixed rain, sunshine, hot and humid temperatures, and insects to torment those in the rigid raider collecting water samples. C.G. Franklin and Vince Hall were on the boat to protect the scientists. Vince was driving the boat while doctors John and Alice Dinsmore took samples with the help of Rachael Hague and Stephanie Morris. None of them saw the huge hippo beneath the surface until it surged up and halfway onto the boat in a savage slashing attack.

John Dinsmore felt the sharp slashing tooth slice his leg wide open as he flew through the air, landing in the water with a loud splash. Vince went into immediate action, snatching up his rifle since he had the best angle, lined up on the hippo and fired one shot, killing the huge beast in the midst of its slashing rage. But C.G. saw something else moving under the boat heading for Dr. Dinsmore. It was the crocodile!

For C.G. Franklin there was no frozen moment of horror, no wondering what he should do. His keen military training kicked in and seeing that he had no shot that would guarantee a kill he ran through several options in less than a second, seizing on the one and only option open to him in time to save John Dinsmore.

Without really thinking about the very real danger, he drew his

130

Cold Steel Recon Tanto Knife from its sheath and threw himself out of the boat on the back of the crocodile, wrapping his legs around its huge sides and hooking his left hand under its powerful left foreleg. Rearing back, he slammed the blade home in the Crocodile's head, his aim exactly right, and to his relief the razor-sharp hardened steel blade penetrated that thick skull. It should have killed the crocodile, but the massive behemoth beast went berserk.

It rocketed straight out of the water the full length of its body and then toppled backwards, landing on top of him as they splashed together in river. There was just enough water where they were to keep all that weight from crushing him, yet he was too busy thinking to give it much thought. Later he would. But C.G. was pulling the blade, and going for a second strike, landing it even as they hit the water. The two bodies sank beneath the surface, all the fight gone from the crocodile as it twitched and died.

Through the entire ten second ordeal that seemed to last a lifetime he had prayed fervently for the strength to penetrate the skull, and the aim to make his strike count. As he felt the death throes of the giant beast, he breathed out a prayer of thanksgiving, even as he thought about where he was and what was happening. He had been aware of the presence of his Lord from the moment of commitment and where no one would see his tears he wept for joy.

C.G. didn't want to stay in the water long, not with all that blood, but they were in a fairly shallow spot. The crocodile stopped sinking just before sinking him in the silt at the bottom of the river and floated to the surface as C.G. disengaged and swam up beside it, pulled out his knife, and with powerful strokes made his way to the boat. As he pulled himself over the side, he saw Alice already tending to John's leg, wrapping it to slow the bleeding, her own face still pale with tears running down her cheeks. Vince grabbed him and pulled him the rest of the way into the boat. As he slid in, he saw Rachael and Stephanie, their faces pale, hands shaking in the fear of the moment, and the relief that he was alive.

For a moment he and Vince looked at each other, their hands still grasped tightly. C.G. knew what Vince was saying with that look.

He was glad his buddy was still among the living, and he approved of the choice C.G. made. They nodded once in understanding and Vince let go.

"Are you crazy?" Rachael Hague snapped, almost leaping on him, working with Stephanie to make sure he wasn't bleeding anywhere. "That was either the most courageous thing I've ever seen, or the dumbest! I don't know what to think!"

"I think it was perhaps a little of both," Stephanie replied, her eyes filled with tears and tears running down her cheeks. "I thought you were dead!" she wept, burying her face in his chest. C.G. held her gently, hugging her tightly, thinking that he'd thought much the same thing. He hadn't hesitated. Breathing another prayer of thanks to God he relaxed completely. Then he grinned.

"Ladies! Step right up! Crocodile purses, shoes, and accessories coming right up!" he said enthusiastically.

"I swear, I'm going to thrash you until you are b-b-b-black and b-b-b-blue!" Stephanie stuttered, half crying, half laughing.

"You could make her a belt. Then she could spank you!" Rachael said with a grin at her friend.

John Dinsmore, pale and shaking, reached a hand over and grasped C.G.'s hand in a firm grip.

"Thanks!" he said, his eyes saying it all.

"Come on doc! You know what Alice would have done to me if I let that monster get to you!" C.G. grinned. He squeezed the doctor's hand and nodded, knowing what John was saying. Once before, when he was wounded and would have fallen into enemy hands, he'd had someone save him. Wade had carried him out of that hellhole, and he'd said thanks in much the same way.

River Venture 3 pulled alongside, and C.G. disengaged from Stephanie and helped Vince lift John up to the boat where he was helped into the sick bay. Leo and Will followed, cut away his pant leg and looked at the gash in his leg. It was bad, cut all the way to the bone. Dr. Penny began barking orders for cleaning out the wound while Dr. Axlerod began to numb the area with local anesthetic.

All the hustle in that cramped space was ordered and necessary and somehow calming.

Jim helped C.G. up to the boat and hugged him fiercely. John was next to hug his friend, and then Wade. Vince, who'd already had his hug stood back and watched. As C.G. stepped back from Wade, Jim put a hand on his shoulder.

"Words could never express how grateful we are for what you risked saving one of our own. Every one of us prayed for you and for John. That act of courage is going to earn you another star on your Medal of Honor. I just wanted to personally tell you how proud of you we all are, and how glad we are that you didn't get dead!" Jim nodded once and shook Clancy's hand.

"Somebody risked it all for me, once," Clancy said quietly, looking at Wade and John. "Besides, there were pretty girls watching. I had to be macho man!" Clancy added, winking at Stephanie. "Excuse me, boss, I gotta go make a belt," he laughed as Stephanie blushed crimson.

Jim knew the reason for the levity. For moments everyone had been frozen in terror and horror, and now that it was over the men needed to make light of it, not because they were shallow and frivolous by nature, but because it eased the horror, and made the terror less than what it was. John, who caught on to what was going on laughed suddenly.

"Make him make a razor strap, Stephanie. Those make more of an impression in a spanking than a simple belt!" C.G. blushed.

The women were all hugging Alice and she'd been shaking and miserable, but the levity helped. She threw herself on Clancy and hugged him fiercely and C.G. hugged back, kissing the top of her head lightly.

In the sick bay John bore the needle making his leg numb and watched the scene unfold. He knew what he owed Clancy Franklin and knew how terrified Alice had been. Grinning he caught Clancy's eye, winked, and the yelled at his wife.

"Yo! Woman! You don't see I'm suffering here? Get your hands off that muscle bound Marine and come in here and hold my hand!" he winked at Clancy again.

"Yo? Woman?" Alice began walking toward him. "John Phillip Dinsmore, you dare address me that way?" John pretended to cringe away from her in fear.

"On second thought, take your time sewing me up, Doc. Give her time to cool off!"

Alice tussled his still wet hair and kissed him gently. Then she hugged him just as fiercely and began to cry. Everyone stood by and watched, knowing that she needed this release, and that John needed it too. He was crying just as unashamedly as his wife as they clung to each other in the aftermath of the horror. Many of the women of the science crew wept with them, clutching Kleenex tissues tightly as they worked through the intense emotion.

Jim felt Cecilia snuggle under his arm and looked down at her. Her eyes were misty, and she reached up and kissed him gently on the lips. He understood. People they both loved very nearly died in a horrible fashion. Folding her into his arms he kissed the top of her head and just squeezed her tightly. For months he would relive that moment of intimacy among his crew and revel in the love they shared for one another.

Finally, he disengaged from his wife and gave orders, and two rigid raiders went out to bring in the crocodile. The hippo they left. Not long after they'd wrestled the nearly one-ton crocodile up on shore a few hippos appeared, but they did not approach. Perhaps it was the presence of so many men, or the presence of one of their herd, dead and floating down the river. Men went to work skinning the Crocodile and taking the meat they wanted. Dorf cut the head away cleanly, using a saws-all with a hacksaw blade to cut through the tough neckbone.

Alistair was there telling him how they would remove the meat from the skull to preserve it as a trophy for C.G. He also told them how to skin the huge reptile to save that valuable skin. Once the skin and meat they wanted was removed they left the carcass for other scavengers to finish it. By the following morning, they knew, most of it would be gone and the vultures would finish the rest.

Eventually the boats began to move upriver once more. Zeke walked up to Jim, who was standing by for the doctors to finish with John. Jim looked at his chief computer expert and realized Zeke had some news he needed to hear. He nodded.

"The river rose two inches last night, and there's a surge of water coming our way that will lift it another three by tomorrow morning," Zeke said, glancing in and waving at John. Now that his leg was numb, he was smiling as the doctors worked to close the wound and allow him to heal without permanent damage. Fascinated by the entire procedure he watched the two doctors work on his flesh, understanding the process of holding it together to heal properly and appreciating the skill.

"I take it the upper Zambezi is getting an unusual amount of rain," Jim guessed quietly.

"More than usual for this time of year, but not a record rainfall," Zeke answered. "However, the season is young, and the record may come. We'll have to see."

"There's more," Jim said, smiling at Zeke.

"Wikffels has paid some local river pirates to attack our boats to delay our reaching Tete," Zeke reported. "These pirates usually don't operate during the rainy season, but his offer was lucrative enough to bring them out on the river in unsafe conditions. They have some larger johnboats with dual outboard engines to move quickly."

"What INTEL do you have so far?" Jim inquired.

"They use guns, Uzi, AK-47, and various pistols. What I can gather of their reputation is all bad. They've been known to take women from local villages, use them, and then feed them to crocodiles for sport. You should know that they kidnapped a French businessman last year for ransom. When his company didn't pay the ransom, the pirates tortured and killed him. In the autopsy undigested pieces of his genitals were found in his stomach, Shep!" Zeke paused for a moment, swallowing hard. "That's all I know so far. What I've seen of their boats suggests that they don't take the best care of their vessels, and my guess is they're careless about the guns too. We won't know that until we get a better look," he lifted his hands.

"Okay. Do we have any kind of time?" Jim asked next.

"They're on their way down river and communicating by radio. There are two boats and they will probably arrive tomorrow night. Wikffels has suggested they attack late at night when we're tied up to shore," Zeke replied.

"Let's talk this afternoon during the rain," Jim suggested. "Get us as much INTEL as you can, please. Keep me posted if anything changes, and well done. *Semper Paratus!*"

"On it!" Zeke declared, departing quickly. He was thinking of the pirates, and what he already knew, and anxious to know as much as possible. This was a group of bad men, and in his mind, they needed to put down like rabid dogs.

Dr. Axlerod was watching the two men as he assisted Dr. Penny with John's leg. Dr. Dinsmore too had been watching the pair and he looked up at Leo with a knowing expression in his eyes.

"You felt the change, didn't you?" he asked with a half smile, wincing at the same time. Leo nodded, his face tense, but he didn't have a chance to reply because John yelled at that moment. "Ow! Watch what you're doing you ham-handed butcher!" he snapped at Will Penny.

"Nurse! Find the biggest needle we have, the most painful shot we can give, and let him have it!" Will snapped at Donna. She made a comical face, rubbing her hands together, pretending to think what would be best to use. Finding a big needle was easy and she filled it with water before returning, looking like she was enjoying every moment of this torture. Then she brought down the house by mimicking Egor, Dr. Frankenstein's assistant from the comedy version of the movie, hunching over and shuffling and speaking with a hoarse whispering voice.

"Yes doctor!" she said, shooting water out of the needle.

"Ye gods! Get that thing away from me!" John laughed.

"There!" Will Penny finally said. "All done with the painful stuff. We can sew you up the rest of the way now," he patted John's shoulder. "Of course, if you revert to calling me nasty names, I'll have Egor put that needle where it will do the most good."

"Yes master!" Donna said, still in her character. John laughed and then grimaced. "How is a man to remain stoic when he's surrounded by this crowd?" he asked. "I am trying to be macho, to impress my wife with my manhood!" Everyone laughed at his quip as he quivered his lower lip.

"Stoic! Didn't I just hear you whining?" Alice said, coming into the room. "What's up? All the soldiers just went into overdrive out there!" she added, kneeling beside her husband.

"Pirates," he said simply. "And these ham-fisted horse doctors are manhandling me, and that crazy nurse is threatening me with a huge needle!" he stuck his lower lip out again and pouted.

"Get a bigger needle," Alice demanded, smiling up at Donna.

"Yes master!" Donna said, shuffling off.

"Did I just enter an alternate reality?" René asked, coming into the room with the x-ray results. She hung them on the board, laughing as Donna smiled and straightened.

"I need to get a fake hump," Donna laughed.

Leo took over sewing up the leg while Will studied the x-rays. No ribs were broken, and no bones in the leg were broken. John had complained about bouncing off the side of the boat when the attack happened, wondering if he'd broken something. His ribs were sore.

"I've got good news, and bad news," Will said turning back to John as Leo finished the last stitch.

"There you are!" Leo said. "Thirty-two stitches inside, and sixty-four outside. You'll have quite a story to tell the grandkids," he added, putting the bloody needle in a container to sanitize it.

"By the time anyone hears it he'll have wrestled the hippo into submission and knocked out the crocodile, saved four maidens, and emerged strong enough to haul himself onto the boat and order us to finish the experiments!" Alice laughed.

"Uh, the good and bad news?" John interjected.

"The good news is that none of your ribs are broken," Will reported.

"I'm afraid to ask!" John said, covering his face. "What's the bad news?"

"Your ribs are probably bruised, and that hurts much worse than broken ribs," Will replied.

"Right now, everything hurts!" John admitted.

"I'll get the needle master!" Donna said, slipping back into Egor.

"This medical plan sucks!" John Dinsmore complained, shaking his head in resignation. Everyone laughed as they helped him to his feet, and he went out of sickbay on a pair of crutches. He put a hand on each doctor's shoulder, keeping the crutches from falling somehow, his face full of emotion.

"Thanks," he said simply. They all understood. In good humor the drama ended.

But John Dinsmore was not one to miss a chance. Later that afternoon Jim passed through the science lab to find him stretched out on a folding chez lounge with all the young and pretty doctors and lab technicians gathered around him, feeding him from a cluster of grapes, and fanning him. Alice came into this scene and stopped dead. For about ten seconds everyone kept a straight face, and then the laughter broke out. Jim was still chuckling when he walked up to the observation deck where he would meet with the military team.

As he walked out of the lab, he heard Alice saying in a stern voice: "Unhand my husband you lazy layabouts and get back to work!"

"But darling! The doctor told me to stay off my leg!" John whined as Jim closed the door with a smile.

His crew was certainly creative, and he understood the fun. It eased the horror of the morning that all of them felt. Alice would need that, as much as the rest of the crew, and Jim appreciated the freedom to allow the crew that kind of antics. Morale was certainly high as he walked among his men. It was his turn to stop and stare.

C.G. stood with the huge knife in his hand, wearing only a makeshift loincloth, muscles flexed, beside him the head of the crocodile, mouth propped open, now just a skeleton, while Bear was snapping photographs.

"Ah!" Jim said dryly. "The hero!" he chuckled as the men broke up laughing. C.G. pulled his pants on and shed the loincloth and grinned sheepishly at him. "How soon will it be posted online for all your friends to see?" Jim asked as he joined in the fun.

"It's already there!" Zeke said, turning his computer so Jim could see.

"I still say it looks like someone put a loincloth on a Mack truck!" Vince laughed.

"He looks that way in all his clothes," Sparks added. The men laughed at that.

C.G. was built like a gymnast, his muscles taught and huge, his chest massive, and his neck seemed to flow into his shoulders. No one could question that he was a powerful man. But Jim knew that muscle was the kind that gave him stamina and speed, not the kind of muscle body builders often developed, like Abe and Sturdy. That kind of muscle slowed a man down. It gave him power and strength, but it slowed him down. Franklin was quick on his feet, and his hands were fast.

"Well, if our hero can step off his pedestal for a moment, we'll get this meeting under way," JR laughed as he arrived.

"Marines, boss! What ya gonna say?" FM commented softly.

FM was no less physically powerful than C.G., perhaps more so, and a former Marine. Jim smiled at the quip.

"They all think they're invincible. That's why we put 'em at the front of the lines," FM added.

"First in, last out!" C.G. said, bumping shoulders with Wade and John. "Ooh Rah!"

Fagan, who had been working hard at a new skill, opened C.G.'s wallet. "Not much to hoorah about in here!" he commented morosely.

"Hey! Give that back!" C.G. said, snatching the wallet back.

"I prefer them lined," Fagan said with a sinister smirk.

"We've created a monster!" Fingers said, shaking his head. "He thinks he is Fagan!"

"Once a villain, I'm a villain to the end!" Fagan said, rubbing his hands together suggestively. Almost every man on the deck grabbed his wallet. They all laughed.

It took only a minute for all of them to switch gears and become intense and combat ready, gathering around to listen to Zeke as he unfolded the INTEL he'd gathered throughout the day. Ideas were presented, weighed, and either shelved for another time, or worked into the plan. Jim noted that Windy and the other pilots had joined the meeting and were actively involved in coming up with a plan. Two hours later, as the rain lessened a bit, the men broke up and headed down to their various duties.

Jim went down to the air-conditioned comfort of the dining room and sat down at the table with his team leaders. The pilots joined them as they went over the plan once more to make sure they had the advantage and firepower to repel the pirates. After hearing of the exploits of these pirates the decision had come down as Jim expected. They were going in hot and heavy. There would be killing.

He hated that he lived in a world where evil men understood nothing less. Founding Father Noah Webster made it clear. Men would need either the Bible or the Bayonet, when it came to keeping law and order. His team was going into battle and every shot they took would be a kill shot. In this case it was high time someone brought justice to those men. Jim was just sad that it would be he and his men meeting out the punishment. God would deal with the justice.

CHAPTER 14

Jim knew that his thirty-six-man unit was the very best especially with the added air support that was such an important component to the mission. These men were the best of Force Recon, SEAL, and SAS in the world. Physically they were in top condition, mentally they worked together as one cohesive unit, and emotionally they were charged and ready to go. Yet he knew the most important part of all was the spiritual aspect. Each one of his men followed Jesus Christ, possessed the Holy Spirit, and that gave them an edge many military units did not enjoy. They were good and moral men who kept the highest standards to please God.

In a sense none of them worked for this agency, for Omega Force. All of them, including Jim, worked for Christ. He was the ultimate boss, the highest commander, and His word was something they all tried desperately to obey. That they all fell short every day they knew. Yet each day they strove with everything to reach that goal, and because of that, they experienced His pleasure and approval.

What that knowledge gave them in the way of a military edge was the knowledge that they need not fear death. Men who were not afraid to die were very dangerous men. His men were such men, knowing that the moment they died they would be in the presence of their Savior. C.G. had proved that when he dove on top of that huge crocodile. At no time did C.G. harbor the sense that he was invincible. Instead, he did what he knew he had to do, what was right, and if he died in the attempt then it was worth it. That was a very good place to be in one's thinking.

Tonight, he or any of his men could be seriously injured or die. Every one of them knew that. As he looked at Cecilia and RJ Jim realized that he was confident God would look after his wife and son much better than he ever could. This gave him a sense of release, that he could do everything necessary tonight for his men without fear, and he gratefully bowed his head and thanked God for that knowledge.

Even more amazing was the fact that Cecilia understood. That morning in their prayers she'd made sure she was surrendered to God's will, that if He took her husband home tonight during the mission it was His choice, and she trusted Him. It didn't mean they both didn't worry. That was human. Both of them did. But behind it all was that sense of being in God's capable hands. Jim remembered Cecilia's words to him after their prayer.

"Honey, just because these pirates are threatening the lives of your wife and son, please don't wade in blood. I know you'll have to kill some of those men tonight, maybe even all of them. Just don't do it in a rage."

"These men have killed countless women and children. It's really hard not to feel rage about that," he admitted honestly. After a moment he continued. "But I think God has moved me past that stage. I notice you didn't tell me to be careful and come back!" he said teasingly.

Cecilia laughed, hugged him tightly and with her face in his chest spoke. "Like that was possible! You would have done what C.G. did yesterday without a second's hesitation. All of you men are that way, courageous to a fault. I won't ask you the impossible!" and she laughed. "Besides, you're a man. To be careful implies thought and care, neither of which is possible for the male gender of this species!"

"Hey RJ! Spit up on your mom sometime today, and pee on her when she's changing your diaper!" Jim taunted, looking over at his son with a grin. Little RJ smiled back and giggled, as though he understood.

As it turned out it had been Jim who received both those presents from his son during the day, and Cecilia had laughed and congratulated her beloved little son both times. Memories like that would keep him strong through the darkness to come.

Thinking about his teams made Jim proud. To lead such men was a privilege and an honor. His own team, Omega 1 included Zeke Kline, Frank Miller, and John Smith. They'd worked as a team for six years now and knew each other so well that on a given mission each man knew what the other was thinking and would do in any given situation.

Jim watched his three men as they went about the day's business. Zeke Kline might have looked like any other computer whiz if it hadn't been for that constant five o'clock shadow, his strong neck, and broad shoulders. He stood an inch over the six-foot mark and weighed 186 pounds. He'd gained a pound in the last year, though Jim couldn't see the difference. The mantra "Any Weapon Any Time" was not an idle boast with Zeke. He was proficient in all of them.

Frank Miller was handy with both machines and explosives, and deadly with weapons. Two inches shorter than Zeke he outweighed his friend by 14 pounds, packing two hundred pounds of hard muscle on his frame. Of the four of them FM was the biggest joker, though Zeke ran a close second.

John Smith was the same height as Zeke, an inch over six feet, but weighed about six pounds less, though when the two stood side by side one couldn't really see that. Like his teammates he was a deadly warrior and when it came to navigation and weather, he was top man in Omega Force.

Team Delta had Dorf Bernard at the leader. Dorf was a giant, six-feet nine-inches tall, two hundred and seventy-five pounds of hard packed muscle adorned his mighty frame. Too tall some thought to be a good soldier he was a force to be reckoned with in the field. As big and heavy as he was, he could walk silently and do most of the things his diminutive friend Mark Drumheiser could do with equal dexterity and silence. He'd proved that many times.

Mark, his second, stood only five-feet four-inches in height, but what he lacked in stature he made up for in skill. Among Jim's men he was the most skilled in martial arts, teaching the other members of the unit every day. Mark possessed the body of a gymnast with defined muscles and power that went with that sport. The two looked quite interesting standing next to each other and made Delta a powerful team indeed.

Jack Boswell, four inches taller than Mark weighed an even one hundred and sixty-four pounds. He'd maintained that weight since he graduated from high school. On that team Jack was the explosives expert, playing second in that endeavor to his other teammate, Bill Kline.

Bill was a doppelganger of his twin Zeke. Identical twins they could use each other for a shaving mirror. Both men competed with each other constantly in weapons and fitness and as a result were impressive warriors in their own right. Known as Sparks among the men because he was their electrician Bill could disarm explosives or set them equally quickly. He often admitted that Jack Boswell was his equal and the two men worked well in the field with explosives.

John Shepherd led Team Zulu. With him were the other three survivors of a Force Recon team that was nearly intentionally wiped out because of important INTEL withheld by an American Admiral. Wade Adams, six-foot five-inches tall, powerfully built, and an awesome soldier he embodied everything that made the Marines famous. The same could be said for C.G. Franklin, a one-hundred and ninety-pound six-footer, and Vince Hall, two inches taller, and twenty-five pounds heavier. In full battle gear those four men could accomplish what it would take twenty other Marines to accomplish.

Jim had two other such teams from the Marines. Bill Dodge led Firefox. He and Vince Hall could exchange clothing since they were both the same height and weight. Dodge was one of those Marines who had been there, seen and done that, and destroyed it completely. He might wear a boyish good-looking face most of the time, but in battle he was deadly. Sid Barrett could shoot the wings off a fly at a thousand yards, some said, and was the unit's best sniper. Sam Colt and Roger Corrigan finished the team.

Looking at them it was easy to see they were a close-knit group. Corrigan and Dodge were equal in height, though Corrigan was twenty-five pounds lighter. Barrett was an inch shorter and much lighter at one hundred and seventy-five pounds. And Colt was the shortest of the four at six foot, weighing in at one hundred and eighty-five pounds. Together they could get the job done.

And then there was Team Bulldog, led by Terrance Red Claw. Chief was deceptive at five-feet nine-inches of height and only one hundred and sixty-five pounds. The man was fast, hard, downright scary in a fight. Gene Hardesty, six-foot five-inches tall and weighing in at two hundred and twenty-five pounds was nicknamed Hayseed because he was a Pennsylvania farm boy. On the battlefield he was anything but a farm boy. Neil Meyers and Mel Pierson stood six-foot and five-eleven respectively, both weighing in at one hundred and eighty pounds, and both formidable warriors. Again, the team was the embodiment of the Marine ideal.

Team Nightfall, like Jim's Team Delta, had all started out in the Marines. Tom Izbicki looking like an all-American quarterback led the team. Izbicki stood six-two and weighed one ninety-six, was a former SEAL team leader, and lived the legend. He had big Steve Coleman, six-four, two twenty-five, and Bernie Finlay who looked like a CPA and was known as Fingers. Finlay stood five-nine and weighed in at one sixty-five. And then there was Richard Kagan, affectionately known as Fagan, at five-seven and one hundred and sixty pounds. It was odd, sometimes, to see men of such disparity in height and weight who could fight as ferociously and effectively as though equals. Jim liked Izzy's team.

Team Knife was the Australian group, SAS forces led by Sean Oxton, a field physician who was first a soldier. Ox stood five-feet nine-inches in height and weighed in at one-ninety. Powerfully built he had distinguished himself in the Australian SAS both as a soldier and field physician. Lee Roy Brown and Chance Edwards were both black, but as different as two men could be. Lee Roy, whose roots were Aborigine stood six-feet tall, a giant among his people, and weighed an impressive two hundred pounds. Chance came from African roots, stood two inches shorter, and weighed in twenty pounds less than his friend. Yet the two seemed cut out of the same mold when it came to being soldiers. And then there was Phil Eustus, an inch shorter than Lee Roy, the same weight as his best friend Chance, another serious soldier. The Aussies were popular among the men because of their humor.

From England Jim had two SAS teams. Raider was led by the SAS definition of soldier, Calvin Weston. A powerful five-foot eleven-inch man weighing in at one hundred and ninety pounds he'd distinguished himself in service. With him were Matthew Banks, Paul Donnelly, and David Carr.

Banks was a solid six-footer weighing in at one hundred and eighty. Paul Donnelly stood above them all at six-feet six-inches, weighing two hundred and sixty pounds. Though much heavier and taller he could move with equal speed and ease with his mates. David Carr made the fourth, five-ten and one hundred and eighty-five pounds of SAS fighting machine.

Team Sniper, led by Norm Geissler, was the final team. Norm was nicknamed Counselor because of his attorney father, and his own serious nature and tendency to listen, rather than talk. At five-ten and one hundred and eighty pounds he was a formidable soldier with an already distinguished career. With him were Lee Ainsworth, Lloyd Brookstone, and Earl Duncan.

Lee was the smallest of his team at five-six but weighted one hundred and sixty pounds. Ainsworth was a distinguished soldier whom his friends called Lord Lee, not because he acted the part, but because he wouldn't let them call him Little Lord Fauntleroy. There was nothing little about him when it came to fighting. Lloyd Brookstone was the son of a polish mother and black Englishman, both college professors. Lloyd was a distinguished mountaineer before he entered the SAS and was quick to distinguish himself in military service. Six feet one inches tall he was an imposing figure weighing in at one hundred and eighty pounds. Earl Duncan was an inch shorter than Lloyd, but weighed two hundred and twelve pounds, all packed into a powerful body trained to the limits of human endurance.

When with the women on the crew, or the children, or victims of disasters they'd rescued, these men were the soul of courtesy and decency. Against aggressors, anarchists, and terrorists they were death incarnate. Jim appreciated the contrast. It gave him a great sense of accomplishment to lead such men of purpose and skill.

He noticed that on days he had to prepare for a mission like this Cecilia often kept to herself, not seeking him out, doing her utmost not to distract him. Any other time she was almost persistent in her attentions. Again, he appreciated the contrast. His wife understood. As he watched the teams, he noted that those with girlfriends were also left to themselves. At lunch he broached the question with Cecilia.

"Did you all get together and decide that leaving us to our thoughts and preparations without distraction was a good idea?" he asked quietly while they stood in line for their food. Cecilia looked up at him, reached up, and kissed him gently on the lips.

"You need to focus during this time, and we all know it. We've discussed it at length and decided this is the best way. I think that Pen and I helped because we understand. But they're intelligent girls. They would have figured it out on their own," she submitted.

Jim filed that away for future consideration. These missions affected everyone, and he wanted a completely healthy crew, mentally, physically, and spiritually. Now that some of the soldiers were cultivating loving relationships with some of the women, he had to make sure everyone could cope. Once more he was grateful for the fact that each member of his crew were followers of Christ. Jesus was the one constant, true refuge in times of trouble. And so far, their studies of the river had indicated there was a lot of trouble.

The Buzi, Pungwe, and Save rivers drain the Zambezi basin. Together the waters of these four river floodplains make up the World Wildlife Fund's Zambezian costal flooded savanna ecoregion.

A mixture of open grassland and freshwater swamp inland from the Indian Ocean they constitute a vast ecoregion. One of the chief responsibilities of the grant issued to *Bring It Up* is determining how best to protect the wildlife in the region, ensuring that pollution is not a major threat to that wildlife.

Cahora Bassa Dam, and Kariba Dam have stemmed some of the annual flooding of the lower Zambezi and caused the area of floodplain to be greatly reduced. But those two dams have not removed flooding completely. Extreme floods cannot be controlled, and even some medium-level floods still happen, especially in the lower Zambezi region. Those floods are important to the wetlands, and the wetlands are still an important habitat.

Aerial photos taken by Windy and Loony from the PBY showed clearly how the wetlands are shrinking. Uncontrolled hunting of animals such as buffalo and waterbuck during the Mozambique Civil War caused severe damage to wildlife. From the photos examined those herds have not yet recovered, though they are growing. Yet further damming would hinder the growth of the herds, which should have been much larger than they were, mostly because the wetlands area was so reduced that it couldn't support larger herds.

Only the Marromeu Game Reserve near the city of Beira is protected. Yet even there the last two rhinos disappeared to poachers while the creatures were on protected land. In underdeveloped countries money always turned a blind eye to things that were illegal. That was part of the problem of the pollutants.

Because they knew the area well Zeke picked out a few spots where someone watching them might radio the pirates that the boats had tied up for the evening. Purposely they anchored on shore in an area where they had wide-open spaces that could be easily defended by those on the boats. Jim and the team did not plan to allow the pirates to get close to his boats. Instead, they planned to strike upriver and out of sight of the boats.

Once the watcher was gone, never imagining he had been seen, the men left the boats in full battle gear, armed to the teeth, and made their way to the strike zone. Here the river was still shallow enough to cross on foot and they boldly walked into the dangerous water and stretched a net in the deeper area where the boats would most probably encounter the barrier. Crocodiles were a real danger here, and even though the men knew this, none hesitated in his duty.

Top ropes were tied off to two trees on shore, spring loaded to straighten and pull the net up when it was time, holding it from letting the boats through. At the bottom they drove in long steel stakes, all along the length of the net, to anchor it to the bottom of the river.

Delta, Zulu, and Firefox were on the far side of the river while Sniper, Bulldog, and Nightfall were on the near side. All twelve men on each side were in the water, just their heads out, snorkels ready for the approach of the boats so they would be invisible until the boats hit the net. Knife had the spring trap on the far side of the river, and Raider the trap in the near side. They would cut the ropes holding the trees bent over at just the right moment, snapping the net into the air, and catching the boats.

Omega 1 was located in front of the net, far enough away that if a boat managed to miss the net, they could take it down. Like the others in the water the men hunkered down, ready to submerge when the boats arrived. Both crocodiles and hippos were in the water, they knew, but so far none had come close to the working men.

Less than an hour later the boats arrived, moving down the deeper channel as expected, and running side-by-side. In the darkness the pirates never saw the men in the water or noticed the snorkels poking above the surface.

When the boats encountered the net that suddenly snapped up before them, pirates were flung forward into each other, into the net, and into the water. Unseen around them the teams rose, night vision goggles engaged, and as they opened fire a nightmare from hell appeared in the sky above: the AH-1W Super Cobra.

Hellfire missiles took out the two boats as the M197 three-barrel 20-mm. gun cut a path three yards wide by twenty yards deep of cover fire. Once that initial assault was completed the loudspeaker from the helicopter ordered in Portuguese for the men to throw down their arms, raise their hands, and surrender.

Stung by the surprise and suddenness of the attack, and the incredible loss of life in the onslaught the pirate's only thought was revenge. One of them opened fire on the helicopter. A three-shot volley from Bulldog's location ended his life. Aware now that there were people around them the men began to fire wildly in all directions. In a matter of seconds their guns were silenced. Two men remained alive, both wounded, and both crying for mercy. But there was no mercy for them that night. The scent of blood in the water lured the crocodiles in and they died a violent death.

Jim got his team out of the water fast, because the blood was coming downstream, right to his men. The other teams were also heading to shore and when they were all together Jim spoke into his COMLINK.

"Sound off!" he ordered tersely.

One by one the men gave their call sign until all thirty-six were accounted for. Two were wounded, taking shrapnel from the exploding boats, but their wounds were superficial. Jim saw Sean heading for the two men to check. Once he okayed the two men for travel the team set off for the boats across the wetlands. During his examination Jim led the men in cutting away the net and gathering it in. There would be no evidence of what happened here other than the pieces of the boats and the bones from dead bodies.

They were careful, walking quietly, checking each step, because at night the danger of poisonous snakes was very real. Their boots were snake-proof, but they took no chances. In a small dugout some distance away a native watched through regular binoculars, counting the men in the group as they moved away from him.

They frightened him. He had come upon the spot just before the attack, heard the boats coming, and held his place to watch. Those men had suddenly appeared between his boat and the pirate boats, without noise, without warning, rising up out of the water like spirits. Now they moved through the brush like spirits, making almost no noise.

Not until they were gone did he dare head back upriver, a trip that would take two days, to reach the person to whom he needed to report. Wikffels waited impatiently to hear from the pirates in his house near Tete. No report ever reached him from the pirates. Later he learned that a military force had met them on the way to the scientists, taken them out, and disappeared. His servants and staff avoided him for the next three days.

Back on the boats the men carefully cleaned their weapons and put them away, washed uniforms, folded, and put them away, and treated their boots from exposure to the wet. It was nearly dawn when they were finished those chores and they made their way to the observation deck to debrief. They were all meeting on the observation deck of *River Venture 4*.

Brookstone and Meyers, who had been wounded, were treated and back with the men at the meeting. Jim moved among the men telling each one he'd done a good job. When he was finished, he presented Brookstone and Meyers with their purple-heart ribbons while the rest of the team applauded and whistled approval.

"Okay men!" Jim began. Everyone grew quiet and waited.

"We're going to get boarded and searched. Somebody was watching. A small craft headed upriver after we left the scene. Inchworm and Wrench, that was excellent work from the sky!" Jim looked at them as the rest of the men clapped and whistled again. "Thanks for getting them back in one piece, Windy and Loony," Jim added.

Windy and Loony shuttled the two for this particular meeting, and they would be returning to the airport shortly with their friends. For the next half-hour the men discussed the mission and how everything went, some sharing the fear experienced just waiting in a river full of hippos and crocodiles, while others shared how their weapons fared in the wet climate. Finally, Jim dismissed them and watched from *River Venture 6* as the PBY taxied downriver and rose into the predawn sky.

John and Wade stood next to him. When the airplane banked and headed north Jim turned to the other two. His two best friends were always nearby, always the last to leave, and he appreciated that respect and honor deeply.

"That net was a good plan, Wade," he commended, clapping Wade on the shoulder. "Do we have a crack team, or what?" he added, clasping John's arm.

"Best in the world!" John said with a grin.

"We even recruited some local help in the end," Wade commented, and then his smile slipped. "That was pretty gruesome."

"Not what I would have liked to see," Jim said. "We did give them a chance to surrender. I'd hoped we could save a few. I guess I didn't consider the blood in the water and what that would do!"

"I worried about you and your team, with all that blood coming down river," John admitted, shaking his head.

"We got gone pretty fast!" Jim replied with a smile. "I swear I could feel a crocodile breathing on my heels!"

"Are you kidding?" Wade laughed. "The whole time I was in the water all I could think about was what I'd do if one suddenly appeared and made a grab for me. Scariest half hour of my life!" he added.

"Yet every man stayed in the water," Jim stated after a moment of silence. "I was never prouder of my men."

"At least in the water no one could see us peeing ourselves in terror! I know I was scared enough!" FM professed, stepping up beside Jim. "Zeke needs to see you," he added.

"Hey FM! If you peed in the water, you're gonna screw up the pollution tests tomorrow!" Wade laughed.

"No Wade!" Vince said, joining John and Wade as Jim and FM walked away. "None of the crocks wanted to get near C.G. Word gets around in the system, you know," Vince was chuckling.

Jim knew that each man had been praying fervently while waiting in the water. Remembering his own fear of what may lurk beneath the muddy surface, and what might happen if a flood surge occurred, had kept his mind busy. But he'd given it to God, in the hopes that they could accomplish their plan without serious injury. God had smiled upon them once more.

CHAPTER 15

In the morning two patrol boats arrived from upriver and politely asked if they could search the boats and see all the paperwork. They were policemen from Sena, ordered by a superior in Tete to search the boats and check the paperwork. Jim allowed them complete access to the boats and asked Finn to fetch the paperwork. While the policemen searched the boat the science team went out again, this time in two rigid raiders with four rifles to guard them.

When they arrived back at the boats the policemen were leaving. Wikffels waited impatiently for a call to tell him what he knew must be true. But when the call came, he learned that no uniforms and no military weapons of any kind were found on board the boats. Angrily he threw his phone into the open pit coalmine and swore vilely. The helicopter had come from Sena, and it was a *Bring It Up* aircraft, fully armed. Yet the soldiers had come from somewhere else! Where?

While the lab technicians worked on the water samples, others counted herds that came down for water, or appeared on the one piece of land still above water in the area. Even while they watched a surge from floodwaters lifted the boats slightly and the area was now under an inch of water. Rain, they all knew, was falling heavily upriver, and more such surges would be coming their way.

Jim knew that local governments wanted more dams to further

control the flooding, but that would only threaten the wetlands and wildlife in the region. His team had to make a very strong argument in favor of protecting those animals. Further threats would come from bacteria ridden waters polluted by sewage effluent.

Thus far suggesting the government spend money to upgrade sewage treatment when flooding will only damage and even wash it away had been futile. So, Jim put some of the team on the job of tackling the tricky problem, and to come up with viable solutions, including teaching the local government personnel how to protect their areas when floods do occur. Wade was leading part of that group because part of the problem required an engineering solution.

It was Windy that introduced the idea of starting a foundation to protect first the people of the floodplains, the wildlife, and ensure infrastructure that would protect the waters from further pollution. Jim sat on the observation deck and sighed when Windy finished presenting his idea. Such a brilliant suggestion had never occurred to Jim, and he chastised himself, because he thought that perhaps he should have considered it much earlier.

Windy got on the Internet with Ken Worthington and between the two of them they put together a board of directors for the foundation that would guarantee it would raise huge amounts of money. Pouring it into the poverty-stricken area through government channels was hardly wise, so Jim sought out the directors of the World Health Organization, the British and American Zoological associations, and began to carefully talk to a member of Green Peace who exercised influence in that organization.

Members of the science team began to talk to their colleagues and soon the idea began to gather momentum and take shape. Most deadly of enemies this idea faced was greed. Corrupt governments in Africa were riddled with greedy men and women seeking nothing more than enriching their own houses. Jim knew that these would represent his greatest challenge in making changes for the better.

His old friend, and former professor of Marine Biology, Henry Booker flew to Mozambique to study the situation. He spoke long with both the President and the Prime Minister about global reputations and managed to convince them that working with the scientists of *Bring It Up* and the world would provide global recognition and the possibility of great aid in the future. Henry had been unanimously chosen to chair the Board of Directors of the Zambezi River Reclamation Foundation.

With the current state of the economy of Mozambique the work of the Foundation was going to be monumental. News of the project began to spread and to gain momentum. Jim knew that this alone would cause certain people and organizations to go on the offensive. He spent hours with his team preparing for any such attacks and was glad they'd prepared.

Wikffels, unwilling to consider the cost of changing his coal industry holdings so that pollution is brought under control launched an all-out attack on the science of the project and the legitimacy of the grant work. Much of the attack came from Gilles Ramanantsoa, remembering the Communist way of dealing with ideas from his days with his father, Major General Gabriel Ramanantsoa. If they could undermine the science and legitimacy of the grant work, they would succeed in shutting down the project. Discredit the science, and scientists, and the world would turn a deaf ear.

Both saw their efforts stymied as major news networks reported on the credentials of the leading scientists, and the fact that their findings included no personal gain for those doing the study. In fact, what these scientists were doing could very well lead to a better ecology, a healthier people, and a healthier economy.

Wikffels turned his attack to the fact that *Bring It Up* was most famous for their efforts in treasure hunting only to have his own family's nefarious connection to the ship recently recovered by the company uncovered. Full disclosure of his family's dealings and activities forced him to back away quickly. Out of desperation he turned to Massoona, giving him a second chance to redeem himself. Massoona was more than willing, and Gilles saw no reason to interfere with such a mission.

That all three men would regret that decision never entered their minds. Massoona's defeat in Alaska was a fluke, poor planning, and overconfidence. In Africa Massoona would have the advantage, for he would be on home ground. Jungle warfare was his specialty. Maximiliano chose twenty of his very best soldiers and began to train for the mission.

All of this transpired as the boats neared Sena, a river port and railway junction with an economy based on sugarcane cultivation and processing. This early in the year the sugarcane was being planted and cultivated and activity along the river was focused on agriculture. Sugar refineries could be seen along the river. Simple observation indicated that the once successful venture was in serious decline.

Sena Sugar Estates, Ltd., a formerly British-owned company was granted a large land subconcession from the Zambezia Company, had estates at Luabo and Marromeu in the Zambezi River delta, also operating a copra (dried meat or kernel of the Coconut) plantation near Chinde, a forestry concession, and a cattle ranch near Luabo. In the mid-1960s it was the largest firm in Mozambique, with more than 10,000 employees.

Centered in Sena, the company built refineries nearby, on the lower Zambezi River, and helped to establish the rail lines to move the product to the capitol. In 1978, after Mozambique's independence, the company was nationalized and its operation was turned over to Cuban experts that followed Communist business paradigms, which consequently failed economically.

During the FRELIMO civil war efforts, the Beira Railway was attacked often, and only in 2010 was service reestablished to Sena. Work at getting the sugarcane industry on its feet again began in 2001 with help from the World Bank. But flood stages made moving anything difficult. Yet Sena was hanging on, if by a thread, and growing steadily.

At considerable expense to the company, *Bring It Up* had a dozen air boats transported to Sena. These were presented to the sugarcane industry as a viable means of transporting people and goods during flood stages. Each craft could hold a crew of a dozen men and move hundreds of pounds of equipment over flooded plains. Goody and

Wrench spent hours training the mechanics for the company in the upkeep of the boats and repairs to the engines and propellers.

Goodwill improved between *Bring It Up* and the Mozambique government when they realized that not only were the boats a gift, but the company was asking nothing in return. Such gestures may cost a great deal of money, but the relationship with the government improved by leaps and bounds, and Jim and his company felt that the expense was justified. Besides, rather than bribe the people, a practical gift of this nature, along with the training provided in repair and upkeep, gave them all an opportunity to meet and get to know key individuals.

After nearly three weeks in Sena, they set forth once more to cover the hundred miles to Tete in full flood. It was indeed a near record flood year and on the first day of their journey they passed a village under four feet of water. It was just a dozen huts but there were people trying to save what they could from the rising waters.

"Why don't they build their houses on stilts?" Wade asked sadly as their boat slid by the village at the rear of the convoy of houseboats.

"Let's ask that question when we get to Tete. Some of these villages would be much better if they were built above the floodwaters. But the huts are pretty crude, poorly constructed, and look like the least amount of effort went into building them," C.G. commented. "That might have something to do with it. Often those in poverty don't think about things like permanent structures protected from floods, or even well-built structures for their homes. Without funds to purchase the tools at least to do better construction they might be hard pressed. Maybe the WHO can come in and provide some help, or Habitat for Humanity."

The men were silent for a few moments, studying the sad little village and its struggling habitants.

"There are some well-established missions out here that we can turn to for help," John said. "Maybe we could use some foundation money to bring some folks in to help build such homes," he mused.

"Not bad for a Marine thinking," Lyn Ross teased.

"Thinking is not encouraged in the Marines!" Penelope joked, joining the fun. "Simply follow orders! Don't think!"

"Actually, because we have to be so adaptable, mostly because we're coming to the rescue of incompetent members of the other armed forces, we are encouraged to think very quickly," Wade retorted. He went slack-jawed and dull-eyed. "Duh! Huh? Heck boy! Kill it quick!" Everyone laughed and he nodded sagely. "Like that!"

"What sir?" C.G. interjected suddenly. "Why did we destroy the entire city? You told us to make sure there were no snipers in any of the buildings! We figured without buildings the snipers couldn't hide in them!" That brought more laughter.

Little by little the ideas rolled in, and the plan grew. Jim kept copious notes and marveled at the creativity of his team. Those on the boats, and those at home working with them began to provide real help for a country in deep difficulty.

Yet Jim knew that the greed of those in political leadership would undermine the overall plan, even threaten its viability. For that he had no ready answer. Sometimes he wanted to take those men by the scruff of the neck and shake them, but knew that would only frighten them, not convince them to change. So, he suggested the one and only answer they had for that problem. The teams began to pray for the leaders, asking God to change their hearts, open their eyes, and help them see the wisdom of acting with integrity in this situation.

God never forces His will on a person. He gives the wisdom, the faith, even the ability to accomplish that will, but He does not force man to do His will. There were always going to be those who seared their consciences so that they no longer felt the prompting of the Holy Spirit to do the right thing. That God would allow them to do terrible evil was always frustrating and seemingly senseless. Yet Jim knew that God's plan was always best, and that even the most-evil forces in the world could not thwart His purpose. Alone, that thought gave him courage and renewed faith.

He struggled with how to respond to the evil he saw everywhere in Mozambique. Injustice abounded. Crime was at epidemic levels. Sickness and disease threatened to wipe out over a third of the population and those in leadership hardly seemed to care. Often, he wondered why God didn't just destroy the entire country out of frustration. Even then he knew that he was no better, no less sinful, violent, or unjust. Sin threatened him as it did all men.

In the end he determined that he would treat everyone with the utmost respect. After all, Jesus died for every human being, giving immeasurable value and worth to every living man, woman, and child. It was a humbling place to live. His sense of justice made him want to retaliate against evil men and women, to teach them a lesson, but he knew there was no lesson he could teach that would reach the heart. Only God could change a heart.

Because they were downriver from Tete they expected heavy deposits of pollution in the water as a result of the coal mining industry. Thiobacillus ferroxidans accelerating the oxidation and acidification processes leaching trace metals from waste fields were evident. Because Mozambique was burning coal to produce energy the country was producing hundreds of millions of tons of solid waste products annually, including fly ash, bottom ash, and flue-gas desulfurization sludge, that contained mercury, uranium, thorium, arsenic, and other heavy metals.

Because open-pit mining requires large amounts of water for coal preparation plants, and dust suppression, precious water from the wetlands was being diverted. Worse, the pollution from these byproducts was leaching into the water sources. In western countries five principal technologies are used to control water flow at mine sites: diversion systems, containment ponds, groundwater pumping systems, subsurface drainage systems, and subsurface barriers. Even with these technologies water pollution is still a major problem. In Mozambique mining companies were taking shortcuts, not using the technologies mentioned, and as a result the water of the Zambezi River was becoming adversely affected.

As they moved along the river the scientists learned of the health issues for surrounding villages and people living close to the mines. Companies like Jindal, Vale, Rio Tinto, and before that Riversadale, all ignore the human element. Because the government of Mozambique acts too slowly to relocate humans near the mines these problems are growing exponentially. Human rights abuses abound with the coal mining industry and the government. Those most affected had no knowledge or power to fight what was being done to them.

In pointing out these failings *Bring It Up* began to meet with more and more resistance from mining representatives and government agents. Because the World Health Organization was pressuring the Mozambique government and mining companies, as well as the World Bank, resistance was not as violent as it might have been. The mining industry needed the funds from the World Bank to operate, and the WHO was an organization with a reputation worldwide.

At Tete they met with the Wozniacs at the mission hospital where the woes of the people were most evident. Only because there was the possibility of help from the foundation *Bring It Up* established did government agencies even give them an audience. Money was flowing freely, greasing palms and turning blind eyes to the real problems that could haunt the country for hundreds of years. Local government agents flatly refused to insist the coal mining industry use established technology to begin to control the pollution.

Prominent members of the WHO promised to increase pressure on the government to establish better controls, but Jim and his team didn't hold out much hope. Corruption was like a cancer. It turned a government against itself and consumed it with greed and avarice until the government was terminated, and there was no more to devour. By that time countless innocent lives would be lost, diseases would mushroom into plague figures when it came to the dead, and most of the rest of the world would shake its head in sadness but offer no help.

It would be Christians, mostly from "evil" America that reached out to help. The Salvation Army and Red Cross and Mission Organizations would offer far too little far too late, but they would fight that uphill battle until they were weary and expended. Jim was proud to be among those who really cared about the people of Mozambique, not just about physical well being, but about their spiritual condition as well. In the end, it would always be hearts changed by a gracious and good God that would offer aid.

Frustration welled up inside Jim as well as he considered the state of his own country. Everyone was so busy trying to avoid offending people they no longer thought about offending God. God is not mocked. Whatsoever a man sows, that he will reap. Jim knew this well and shuddered to think of what might come if God removed His mighty hand of mercy from America. Already the country was plunged into wickedness so dark, it defied God with a willing heart and encouraged others to do the same.

The words of Joshua came to his mind. "As for me and my house, we will serve the Lord." Considering his part as the spiritual leader of his family he decided that he had a lot of work to do to make that a priority. His children needed to see him leading in this, reading his Bible with Cecilia each morning and evening, and hear them praying over the children as well. It was a tall order, but he wanted it more than anything. He wanted his children to grow up knowing that their father, flawed as he was, walked the talk to the best of his ability, and admitted when he failed.

"Lord, let that be my family's mantra!" Jim breathed quietly.

CHAPTER 16

As he finished that heartfelt prayer his phone beeped on his desk, and he lifted it.

"I have Admiral Runion on the line, Shep," Ives said. "Line one."

"Thanks, Ives," Jim replied, hitting the line next to the blinking green light.

"Admiral! Great to hear your voice!" Jim said enthusiastically.

"And good to hear yours, you pirate!" Admiral Runion said with real feeling in his voice. "We've got some INTEL for you," he added immediately. "I've sent the information along to Zeke, but I thought you'd like to hear what we discovered before that techno wizard stole my thunder," Jim smiled.

"I'm all ears," Jim invited.

"Right! Wikffels is attempting to purchase all the blue diamonds and blue diamond chips in the world, giving him a monopoly. His friend, and business partner Giles, is planning to steal those diamonds, and kill Wikffels in the process. He plans to use the diamonds to fund a daring plan to force board members of Ilmenite mining to sell shares to him, gaining control of the Ilmenite mines of Talanaro, Madagascar. With that power he plans to administer a coup and take over the government of Madagascar. He owns a compound in Malawi along the Shire River near Myela where he provides tour boat

162

trips on Lake Nyasa. My guess is that once he steals the diamonds, he will take them to his compound. Here's where the plot thickens!

"Our friends in the Zhanzhu Triad have set plans in motion to steal the diamonds from Ramanantsoa, kill him, and take control of the latest technology titanium prototype laser capable of targeting all current foreign communication satellites, leaving the companies they control as the sole providers of satellite communication.

"I'm aware you know about most of this, so I'll get right to the nitty-gritty details of this nefarious three-way drama. This would make for a good fiction spy novel! Gregor Vasovitch is somewhere down there and has eliminated Giles' man spying on the Triad. He's the new assassin for the Zhanzhu family. When this deal goes down, he will be leading the troops, so you be careful. Since he has proven he is good enough to stay out of the hands of the CIA and NSA agents trying to bring him in he's going to be a handful. Don't get dead!"

Jim smiled at the order, a familiar one from his former boss in the Navy. It wasn't safety he sought, but faithfulness to God. He was safe in God's hands.

"He's slippery. We'll try to get eyes on and keep him in our sights, Admiral," Jim promised seriously. "That's not someone I want sneaking around unnoticed."

"Indeed!" Admiral Runion agreed. "How are the boys?" he asked, business over. Jim grinned.

"You won't believe how fast they're growing. Both of them are walking now, and our wives are pregnant again. All three of them!" Jim reported with a chuckle.

"Who would have thought that Wade Adams would be a dad!" Admiral Runion laughed. "Like you and John, he'll be a good one. Have you seen the Wozniacs?"

"Yes. They're here at Tete. We shipped in some much-needed supplies and Wade is helping them create a place where they can hide the medical supplies to keep from having them stolen. I'm also letting it be known in local circles that if the good doctors of this clinic are bothered by criminal entities, those entities will cease to exist. I don't think they believe me," Jim added.

"No. But if you make one example the rest will figure it out," Admiral Runion stated.

"We'll make it an extreme lesson. That seems to be all these people understand. I normally would say I hate that part of the job, but this lot has made it easy not to feel a bit sorry about making an example," Jim revealed seriously.

"How about the pollution study?" Admiral Runion asked, switching gears.

"It's dire. This river is in serious danger, and so is the Indian Ocean. We're probably going to have to get all the surrounding countries that will be affected by the currents carrying this to their borders to put pressure on the Mozambique government to put a stop to it. The trouble is what has happened already will affect our waters for hundreds of years. The damage is already done!" Jim rejoined with real frustration.

"John and his team of marine biologists are working around the clock to make this report such that it stirs up a hornet's nest of response. I've got a good science team here. We'll be leaving in a day or two and traveling our third stage of exploration."

"You're in the most danger on this stage of your trip! Be careful!" Admiral Runion grunted. "Give my grandkids a hug!" he added before hanging up the phone. Jim looked at the dead receiver with a tolerant smile before replacing it. Technically the Admiral wasn't their grandfather, but he had adopted them, thereby telling Jim that he considered himself family. Family was important. Honor was what he felt when he thought about a man like Admiral Runion adopting him as family.

Picking up the map on his desk he studied it for several minutes, noting every detail, memorizing what he saw, something he'd trained himself to do. After careful study that lasted nearly half an hour, he laid the map down and stood up, looking at it with a new understanding and perspective of the enormity of the task before him. Finally, after about five minutes of studying it from a standing position he sat down, folded it, and took out a notebook.

As far as the Zambezi basin was concerned, there were four rivers to consider. Along with the Zambezi the Buzi, Pungwe, and Save Rivers drain the basin. Together the floodplains of these four rivers make up the World Wildlife Funds Zambezian costal flooded savanna ecoregion. Here was a mixture of open grassland and freshwater swamp inland from the Indian Ocean in Mozambique.

Although the dams have stemmed some of the annual flooding of the lower Zambezi and caused the area of floodplain to be greatly reduced, they have not removed flooding completely. Extreme floods cannot be controlled, and even some medium-level floods still happen. But the wetlands were an important habitat. Shrinking wetlands and uncontrolled hunting of animals such as buffalo and waterbuck during the Mozambique Civil War caused severe damage to wildlife, and it was slow to recover. Further damming would hinder that.

In all that vast area only the Marromeu Game Reserve near the city of Beira is protected. That was why one of the chief responsibilities of the grant issued to *Bring It Up* is determining how best to protect the wildlife in the region, ensuring that pollution is not a major threat to that wildlife. Jim sighed.

Local governments wanted more dams to further control the flooding, but that would threaten the wetlands and the wildlife. *Bring It Up* was faced with resistance to spending money to upgrade sewage treatment when flooding will only damage and even wash it away. Governments rarely could see past their tax revenues. He wrote a few notes in his notebook, closed it, and stood up.

"Ives, I'm going down to the Science Lab. Would you mind asking Wade to join me there, if he's not already glued to his wife's lips?" Jim smiled at Ives as he walked out, and Ives laughed. He'd been talking to him on the COMLINK, and everyone heard the comment.

"I think we need a medic in the Science Lab!" Alice spoke up. "Dr. Adam's appears to be suffering from something. Her face is very red!"

"I'll kiss it and make it better!" Wade's voice came over the COMLINK next. "Hold on baby! I'm coming! Bet I get to the lab first, Jim!" there was a pause. "Jim?"

"The captain's lips are busy at the moment!" Cecilia's voice came over the COMLINK, obviously just after a kiss.

"I may be a few minutes, Wade," Jim testified, laughing as Cecilia giggled in his arms.

"Our son is supposed to be taking a nap," Cecilia said. Jim could hear the light noise from the baby monitor. "I came to remind you to check in with the Wozniacs," she added after another kiss.

"Pippi and JR are watching the clinic. If anything happens, we go in 12-Teams." With thirty-six men in his unit Jim could divide them into three very effective teams of twelve. In this instance they intended to make a statement that no one would miss, and a military response with three teams and air support would make that statement definitively.

"Who has JAS?" Cecilia asked.

"Mom has him," Jim smiled. "Want to come down to the lab and have a kissing contest with Wade and Angela?" he suggested. She snuggled into his chest, giggling again and finally reached up and gently slapped his cheek.

"As you can probably hear, I need to return to our stateroom and lower the boom on our son. That's a nautical term for discipline," she added as FM hurried past.

He stopped and turned, pulled out his pocket notebook, puled the stylus from the side, and looked up with it paused above the screen. "You spell that n-a-u-g-h-t-y-c-a-l, correct?" he grinned spelling out the letters.

"It's the influence of people like you that so readily lead my son astray!" Cecilia said, pointing an authoritative finger at him. "I outrank you, PO1 Miller!"

"Geeze, boss!" Frank stuck out his lower lip comically. "All I did was ask how to spell the word!"

"Did we have to bring him?" Cecilia asked, laughing, and laying a friendly hand on FM's arm. "Get back to work, you miscreant," she snorted. "Were you finished kissing me, dear?" she asked, and Jim chuckled.

Jim continued to smile happily as he headed down to the science lab. FM was a clown, and no mistake. He often wondered how FM thought of those things so quickly. When he got to the lab Angela's face was still flushed. Looking at her he shook his head.

"Wade, you made it worse. Where's the doctor?" Angela blushed even more deeply as everyone laughed.

"He's busy!" D.J. said, coming into the room holding her husband's hand. "There's an epidemic on board this ship. We've isolated it and named it lipsmackeritis," that brought a chorus of laughter to the room. From behind her back she pulled a needle she must have had someone make for her. It had to be four feet long with an even longer needle at the end. "A shot of this will cure it!" she said, hunching her shoulders and shuffling across the floor. "Bend over, master!" she mimicked the famous Igor of Dr. Frankenstein fame, waving at Wade.

When the laughter finally died down Jim waved everyone to silence, still grinning. He suddenly understood. At any moment the unit could be called out to protect the clinic where the Wozniacs worked. Everyone felt the tension keenly at times like this. Everyone was doing his or her part to keep the tension manageable. At that moment his respect and love of his crew went up another notch.

"I need four things," Jim stated. "First, we need a sewage treatment facility that can withstand flooding. Second, we need a dike or wall around that facility that will keep it from mixing with the rest of the water until the sewage is fully treated. Third, I need funding to build it that doesn't come from the government of Mozambique. Fourth, and finally, I need a plan to lure in reputable companies to build and maintain the facilities that will be built for every major city and town that influences the Zambezi River and I want the WHO funded to constantly monitor the facilities."

"Struth!" Dr. Dundee said after a shocked silence. "You don't want much, do you, mate?"

"Actually, I want coal mining industries to adopt the same pollution controls we use in the United States too, but that's going to take a little more than this team can provide at the moment," Jim states seriously.

"Sure, Jim!" Wade said nodding. "We'll just whip that up for you by lunch. Everybody agree that lunch is a good deadline? Lunch on say July 1, two years from now!" he added.

"Listen ladies and gentlemen!" Jim said, holding up his hands as if to fend them off. "I don't believe that God sent us here to flex our muscles, shoot some bad guys, and leave. I've got the most talented and amazing team in the world, second to none! I believe God sent us here at this moment because we can actually do something to help the people of this country. We all know this government will never agree to building those facilities and putting in the infrastructure to carry sewage to them for treatment. They just don't understand the need, or won't understand it, maybe. But we do! Let's shock the world!

"Remember Jim Elliot's prayer? Oh, that God would make us dangerous! Well, I believe that this crew is serious about that. I know I am! Let's accomplish something that will help the people of this country in a real and effective way! What do you say?"

"It's only a drop in the bucket, but a drop starts things moving out in ever increasing ripples," John Dinsmore said quietly. "You do realize that this will take a miracle?" he added, looking at Jim.

"My God does miracles every day," Jim replied just as quietly.

"Oh well!" Dr. Dundee said. "If you're going to bring God into it, then of course it's possible!" he grinned as he said it.

"Wade can study the designs of other facilities that have to deal with floods. If anyone can design a facility that will work here, Wade is our man!" Jim said. "All of you are experts on breaking down and treating bacteria. Who better to put it all together so we can sell it to a funder?" Jim spread his hands.

"You think a great deal of us, Captain," Alice commented, smiling at him.

"That I do, Doctor!" he replied.

"In that case we'd better get cracking!" Alice said turning to face her staff. "Mr. Adams! Unhand that scientist. I need her!" Alice added with a wink at Jim. He was trying unsuccessfully to hide a smile and Wade smirked at him. Alice shook her head, looking at the two friends, and thinking that she was very fortunate to know such men.

Wade raised both hands and moved to a computer station. Shaking his head in amusement Jim left the science lab and headed back to his riverboat to talk to Zeke. At the moment all six boats were tied bow-first to the shore and close enough to merely step across the stern decks to move from boat to boat with ease. Without mishap Jim returned to his own craft and moved into the CIC.

Zeke, seeing him enter, held up a finger while he listened to his earphones for a few moments, before taking them off and nodding. Making an entry into his computer he finally turned to face Jim.

"I was about to call you," he said without preamble. "John saw our friend Tambwe checking out the clinic. His organization is the most powerful in this part of the country."

The words *organized crime* always struck a chord in Jim's heart. Here the people were so desperate and so impoverished that the last thing they needed was organized crime. And yet over the past few years it had gone international, and the drug and sex trade had the one thing that made the organization almost invulnerable. Money.

Zeke, who had been watching his commanding officer's eyes, almost drew away. "Geeze, boss, get those thoughts out of your head before we go after this bozo and his organization! These guys own the government here! Let's remember that! And this government likes its bribes! No! Come to think of it, let's take that money away. Who knows, it might improve things!"

"We're ghosts, remember?" Jim replied, his eyes not changing one bit. "I want this to be an example no one will ever forget. I want the people of Tete and Mozambique to believe that it was an international force that came to the aid of the clinic, a new anti-terrorist force."

"And if we lose a man, everyone will know it was us, Jim," Zeke pointed out soberly.

"Let's be sure no one gets dead!" Jim grinned at his friend. Zeke grinned back. There were no guarantees, but Jim knew his men would do their utmost to stay alive and succeed in this important mission.

"Remember, these guys like to attack during the daylight hours, to be seen!" Zeke reminded him.

"Yes. And they all gather the night before to prepare for the raid.

If someone can give me the day of the attack, we'll plan to hit their compound the night before," Jim replied.

"That's why I was going to call you. I've been sampling cell calls since the sighting. They are meeting tonight and will attack tomorrow. Tomorrow is when the shipment arrives with all the stuff they need at the clinic. You were right to make that public," Zeke reported. "It told them what we wanted them to know and now they're moving.

"How will we deal with the publicity?" Zeke asked after a pause.

"Ever see a Crock feeding frenzy?" Jim asked.

"None of us fancy digging in the mud!" Zeke said with a shudder. In his mind he saw the ditch dug in the mud bank at the river's edge. He realized it would be dug today, and tonight their captives would all be lined up, headless, in that thick nasty-smelling mud. After that the scent of blood would bring the crocks. In a feeding frenzy, crocks were downright frightening! Feeling slightly queasy he turned his mind to the job at hand.

"I'll get the men digging right away," he offered. Jim nodded, his own face bleak as he thought about the horrible death these men would face. It would be quite fitting, however, since they prided themselves on beheading and displaying the heads of their victims for all to see. Pressing his COMLINK he spoke.

"Tonight, is a go mission Omega Force! Team gathers at 21:00. Get what rest you can," he clicked off and went to his bunk to rest.

CHAPTER 17

Tambwe proved to be a good INTEL source for Zeke. Not long after dark, unseen beyond the compound where his soldiers were gathered a force of thirty-six soldiers moved silently toward the objective. Thinking himself secure in his compound Tambwe posted only minimal guards, and all five of them were smoking, and looking more often toward the inner part of the compound than outwards.

Because they continually looked to where there was light, when they looked out, they could see very little. They had grown secure and careless over the past year. No one dared oppose them. Mark and Jack, Jim and Frank, Terrance and Neil arrived at the compound wall first. Their job was to neutralize the guards. Behind the five-foot wall the guards stood and with the light behind them gave an amazingly easy target.

Five shots sounded from silenced weapons and the guards dropped, the sound of their falling bodies drowned out by the noise within. In minutes all thirty-six men were within the compound. Frank and Zeke now moved apart, planting charges, while Sid and Roger did the same thing in the opposite direction. When they met in the center, they rejoined their respective 12-Team.

Now the most dangerous moment came. For three seconds the 12-Teams closed their eyes as the explosions went off all around the compound. It was dangerous for two reasons. First, if they were discovered they could be shot before opening eyes, and second, shrapnel was a real danger. Counting off the three seconds the men pulled down their night vision goggles and opened their eyes to pandemonium. Within the compound the lights were all gone, the generators blown, along with the back-up system. There were no fires. The explosives used prevented fires.

Thirty-six agents of death rose out of the darkness and picked off the solders with quick three-shot bursts. In panic Tambwe ordered his men to fire, and half his troops went down from friendly fire before he realized his mistake. By then it was too late. Taking advantage of the confusion and mayhem *Omega Force* finished the battle in three minutes. When the gunfire silenced only one of Tambwe's soldiers lived. He was, at the moment, being held securely by Bear while Hobbs bound his hands and feet tightly with plastic restraint zip ties.

Bear used his video camera to record the one hundred and thirty-nine heads being removed. This was a grizzly task, using bolt cutters to sever the spinal cord, and a power-saw to remove the head. Just outside the compound the bodies were arranged on the bank of the river, headless necks lying just beneath the surface. The smell of the blood would bring crocks to dine, and other denizens of the jungle plain. This too was put on digital record. At the front gate the heads were placed on stakes driven into the ground for that purpose. When the gruesome task was done the lone survivor was brought out and turned to face the gate. There his blindfold was removed, and he stared in horror at the heads of his comrades.

Calvin Weston grabbed the back of his neck savagely. "See this?" he hissed savagely. "Anyone who attacks the clinic at Tete, anyone who steals medicine from those doctors, suffers the same fate!"

Terrance Red Claw stepped up, drew his knife and put the point against the man's eye. In Blackfoot he made his threat, while Jim translated into Portuguese. "Never forget what you saw here. You did not know we were with you tonight; you will never know we are there. Death will come swiftly to any who disobey."

Bear replaced the blindfold. The prisoner felt the hands holding him loosen and disappear, but he dared not move. In silence he waited until finally he cried out that he would pass the word. But there was no answer. It took him the better part of half an hour to get his hands free and remove the blindfold. When he looked around fearfully, he discovered he was alone, though all around him the sounds of predators filled the night air with groans and grunts, growls, splashes, and hideous other sounds. Terrified he backed away down the road, and finally turned and sprinted away. It took him most of the night to reach civilization.

Back in their teams the men made their way silently and unobserved by any humans to the boats. Tambwe promised to send men to watch the boats early in the morning, to be sure the men from *Bring It Up* did not interfere with their robbery. No one was watching and with the exception of a few dogs and chickens none observed the passage of each team. Once on board they worked fast to break down their weapons, clean and prep them, stow them carefully, with the night camouflage gear, gloves, balaclavas, and vests.

Not until that was done did the men take a refreshing shower to clean away the sweat and blood from the night's raid. Once everyone showered food was provided on the upper deck of *River Venture 4*, a sumptuous early breakfast, where Jim debriefed the men. He watched them come, in small groups, and realized that his men had once again proved that training and preparation made them more than formidable. *Omega Force* was indeed second to none, and it filled him with pride.

"How did these pelicans ever get to be so feared in these parts?" Ox asked when Jim asked for comments. "The inside of their compound was completely open, no enclosed areas for protection, bright lights, just begging for some blokes like us to come along and mop up!"

"They've been the big noise down here for a year or so," Hobbs said, looking over at Ox with a serious expression. "They have . . . uh, had guns, more guns than anyone else."

"Technically they still have the guns, they just won't work," Sparks added with a grin. "Hydrochloric Acid in the works makes a mess. One cannot just replace the works after the Acid eats away at everything."

"That was a good idea," Jim said, nodding at Wade. "And the explosives were well placed and timed, no fires afterward, just darkness."

"We rule the night!" Chief said solemnly. "Poor sods never had a chance."

"Was anyone injured?" Jim asked. "We all worried about the shrapnel from the explosions and the wild shooting."

"I took one in the vest," Sam Colt said, rubbing the spot on his abdomen. "It hurt some at first," he added unnecessarily.

"Anyone else?" Jim asked looking around. His men seemed calm and even more deadly if that were possible. He could see a few rubbing spots that hurt and waited for them to answer, knowing they would play down the injuries.

"One bounced off my knife, but it didn't hurt me. Startled me some," Lee Roy stated flatly. "Didn't break the blade though," he added.

"Thank God for Kevlar!" Dorf said quietly.

"Amen!" A chorus of voices replied. Jim looked around the room with some pride and finally spoke again.

"When all those bullets were flying every one of you did what he was supposed to do. We were successful because we worked the plan flawlessly."

"*Nulli Secundum!*" Roared around the deck.

"However, let's remember to never underestimate our enemies. So far, we've seen carelessness from most of them, but we can't count on that. Tambwe played into our hands last night. When word gets out, we'll be searched. I want everyone busy as usual when that happens. Zulu and Bulldog have watch over the science crew. Well done tonight. Dorf, will you lead us in a prayer of thanksgiving, please?"

The deck grew silent as men bowed their heads and Dorf led them in a prayer thanking God for the skills they'd learned that had protected them, and the dedication to training He'd given all of them, and then thanked God for watching over them so carefully, as He always did. A quiet "Amen" followed his.

At ten o'clock six SUVs arrived near the bank where the boats were tethered. Kaki green in color they bore the logo of the Zimbabwe military. A tall heavy-set man in the uniform of a general exited the lead vehicle and approached the boats. Jim stepped off the bow onto the ground and met the general a few feet from the boats. His eyes swept over the troops getting out of the vehicles, four in each vehicle with a driver, making a total of thirty soldiers.

"You are Captain James Shepherd?" the general asked.

"I am," Jim replied. Jim was dressed in jeans, a clean T-shirt, and wore no insignia of any kind indicating his rank.

"May I have permission to come aboard and search your boats?" the general asked.

"Our boats are always open, general. The folks of Tete have been on and off them many times. We have nothing to hide. I ask only that your men conduct themselves as gentlemen around the ladies on my crew. Any untoward actions would result in an international incident that would reflect badly on your government, and the man responsible would answer to me, as would you as a superior officer," Jim stared into the general's eyes and had the satisfaction of seeing him swallow nervously, and then recover quickly.

"You dare to threaten me?" the general drew himself up to his full height and glared down at Jim.

"I do," Jim retorted flatly. For a moment the two men stared into each other's eyes. Jim sighed inwardly. He was going to have to prove it. "We're done here," Jim said, turning away and walking back to the boat.

The general waved his men forward and they went to each boat. Jim pressed the COMLINK. "If anyone misbehaves, he answers to me. I don't care if he's already been roughed up a bit," he added.

He walked onto the front deck and stood beside the door, just behind Cecilia and RJ. FM took a stance to Jim's left, arms folded across his massive chest, and balefully watched the men file past. The general was with this group, and he watched his men search the boat thoroughly. Zeke, in the CIC cooperated in showing them the equipment they were using for their scientific research.

Forty minutes later the general listened to the reports on his walkie-talkie with frustration. Inevitably it was on *River Venture 3* that an incident occurred. One of the soldiers had grabbed Elizabeth Minor's bottom as she bent over a microscope. C.G. Franklin was closest, and he had the man in a submission hold before anyone could blink. At the same time Vince keyed his COMLINK.

"We have an incident in the science lab, boss," he said. Jim stepped up to the general.

"Will you come with me, please?" he asked politely.

The general, who had been advised of the same situation through his device nodded and waved his men to follow. Jim said nothing. They walked off the bow and over to *River Venture 3* and into the lab. Four soldiers had their guns pointed at C.G., who was holding the perpetrator in such a way the man was screaming in pain.

"Take him on shore," Jim commanded.

"You will instruct your man to release him, or you will be shot!" the general said, pulling his side arm. His eyes opened wide as Jim moved, taking the gun away easily and shoving it against the general's neck. The general heard the click of the safety and realized he was in grave danger. He stared down into green eyes that were as hard as stone. It had been a long time since he had tasted fear, but he tasted it now.

"You'll die as well," Jim stated. The general realized that Jim wasn't even sweating and didn't understand. He looked around only to discover that all of his men had been disarmed!

"Now that you know your situation, you will give the order for your men to step off the boats, put down all of their weapons, and walk to the vehicles. If one of them fails to follow your orders I will kill you first. Do you understand?" again, those eyes stared into his and the general licked his lips.

"You risk everything!" the general sputtered. Jim drew back the hammer of the pistol and the general finally understood. Grudgingly he gave the order. Slowly Jim walked him backwards off the boat, never letting up on the pressure to his neck with the gun. C.G. brought the perpetrator last, still screaming from the pain in his arm and shoulder.

Angrily the soldiers watched as Jim handed the general into the hands of Dorf, who towered over the man, dwarfing him with his physique. He turned to the soldier C.G. held and nodded.

C.G. let the man go and immediately the man spun to attack C.G. He went down hard and stayed down. C.G.'s blow had been fierce. He looked up at Jim and shrugged his shoulders.

"Sorry, boss. I kinda got carried away in the moment!" he admitted sheepishly.

"General, since this man cannot take his just punishment from me, do you have anyone else who would like to champion his cause?" Jim asked without looking at the general. Had he done so he would have seen the look of cunning that came into the general's eyes.

"George! This man says he will fight you instead!" the general said, his smile now smug.

George was a killer at heart, the fiercest warrior the general had at his command, and though he wasn't the biggest man in the unit, he'd beaten every one of them in hand-to-hand combat. Without hesitating George came forward. Jim slowly turned and faced his new combatant. There was no swagger in this man, just a lust for blood that Jim sensed immediately. He was not surprised when the man drew a small knife from his boot that fit in his fist, between the forefinger and middle finger.

For about thirty seconds Jim measured the man as he avoided the slashes and attack, determining his skill. The general watched with a smile until suddenly the battle changed. Blows, landing so quickly he could not follow, stopped his killer cold, stood him straight up, and then a foot connected with his head and the man went down like a rag doll. It had taken Jim Shepherd all of three seconds to render his best warrior unconscious! Not only that, but his trained killer had flipped in the air and landed without making a sound, unconscious, and badly injured by the looks of things and sounds of his breathing.

"Who are you?" the general asked as Jim walked up, tossing the little knife up and down in his right hand.

"Okay, gentlemen! Take them down!" Jim said loudly in response. Dorf let go of the general who turned to watch his men go down as George had.

"My men are all former military, and far more advanced in hand-to-hand combat than anything you can muster. Your punishment is to help your men into the vehicles and leave, humiliated in front of the people of Tete. Be glad your punishment does not include a caning in public," Jim added evenly when the general began to sputter. He watched the fight go out of the man. "And don't order any of the folks watching to help you."

The general glanced at his watch and raised his eyebrows. Jim guessed, correctly that he knew of the raid by Tambwe. Again, guessing, he thought that perhaps the general didn't know about what had happened at Tambwe's compound. The idea formed quickly in his mind, and he smiled to himself. He took a wild shot.

"Yes. You'd better hurry so you and your men are not around for Tambwe's raid on the clinic. He might think all those bribes had been wasted and do something about it!" to his utter delight the shot went home.

"How do you know of this?" the general asked.

"Medicine and medical supplies just arrived, general. We're not fools."

Glaring at Jim the general turned and began to work on getting his men into the vehicles. Most of them were regaining consciousness, but a few had to be lifted into their seats. By the end of the half hour all were in place and to the jeering of the crowd the military drove away, glaring hatred at Jim's men and the townspeople alike. Laughing at the glares Jim waved as the SUVs pulled away, and his men followed suit.

Out of sheer contrariness Jim turned to his men. "What are you standing around waving for?" he barked. "Play time is over! Get back to work!" he was grinning as he said the last. FM, predictably, responded.

"Dog pile on the captain!" he yelled. Jim found himself beneath a host of heavy bodies as he laughed, shoved, and fought in the uneven battle. At last, they got up and he lay on the ground, arms spread wide, unmoving.

"Did anybody get the license on that bulldozer?" he asked.

"This is no time to be lying around lollygagging, mister!" Cecilia's voice interrupted his thoughts. "There's work to be done. Jump to it!"

Jim shot to his feet and saluted his wife and laughed when she widened her eyes at the state of his clothing.

"Look at you! You're a mess! How can I expect to raise my son to dress respectably when you go around in public looking like that?" Looking down at RJ she giggled. "Pay no attention to the dirty man. We don't know him!" RJ laughed happily.

Leaning forward Jim gave Cecilia a kiss and went to the boat to shower and change. He felt that scrimmages like that should end in a moment of levity, and Cecilia had provided that, after his men's offering. He decided he liked Cecilia's better, grunted from some forming bruises, and dressed in his full uniform. The next visit, he knew, would be by a diplomat. He hoped the diplomat had sense enough to be diplomatic.

Going into the tiny office he waved at Nelson and sat down at his desk to a stack of paperwork requiring his signature. Even sharing the responsibilities with his brother John, the paperwork never seemed to end. Fortunately for both of them, their administrative assistants were the best, keeping the paperwork to a minimum. Dutifully Jim busied himself with his least favorite task and was just finishing up when Zeke arrived to tell him an ambassador was asking permission to board.

Transferring the finished work to his able Lieutenant he sketched a wave and went out to greet the ambassador. Cecilia, in her uniform, carrying RJ, joined him and he nodded approval. She smiled, knowing a pretty face and a woman with child and with a child would defuse any message of threat or reprisal. Judging her husband's mood, she decided he probably wasn't going to thrash the ambassador.

The ambassador was wiping sweat from his bald head, perspiring in the heat of the day, but his expression was guarded. He shook hands with Jim, bowed over Cecilia's hand properly and cleared his throat.

"Our government is not pleased that you saw fit to publically humiliate a general and some of his troops this morning, Captain Shepherd," he began. Cecilia cut him off by clearing her throat and speaking quickly.

"My husband has already had to defend the honor of one of our female crewmembers against the audacious and heinous offense of your general and his men. I think he acted with restraint, and unless you want to join the ranks of those who get properly thrashed, I suggest you offer an official apology for the gross conduct of your country's soldiers, and the miscarriage of justice that occurred when a respected team of international scientists here to help your country was treated with such disrespect, boarded, and searched without cause!" she could see by his body language that he was going to make a grave error. His words sealed his fate.

"In England woman may have the right to speak as you do, but here ..." His sentence ended when Jim's fist connected with his body, just below his heart, causing his knees to buckle, and as he fell, he tried to breathe, his eyes open wide, the pain in his chest frightening him.

"I did warn you, foolish man!" Cecilia said, smiling down at him like he was some errant child. His thoughts were of revenge until he looked into those of her husband, and he changed his tact immediately. After a period of time in which he was sure he was going to die his breath came back and he cried out in pain. Jim leaned down, grabbed the lapels of his jacket and hauled him to his feet.

"Most diplomats know enough to be respectful. Leave now," Jim motioned to Cecilia and the two of them turned and walked back to the boat. As a rebuff Cecilia thought it perfect as they walked away, backs turned, as if the man was unimportant.

"But I am not finished!" he said painfully, rubbing his chest.

"You are!" Jim said tersely, turning to face the man. "I'll talk to anyone who is polite and professional. That means I don't talk to you. And I don't repeat myself," he took a step toward the diplomat who backed away quickly, waving his arms ineffectively in the air in front of him. All Jim could think as the man scrabbled backwards was what a coward he was.

The next diplomat was a diplomat, a senior man with greying hair and a pleasant smile. He introduced himself as Dr. Hamnebo of the Zimbabwe government. His handshake was firm, and his eyes twinkled as he looked at Cecilia.

"A most unfortunate incident, my dear friends. Most unfortunate. My government heaps apologies for the behavior of our general and the junior diplomat who came to see you earlier. Could we talk perhaps where it is a little cooler?"

"Follow me, sir," Jim invited respectfully, leading the man onto the boat and into the dining area where they sat at the table in air-conditioned comfort. Everything around them was spotless, saying volumes for his crew. Jim smiled.

"My government is not always subtle and advanced in its ways, I am afraid," Dr. Hamnebo said as he sipped a glass of cold beer. He looked at the bottle. "This is very good beer," he said with appreciation. "How much did you know about Tambwe and his organization?" he asked after a pause.

"What most folks around here know. He planned to take the new medical supplies we delivered to the clinic here. We've been expecting him all day," Jim replied.

"He will not be coming. At the moment his head is impaled on a spike in front of his compound, along with the heads of all of his men, except one. That one was told to pass the word that the clinic was protected. Was it a NATO force that violated our borders?"

"Why are you asking me?" Jim asked feigning innocence. "We did not contact anyone. Surely you could determine that."

"Hm, yes," Dr. Hamnebo said slowly. "We did ascertain that no one on these boats contacted anyone outside the country, nor did the doctors or nurses at the clinic. At your request they are in hiding today."

"We learned that Tambwe was going to make his attack today and warned the doctors and nurses. They closed the clinic and went into hiding. How large was this force? Tambwe had over a hundred men we've heard," Jim asked.

"Our witness does not know. He estimates that at least three times the number of his troops invaded the compound. What we did get out of him was that the force was international, speaking Portuguese, French, German, English, and a language he does not know. He thought it might be Russian," Dr. Hamnebo said guardedly.

"Hats off to the good guys!" Jim said, lifting his Diet Coke.

"You, of course, do not know who they were?" Dr. Hamnebo asked softly.

"Whoever they were, they did this region a service. They protected the medical supplies at a much-needed clinic, and probably made sure no one else will bother the clinic in a long while. I doubt they were NATO forces, though. NATO forces would have alerted your government, even though it would have tipped off Tambwe and made the attack a failure."

"You do not think very highly of our government, do you?" Dr. Hamnebo asked bleakly.

"Dr. Hamnebo, please don't insult our intelligence. Your government has fought us every step of the way, and we are here to help. Government agents have acted atrociously and illegally all along the river. Tambwe and his organization bribed government officials to allow them to terrorize this region mercilessly. Your people are suffering from extreme poverty and disease. The coal industry is ignoring protocol to protect the environment, poachers have been allowed to almost wipe out species here on protected lands. That same government has built dams without proper studies that now threaten all of the delta area of this river and the flood plains. Pollution is at an all-time high in the water, accompanied by red algae that is now polluting the Indian Ocean and killing fish and threatening the whale population. Please tell me, of all those statements, which generates respect?"

"Unfortunately, that bleak picture of our government is very accurate. However, governments do have power," he stopped as Jim raised his hand.

"No sir, they do not," Jim said emphatically. "To have power one must have authority, and there is only one authority in the entire world. God Almighty has authority, and therefore He has power. Governments have military might, law enforcement, but without God's blessing and power behind it such things are an illusion. How many different governments have you had in the last twenty years? Three? Which of them had any power? None! Is anything left of the two former governments? No!

"If your government chooses to act against us there will be such an international reaction that the economy of this government would collapse. You know it, and I know it. Sanctions against your government would cripple it over night! Should your government decide to treat us with respect, we will respond in kind."

"You are very bold, Captain Shepherd," Dr. Hamnebo said. His eyes twinkled again. "It is rather refreshing to meet a person of your caliber. The group that took down Tambwe used silenced weapons. There are none aboard your boat, on any of your aircraft, or aboard your ship. They also wore camouflage clothing, and none of that has been found on the various searches. Two of the searches have been most thorough. I must tell you that you are not suspected in this act, but you can see how it worries us that a force of this nature could appear and disappear without knowledge?"

"They did you a favor," Jim repeated. "Be thankful."

"Ah well! As to that another organization will eventually muscle its way in, and it may be worse than Tambwe's!" Dr. Hamnebo's face was clouded with sadness.

"And your government is powerless to prevent that," Jim answered gravely.

Dr. Hamnebo nodded sadly. "What you say is true. We are powerless. As long as corruption exists, there will be no blessing from God, and there will be no real power, only more fighting," for a moment his face was sad as he thought about that truth. "I had hoped that after our civil war we would see an end to it, but alas, it is not to be. You must be very careful on the next leg of your journey,

Captain. Powerful forces are gathering against you, not the least of which is Gilles Ramanantsoa and Martin Wikffels."

"Dr. Hamnebo, you have just convinced me that you are a true diplomat, and a friend," Jim professed solemnly. "I accept all apologies and I give you my respect, sir, for you alone thus far have earned it. We know about those two miscreants and will deal with them accordingly," Jim promised.

The smile that lit Dr. Hamnebo's face changed his features, and he squared his shoulders before speaking. "It is I who am honored, Captain Shepherd. I am a good judge of character, and to be called a diplomat and friend by one such as you, is high praise indeed. I thank you," he offered his hand and Jim took it gladly.

"We will continue to do all that we can to help your country, and if opportunity presents itself, perhaps remove some of the more dangerous elements to your government and future peace," Jim promised after a moment's pause.

"Now you convince me that you are a friend to my country as well. I thank you," Dr. Hamnebo said. "I shall struggle to write my report now, to satisfy both my government, and your worthy company. God speed, Captain."

Jim escorted Dr. Hamnebo off the boat and all the way to his vehicle, noting that it was an ancient Volvo, not something new and fancy. Opening the driver's door for Dr. Hamnebo he was not surprised to find the interior pristine. As the good doctor drove away Jim saw Gregor Vasovitch out of the corner of his eye. A silenced pistol was in his hand, but it was not raised. From the boat a voice came loud and clear.

"Mr. Vasovitch drop the pistol now. I have you in my crosshairs," it was the voice of Scope, one of their best snipers. Vasovitch dropped the pistol and charged, his face a mask of rage and hate, and Jim calmly stood and watched him come. When no shot stopped him Vasovitch began to smile a ferocious smile of triumph. His leaping kick was vicious and aimed to take Jim out of the fight with the first blow. It was everything Jim expected from such a man, but it also told Jim that the man's age was slowing him down.

His eyes widened in surprise as Jim seemed to flow into the air, spinning, just beneath his own extended leg now snapping out for the final motion, and then opened all the way as a scream escaped his lips. Jim's foot landed between his legs with the force of a pile driver, stopping his forward motion instantly, and as his face hurtled toward the ground a back kick smashed his nose, turning his head sideways, and causing him to spin awkwardly. Even before his body fully landed another kick slammed into his solar plexus, driving the air from his lungs and flinging him several feet backwards.

Gregor wasn't done yet. He rolled, trying to find some purchase, but even before he could get his hands down a foot connected with his neck, just below his ear, and he went down and out, his body dropping like a rag doll. For a moment Jim crouched, ready to strike again, his fists clenched, body in a position to go any direction. But Gregor was out. Finally, Jim relaxed, breathed out, and loosened his shoulders and chest.

Dorf and Wade came running up with plastic zip restraint ties and within seconds Gregor Vasovitch was trussed and heading back to the boat on Dorf's shoulders.

As they reached the boat Jim looked up and gave the orders to disengage from the shore and head upriver. People who had watched the battle on the shore turned away as the boats headed upriver. There were none to report to the Zhanzhu agent what happened to Gregor Vasovitch. That agent had not been present, and he would have tried to dissuade Vasovitch from making an open move against the men of *Bring It Up*. He would have been astounded to learn what really happened.

Jim watched Dorf dump Gregor to the deck floor, none to gently, and then looked up at team Raider, all four of them standing there. He nodded once.

"He's all yours. Take a rigid raider and do what you have to in order to get the information we all need. We've voted and he's a sanctioned kill, so when you're finished make sure there is no evidence and rejoin us," Jim said. The vote had come after intelligence came in of his activities while here in Zimbabwe. Gregor was vicious, his acts of attrition against innocent people always ending in horrible deaths.

"Surprised me a bit when Sir Edward added his vote to the sanction," Hobbs said, looking dispassionately on Vasovitch. "I thought he'd want a crack at what's in this one's head."

"He knows you'll pass on what you learn," Jim said quietly. He saw the distaste for what he was about to do on Weston's face and nodded. It had to be done. He knew Weston would do his duty. After Raider left with the prisoner Jim went to talk to Cowboy and Gearhead, his two physicians. They needed to be ready now for any eventuality, and though Jim knew they were already in that frame of mind, it was his duty to remind them.

CHAPTER 18

Moatize was dismal. Most of the coal mining is open pit mining, which produces health issues for surrounding villages and people living close to the mines. Research had already demonstrated that companies such as Jindal, Vale, Rio Tinto, and before that Riversdale all ignored the human element. They were not alone. The government of Mozambique acted far too slowly to relocate humans near the mines, allowing them to live in dangerous conditions with total disregard to their plight.

In his report Jim summed it up with this simple statement: *Human rights abuses abound with the local coal mining industry and government.* The Wozniacs already warned him about the health conditions, black lung prevalent even in younger children, and other problems.

Fearing the worst their fears were confirmed as they tested the waters. Pollution here, as at Tete, was spiking to alarming levels. Jim interpreted again for the scientists of his crew as they addressed the owners and managers of the coal mining concerns in the area, along with a few government representatives.

Wikffels was present, wearing his yellow suit, sitting quietly beside his silent partner Ramanantsoa. Neither spoke. A spokesman hired to represent them was quick to point out how much revenue for the country this industry was providing, revenue that could be used to move those affected to safer living areas. He also pointed out that they were within the parameters of this governments EPA requirements.

Jim was quite pleased with Alice Dinsmore as she shredded the spokesman's claims with facts showing that whatever revenue the mines had made for the government would soon be used up in expenses to clean up the river, the Indian Ocean, pay the lawsuits that were bound to follow by other countries affected by the red algae and pollutants. She too used facts; facts that made it clear that Zimbabwe was in for huge financial losses in the very near future.

With a smile Jim watched Ramanantsoa drag Wikffels from the room sputtering in rage. Ramanantsoa, at least, realized that they faced a very deadly enemy in this study, but at the moment was willing to bide his time, knowing that Massoona would soon be ridding him of this nuisance. What he didn't want was another public embarrassment with Wikffels in one of his rages. It took him some time but he finally calmed Wikffels down and sent him away with the knowledge that the mercenary Maximiliano would soon solve this problem once and for all.

Once he'd gotten Wikffels away to take out his anger somewhere else he made a call before returning to the conference room. Zeke, as always, was ready for that and traced and recorded the call. Ramanantsoa may use disposable cell phones, but with the right technology Zeke was able to program a voice recognition code into his Cray computers that recorded all calls matching that code. Later that day what they heard when they listened to the recording was the voice of Ramanantsoa telling Massoona to use at least one hundred and twenty mercenaries and to make sure that no one on the *Bring It Up* crew was ever seen again.

Massoona argued against the idea, thinking that his original twenty was enough, but he was wise enough not to argue with Ramanantsoa. Instead, he negotiated for a higher rate, and permission that he and his original twenty men from the Alaska failure would do the actual killing. Jim, John, Wade and Andrea listened to the recording with bleak faces.

Later that night they shared the recording with everyone on the crew. After listening to the recording, a decision was reached that Massoona's mercenaries would never leave the jungle, and no trace of them would ever be found. The vote was unanimous, and the sanction was given. Jim sighed, feeling that too many people had already died on this mission, but there was little he could do. He did ask Abe to pray for their protection.

Team Raider traveled up a tributary to the Zambezi River into a remote area until they found what they were looking for. Gregor Vasovitch was Spetsnaz trained which meant he had been trained to endure torture. What Raider knew was that very few men could withstand it for any length of time, and there were things that could be done to quickly lower a man's resistance to torture.

Finding four sturdy trees they secured the prisoner upside down, his head just touching the ground, arms and legs stretched tight and spread as far as they would go without coming out of the socket. Cutting off his clothing they left him there for most of the day, letting the sun burn his skin and areas that had never been exposed to it before.

Just before nightfall Bear poured a bucket of sugar water over the prisoner's face, letting much of it go up his upside-down nostrils until the man was choking and spitting furiously. It didn't take long for the ants to find the sugar water and through the night Vasovitch screamed and struggled as they crawled into his nostrils and over his face, stinging him painfully and chewing parts of his skin away to take back to their nest. Relentlessly the ants fed until the man was sobbing and moaning, begging for mercy.

In the morning he was bleeding and hoarse from screaming, his hands looked like white pieces of meat, swollen and bloodied around the wrists where he'd tried to escape. His eyes were swollen and painful from bug bites and his head ached miserably. When his feet were released, he thought he was going to have a reprieve, but his curses soon grew as his body was stretched out, just a few inches over the ground.

He screamed once when Hobbs made the cut and stared at his

manhood dripping blood from a slender cut. Hobbs squatted several feet from the soles of the prisoner's feet where he could see his face.

"Crocodiles can scent blood from a great distance, yeah mate? We caught a small one, not big enough to eat you, but big enough to rip some things off. We've been poking him all night long and he is very angry. I'm going to let the boys release him now. Let's see how you handle this," Hobbs said conversationally.

Bear appeared, holding a baby crocodile, no more than two feet long, and as soon as he put it down it rushed toward Vasovitch who screamed in terror. As Hobbs thought, the scent of blood led it straight to the bleeding member and it bit down hard. That was when Bear grabbed it, so that it couldn't thrash about too much, and Carr slowly pulled its jaws apart. The Crocodile was now snapping its teeth just inches from Vasovitch and he screamed. That was when Banks plunged the needle in and pushed the plunger of the hypodermic needle to the bottom.

By late afternoon that day Vasovitch was broken and talking. Banks stood nearby with a digital recorder taking it all down while the Russian sobbingly recited his deeds for the Zhanzhu Triad. Tao Ling Zhanzhu ordered the death of Hobbs cousin, and Vasovitch admitted that he hadn't broken under torture, making Tao so angry he had finally killed him with Tao's ceremonial sword.

It took hours to get the whole confession and when it was over the four men looked at each other with horror. The smell of blood was bringing the predators closer to them, so they released Vasovitch, who could no longer see, and walked away, leaving him to face the horrors of predators far better at killing than he would ever know. From a distance they watched a pride of lions bring him down and finally drag his carcass into the jungle growth. His death had not been easy or quick.

"I'm getting too bloody old for this," Hobbs finally sighed as they sped down the tributary toward the Zambezi. Rain was falling heavily, and his men just nodded, looking spent and depressed.

"We should have fed him to the ants!" Donnelly snarled with feeling.

"Yeah. Dying by lion attack was just too quick," Carr added.

"At least we didn't have to kill him," Banks said sadly. "God, he was vile!" he added.

"That's why we do what we do," Hobbs nodded after a pause.

Late the next day they rejoined the boats, showered and changed, and ate, and then spent several hours with Zeke, Jim, John, and Wade. The information was copied and sent out, but not until after the eight men spent a few hours sifting through it all. At last Jim sat back and put a hand on Hobbs shoulder.

"You okay?" he asked. "Sorry! What a stupid question," Jim admitted immediately. "How are you holding up?" he amended.

"It takes a toll, doing what we do. We needed the information and I got it, but I did things that will haunt me. We all did," Hobbs indicated his men. "What we did would break any man, and it nearly broke us to do it, Shep. It had to be done, and for my cousin's sake it was fitting, but God Almighty!"

"Yeah. What we do is pretty horrible. All of us had a part in that, Hobbs. Don't bottle it up inside. Okay?" Jim replied.

"Yeah, Shep. I have to learn how to use a sword now, so I guess I'll pour myself into that. That should help," Hobbs grinned lopsidedly.

"Just a sword isn't enough. Kensyobudo is a good art to study. A sword is a good weapon, but it is no match for a quarterstaff. Learn Kensyobudo first, and then learn the quarterstaff. No Japanese swordsman will be able to touch you," Jim advised soberly. "They never believe that a quarterstaff is better than a sword, by the way."

"Kensyobudo is a form of Kendo, isn't it?" Bear asked quickly.

"That it is, but it focuses more on the use of swords and spears. As in all disciplines of this nature it is a bit narrow and those who rise high in the art are often disgruntled and even angry when defeated by non-purists. A non-purist would be one who studies more than one art and combines the disciplines. We've been doing that for years, which is why Western Europeans are so often world champions in the martial arts major events," John answered. "We don't just practice the dance steps and moves routinely, we experiment and try new things, invent ways of combining disciplines. It makes us unpredictable and deadly adversaries."

"Yeah. I noticed your wife trying out some of those new moves the other day in training. We all feared for your life, mate! Pippi seemed quite agile and effective!" Wade laughed.

John laughed with him, and shook his head, unaware his wife was now standing in the door. "Truth be told, she's much more skilled than I am, but I'm stronger, and I sometimes take chances I shouldn't. She tends to take advantage of that," he rubbed his chest where she'd landed a particularly devastating kick that morning.

"Which is my Segway to tell you gentlemen that this man needs his rest," Penelope suggested, putting her arms around her husband's shoulders from behind. She looked for a moment at Calvin Weston and his men and spoke. "Calvin, why don't you take your men to Abe, spend some time in prayer, and then get some rest. We can hear all about it tomorrow."

"I should remind you gentlemen that my wife is with child, so I had to go easy on her this morning," John quipped as soon as she finished. Pen grabbed his ear and hauled him to his feet, and he pretended severe pain as she dragged him from the room while the other men laughed. When the laughter died down Jim nodded at Calvin. Pippi had been correct. Smiling and nodding he spoke.

"Her advice was good. Take it. Well done, men," he rose to his feet and left the room, Wade following close after.

"I liked her advice," Calvin claimed with a sigh. "Let's go see that muscle-bound cook and see if he can pray some peace into our hearts," he rose, clapped Zeke on the shoulder and his men followed him out.

For several minutes Zeke remained, silent, his thoughts racing. Vasovitch had known a great deal about the Triad, and Zeke knew that they represented a real threat, not just to *Bring It Up*, but also to the world. Getting the information out would be the easy part. Putting the Triad out of business would need some serious thought, and a lot more INTEL. Sighing he stacked his notes and slid them in a file folder. The Triad folder was growing thicker by the day. China protected the Triad, and that could prove the greatest detriment of all. Sighing again, Zeke left the room.

A text message alert appeared on the phone they'd confiscated from Vasovitch. It would probably be the only text that phone would receive. It was coded, but Zeke already had enough information on the Triad's codes to easily crack it, responding with the same code. Carefully he copied the cryptic style of the assassin in his response, buying some time for everyone. It would be several days before they guessed that Vasovitch was no longer among the living. Even then they'd have to make sure, and that would take some time. He grinned as he sent the message.

"Three days," he typed in the message. "Let them figure that out!" he thought with another smile. Knowing they would wait three days for the next message he destroyed the phone by simply taking it apart, destroying the GPS device, and keeping the rest of the parts. Carefully he stored them in the little plastic cabinet he kept for computer and phone parts. The actual casing was taken to the galley and melted in the incinerator they maintained. Raider was gathered around Abe and Sturdy at the table in the dining area, deep in prayer. He slid into a seat and joined the prayers.

CHAPTER 19

Reaching the Cahora Bassa Dam turned out to be one of the more pleasant segments of the journey. Shortly before reaching the Cahora Bassa Rapids the boats pulled to shore and waited for the hired Sikorsky-S64 to lift each one up to the lake. Once past the coal mines near Tete the pollution levels dropped significantly. As they ate dinner that evening the main discussion around the tables was Project Cahora, a MEDC Lda application for license 5084L.

Encompassing an area of 8,680 hectares, a large portion of which is occupied by the waters of the Cahora Bassa Lake. Terrestrial areas elevated above the lake waters account for over 2,650 hectares which are comprised of sedimentary lithologies of the Cadzi Formation, postulated to cover the entire concession. Below the Cadzi Formation like the Matinde Formation, followed by the Moatize Formation, both of which are known coal-bearing Lower Karoo units. It was only a matter of time before the government issued the license and coal mining would begin in earnest, possibly destroying the beautiful lake and surrounding area.

Wildlife in the area would be adversely affected as well. Some of the best hunting in the area was done along the shores of Cahora Bassa Lake. Pollution and the increasing presence of man in the area would have a major effect.

There were those in the group that were passionate about needing to block further coal mining, and it was their voices that spoke the thoughts and feelings of the more analytical and amiable members of the group. Everyone agreed that it would not be the crew of *Bring It Up* that could halt such wanton destruction. Only pressure from international sources could provide that. With the threat of red algae in the Indian Ocean many were hopeful that measures would be taken. However, Jim was fairly certain that too much time would pass before the actual pressure was exerted, and that by then the coal mining industry would have already begun its destruction.

In the morning the CH53 made two trips to shuttle passengers to the lake, while the strange looking Sikorsky-S64 lifted the boats. Each boat was designed with four shoulder eyebolts at each corner of the craft, bolted into the lightweight frame, so that a sling could be attached, and the boat lifted and transported. Everything in the boats had to be secured for this part of the operation to ensure that nothing was damaged in the transportation. Jim, John, Wade, and Andrea made a careful inspection to make sure all was as it should be before leaving the boats. None expected to find anything overlooked and their expectations were correct.

Once the boats were on the lake the mechanics and electricians checked them over and declared them safe and ready to use. The inspection Goody, Inchworm, Wrench, Hammer and Loony gave the boats took the entire first day, and for good reason. It was decided to leave the boats unguarded, a move they were sure would demonstrate they had nothing to hide, and also give some others a chance to sabotage or bug the boats. Since Zeke had hidden cameras everywhere, he and News watched their computers, smiling grimly as nefarious characters first searched, and then planted their various devices.

Wikfells' man planted explosives on the pontoons of every boat, a few nasty surprises in the galley and computer center, and some explosives near the fuel tanks. A soldier of Zimbabwe planted listening devices in the CIC and dining areas of the boats. No one representing the Zhanzhu Triad appeared because Vasovitch had been tasked with sabotaging the vessels. They did not yet know that their agent was no longer among the living. All this was recorded for future reference, and the devices were defused, removed, and disposed of during that first day. No one hurried when doing something of that nature, which was why an entire day passed.

Martin Wikfells appeared in person to detonate the explosives the following morning, and when he was sure everyone was on board, he opened the covers on the electronic box, and toggled all the switches to detonate the bombs. After a few moments of irritated waiting, he threw the box across the room, smashing part of the wall and shattering the box, scattering pieces all over the room. Following that Wikfells shot his man who had planted the explosives and fled back to his house near Tete.

Zeke, ever ready to play a prank, kept one of the listening devices and attached it to a seven-hour loop of a *Three Stooges* episode from an early television broadcast featuring the three men in a parody of safari gone wrong. The two men assigned the task of listening to the devices looked at one another in consternation, began to laugh, and then offered the earphones to the captain that planted the devices. He listened for a few moments, said something unprintable, and promptly shot the recorders. The two men who had been tasked with listening wisely fled the room.

Tracing the signal Zeke picked up a call from a landline at the location. He now had a voiceprint of the captain, and of his superior, a General in Harare. The captain's report was short and to the point.

"They found and disabled all of our listening devices," he reported angrily when the General picked up his extension.

"Search the boats at Kanyemba!" the General ordered tersely. "Make a public example of Captain Shepherd and then take the women as prisoners!"

"I will personally kill Captain Shepherd," the captain purred with pleasure. He didn't like being made to look a fool.

"Behead him and bring me his head!" the General demanded and hung up.

"Yo Shep!" Zeke said into his COMLINK.

"Go Zeke," Jim replied.

"I have a recording for you to listen to in the CIC. If you could peal your lips off that pretty wife of yours, could you make your way here, please?" Zeke replied.

Jim had indeed been kissing Cecilia at that moment and he looked up at the camera with an expression of exasperation.

"On my way, Seaman Kline!" Jim said with a straight face.

"Demoted!" sounded from a dozen voices in Zeke's ear and he grinned. His fingers flew over the keyboard in front of him and the next man to speak sounded like Donald Duck. Another spoke, sounding like Goofy. FM, who had been the latter, mimicked the Disney dog character perfectly.

"Well gosh, Zeke! Somebody took my bone!" he said, sounding just like the Disney character.

Loony yelled for FM to shut up, sounding just like the cartoon character Yosemite Sam. When he heard his voice, Loony shot back at Zeke. "I'm a commin', and I'm a bringin' my guns pardner!"

Jim entered the CIC laughing as the voices went on. He knew that everyone on the boat would have to see what voice they'd been given. Zeke, he saw, was recording the conversations. Shaking his head, he motioned for Zeke to take off his earphones. Zeke did so with a wide grin.

"If I restore you to your present rank, will you put a stop to this nonsense?" Jim asked with a grin.

"In a while," Zeke agreed easily. "Listen to this, while I continue to record!" he was laughing as he handed Jim another pair of earphones and let him listen to Captain Kananga of the Zimbabwe Defense Forces.

"What INTEL do we have on this guy?" Jim asked when he was finished listening.

"He was with the Zimbabwe African National Liberation Army, or ZANLA, to use the acronym, before they put together the defense forces. His reputation is all bad. You saw him on the monitor. He's as tall as Bear. Word is, he likes hands-on killing," Zeke replied.

"ZANLA had a bad reputation everywhere they went, and this guy was one of the main reasons."

"Kananga is going to be very disappointed when we stop at Zumbo instead of Kanyemba," Jim mused quietly.

"I don't think that will stop his attempt to get at you," Zeke said, shaking his head.

"No. He'll cross the river and try to bribe the local police to allow him to take us captive. As soon as we know his plans we go to full military response," Jim shrugged his shoulders. "Hopefully it will be dark."

"We're talking a pitched battle!" Zeke said.

"Yes. But we may be able to avoid all of it if we load and leave. If they send patrol boats after us, we can handle that," Jim replied.

"We'd better get everyone up to speed on this new threat," Zeke noted.

"Right. See if you can break through the cartoon network and arrange a meeting just before lunch," Jim grinned and left Zeke to end his shenanigans with the COMLINK system.

Just before lunch they all gathered on the observation deck of the garbage scow and Jim filled them in on the new threat. Zeke played the recording, and everyone listened carefully. Opening laptops, they all looked at photographs of Kananga and read his file. After about ten minutes of silence Viper spoke up.

"The only real challenge is a daytime attack," he said.

"I agree," John said.

"How long will it take us to load our supplies at Zumbo?" Pippi asked.

"Most of it is food, ammunition, and medical supplies," Rock 'n Roll replied quickly. "It will probably take us twenty minutes or less if it is at the dock as requested."

"What about taking the Sea Stallion to Zumbo, picking up the supplies a day early, and loading up on the water?" Pippi asked.

"That would work," Zeke replied quickly.

"I think that's probably the best idea we'll have," John added. "It will avoid our having to stop at Zumbo."

"And if Kananga comes in a patrol boat?" Jim asked, grinning at his brother.

"We could alert Zambia that we have INTEL that Kananga is going to steal the supplies we bought at Zumbo. They would take that as an insult and are sure to respond," Inchworm spoke up.

"That could work," Zeke said with enthusiasm.

The ideas continued and Jim listened to each one, filled with pride to lead such a crew. By the end of the meeting, they had a plan in place that everyone agreed was the best plan. After a quick lunch everyone went back to working with the science crew as they continued to study the waters of the Cahora Bassa Lake.

In the deeper waters they didn't have to worry about hippos. All six rigid raiders were on the water with the six biologists, each with at least one lab assistant, a driver and two men for security. Other members of the crew went along, so that the boats were half full. Those on the research boats kept a close watch for danger and continued with their other responsibilities.

Cup Cake was with Dr. Putnam's boat, following his instructions. In his boat he had the men from Firefox with him, copiously taking notes and listening as he instructed them on what he was looking for. Viper, Scope, R.C., and .45 were good students, and he enjoyed having them along. Two men from Bulldog stood at either side of the boat, one in front, one in the rear, both holding rifles. Hayseed and M.P. listened, but their eyes were busy scanning the water around them.

SOS was with Dr. Copeland. Nightfall was with them and the two men providing security were from Omega 1. Jim and F.M. had the watch, and though they both listened carefully to Dr. C as she expounded on what she was finding, their eyes were busy scanning the water. Jim noticed that F.M. looked often at Stephanie Morris, whom everyone called SOS. He wondered if there was romance budding there. But F.M.'s looks were quick, and his eyes continued to move as he scanned for danger.

"I wouldn't suggest swimming in this water," Dr. C. replied to a comment from Santa. "Besides, the usual bacteria your body isn't prepared to fight off, another threat remains that will give you pause for thought. There are schools of bull sharks in these waters."

"Bull sharks!" Coleman said in amazement. "In fresh water?"

"Yes. There have been attacks recorded. We read about a few of them while we were supplying at Cahora Bassa," she replied without looking up from the microscope she was studying at the moment. "There is a plethora of Kapenta in the lake, so they have plenty of food, and yet people have been attacked and bitten, some badly."

"I wonder how they get along with the Crocodiles?" Fingers asked with a grin.

"Smaller ones I'm sure are prey to the sharks, as the smaller sharks are prey to the Crocodiles," Dr. C. replied, looking up from her microscopic study. "I would like to know if the Crocks have realized that they can't take the bull sharks down for a death roll, but if they hold them still can kill them. When two species that don't normally come together are thrust together like this the results can be interesting."

"What about the saltwater Crocks? How do they deal with sharks?" Izzy asked.

"I've seen photos of a saltwater crocodile with a bull shark in its mouth. It was probably eighteen or twenty feet long. Somehow it had pulled the bull shark up on the sand and had its head in its mouth. All-in-all it was pretty impressive," Dr. C. alluded. "Those saltwater crocks can weight up to four tons!" she added.

Just then three fins broke the surface of the water as three bull sharks circled the boat. Everyone reacted differently and Jim and FM raised their rifles but didn't fire. If the sharks attacked the boat they certainly would, but until then they remained at the ready.

"Where's a crock when you need one?" Kagan asked.

"Better yet, where's C.G.?" Dr. C. asked with a grin.

"Hey C.G.!" Kagan spoke into his COMLINK.

"Go Fagan," C.G. replied.

"Got three bull sharks circling our boat. Crocks can kill them, and since you killed a crock, we thought you might like to come to our rescue!" Fagan replied. "I'd jump in and take care of it but . . .

I'm reviewing the situation!" he sang the last four words from the popular musical *Oliver* version of the villain.

To everyone's surprise C.G. appeared, hanging from one of the support poles from the observation deck, wearing nothing but a loincloth and shorts and brandishing his knife. He put his knife in its sheath, beat his chest and gave off a television version of Tarzan's challenge. Pretending to see a shark he pointed, screamed in a high-pitched voice, and clung to the support pole shaking. Jim broke out laughing with everyone else when Dorf appeared, arms crossed, shaking his head and motioning C.G. back in the boat. Jim never got tired of the shenanigans of his men and enjoyed this drama as it played out.

C.G. leaped into the boat and hid behind Dorf, peeking out to either side and looking at the water as though terrified. Shaking his head Jim continued to watch the sharks, glad his crew was creative and theatrical at times. Listening to the chatter on the COMLINK he grinned at the more expressive element as they bantered back and forth.

Back on the boats more studies were done, and the results entered into the computers. After dinner that evening, before the games, the biologists gathered on the observation deck and took everyone through what they had learned about the waters of Cahora Bassa Lake. At the moment they were anchored, the chains stretched against the current, the four in the center almost touching stern to bow. Only about six inches of space between each boat made moving through them simple and safe.

"We've got good news and bad news," Alice Dinsmore said, stepping up to the front. Her blonde hair was matted to her head with the humidity, and she had it tied in a ponytail at the back. Without makeup she still looked vibrant with her big smile, prominent cheekbones, and pretty eyes. Her husband was working the computer and the Smartboards came to life. There were three of them so that everyone on the deck could see the results clearly.

"Pollution in these waters is less than that of the waters below the dam and south of Tete, suggesting that the coal mining industry and sugar cane industry contributes a great deal more than studies originally showed. However, sewage effluent is still far too high, and the Kariba Dam seems to have reduced nutrients that used to be found in high volumes in this water. Levels aren't too dangerous yet, but they are nearing that threshold," she looked around the deck and saw that everyone was focused on her. "Dr. Copeland will share what she learned." Dr. C. stood up and came to the front.

"Most of the reason for the reduction of the alluvium or silt deposits can be attributed to the dams that have been built along the river. Silt is really fine sand, clay, or other material carried by running water and deposited as sediment, especially in a channel or harbor," she taught. Seeing Bob Neff's hand raised she nodded to him.

"Do we have an idea of the percentage of loss?" he asked.

"At the present time our estimates are a reduction of silt by a third of the normal deposits," she nodded with a pleased smile. It had been a good question.

"Those materials are vital in supplying nutrients that the lowland flood plains need to maintain a healthy system," Bob spelled out.

"Correct!" Dr. C. turned the full wattage of her smile on him, and Bob blushed deeply.

"In building the dams they have managed to control some of the flooding, but the cost to the ecosystem is high," she put up a chart showing a ten-year projection of what that might mean to the flood plains. The silence on the deck was all the evidence she needed that the bleak picture spoke volumes.

"Whenever we try to improve our world the thinkers and movers of such grand plans rarely consider the affects these improvements might have upon nature, or man. A hydroelectric plant and a dam to help control flooding seemed a good idea. The cost of this venture may be the ultimate destruction of the flood plains. That would affect people, plants, animals, fish, birds, insects, and the ocean! I can honestly say that few, if any, have considered the full rationale of this evidence. Even now, if we bring it to the public, I doubt if they will heed our warnings. More damming is planned in the future, and I think that will spell the end of the wetlands," she spoke the last truth sadly. "If any more interruptions in the natural course of things occurs, it will tip the scales."

"Thanks, Dr. Copeland. Dr. Dundee, perhaps you could share next?" Alice made it a question, and Mike nodded and stood easily.

"Man-made lakes often create micro-organisms that can affect all of life within the waters. I think I've isolated the organism that is causing the epizootic ulcerative syndrome, which from this moment all we'll call EUS to simplify things. This particular bacterium only appears at the end of the dry season," a microscopic organism appeared on the Smartboard. "Because this was not originally a lake, but is man-made, there are toxic plants that are decomposing beneath the surface, creating this bacterium. It needs the water to reach a temperature of 23 degrees Celsius. That would be just below 74 degrees Fahrenheit for you Yanks."

"Fish eat the plant food, thus ingesting the bacteria which generates the ulcers. Those plants don't normally occur in a lake, so the fish are affected. Once the bacterium is ingested, the fish may be eaten by a larger fish. The ulcers will not appear on that fish. It seems to be a direct plant to stomach reaction. So, I think we can let people know that there is no danger to humans yet," he nodded to FM whose hand was up.

"Uh, Doc, that word yet has an ominous sound to it!" he commented, raising his eyebrows in question.

"Yes, and it should. Bacteria can mutate. It does all the time on a microbiological scale. Birds that eat the fish mutate the bacteria into something much more dangerous. Remember the birds we found along the shore in Quelimane? All of them had a new strain of this bacteria in their digestive tracts. Other carrion birds ate those dead birds, thereby mutating the strain even further. To what I won't know until we study one. This bacterium could eventually become as dangerous as Ebola! I just don't have enough data yet to determine how it is mutating. This particular bacterium comes from *Strophantus amboensis* (Omuhundure), which I understand is used as a poison for arrows and spears by some tribes in Africa," Mike stopped and looked around. When no hands were raised, he motioned to Alice.

"Perhaps Dr. Adams could go next," she waved Angela up and Angela walked to the front.

"Stand up, we can't see you!" Dorf said from the back.

"I am standing, thank you!" Angela snapped, shaking a finger at him. "Be quiet or I'll have my husband thrash you!" she added.

"Shut up or I'll thrash both of you!" she said as Wade opened his mouth. Everyone laughed. Angela was tiny, just shy of five feet tall, and her facial features made her look much younger than her years. Hearing the diminutive Dr. Adams threaten to thrash two of the biggest and strongest men on the team was funny. Wade made a motion as if zipping his lips closed and cowered back from her, making everyone laugh even harder. She stamped her foot.

"Now!" she admonished above the laughter, and slowly it got quiet. "I checked for red algae in the waters today and found none. That means the source of the red algae is south of here, probably a result of the coal mining industry, coupled with the sewage situation. This is not good news because forcing the coal industry to change what they're doing is going to require international pressure from every country boarding the Indiana Ocean. That, and only that, will cause the government to insist on change," she suddenly grabbed her abdomen and winced.

"If this kid kicks me like that again I'm going to have to run . . . oh never mind! I have to go to the bathroom!" she grimaced and made her way to the steps and down to a restroom.

"Kick her again kid!" Dorf yelled from the back.

"I heard that!" Angela yelled from the stairs.

CHAPTER 20

"**J**ohn, perhaps you can address this unruly crowd," Alice said without getting up. John shook his head but got up and faced the group. Quickly everyone got quiet.

"There are not many species of fish in the lake, less than I would have imagined. Tiger fish are plentiful, some weighing up to 14 kg. The lake also contains various bream species, including Mossambica, three-spot and red-breast, plus catfish and their man-sized cousins the vundu. The other-worldly Cornish Jack and smaller members of the bottle-nose family are also present, as are chessa and nkupe, both of them small-mouthed, rough-scaled and extremely hard fighting fish. Those of you who are avid fishermen might enjoy fishing on the lake for that very reason. Of course, there are Kapenta and bull sharks in the lake too.

"This lake was not deforested when it was filled, which I believe is another reason for some of the conditions in the water. Plan to snag your lines if you're going to do any fishing, but don't dive in to unsnag them! As beautiful as this lake is, I believe that swimmers will always be in danger, especially in the shallower waters. Several people have been killed by Crocodiles and even more from attacks from hippos.

"What I really noticed was that the decomposition of the foliage beneath the surface is adding effluents that aren't common in other lakes of the region. The fish seem to be thriving in this element, although that bacteria Mike mentioned is causing some problems. I've seen several species with EUS." Photos of the fish appeared on the Smartboards as everyone watched and wrote notes on iPads, laptops, or paper. John continued.

"In South Carolina and other places in the U.S. lakes were formed without deforestation and the wildlife has adapted and thrived in those areas, and I expect no less here. This is really a wonderful place for fish to live. There are leaches in the water as well, and I've noticed some fish with leaches attached. The leaches are three times the size of normal leaches! We're going to take some samples and dissect some of them to determine why. They range in color from dark brown to jet-black and appear to be more aggressive than they should be. That's another good reason not to swim in these waters without proper protection.

"This lake is about one hundred eighty-one and a half miles long and 23 miles wide, giving us a surface area of 1702 square miles! That's a lot of territory! The average depth is around sixty-eight and a half feet, and the deepest part is close to 86 fathoms, or five hundred and fifteen feet!"

As he sat down a buzz of conversation started up and then quieted as Alice stood again. She nodded to John, and he put up the last slide on the Smartboard. It was a picture of a person with about forty leaches attached to his body. In the stunned silence that followed she smiled.

"We're diving tomorrow to have a look beneath the surface and take some deeper samples. Also, we'd like to see how the leaches do with human food and we need volunteers," for a moment she looked around the deck and then sighed. "Very well. I'll select one of you to be the lucky Guinea Pig! Dr. Adams, did you have anyone in mind?" she asked.

"Lieutenant Commander Bernard!" she replied immediately. "He encouraged my child to mischief!" she added.

Jim chuckled, wondering what drama this might cause the following day. Several hands went up and Alice nodded to FM.

"We should probably tether you when you dive tomorrow," he said. "Depending on how deep you go we won't be able to see you from the boats! If one of those leaches gets you, or a bull shark, or something else, we'd like to bring the remains to the surface."

"I was using the "royal we" when I spoke, Mr. Miller. You might be one of the divers! The captain has that decision, of course. He assures me that each of the marine biologists will have four divers with them tomorrow, so I'm guessing he's already decided which teams will go," Alice replied. "If you want to be tethered to the boat, I suggest you work that out with your dive buddies."

FM began clearing his throat, coughing, and holding his neck with his hands. It appeared as though he was suffering some malady. Donna Penny pulled up the huge hypodermic she'd found somewhere and pointed the needle end at FM.

"Bend over, love. I'll give you a shot that will make you forget all about your other symptoms!" she said lightly.

"I feel much better!" FM said immediately.

Everyone laughed at the interchange and Jim felt that this was the way such meetings should end. Good fun was always appreciated. He finally stood as the laughter died down and immediate quiet settled over the group.

"Zulu, Firefox, Knife, Raider, Sniper, and Nightfall will dive tomorrow. Dr. Copeland has Zulu. Dr. Alice Dinsmore has Firefox. Dr. John Dinsmore has Knife. Dr. Lowe has Raider. Dr. Putnam has Sniper, and Dr. Adams has Nightfall. Tomorrow's dive goes no deeper than one hundred and twenty feet. Dr. Dinsmore wants divers to stop every ten feet to take samples and record water temperatures and current speeds and direction.

"I'm going to ask Abe to lead us in prayer as we end tonight's meeting," Jim nodded to Abe who stood. All the men stood, as they always did, bowed heads, some folding hands, others remaining at ease with their hands in pockets or at their sides. Abe's prayer was focused on everyone trusting God for whatever situations they might face tomorrow and a request to help them find ways to encourage the governments of this area to seek changes that would protect people first. Not once did he ask for safety, for all of them knew that they were always under His protection, and even if they faced death, He would be there with them. Jim loved listening to Abe pray, because the man's faith was deep and real. A soft "Amen" followed Abe's close to his prayer.

Divers went down the next day at eleven, when the sun was high, and visibility would be at its best. Even so, the currents stirred up silt and made the waters seem almost muddy. Visibility would be about ten to fifteen feet. Jim watched the divers enter the water from the rigid raiders, falling backwards and sinking quickly beneath the surface. The raiders took up a position in a rough circle around the area where the divers were, to protect them from boats, though there were few in the water because it was near the close of the rainy season.

Beneath the surface the divers watched their depth meters, stopping every ten feet to measure water temperature, current speed, and take samples. It might have seemed monotonous to anyone watching them, but no one was bored. Each team surrounded the biologist, looking outwards, spear-gun/shock-rod at the ready. These were designed so that the shock fork was above and stretched beyond the end of the spear.

A few bull sharks circled nearby but didn't come close to the divers. One team noticed a lone crocodile swimming just feet beneath the surface. It was average in length, about six meters long, its tail propelling it smoothly through the water. If it noticed them, it paid no heed and continued on its way. Tiger fish, their jaws jutting open showing their sharp teeth, flashed by occasionally but did not come near. Some bore the EUS, while others were untouched by the bacteria. Other fish were evident, but did not come close enough to identify, other than a flash of scales as they scurried away.

Each team was tasked with finding one with leaches attached, spearing it, and bagging it. That was not as difficult as many thought, because some of the fish came close enough to be easy shots, and their silvery sides made spotting the leaches easier. Each team speared and bagged one. The bag would keep the leaches from detaching and reaching any of the divers.

The deeper they went the better visibility got, until they were at the tops of the trees rotting at the bottom. All the leaves had been stripped or rotted away and they stood like hoary old skeletons of scarecrow figures. Even at this depth the water temperature was close to sixty degrees Fahrenheit. At this depth the current was slow, and the water clear enough that they could see fish swimming among the branches and near the bottom, nibbling at the flora that remained, stirring up little pools of silt as they pecked at the bottom in search of something to eat.

As they moved in a slow circle, they discovered the bones of an elephant that must have drowned when they filled the lake, and several species of monkey and even a gorilla skeleton. At last, they moved together in stages toward the surface, the teams ever vigilant against attack by bull shark or crocodile, especially as they drew closer to the surface itself. However, all six teams climbed onto the rigid raiders and deposited their samples without incident.

Jim watched from his research boat as a large bull shark circled the boat several times before moving toward one of the rigid raiders, but all the divers were in the boat by then. The noise of the motors seemed to attract the sharks, but none approached the boats themselves. Once all the divers were on board, and the boats secured to their tow cables, divers put their equipment away carefully, writing on a chart the amount of air left in each tank, showered and dressed, and came to the dining room for lunch.

The boats were once again on the way, moving at a faster pace now that they were on the lake, still just four feet separating them as they moved in perfect synchronization at a speed of twenty knots. In the afternoon the wind often produced waves on the lake, but this morning it was smooth as glass, and everyone grabbed lunch and headed up to an observation deck to watch the shoreline of Zambia slip by. Vistas from this viewpoint were magnificent and filled with exciting sightings.

In places the jungle grew right out into the lake because it was at flood stage and struggles of life and death went on with great splashes, mighty roars, and screams, hidden in the shadows of the trees. Other places the shore was lined with crocodiles sunning themselves, some as large as twenty-five feet and weighing in at over three tons. Lions, leopards, cheetah, spotted hyena, and jackals were observed and pointed out with excitement. Reedbuck and the migrating eland were plentiful on the plains, while hippos moved among the shallows in number.

A herd of Zebra thundered over the plain, leaving a trail of dust, spooked by one of the carnivores. Water buffalo and giraffes were evident in herds as well. Although they looked carefully no one spotted a herd of elephants, though one large male was seen at the edge of jungle growth looking out over the plain as if studying it. One of his tusks was broken in half and the other seemed long.

During a journey in close to the shore they spotted Pintails, Garganey, African Openbill, Saddle-billed Storks, Wattled Crane, and even some Great White Pelicans. What most appreciated was a plethora of endemic butterflies fluttering over wildflowers and filling the air with a myriad of bright colors mixed with dark contrasts. Vivid yellows contrasted against reds and browns, white contrasted against brown, orange contrasted against greens and browns, and vivid greens were visible everywhere they looked. Alistair Gregg told everyone there were over nine hundred species known from Zambia, twenty-seven of which are endemic, or unique to Zambia. Not being an entomologist, he couldn't name them so those of the crew who took an interest set aside time to research them.

Jim was not surprised to find FM shoulder to shoulder with Miss Morris later that day in front of a laptop taking notes on the butterflies. Cecilia, walking beside him, nudged him and smiled at the couple. It seemed impossible that FM would end up married, yet the relationship between the two was blossoming. S.O.S. certainly seemed to appreciate his keen intelligence and curiosity, and the two were constantly discussing various scientific theories.

Smiling down at Cecilia he continued on through the boat to the front deck, pulled a bottle of water out for his wife, and a Diet Coke with Lime for his pleasure, and the two sat and drank, taking in the beauty of Africa around them. Jim had RJ in his arms but here he could put him down and let him wander about the deck without fear that he might be hurt or lost overboard. The barrier around the deck was Kevlar lined and made of a fiber said to be stronger than steel, yet lighter than aluminum. RJ would be quite safe in his meanderings.

He watched RJ toddle about the deck holding his blanket and favorite toy. The toy was a plastic rendition of Noah's Arc with wheels. When new it was filled with animals, but those had all been tossed in his toy box because he seemed content with just the horses to play with and move up and down the ramp that folded outwards from one side.

Pippi and John arrived with JAS and soon the two boys were busy on the deck. JAS had a pirate ship with wheels and in their little world they played happily with their toys or walked to stare out at the water slipping by. Both could climb on a chair and look over the railing. The Mosquito netting made sure they were still securely protected inside the forward deck. Parents worked hard to train the boys not to lean against the netting, for the mosquitoes could suck blood if they did that, and the boys had learned the lesson. Their parents sat and talked for nearly an hour before they finally headed back to their work.

Jim loved those hours he spent with his wife and son, and especially when John and Pippi joined them with JAS. The grandparents often came up during those times if they weren't busy teaching or researching. This morning it had been just John and Pippi and the four had enjoyed the quiet beauty and peaceful talk of nothing important. Yet it was time for some work to be done now, so Jim pulled his mind back to the tasks at hand.

Stopping in at the CIC he noticed that Zeke and News appeared excited. They looked up as he stepped into the cool interior.

"Good! You're here!" Zeke said.

"Well! I saw that you had something for me, so I came right away," Jim said.

"What?" News asked.

"Captain Jim is watching you!" Jim said with a wide grin.

"Somebody put a bun on that hotdog!" Zeke said with an answering grin. "That's my line! Anyway, we have a lead on our friend Maximiliano. He has shipped some crates to Senanga. A dozen six-wheelers are being delivered from Ngulwana and Mbanga and will arrive at Senanga about the time we're being lifted over Victoria Falls. Our friend Kananga has ordered a patrol boat ready to take him across to Zumbo when we arrive."

"You have an odd idea of what the word *friend* means!" Jim replied after a moment of thought. "So Massoona Maximiliano will hit us between Sesheke and Sioma! What INTEL do we have?"

"He can only hit is in one place," News piped up. Jim grinned as Zeke blinked once, surprised that he'd been upstaged.

"Yes," Zeke continued, glancing at News. The latter smiled at him, and he grinned back. "It has to be where the Njoko empties into the Zambezi River. Nawinda Kuta is to the north and there is a road of sorts he can use for a quick exit. From there he can fly to Mulobezi and catch the train to Livingstone and points south. That train only runs once a week, so we can pretty much figure out which day he will plan to hit us and plan accordingly."

"Any ideas on how to handle Kananga?" Jim asked as he studied the maps on the computer screen before him.

"Chiwatuku is in bed with the Russians and he's the head of the MIU, or Military Intelligence Unit, which in this case is not an oxymoron. This MIU is so clumsy and so lacking intelligence it's ludicrous! Let him wake up to Kananga's head in his bead and he might get the point!" Zeke reported with derision.

"You need to switch to decaf in the morning!" Jim teased with a chuckle. News laughed aloud.

"No, I think that I'll take Kananga prisoner from his own boat, show him the film of what Hobbs and his team did to Vasovitch. Edit out Bear grabbing the crocodile and start the tape again when Vasovitch starts pouring out his life. We'll let him see the end, while Hobbs and his team stand staring balefully at him. I'm sure he'll get the point. After that I'll let him have his knives and have a shot at me, then turn him over to Raider. At the last minute I'll have a change of heart and just turn him loose," Jim added.

"Dang, Shep! That's diabolical! When I grow up, I want to be able to think like you!" Zeke joked. Cecilia had entered at that moment. She looked at Zeke and shook her head.

"You'll never grow up," she said.

"Probably not. Our Captain doesn't encourage it," Zeke shot back.

"Naturally! Men are just tall boys who play with more expensive toys," she smiled at her husband as she said it and sat down. "What are we discussing?" she arranged her hair carefully, tied it back in a ponytail, and looked up at her husband. Jim was smiling down at her and nodding as though he agreed completely.

"Putting the fear of mortality into Captain Kananga," News replied. "Your husband is diabolical when it comes to frightening people!" he added.

"That's because he's had to deal with you all these years," she teased, smiling at News as she said it.

"She doesn't have a very high opinion of us!" News said to Zeke in mock amazement.

"The longer you keep me from her the worse her opinion will become," Jim retorted.

"Uh! We're done here, boss," Zeke said, swallowing dramatically and casting fearful looks at Cecilia. She began to laugh.

"You are too much!" she said as she rose. "I'd better get you away from this bad influence, dear," taking Jim's hand, she led him out of the CIC. He paused at the door.

"Get me all the INTEL you can on Massoona and some INTEL on the terrain around where he wants to hit us, please. Thanks guys. Job well done! Let's call a meeting of the team for after dinner tonight. We should get everyone up to speed and ready. Does that seem reasonable?"

"Got it, Shep," Zeke agreed with a wave, already turning to his computer consol. Smiling, Jim let Cecilia pull him from the CIC.

"How bad is it?" she asked as they made their way to their cabin.

"Bad," Jim replied easily. "We'll sort it out," he added gently. "God will see us through."

"You know, until my parents and brothers were murdered, I didn't really know what that saying meant. I do now," Cecilia said with a hint of sadness in her voice. RJ picked up on it immediately and hugged his mother. Jim patted him.

CHAPTER 21

In the morning, according to plan, the CH-53D Sea Stallion flew into Zumbo to pick up the supplies. No one in Zumbo gave the appearance of the helicopter a second thought, or that the supplies were being airlifted to the boats. Kananga hadn't contacted Zumbo officials yet, which was to their advantage. As soon as everything was properly loaded and strapped down the chopper lifted off and headed out to the lake, landing near the boats.

One-by-one the boats moved to the chopper, transferred the goods, and moved away. In the air again the chopper set off for Chirundu where the AH-1W Super Cobra and PBY waited. The two choppers would be locked in a hangar the company rented for that purpose and the PBY would ferry them back to the boats.

It was almost evening when the Catalina appeared in the sky, circled, and made a textbook landing into the wind, coasting to a stop only a few feet from the lead boat. Jim admired the flying boat as it split the water and smiled when it came to a stop. Windy was becoming quite adept at flying the old machine, and he loved flying it almost as much as he loved working in the kitchen. From the window Jim could see him smiling and waving and Jim waved back.

The plane would be towed behind the last boat until they were a mile from Zumbo. Once they passed Zumbo Windy, Loony, and

Ives would go up in the PBY and keep watch from the air for the approach of the patrol boat, warning Jim in plenty of time to make his move. They all guessed that Kananga would move at night, rather than in daylight.

Lying on the north-east bank of the Zambezi-Luangwa River confluence, Zumbo is a border town, with Zambia (and the town of Luangwa, previously called Feira,) across the Luangwa River and Zimbabwe (with its border post at Kanyemba) diagonally across the Zambezi and 2 km upstream. Jim remembered that the Portuguese established Zumbo as a trading post in the last part of the 17th century. It became prosperous as it traded along the middle Zambezi and into Zimbabwe, and up the lower Luangwa, trading for ivory as far away as Lake Bangweulu. Dominating the area, traders from Zumbo settled in Feira. The town declined after Northern and Southern Rhodesia (later Zambia and Zimbabwe) became part of the British Empire, cutting off its trade with those territories.

After that, things got even worse for the border town. The town's strategic location meant that in the Mozambican War of Independence and Mozambican Civil War, guerrilla warfare was active in and around the town and many landmines were laid. Zumbo was abandoned for a time in the civil war and partially destroyed, and now, after all the chaos and loss, reconstruction was ongoing. Some of the construction was obvious, but at flood stage most of it was halted.

As well as fishing in the river and lake, economic activity relies on trade with the neighboring countries, inevitably involving smuggling as well. There are small coal mines near the town, and the main crops grown on the fertile banks and floodplain of the rivers are rice, cassava, and beans. Sighing as he watched the town slip past Jim moved away from the wheel of the boat, his holographic image taking his place.

Omega 1, his team, was tasked with taking Kananga. Raider would be backing up his team and he nodded at Hobbs as they passed each other in the corridor. Suiting up and preparing for battle was something Jim did alone and in absolute quiet, and Cecilia kept away from the cabin for that reason. She was on John's boat at the moment, having kissed her husband earlier, hiding her concern as best as she could. For a moment Jim had touched foreheads with her, a tender moment for both.

Now he stared at himself in the mirror, dressed for battle, his face painted, weapons in place. Nodding once to his reflection he patted his H&K Mark 23 and left the cabin. At the rear of the boat eight men stepped onto the rigid raider, pulled close for boarding, and with Frank Miller at the wheel the raider pulled away, speeding up and racing ahead of the boats toward the Zambia shore.

"Omega 1 and Raider are clear," Jim reported into his COMLINK.

"Roger that, bro!" John's voice returned. "Don't get dead."

Soon they were tethered to the shore, beneath a camouflage net, awaiting the passing of Kananga's patrol boat. As the sun set the men sat silently, watching the crocodiles and other predators cautiously. Above them the PBY flew over once, low to the water and then rising gracefully into the darkening sky.

"Patrol boat leaving Kanyemba now, Shep," Windy's voice was calm. "Loony counted an even dozen soldiers," Jim thought about that for a moment before responding.

"Roger that, Windy," Jim replied. "Land safely, bud!" he added. Windy was confident he could land the craft on the runway at Chirundu, even in the dark. Wrench and Inchworm were at the landing strip preparing to light it up at both ends when Windy was close.

"Don't worry, boss. I won't let him scratch this beautiful antique!" Loony assured Jim through the COMLINK.

"You shouldn't talk about yourself as an antique, Loony!" Zeke's voice sounded over the COMLINK.

"When you get to be my age you can say that," Alistair's reply brought laughter.

Jim and his men listened to the chatter with smiles but soon settled into listening for something else. It came, long before they saw the running lights, the sound traveling over the surface of the water as the patrol boat approached. Even before it reached them, they removed the netting, packed it carefully away, and headed out onto the river, David Carr now at the wheel.

They approached from behind, easily pacing the patrol boat, until Jim's team could step onto the enemy boat, hidden in the darkness. Frank and Jim slipped up either side of the boat and found that all but the pilot went below decks, probably to minimize the irritation of the local insects. Portals on the sides were open to allow the air to flow. Two gas grenades dropped to the deck but before the men could react, they lost consciousness. The pilot froze when the cold steel barrel of a pistol pressed against the back of his neck.

"Pull the boat to the shore on the Zambia side," Zeke said in Portuguese.

When they were close to the shore Zeke sprayed the man in the face, catching him as he dropped unconscious. A moment later he removed his breathing device, stepped to the wheel and gunned the engine. Here the water was too shallow, and the boat tipped away from the land as the bottom hit rocks. Beneath the propeller was torn to shreds and the shaft bent. Disabled and with holes in the hull the boat settled to the bottom. Zeke quickly disabled all the radios on board while Kananga was transferred to the Raider.

Twelve hours later Kananga awoke with a start and then winced in pain. His head ached worse than any hangover. He could feel shackles on his wrists and ankles. Opening his eyes, he looked down to realize that he was naked, seated on a steel chair, shackled to the arms and legs. Leaning forward he saw that the chair was bolted to the deck. That the boat was moving was obvious, though he could hear little sound. In front of him was a door. For a moment he tried to understand what had happened.

What he couldn't know was that he was in a hurriedly erected cell on the observation deck of *River Venture 1*. The door opened, emitting blinding light from what he thought must be the morning sun. Out of the blinding light Omega 1 and Raider entered the cell. There was just enough room for all eight men and the prisoner. As the last man entered the door closed.

"It's a beautiful sunset. Sorry you're missing it," Captain Shepherd commented. He turned to another soldier. "Zeke."

"Just watch," Zeke instructed, opening his laptop and setting on Kananga's thighs. The tape had been expertly edited and ran now a full twenty-eight minutes and eight seconds. Kananga watched as the scene unfolded, watched the insects crawl into the man's nose and ears, and into his mouth when he opened it to scream. The twitching body told all as the ants stung him again and again. In short order the man's skin was covered in blood. Kananga watched it all, looking up occasionally at the men in front of him, all four from Raider, recognizing them, seeing the baleful stares as they stared back into his eyes.

These were the men who had done this to another man! Who was he? And then the crocodile rushed in and clamped down on the man's genitals and he screamed the most horrified scream yet. Soon he was blabbering his story and Kananga realized that this man was a Russian, a professional soldier, and when he heard his name his mouth opened in shock. Vasovitch! As he listened to the confession, he realized that these men had broken a real professional, and they'd done it quickly! Were they going to do the same to him? He looked at them and looked away, frightened by what he saw.

At last, Vasovitch, blind and crippled, was released and the lions took him. Zeke picked up the laptop, turned and left, followed by Miller, and Smitty. Now Jim moved to the front again, looking down at Kananga.

"Word is you're looking for my head," Jim said conversationally. He seemed completely at ease, unafraid. His demeanor unnerved Kananga, and he swallowed, his mouth suddenly dry. "That is what General Chiwatuku ordered, wasn't it?" Jim smiled. "Perhaps not as easy as you thought?"

"What have you done with my men?" Kananga finally managed to ask, his voice hoarse, his head pounding even worse with the effort of speaking. Running his tongue over his mouth didn't help ease the dryness.

"They are still on your patrol boat. I imagine about now they're realizing that you are no longer among them. The boat is sitting on the bottom of the river in about three feet of water, prop gone, holes in the hull, and all radios destroyed. We took their guns and ammunition and all their gear and left them naked. I imagine they'll find it difficult to get help unless someone comes by in a boat," Jim replied.

"What are you going to do to me?" Kananga managed to ask.

"After you've recovered from your headache and feel better, I'm going to feed you, and then let you try to take my head. I kept your knives for you. If you can take my head, you will be freed. Should you fail, I turn you over to them," Jim inclined his head toward the four men staring down at Kananga hungrily. "Their task is to take you out in the wild and do the same to you they did to Vasovitch, recording your confession, and then turning you loose for the carnivores to exact justice."

Jim turned and left, and another man came in, young, tall, with a bottle of water and a straw. Kananga drank thirstily. He was offered some pills to help with the headache and accepted them gratefully. An hour later his headache was gone, but the fear inside him was mushrooming. Those four men stood with arms folded, saying nothing, simply staring at him. In their faces he could read nothing but disdain, and it unnerved him. Kananga was used to being feared by all who knew him, and in these men, he saw no fear at all, and he remembered the ease with which he'd been taken.

Once again, the door opened, and Kananga saw it was dark outside. An older man came in bearing a tray with food. One of the men stepped forward, turned a key in the shackle of Kananga's left hand, and stepped back. Holding the tray with his shackled right-hand Kananga attacked the food hungrily. He knew he needed his strength for the fight. Would they really allow him to try to take the captain's head?

When he was finished one of the soldiers removed the tray and took it outside, returning immediately to take his stance with the others, arms folded, simply staring. Kananga began to feel the necessity of a bathroom and asked if he could use one. Just as he finished asking Jim stepped into the room again.

"Your clothes are behind you. We took the liberty of washing them. Get dressed," Jim turned to the four men. "Take him to the forward head and then bring him to *River Venture 3*. Give him his knives at the steps to the observation deck. I'll be waiting there," Jim spun and left.

Kananga dressed, his uniform clean for the first time in over a week, aware of the four men staring at him. Finally, he straightened and one of them opened the door and stepped out, the tallest and strongest of the four, so he was forced to walk through the other three. Trying hard not to see their baleful stares he squared his shoulders and followed the man as tall as he down a flight of steps, forward to a bathroom, where he was nodded in.

After relieving himself he splashed water on his face and breathed deeply. Rotating his shoulders, he felt his strength and smiled grimly. The captain was a fool! Feeling sure of his skill with his knives he walked back out into the corridor to the baleful stares of the men. He pointed at each.

"After I kill your Captain, I will kill you," he boasted proudly.

"Good luck with killing the captain, mate," Hobbs said, showing no emotion at all. He motioned for the tall man to lead the way and Kananga fell in behind him. Kananga looked at the man's hand and realized he was holding an H&K Mark 23 complete with silencer and suppressor. Kananga followed Bear.

Had they realized what he was thinking? He'd thought of attacking them, getting his knives, and escaping to kill the captain another time. The man with the gun was far enough away that if Kananga turned, he would be shot before he could do anything. His confidence slipped. These men were careful, too careful. Perhaps this was all a ruse.

Two boats back the tall man stepped aside. As he did so he produced Kananga's knives. Kananga did not miss the sound of the hammer of the Mark 23 clicking into the firing position. Smiling wanly, he took the knives and mounted the steps. He came out on the observation deck and saw the captain standing at ease near the bow. In the boat behind a large crowd had gathered, and in the boat ahead were others. It looked as though the entire crew had gathered to see the fight. Good!

Kananga didn't hesitate. Like a raging bull he went from walking to sprinting, his knives weaving in a deadly arc. Captain Shepherd went from standing at ease to motion, easily slipping away from the initial attack, his kick stunning Kananga's left arm so that he could barely move it. It was obvious they knew he was left-handed!

Spinning to his right he slashed out at Jim again, but Jim slipped beneath the cut striking just above Kananga's elbow with one hand, and the other connecting with Kananga's throat. That straightened him up, and the knife fell from his right hand. Jim's next kick landed squarely between Kananga's legs, and he buckled to the deck, managing to hold on to his knife in his left hand, choking and groaning in intense pain.

He couldn't see! Lights danced in his vision for a moment before it cleared. The captain had gone still when Kananga went down. Desperately he lashed out with his knife, but his left arm still didn't work properly. Jim's boot came down on his wrist, shattering the bones and Kananga screamed. Hands hauled him to his feet and pummeled him so quickly he couldn't follow, couldn't breathe, couldn't think. He went down when a foot connected with his neck, his body flipping in the air, landing with bone jarring force, driving the wind from his lungs.

Finally, air rushed into his lungs and Kananga screamed weakly. It hurt just to breathe! Jim squatted down where Kananga could see him. His green eyes were cold, and Kananga thought of a cold grave and shivered.

"You're not very good at taking heads. Maybe you should try another line of work. I'm not like any of the victims you've attacked and killed in the past. I'm a trained soldier. Every one of my men could eat you for breakfast. I have thirty-six men. You brought twelve less competent than yourself. You didn't do your homework, you didn't try to discover anything about your enemy, you simply decided you could take my head and set out to do so. Your incompetence sickens me! Just so you know, if you had an entire army, my men would still destroy you," Jim stood up.

"Hobbs! Get this garbage out of my sight!"

Kananga almost whimpered as Hobbs and his men appeared. They were not gentle in raising him to his feet and dragging him down to the Rigid Raider. The big one lifted him easily and tossed him into the raider, causing more damage. Kananga lay there like a rag doll, trying to find some glimmer of hope. There was none.

Just as the men were getting ready to untie the craft Jim appeared above.

"Wait!" he said. "I've changed my mind. This incompetent jerk isn't a threat to us. Take him to within a few hundred yards of his boat, take his clothes, and make him swim to shore. If he survives and reaches his men and his boat, he can go his way," Jim looked down at Kananga, pointing his finger. "Next time I see you, I kill you," he promised, turning away.

For the first time Kananga realized that all four of his captors now wore full military garb, and they faded into the darkness like four ghosts. Swallowing hard he lay where they had thrown him and prayed that his men had found some weapons and would be ready. He knew they had not. Like him, they knew the dangers of where they were. Their boat was their only safety. Without hope he lay for almost an hour, casting away plan after plan as futile and dangerous, until the boat began to slow and head closer to shore.

Bear pointed his MP5SD at Kananga and told him to disrobe. Struggling with his broken wrist and bruised body he managed to get out of his clothes. They had to help him with his shoes. When he was naked Hobbs pointed to the shore.

"The shore is that way," Bear pushed Kananga over the side and the boat immediately moved away. The men on the Raider heard the weak horrified scream as the crocodile took Kananga in a death roll. With their night vision glasses they'd seen the disturbance on the surface. The crocodile did not resurface.

"Fitting," Banks said slowly. "I think his men are still there! Yes, they've come up to look. There are only seven of them!" he said, turning to the others.

The roar of a lion echoed in the darkness and the men scampered for the cabin of the sunken boat quickly. A blur of motion appeared, and the last man screamed as the lion's jaw closed on his neck. He was quickly dragged off the boat and to shore.

"And then there were six," D.C. said softly.

"Lions don't usually attack people!" Bear spoke quietly as he moved the boat back upriver.

"We'd better tell everyone. Things have changed in the National Park!" Hobbs replied. "That lion knew those men were vulnerable and it didn't hesitate!"

"Now we know why there were only seven left!" D.C. said sadly.

"Maybe!" Bear replied. "Some could have tried to go for help. That might be what led those lions to that boat."

Cecilia looked up at Jim as he stepped out of the shower. Holding RJ in her arms she rocked him gently as she studied her husband. At last, she spoke.

"Why do you do it?" she asked.

He knew immediately what she was asking. Why had he faced Kananga alone? Smiling lopsidedly as he dressed, he thought for a moment.

"I knew I could take him, knew that any of my men could take him, but didn't wish to risk any of them. Besides, after looking through the INTEL on that beast I wanted to hurt him. Two years ago, I might have killed him," Jim sighed, thinking that Cecilia was correct. In light of eternity, was the risk of what he'd done worth it? He didn't think so. He needed to stop risking himself that way.

"I'm sure that made sense to you and your men, but to me, RJ, and your unborn baby, it didn't make any sense at all!" Cecilia had tears in her eyes as she spoke, and RJ looked at her with concern on his little face. Jim sighed again, folded all three of them into his arms.

"I'll try to change that part of me," he promised softly. "I guess I need to think seriously about putting myself in that particular kind of danger," he admitted.

"I don't know that you can, but thank you for thinking about it," Cecilia rejoined, and hiccupped. Jim gently wiped her tears away.

"I love you," he said simply. Folding her into his arms again he hugged her fiercely and she sighed, still feeling conflicted.

CHAPTER 22

In the morning Jim met with News and Uncle Zeke in the CIC. Both had that smug look of knowing something no one else knew and Jim was immediately interested. He looked at the two men with a smile.

"Okay! Dazzle me with your brilliance!" he said with a low laugh.

"You are truly a wise leader of men," Zeke mocked, bowing slightly.

"Well said," Jim retorted, patting himself on the back. News laughed. Jim was rarely this demonstrative.

"A General from Zambia is coming to inspect our boats, crew, and paperwork. He's top man there and he absolutely hates General Chiwatuku. His name is General Banuuto, and he recently made overtures to the UK because of the Russian presence in Zimbabwe and General Chiwatuku's obvious infatuation with Russian help. Apparently, he has an agent in Chiwatuku's organization close enough to the General to know everything that goes on. His INTEL has proved very useful," Zeke grinned.

"And he's coming here to inspect our boats, paperwork, and crew?" Jim mused. "Do you think this agent would be willing to do a spot of work for us?"

"If his General tells him to do so, he will most definitely do it!"

News replied. "They're connected in a powerful way. Both lost sons to Chiwatuku during the revolution."

"Do we still have the laser pointers that can be activated remotely?" Jim asked Zeke.

"Why?" Zeke asked, curious.

"In the General's dining room, where he eats breakfast every morning at 08:15 sharp, dressed in his uniform, facing a gilded mirror, are a set of windows, set high up in the room to provide ambient light. These windows have a ledge almost a foot wide. If Banuuto's man can position them so that three point at the General's heart, and the fourth at his forehead when he sits up straight in his chair, we could have a little fun, and possibly even put him in such a compromising situation he could be removed!"

"How do you do that? We give you INTEL and you turn it into a foolproof plan!" News exclaimed, shaking his head in admiration.

"When General Banuuto arrives let me know. I'll talk to him directly," Jim said with a grin.

Later, Jim made the phone call from the CIC while General Banuuto stood beside him with a feral grin on his face. The number he called was that of General Chiwatuku's private cell phone and he made the call with Kananga's phone. Knowing something about the General's schedule, Jim knew he would be enjoying his breakfast at this late hour. The General picked up the phone on the fourth ring.

"Tell me you have his head!" the General said, recognizing the number as that of Kananga.

"Good morning General Chiwatuku. This is Captain James Shepherd of *Bring It Up*. My company is an international company, with holdings in the United States, the United Kingdom, and Italy. Any further action against any member of this crew will be considered an act of war. Like Kananga you will be crushed."

A long silence stretched and finally the General found his voice. "Empty threats! Your government would never act against another sovereign state!"

"I wasn't talking about any government, General. Look in the mirror." The General looked in the gilded mirror hanging across from where he sat. To his horror three bright red dots lit up a spot that outlined his heart. They were coming from the ceiling windows, but when he looked, he could see no one.

"Kananga is dead. Six of his soldiers are also dead, but not by my hand, or the hand of anyone on my crew. Kananga died in a crocodile attack, and your men were attacked and killed by lions. If you look hard enough, you'll find the evidence that I speak the truth. The patrol boat is about five kilometers from Zumbo on the Zambia side of the river. Those men need to be rescued in the daylight," Jim reported.

"You killed those men! This I will prove, and I will personally hunt you down!" the General's face lost all color as a fourth red dot appeared in the center of his forehead.

"My best sniper has you in his crosshairs, General. I'll give you to the count of three to reconsider. One, two . . ."

"Please don't kill me!" the General sputtered, holding up both hands.

"Not this time, General. Make a move against me, or anyone on my crew, and there will be no warning. Am I clear?" Jim's voice was steel.

"Yes! Yes! Please!" the General pleaded. As suddenly as they had appeared all four dots went away.

As Jim suspected, the General made the call immediately, reported that four of the *Bring It Up* crew had just targeted him with laser targets. Banuuto smiled as his phone rang. His office had received the warrants. Chiwatuku was insisting that he arrest James Shepherd and extradite him to his side of the river. Smiling at Jim he accepted the call and explained what had really happened. Later that morning Chiwatuku received a call from his counterpart in Zambia.

"You sent out a bulletin regarding the *Bring It Up* crew this morning at eight-thirty-eight. Is this correct?" General Banuuto asked politely, nodding at Jim.

"Of course, it is!" Chiwatuku sputtered. "Do you have them?" he begged eagerly.

"Actually, at eight-thirty-eight this morning I was on one of their boats and taken on a tour of all six boats. Every crewmember was on board at that time. To this I can attest. My government searched the boats and examined everyone's passports and the paperwork regarding the most excellent work this crew of scientists is doing. I'm sure that before long you'll be receiving some calls from your Russian friends, and probably ambassadors from three other countries.

"Should you decide to carry out your threats, I would consider it an act of war. Do I make myself clear?" the Zambian General smiled and nodded again to Jim.

"This is impossible!" General Chiwatuku sputtered.

"Are you calling me a liar, my friend?"

"No! No! I did not mean that!" Chiwatuku back-pedaled quickly. "Thank you. I will withdraw the wants and warrants immediately."

No sooner did he hang up than the Russian ambassador called. He was very emphatic that General Chiwatuku must leave *Bring It Up* alone. Calls from the government of Italy, England, and the United States followed. Even more puzzling, when the police investigated, they found four laser pens positioned inside the window on the sill above. Apparently, they were activated by some kind of remote switch. When Chiwatuku saw them, he spun and left the room.

Later that day the mangled bodies of Kananga and those six unfortunate men arrived courtesy of Zambian wildlife officers. After a detailed autopsy of the bodies, and the recorded testimony of the six men that were left alive, it was evident that six of the men died by lion attack, and Kananga died in the jaws of a crocodile. All six of the witnesses remembered the scream of terror in the night that must have been Kananga, trying to make his way back to the boat. None could explain why he was in the water. It was suggested that he was trying to get help. No one believed it.

By afternoon of the next day Chiwatuku resigned his position under pressure. Because some of the dealings by the Russians were of a specifically clandestine nature, Chiwatuku never made it out of the city. His body was found in a ditch some days later. Jim read the report shaking his head. Someone shot Chiwatuku three times in the chest and once in the head. The weapon was a Ruger .22 with bullets that fragmented once they entered the body. It was the weapon of an assassin. The Russians were ever direct.

Now that he knew his crew and mission was safe until they reached the part of the river between Sesheke and Sioma he relaxed a little. Zambia had received them with courtesy and respect, and the General had been more than happy to cooperate against a General he despised. It helped that Jim understood that a national park that spanned more than one country would not work. Furthermore, promised medical help from the Wozniac's and WHO helped to cement good relations.

General Banuuto was treated to a wonderful dinner, eating with the crew, and treated as a friend. When he finally left *Bring It Up*, he was in good spirits. Jim was not surprised when the General called to inform him of the death of Chiwatuku.

With the waters at flood stage *Bring It Up* had the only craft out on the river. Although it rained every day, there were hours when the sun shown, and they could line the railings of the observation decks, and stare at the wonder of Lower Zambezi National Park. Often, they passed pods of hippos, the alpha male obvious, much larger than the rest, some weighing over two tons! Once in this region there had been pods as large as a hundred animals. Today most of the pods were between ten and fifteen animals.

Small elephant herds were also in the water occasionally, trumpeting, spraying water at each other, and playing together, especially in the heat of the afternoon. Once, in the late afternoon, everyone on the crew had gathered on the observation platform when a cheetah appeared, chasing a herd of Zebra. The drama on the plains unfolded very quickly. In less than ninety seconds the cat separated and ran down a colt, killing it easily, and then quickly dragging it away. It had been a savage moment when the colt died in the jaws of the cheetah, yet the grace, speed, and skill of the hunter had been the subject of most conversations after the boats continued upriver. Its speed and agility had been inspirational to witness. That final burst of speed at the end had been amazing.

Bear, naturally, photographed the entire episode in high definition and his video went viral on the Internet overnight. Still photos of amazing birds, reptiles, amphibians, mammals, insects, and arachnids were copyrighted and sold to Getty Images, the Audubon Society, and other naturalist publications. Since there was a fully equipped darkroom in the lab area, Bear enlarged several of his better shots and prints hung all over the boat, tacked to the walls by a sticky substance that didn't leave marks and could easily be removed.

Using infrared technology photographers caught crocodiles, their eyes bright green in the night above the water, inches away from prey. Since many of the carnivores hunted during the night occasional shots of a lion, its eyes glowing by the riverbank among the bushes, the shaggy outline of its mane identifying the huge cat produced interesting comments. There were those on the team who thought that hunters hunting the great lions should only be allowed to hunt at night, while others shivered at the gleaming eyes and huge cats glad that they were nowhere near his territory.

Screams filled the jungle at night, screams of rage and death, fear and despair, challenge, and terror. Early one evening the challenge of an anthropoid ape echoed across the water. It was Dr. Gregg that identified the scream. FM, sitting quietly on the observation deck with his back against the outside railing cleared his throat.

"That's rather disappointing!" he said. Dr. Gregg looked at him.

"Why do you say that?" he asked.

"That Tarzan character was a fraud! He never sounded like that!" Amused laughter filled the night and for a moment all sound ceased in the jungle, and then picked up again.

"Yes! Well! The human throat is not capable of making that sound, so he had to improvise," Dr. Gregg said softly.

"I imagine today the movie industry could dub the sound in," Stephanie suggested, putting her delicate hand on FM's arm.

"Yeah! And every woman and kid in the theater would wet their pants!" FM quipped. "I know I did!" he added just before she hit him. That got more laughter and once again all sound ceased. It was eerie how it just stopped, and then started again. The ape screamed its challenge again.

"We're gonna need bigger guns tonight, boss!" Lloyd Brookstone stated in a quavering high-pitched hoarse voice.

"Don't you dare shoot one of those magnificent creatures!" Mary Ann said hotly.

"Maybe we should hold his hand while he's on duty!" Barbara said to her friend.

"Sure!" Lloyd replied. "If one comes along, I'll let you talk it out of attacking us, so I don't have to shoot it. If it eats you, I'll shoot it!"

"Horrid man!" Barbara retorted. "I shall see you are armed with a pea-shooter!"

"Do they like peas?" FM turned to Dr. Gregg.

"Yes. They are omnivorous, so if you shoot enough peas at it perhaps it will get filled up and not need to eat you," Mary Anne chuckled.

"They eat omnis!" Lloyd exclaimed in mock surprise. "I don't think we have any of those!"

"Why would it eat *Omni* Magazines?" Wade asked when the laughter died down.

Jim listened to the chatter with a smile playing around his face. RJ was on his lap, sound asleep, warm, and pressed up against him, and Cecilia was nestled under his left arm, her arm around the baby. Both had jerked at the roar of the ape, but slept on, and he felt strangely at peace. The bantering continued, some of it quite clever as his crew, more a family than close friends, teased one another outrageously.

Abe and Sturdy had a fine lesson from the Bible that night, with help from Alistair. Dr. Gregg described in vivid detail how the lives of Daniel, Mishael, Hananiah, and Azariah changed once they were taken captive. Going from a culture that followed a loving Heavenly Father to a nation filled with brutal religions became clear in the thinking of everyone on the crew. Adding to that the changes in their names, from wonderful names that had rich meanings to worthless names reflecting gods that didn't even exist captured the imagination and made Jim think.

Jim found himself thinking that those four men must have had great dads who taught them to expect the unexpected, to remain loyal to God no matter what the cost personally, and he found himself wanting to be that kind of a father to his sons and daughters. Recently he'd been reading everything he could get his hands on relating to that subject and realized that being a father required discipline and hard work.

When it came to disciplining his men, he'd learned early on that harsh words and unreasonable demands only bred resentment. Somehow, he'd picked up on the fact that many officers in the Navy and Marines were harsh because they were taught to be harsh. There were times when a man needed to be obeyed immediately, but Jim learned that if his men knew he was willing to do, and often did anything he demanded of them, they responded with immediate obedience and intense loyalty. Through the grace of God, he'd learned a secret few officers came to realize.

He knew, with great pride, that his men not only respected, but also accepted him as one of them, one who had earned the right to lead them, and they would follow, even into death. They did that because they knew that Jim would be right there with them. Pushing himself to be the best, to seek his highest level of achievement, he'd set an example his men followed. Many of them would have done the same, because of the type of men they were, but his example provided that extra impetus. That was why his team was second to none.

He wanted his sons and daughters to feel much the same way. To see him as someone who was not perfect, but trying his best at all times, and to realize that he respected and loved them, and would sacrifice anything for them. Listening to the questions Abe and Sturdy were fielding he realized that he was not alone in this quest, and it filled him with great joy and pride that he led such people.

Later that night he lay in bed with Cecilia, gently rubbing her back and shoulders to ease the burden of carrying their second son. RJ slept peacefully in his crib, his body still, his breathing steady. Cecilia sighed with pleasure and turned her head to look at her husband.

Jim Shepherd was one of the strongest men she knew, his body hard, and yet his hands were gentle whenever he touched her, and those stormy green eyes always softened when they looked into hers.

Smiling she stretched for a kiss and turned her head back, closing her eyes.

"You're going to be a great dad, dear. Stop worrying about it," she said softly. "I love you."

He chuckled. "You always know what I'm wrestling with," he said, shaking his head. "I love you too, Cecilia."

Knowing that John and Wade were probably wrestling with the same thoughts, and aware they might be having the same conversation with their wives, he smiled and bowed his head. When it came to prayer, he was much more confident that ever, and he prayed a simple prayer for a broken heart that God could use, and a willing spirit to be the kind of man God intended. Despite all the questions that request raised it was enough and he slept peacefully until it was his turn to take the watch.

Jim liked the two-hour watch. While his eyes were busy scanning the water and shoreline his mind was busy with the problems they faced. Massoona and his thugs were getting ready to attack his boats and crew, wipe them out, exacting revenge, all for money and pride. Wikfells, Ramanantsoa, and Ke Yi Zhanzhu and the Zhanzhu Triad were seeking world domination. All three were world-class criminals, the kind of men who killed without remorse, ever seeking a treasure they would never acquire. Power. It was really that simple.

Jim knew that no one had real power. Power came with authority, and there was only One who had absolute authority, and that was God. He alone was omnipotent, and for any man to believe he had any kind of power was self-deceiving. If all power belonged to God, then there was none for man. It would not be by his might and cunning that Jim would defeat these men! Knowing that instinctively Jim turned to God for help at every opportunity, always thanking Him for providing that help even before Jim knew Him as Lord and Savior. Not that he hadn't known God was there, indeed, he had, but there had not been this close personal relationship.

By the time his watch was over he knew how he was going to handle Massoona and his army of one hundred and twenty thugs. Though it saddened him deeply he knew that this would be a fight to the death. In a way, it was fitting that Massoona, and his men would die in the jungle. He who lived by the sword died by the sword. And God is not mocked! What a man sows he shall reap. Massoona sowed hatred, brutality, and death. Every ship he took as a pirate involved killing everyone on those ships. When the vote had been cast, it had been unanimous. Massoona and his men were sanctioned kills.

Jim also knew he wasn't doing God's work in this. God's work would be done when Massoona came face to face with the one true and living God and judge of all men. It would not be until that moment that he would realize that all power belonged to God, and to Him alone. At that moment he would know that he had been given every opportunity to receive the free gift that God offered to all sinners, but he had refused. Knowing full well that he too could have faced God in that condition Jim thanked Him once again for his salvation.

When it came right down to it, it was always all about God. Man did nothing, could do nothing for himself related to deserving salvation. The Bible was very clear about that. There were no righteous men, none who sought God, none who did good, not even one! And yet, while he hated God, God had loved him unconditionally!

Jim relieved Hobbs and two hours later he heard Goody mounting the steps to relieve him. Glancing over he saw that Goody had an apple in his hand, several bites already gone. His senior chief petty officer loved apples. As Zeke approached Jim lowered his night vision binoculars, picked up the log, and began to fill in the last lines for his watch. Goody stood quietly, looking out into the darkness before he picked up the hunting rifle, checked it to be sure the safety was engaged, and checked to see if a shell was in the pipe. Not until Jim finished writing, did he speak.

"How you holding up Shep?" he asked, smiling up at the Captain. A trim five-feet six-inches tall Zeke weighed in at one hundred and fifty-five pounds, and despite his thirty-nine years of age the man was still in top condition. Jim grinned at him.

"I've been realizing just how insignificant I am compared to God," Jim laughed softly.

"I get that," Zeke said easily. "Everything we accomplish is by

His power and grace. It's never about us. Humbling! And then we get to look out at all of this that He created and realize that His wisdom and knowledge is infinite! So, what does He do? He shares it all with us out of love," the chief mechanic punched Jim lightly on the arm. "That is pretty cool!"

"Indeed, it is, Goody," Jim replied. "Sunrise in twenty-eight minutes. Mind if I keep you company to watch it?" he asked.

"If that anthropoid ape is out there screaming, I'll be more than happy to have someone about!" Zeke replied easily, taking the binoculars from Jim. He marked the time he began his watch and checked to be sure Jim had clocked out. Then he put the clipboard back on its hook and looked through the binoculars at the water in front first, circling to his right slowly.

Jim simply stood looking toward the east where he could see that a pale line of light was beginning to show. Heavy clouds covered the area they occupied, but to the east the sky was clear. Rain began to pour at that moment, a deluge that seemed to fill the air with moisture. Both Jim and Zeke worked their lips and tongues, almost tasting the moisture.

On shore a small pod of hippos appeared, entering the water quietly, moving out until only their backs and heads stuck out of the water. Although they weren't social creatures, in the water they always seemed to huddle together, and both men knew no one had an answer for that. Jim thought it was perhaps wrong to consider them unsocial, despite their behavior. The male ruling this pod appeared to weigh in at over three tons, a huge old fellow with one broken tooth showing when he opened his mouth. Smiling as the huge animal opened its mouth fully to warn off the boats passing by Jim shook his head.

CHAPTER 23

With the rising of the sun, despite the rain, a cacophony of noise erupted from the jungle trees nearest the water as the birds, monkeys, and other denizens of the jungle announced the coming of the day. Today, he knew, his science team would be testing the waters for changes that occur only during flood stages. There was still one dam to cross at Kariba, and they wanted to know how the dams affected the reduction in emplacement of silt and associate nutrients in the delta. This part of the study, and the third and final part, would give a definitive answer to the question of how the dams hinder the natural displacement. Once again, they would prove that when man tries to improve something, he generally creates more problems than the one he might have solved!

RJ was an early riser, and Jim was not surprised to find him sitting up in his crib when he returned to his cabin. The noise from the jungle probably brought him awake. Jim lifted him gently, noting how warm his body felt, and put him on the changing table. He'd no sooner taken off the wet and messy diaper than RJ began to pee again. Learning from several other occasions Jim had a diaper over him and he grinned at his son.

"Missed me, pal!" he said, at which point RJ grabbed the diaper and pulled it off, causing Jim to rear back to avoid the flow. "Scamp!

How dare you pee on your Captain!" Jim teased with a huge grin at his son. RJ giggled joyously, a sound Jim had come to love, and he completed cleaning up his son and putting clean diapers on before another accident occurred. After wiping clean the changing table, and washing his hands, Jim picked RJ up and carried him to the bed, where Cecilia sat to receive him. Leaning down he kissed Cecilia before depositing JR in her lap.

After his morning bottle RJ played on the floor with his daddy until Cecilia was changed into her uniform and ready to head down to breakfast. Holding her hand and carrying RJ Jim moved out of the cabin, down the steps to the main deck, and made his way back to the Garbage Scow. Cecilia carried both plates back while Jim held RJ and they were first at table in their boat, joined shortly by the rest of the crew, with the exception of Goody, who was still on watch.

For a few minutes no one spoke as everyone dug into a delicious and nutritious breakfast provided by the kitchen crew. Abe and JimJim always provided delicious and nutritious food, changing up the menu often enough that no one got bored with the food, as they often did when out in the field and eating MREs. This morning Jim ate basted eggs, bacon, a fresh fruit salad with some of the local fruits included, a large glass of ice-cold milk, and some fresh fish from yesterday's catch.

Many of the men enjoyed an hour or so of fishing each day as evening closed over the river, and their catch provided food for all three meals the next day. Today's recipe was new, something one of the chefs found on the Internet, or in a cookbook for that type of fish. Jim liked the subtle flavor of lemon and lime and the seasonings that enhanced the flavor of the fish. The edge of his plate was soon littered with small fragile bones he'd either picked out with his fork or pulled from his mouth.

After breakfast he walked back to *River Venture 4* and complimented the crew on breakfast, and on the fish recipe. Abe nodded to JimJim to signify it was his recipe. JimJim told him where he found the recipe and thanked the captain for stopping in to tell them he'd enjoyed it. Bull and TP wandered into the kitchen area and caught sight of Jim.

"Oy! It's the brass. Look busy!" Bill Franklin said to Tom Patterson. Both had their arms full of pots and pans they'd just washed ready to hang back in place.

TP pretended to fumble with his armful and almost trip and Bull rolled his eyes. Jim grinned at the pair. When they'd first joined the crew, they never would have acted this way, clowning around, trusting that he would appreciate their humor as much as their hard work. Both men had become as close as family and they trusted the crewmembers equally.

"You drop my pans and dent them I dent you!" Abe pretended to be stern, shaking a finger at TP.

"Yes sir! Warrant Officer Lincoln, sir!" TP said, snapping to attention and trying to salute while the stack of pans swayed dangerously. Jim reached out a hand to steady the stack.

"Exemplary discipline, Mr. Lincoln!" Jim said, twisting one of the pans so that the handle poked TP in the nose.

"Oh, my goodness!" JimJim exclaimed. "Get your nose off that handle. It was clean! Now you have to wash it over again!"

TP hung up the pans, and when he'd finished, he took the one that had poked him in the nose, licked the handle, and wiped it off with his sleeve. JimJim clapped him on the back of the head.

"Don't let the captain see how we wash our pots and pans!" he whispered loudly.

Jim threw his head back and laughed as TP took the pot back to the sink to wash it again. TP was grinning broadly, and Bull was laughing too. "I'm telling everyone what I just saw!" Jim said through his laughter.

"Captain! You wouldn't! It would ruin our sterling reputation!" Windy said, striking a pose.

Sturdy appeared with a rotting piece of fish on a plate. "You plannin' on fish for lunch, Captain?" he asked. Everyone wrinkled noses at the stench.

"Uh, I just decided, no one really needs to know how things are done in the kitchen," Jim said pretending to hold back vomit.

"Good!" Sturdy replied, winking at him as he dumped the fish into the garbage. "That one won't go on your plate then!"

"Well done, men! Well done!" Jim pretended to be very nervous as he slowly made his way out of the kitchen. They all laughed together as he turned to go, shaking his head.

After inspecting each boat, he returned to sit on the front deck with those who had gathered there to watch the beauty of the Jungle. Rain still poured down in a steady stream. It was going to be a record year for rain. One of the Rigid Raiders passed them as Jim pulled a Diet Coke with lime from the refrigerator and sat down next to FM. The science crew was beginning its day.

After finishing his Coke, Jim rose without saying anything and headed in to take care of his morning workload. John and Wade were already in the office, their desks arranged so that they could look at each other as they worked. Finn and Ives were typing away at computer keyboards. In the past Finn would have stood up and yelled at the top of his lungs "Captain on deck!" Today he merely looked up and nodded, a marked improvement.

Looking at the "in" box on his desk Jim realized that the paperwork was less than he expected. Working through it carefully he held up the last report and looked across at Wade.

"We're really that far below our estimate on fuel consumption?" he asked.

"Neat, huh?" Wade replied. "The hydraulic system is saving us thousands of dollars!"

John looked at the two of them with a broad grin. "We'd better not make those records public. Oil companies wouldn't like that!"

"Where did you guys get the idea for a hydraulic system to run boats, trucks, and Jeeps?" Jim asked, signing the report and putting it in the "out" box.

"Back in the 1950s a technical school came up with the idea and actually converted a huge old Oldsmobile into a hydraulic car. Hydraulics work on pressure, and that can be dangerous, so the whole idea never got off the ground. Besides which, the car companies couldn't change their paradigm," Wade supplied. "TRT studied several other hydraulic systems and came up with this one, and he asked me to design it, so it had built in safety measures. I did some studying, and you are seeing the end result."

"How did you guys figure out how to use it in the arctic? Doesn't extreme cold thicken the fluids?" Jim asked.

"It does, so we used a solar heat pump to keep heat to the lines. All of the hydraulic lines are inside an insulated pipe that can either heat or cool the lines, depending on where we are," Wade answered.

"You always were a geek," John said playfully.

"Yeah, and if I hadn't helped you two in Algebra, Geometry and Calculus, where would you both be?" Wade replied.

"Probably still in High School! Oh gosh! We'd still be dating! What a horrible thought! All those raging hormones," John joked. "So how come if you take Algebra I twice, the second time around it isn't Algebra II?"

"One squared, is still one," Wade shot back. "One times one is still one."

"Yes, math geek, but one plus one equals two!" John replied. To demonstrate he wadded up two pieces of paper, and threw one at Wade, and then the second. "See! Two!" he finished.

"Try to make him understand," Jim said, patting Wade on the back as he left the office with a huge grin.

In the CIC he leaned down and kissed Cecilia. Zeke and News said nothing because at the moment they were glued to the multiple screens before them. Cecilia smiled as Jim went over and lifted JAS and RJ into his arms one at a time to toss them and tease them, making both of them squeal with joy. He gently lowered them back into the play area and turned to look at the computer screens.

"What are you two studying so carefully?" he asked, stepping between them.

"Massoona is building a base camp and improving the escape route," Zeke said, pointing to one of the screens. Jim could see almost a hundred men working on the road that led to the river. It was really just two tracks, most of it overgrown, with deep holes that needed to be filled and ditches that needed to be bridged to allow the six-wheel trucks to pass.

"Wouldn't boats serve better?" Jim asked no one in particular.

"I think he plans to move his men into position with the trucks, using them to escape," News said slowly. "He's also moved in a lot of explosives," he pointed to a shed in the base camp. "That's full!" he reported.

"Keep an eye on that stuff. We'll blow it a day or two before he decides to attack," Jim replied, studying the camp layout. Whatever Massoona was, he wasn't a tactician! The camp was haphazard and offered several problems if his troops were surrounded and attacked while occupying the camp.

"He must be pretty sure no one is going to reach his camp to attack," Jim muttered.

"Nobody even knows he's there!" Zeke said easily. "During flood stages that whole area is deserted for higher ground. All those rivers and streams that empty into the Zambezi flood too!"

"What's your assessment?" Jim asked.

"Massoona is lazy. He likes power, and he treats his men poorly. They have no scouts out and some of the bridges they've constructed are so poorly built I doubt if all his trucks would get back to base camp even if he had the chance," Zeke replied.

"Who paid for the trucks?" Jim asked.

"Wikffels' coal company bought four of them, and Ramanantsoa bought the other three," Zeke replied quickly. "They're REO vehicles, but obviously bought from a surplus dealer. Six of them have had major engine problems and one dropped an axle!" Zeke laughed. "Seven out of seven fails!"

Massoona took them into the field without testing them or inspecting them?" Jim exclaimed, surprised.

"Like I said, he's lazy," Zeke replied.

"Are his men training at all?" Jim asked.

"Not yet," Zeke replied with a significant look at Jim.

Both of them knew that constant training was important to riding that wave of perfection every soldier sought.

"How are you getting such a clear picture?" Jim asked suddenly.

"There's a NASA satellite that is being used to do a study on the effect of sunspots on the local weather. I've isolated one of their cameras that was not being used, turned it on, and am monitoring things," News replied, looking over his shoulder at Jim with a grin.

"And why isn't NASA using that camera?" Jim asked, raising an eyebrow.

"It malfunctioned, so they shut it off until they can figure out what's wrong. Tomorrow another camera will malfunction and this one will miraculously recover!" his grin was devilish now. "You should see their comments on what's happening. Two of them think aliens are playing with the system, and the rest have ideas about the sunspots affecting the wiring or overheating occurring," he laughed.

"There's a Russian satellite up there we can use when this one moves in its orbit," Zeke said. It was obvious he was unconcerned about discovery.

"Giving you two a Cray was like handing a gun to a delinquent and suggesting he go mugging!" Jim commented, shaking his head.

"Yeah, well just remember that when we get there neither satellite will be available. It will be eyes on only," Zeke warned darkly. "I hate the jungle!"

"It probably doesn't like you either," Jim replied with a grin, rubbing his head. "Keep me posted on whether or not those men start training and what training they do," he nodded once, turned, and kissing Cecilia once more he left to go back to the Science Lab.

"I'm scheduled to ride shotgun on one of the Rigid Raiders," he said to Cecilia as he left the room. "See you when I get back."

On the Rigid Raider he had a very special rifle at his disposal. His choice today was the Remington Model 700 XCR II. He liked the stainless-steel barrel and receiver coated with matte black TriNyte for a more classic look with less glare for superior stealth. Every bit as impervious to extreme conditions, with the same proven track record in accelerated saltwater testing that opened the world's eyes to the power of the patented technology, simply put, TriNyte delivers scratch and corrosion resistance dramatically superior to standard stainless steel as well as any protective coating by any other manufacturer.

The Model 700 XCR II is also optimized for sure handling in adverse climates. Its feature-laden olive drab green synthetic stock is a technological marvel that looks and feels the part with patented Hogue® rubber overmolding featured at the grip and fore-end areas. These revolutionary enhancements gave him a positive grip in the slickest environments. And shots were made infinitely more comfortable with Remington's SuperCell™ recoil pad - the most effective on the market. Remington's X-Mark Pro° Trigger System gave him a level of crispness and shot control once only available through high-dollar customization. Choice from a wide range of hard-hitting big and dangerous-game cartridges, all delivered with the track-driving accuracy only a legendary Model 700 barreled action could produce made it the perfect rifle for today's work.

On the opposite side of the boat FM had chosen the 416 Rigby for his rifle. Both men kept eyes on the hippos near the shore and any crocodiles. The Rigid Raiders were large enough that most hippos and crocks left them alone, but one never knew with wild animals. Today FM had the side away from the shore, so he had the added responsibility to watch the water of the river that direction for danger. One never knew from where danger would come in this country.

Aboard Dr. Copeland and Dr. Putnam worked together to collect the samples, while lab technicians Rachael Hague and Elizabeth Minor catalogued and labeled each bottle. At the wheel Driver seemed relaxed as he either moved or held the boat where the science team directed. Moving out in front of the riverboats the Rigid Raiders were almost as quiet, and Jim listened to the various noises from the jungle.

At one point they came upon a meadow that emptied on the riverbank. A small herd of elephants played in the water while the alpha male kept watch, his attention as much on the water as it was on the meadow and jungle around them. Beyond the elephants a small pod of hippos wiggled their ears to keep the ever-present bugs from settling. When the alpha male hippo caught sight of the boat he lunged forward and roared a challenge.

Instead of slowing he continued swimming out toward them. Jim slid a shell into the barrel of the rifle and raised it, shooting the bolt action down to lock it in place. He didn't really want to kill the hippo, but if it didn't stop, he wouldn't hesitate. Ten yards from the boat the hippo dipped beneath the surface. Jim warned everyone to brace for impact. But Driver spun the wheel and hit the throttle, the boat leaping from the water and moving forward fast. Coming up behind its intended target the hippo thrashed for a moment, and then turned and swam back to its pod. Carefully Jim ejected the shell and breathed out in relief. He looked at the bullet and nodded once before putting it back in his leather holder.

"Would you have killed it?" Elizabeth asked quietly when they were once again busy with collecting samples.

"Yes," Jim answered simply, his eyes busy with the shoreline. For a moment her green eyes studied the captain and she looked significantly at her lab partner. She'd heard the sadness in his voice. These men, military men who often faced death and dealt death, were deeply saddened because of its necessity. Yet when the time came, they were ready to do their duty, regardless. Feeling suddenly safer she sighed.

"Thanks," she offered simply, and he looked at her and nodded, understanding.

CHAPTER 24

A t the rapids the boats were once again airlifted up to Lake Kariba where they were docked and resupplied at Kariba, the town built originally to house the construction workers on the dam. Until 1958 there hadn't been a town there, and today nearly twenty-four thousand people inhabited the small city. Because it is the center of the tourist industry for the Lake Kariba region it provides accommodations in various hotels and lodges along with two casinos and several restaurants.

Located on the Zimbabwe side of things Jim kept the crew close to the boats and as soon as everything was loaded the helicopters lifted off and headed for Livingstone where they would wait for the boats to make the nearly one-hundred and forty-mile trip the length of the largest man-made lake in the world. Shortly after the choppers left the Catalina swept across the waters and lifted into the air to shuttle the pilots back to the boats. Windy wiggled the wings twice at those watching and waving as he expertly piloted the restored classic.

All that day the crew worked hard to store everything properly and the boats, engines, and rooms were carefully inspected. No electronic listening or watching devices had been added on this trip and nothing had been tampered with. Still, Jim was unwilling to take even the slightest chance and made sure everything was checked.

As sunset arrived the boats set out, towing the PBY Catalina behind the sixth riverboat along with its Rigid Raider.

They had to be careful as they made their way past the drowned forests that lined the shores, leafless, black skeletons of once beautiful denizens of the jungle fauna they now stood stark and grim, like scarecrow frames after a fire. It was an ugly reminder of what had been lost when the lake was created. Yet they still provided important habitats for many species of bird including fisheagle, cormorant, darter, pied kingfisher, duck, and geese. Jim decided it was like gliding through a graveyard of trees.

Once beyond the trees they dropped anchor, ate dinner on the observation deck of the Garbage Scow, and after helping with the cleanup held a general meeting. Alistair stood up when Jim called everyone to order and as the crew quieted, he cleared his throat.

"Kariba dam is one of the largest in the world. This so called "modern day wonder" that we just saw close up is one hundred and twenty-eight meters high and five hundred and seventy-nine meters long. Its construction rivals that of the Hoover Dam," he began. FM immediately raised his hand and with a grin Alistair nodded to him.

"Yo! Dr. Museum! Can you translate that into English numbers, please? I'm not real familiar with Mr. D'Metrics," he pronounced D'Metrics, deemeetrics, faking a Greek accent. Everyone chuckled.

"Very well, Mr. Miller," Alistair said lightly. "To convert meters to feet simply multiply the number of meters by 3.2808. So, we're talking about a dam that is approximately 420 feet high and 1,900 feet long. Does that help?"

"So, either way you measure it, we're talking about a big water retaining facility. I can't use the other word because I'll have to wash my mouth out with soap," FM quipped.

"The water retaining facility is spelled d-a-m, and the swear word is spelled d-a-m-n. The first means something that prohibits the flow of water and the second means condemnation from God. You shouldn't ever use that word, but you can say 'dam' without any worries. Now, if you interrupt my husband again, I'll wash your mouth out with soap!" Gwyneth threatened, pretending to be stern and pointing her finger at FM. He hunched into himself as if terrified.

"Sorry, Mrs. Museum! I'll behave!" he said in a shaky voice.

"I'll believe that when I see it!" she retorted with a snort.

"May I continue?" Alistair inquired, raising an eyebrow at FM. FM pretended to zip his lip shut and nodded.

Alistair liked this young man very much. FM always had something funny to say, and he was smart, much smarter than most people thought. Because he was so muscularly developed, and such a clown, most people underestimated his intelligence, but Alistair knew he had a keen mind, much like his bonus sons. Honored to be part of this group he continued.

"The Kariba dam was initiated by the Federation existing at the time between British ruled Northern and Southern Rhodesia (now Zambia and Zimbabwe) and Nyasaland (Malawi). Construction began in 1955 and was completed in 1959. Once the waters began rising the river people, or Tongas, were forced to relocate to higher ground. For sound reasons the Tonga's were very much against this as they felt they were leaving their ancestral burial grounds and their very way of life, dictated by their religious traditions. However, they did concede that they had to move, and held ceremonies to honor their gods before they began their journey to new lands.

"Naturally, the British built schools and clinics in some of the new areas and even installed wells for their arrival. Some of the new villages were relocated close to the water's edge and these have prospered with the new fishing opportunities on the lake. But for the most part, as in every one of these sad scenarios, the relocation disrupted the Tonga's way of life and the compensation was minimal at best.

"The other problem that was created was that thousands of animals were stranded by the rising waters. Operation Noah, led by Robert Fothergill, a noted game warden, along with other wardens, utilized the funds raised to purchase boats and equipment necessary for this mammoth rescue and relocation of the animals. One of the islands created when the lake was filled is named Fothergill Island in honor and memory of Robert.

"I would have been fascinated to be here during that time. They had to rescue elephants and rhinos, a huge undertaking, and the tiny bushbabys and snakes indigenous to the area. I think it might have been very dangerous, for the animals were experiencing great disturbances.

"Before the lake was filled some one thousand square kilometers (that's 386 square miles for you, Mr. Miller) of vegetation was cleared of trees. Many believed at the time that this would have an adverse effect on the lake's ecosystem. What in fact happened was exactly the opposite! The lake actually became rich in chemicals from the burnt trees and the remaining trees provided habitats for many animals that found their way into the lake. That just goes to prove that science doesn't have all the answers!

"The lake itself has a surface area of 5,580 square kilometers (2,154 square miles to you, Mr. Miller) and a catchment area of 663,000 square kilometers (255,984.3 square miles)!" Alistair smiled at FM and winked at him as he made the conversions, thinking that this savvy soldier could probably do the calculations in his head. He paused to take a drink of water before continuing.

"This lake is forty kilometers wide, or twenty-five miles, and two hundred and twenty-three kilometers long, or one hundred and thirty-nine miles. The average depth is twenty-nine meters, or ninety-five feet and the deepest spot has been determined to be ninety-seven meters or three hundred and eighteen feet. That makes the water volume of this lake 180 cubic kilometers or 43 cubic miles.

"Here's an interesting tidbit! The Tonga people believe the building of the Kariba Dam deeply offended Nyaminyami, the Zambezi River God or Zambezi Snake Spirit. In their legend his wife travelled down the gorge, and during her absence the dam wall separated Nyaminyami from his wife. Construction was halted in 1957 due to the worst floods ever known on the Zambezi. In 1958 heavy rains accompanied more flooding and the Tonga believed this was the wrath of Nyaminyami. You'll see pendants on jewelry, usually carved out of wood, stone or bone, occasionally ivory, silver or gold, both as a fashion accessory and as a good luck charm. Sad that these people worshiped the creation, rather than the creator."

"Perhaps the saddest note on all of this is the Matusadona national park. Just recently the last known black rhino was hunted and killed for a trophy animal in the park! Smaller than the Lower Zambezi national park, it should have been five times larger. However, as is usually the case, even a national park here provides no real protection for endangered species.

"We have reached the half-way point of our sixteen-hundred-mile journey to the source of the Zambezi in a marsh in northwestern Zambia. Now that you know a little about where we are, I'll turn the rest of this discussion over to Dr. Dinsmore," Alistair folded to the deck beside Gwyneth and leaned back against the railing with a satisfied sigh.

Dr. Alice Dinsmore stood up. "Thanks Alistair," she said, smiling down at him. "The Zambezi valley has always supported a kaleidoscope of wildlife, birds and fish. We'll see the hippos and crocodiles, monitor lizards (which we haven't sighted thus far), buffalo, zebra, giraffe, elephants, lions, leopards, etc.

"One of the studies we're supposed to do is a plan for a national park that spans more than one country. This, we have already decided, is quite impossible. Our recommendation will be two national parks or preserves located on either side of the river, but operated by separate governments, and overseen by the organization that provides the funding for such a project.

"Zambia's wildlife rangers have already been invaluable to us in identifying the most endangered species and where they can be found. That will help considerably. However! There is still a great deal of work to be done, especially in surveying land and determining which parcels will best serve those populations.

"With that we have the usual water samples to study. I'll turn the next part over to Dr. Copeland. She'll tell you what inhabits this lake and what we need to know for proper caution," Alice motioned with her hand to Iris, who stood gracefully.

"A number of fish species have been introduced to the lake, notably the sardine-like Kapenta, which were transported from Lake Tanganyika. Kapenta supports a thriving commercial fishery. The tigerfish, which was among the indigenous species of this river system, now thrive on the Kapenta, which unfortunately encourages tourism. Some of those tourism industries have begun feeding the crocodiles from the tour boats, showing people how they can propel their bodies out of the water and other things.

"This has made the crocodile population much more dangerous to smaller boats, like our Rigid Raiders if we go close to shore for any reason. Game wardens have warned the tour boats of this danger, but they continue the practice because tourists want pictures of crocodiles coming out of the water. Tour boats are big enough to go in among the small pods of hippos too, which doesn't bode well for smaller craft.

"We're going to have to be doubly vigilant as we gather samples. There have been many crocodile attacks and several deaths, especially among the tourists. Because the latter often feed the crocks from their houseboats to entice them close enough for a good photograph our lives are going to be very interesting. Several tourists have learned the hard way that a crocodile is not selective about food, taking it where it can find it.

"Crocodiles are the most social of reptiles. They tolerate each other during basking but are fiercely territorial when it comes to hunting. A Nile crocodile will not tolerate another male in its hunting area. These crocs are big and dangerous so beware! They have the advantage of attacking before we can react, so we are going to take precautions whenever we are out in the boats gathering samples. I don't want anyone losing an arm or leg or anything else to these deadly predators.

"We also want to check the fish we catch, examining them for parasites and any other indicators. Most of the fish we catch will be healthy and safe to eat, but we do want to be careful. We also want to take the usual precautions against insect bites. I think that's all we have to say. Captains, do either of you want to add anything?" Iris looked at Jim and John and it was John who stood up.

"Getting the boats up to the lake was done without mishap and I want to compliment everyone on getting everything in the way of supplies stowed properly. Also, our flight crew did an excellent job of ferrying the choppers to Livingstone. We hired a special service to guard the birds while they're on the ground. Massoona may very well try to tamper with them, but he won't if they are closely guarded and watched. Ira Lehman provided the team as a special favor.

"We all know our assignments. Those of you who wish to fish tonight may do so. All the proper licenses have been provided. However, I want to make sure you fish from the observation decks, just in case a crocodile decides to try to take your fish before you can land it. No one fishes from the rear decks, and when crossing from boat to boat we will do so from the observation decks. Each is equipped with a safe, railed, gangplank. Let's keep everyone safe," John smiled and nodded to Jim who stood beside his brother, holding RJ. As he stood John stooped and gathered JAS into his arms.

"This is going to be an amazing body of water to study and I'm looking forward to spending the time we're here enjoying it. Because we'll have fairly calm water, unless there's a storm, we'll have a chance to catch up on some of the reports we'll need to complete this grant. So far, we are a little ahead of schedule on that, and the information we've gathered should help future generations make better decisions about the Zambezi River and this incredible valley. However, we can't make people see the truth. All we can do is tell the truth, and we're doing that.

"For those of you who want to swim during the hottest times of the day, we will be lowering the swimming pool from one o'clock in the afternoon and pulling it back in at five o'clock." There was a cheer from the crew at this news.

The swimming pool was really a shark net with sides that went down thirty feet, and a netted bottom with strong aluminum alloy rods that were assembled by divers at the bottom and sides of the net to keep predators from penetrating sides and bottom. According to Goody a great white or thirty-foot crocodile would not be able to break through that barrier. Along the top of the pool were inflated floats, made of the same material as the pontoons on the riverboats, also able to withstand predators. With the boats parked around it people could dive from the observation decks and swim without fear.

Mornings were spent taking samples and working on the grant reports, but the afternoons were set aside for rest and recreation. Once the pollution levels of the water had been tested, and proven to be minimal during flood stage, most of the crew spent the afternoon swimming in the cool waters or watching the amazing thunderstorms that swept across the lake from the safety of the boats. The latter were accompanied by impressive pyrotechnic displays of lightening and thundering roars from the clouds.

Jim found that RJ loved the water, and so did his mother, because in the water her pregnancy didn't weigh on her as much. Five families from the UK that saved together and rented a large houseboat joined them one afternoon, curious about their swimming pool, and spent the afternoon swimming in the safety of the pool with the crew. All of their children were young or older teens, most of them girls, and the men of *Bring It Up* entertained them in a game of water basketball, cannonball tag, and Marco Polo.

That evening they ate with the crew, amazed at the incredible dinner, and listened with rapt attention as the work of the crew was outlined. It turned out that all ten parents were teachers at various levels who were fascinated by the study. Alice, aware that these people had no concept of Christianity or creation invited them to tag along if they wished.

They did not stay for the Bible Study, but they did participate in the evening games. Jim was disappointed that they had no interest in spiritual things, but he felt that they had made a good enough impression that they would get several chances to enlighten them. During the prayer time the families were brought before the Lord with the desire that the men and women of the crew would live in such a way that their lives would be a beacon, drawing the family toward Christ. Proud of his crew Jim prayed fervently that their request would be sweet before the Lord.

CHAPTER 25

Morning dawned on Lake Kariba, casting a golden glow across the smooth waters, and amidst the gathering storm clouds blue sky beaconed. Andrea, Jim, John, and Wade stood on the observation deck of *River Venture 1* with Bear who had the watch. Jim appeared first on the deck with a steaming cup of coffee for Bear, and his usual glass of iced tea in the other hand. Now they stood together watching the dawn throw back the darkness of night and fill the world with light. With a critical eye Jim looked at the clouds.

"I'd say we're in for some rain this morning," he predicted conversationally.

"I looked in at the CIC weather monitoring system this morning and forecasts are for heavy rains most of the morning," Wade agreed.

John pulled his coffee cup away from his lips, enjoying the smell and taste of the coffee before replying.

"Anyone want to wager on record rainfall this year?" he asked. "At the present moment we're about a quarter inch above normal and the worst is yet to come."

"I would agree," Andrea said, rubbing his knee. "My knee tells me it will rain this morning, and rain hard. And I feel that the weather is changing."

Jim looked back across the five boats behind him and spotted the houseboat of their new friends anchored near the last boat. No lights showed in any of the windows and the boat lay quiet on the still morning waters. He turned back and looked at the storm clouds now rising quickly.

"Shall we set off after breakfast and hope the rain clears so we can gather some samples?" Jim asked.

"We're not sending them out if there's lightening!" John laughed.

Wade glanced down and saw four crocodiles gathered beneath them. He pointed to them.

"Looks like they're looking for some breakfast," he said. Bear too had been watching them.

"They showed up when you three started talking," he explained quietly. "That's just down-right dangerous!" he added. "They're too familiar with boats and people!"

Bond came up the stairs at that point, wearing his hot weather uniform with short-sleeved shirt and lightweight pants. His shoes made no sound as he walked across the deck. All Jim's soldiers walked lightly when they walked, something they'd learned, a skill developed and carefully honed and constantly practiced. Seeming to glide across the deck he came to a stop, looking from face to face with curiosity. Grinning at the three officers on the deck he winked at Bear.

"In trouble with the brass again, yah?" he asked facetiously. He sauntered past the three ranking officers, looked down at the crocodiles and up at Bear who towered over him. His Walther PPK appeared in his hands in a lightening motion, and he pointed it at the crocodiles.

"Bond! Banks Bond!" he said dramatically, raising the weapon and replacing it.

"That pea-shooter will just make them angry," Bear grinned at his team member. "Notice how frightened they became?" he asked facetiously.

"Shut it, you great lump of muscle. Let's see what you've done the last two hours, eh?" Banks grinned at his friend and picked up the clipboard. Bear grinned back. After checking the log Banks checked the rifle carefully and nodded, logging Bear out and himself in.

"Breakfast?" Bear asked the other three.

"I'm starving," Wade sighed, nodding.

"Me too!" John grinned. The four walked to the back of the deck together.

An aluminum alloy gangplank connected the observation decks. It could be operated electronically, or in the event of no power, cranked out. Wade operated the controls and the plank slid silently out from beneath their feet, snapping up three inches to become level with both decks with a loud clank. The crocodiles reacted to that noise.

Lee Ainsworth was on watch and Rock was just going off. He joined them as they continued back to *River Venture 3*. There they gathered PU, who had just been relieved by Chance, and moved to *River Venture 4*. Following Santa down the steps they entered the galley and joined the growing line for breakfast.

Jim listened to the comments of the men around him as he loaded eggs, bacon, and fruit on his plate. Despite the length of their mission, the spirit of the men was high, and their mood was good. The usual bantering and joking going on all around him, and friends greeted friends happily as they joined the line. Cecilia came in carrying RJ who had fallen asleep on her shoulder and Jim helped her carry her plate and drink back to *River Venture 1* where they sat around an already filling table to eat. Jim didn't insist his crew get up at 04:30 every morning, yet almost every one of them did, or at the latest 05:00. Cecilia and RJ sat to his left. Zeke Kline, Calvin Weston, Bill Kline, Richard Nelson, John Smith, Zeke Good, Frank Miller, David Carr, and Paul Donnelly filled the table by 05:00. Banks was up on guard duty.

After breakfast Bear took a plate up to Banks and kept him company while he ate, helping with the watch duty. That duty done Bear went down to the cabin to grab ninety minutes of shuteye. After a shower and a fresh uniform, he appeared on *River Venture 3* to go out with the boats. Rain fell heavily, but there was no thunder and lightening near their area. Transferring the scientists, lab technicians, and armed guards to the Rigid Raiders went smoothly and the Raiders moved out ahead of the riverboats.

Despite the heavy rain the science teams collected the necessary water samples, including some of the rain. Drenched and dripping they returned to the science lab with their containers before heading into their respective cabins to dry off and change clothes. Wet clothing was placed in a net bag and sent back to *River Venture 4* and the laundry facility. Fingers, Fagan, Spanky and Babs had laundry duty that day. All clothing was contained in marked bags, so everyone received his or her own clothing back at the end of the day. Everyone shared laundry duty, including Jim and Cecilia. Laundry was usually done by lunch, and the men washed men's clothes, while the women washed women's clothes, though they tended to help each other if the loads were larger than usual, and one group finished before the other. It was a good system that had been suggested by crewmembers. So far on this journey it had worked perfectly, despite the change in the type of washers and dryers.

Once again, the five British families joined them for an afternoon of swimming and fun, and they stayed for dinner. Most of the parents watched the activity in the science lab while their children, safe in the swimming pool, played with those who had no or light duty that afternoon. Jim came back to see how the studies were coming along and stayed for almost an hour to discuss the findings with his marine biologists.

Alice had the floor at one point and Jim listened carefully as she recapped their findings.

"We've isolated the bacteria that is causing the EUS on the fish and thus far none of the fish caught in this lake have that bacteria, so it was introduced further down river. My guess is the plant causing the bacteria only lived in that region. If those fish are eaten most humans have the bacteria fighting mechanism to protect them. However, carrion birds will eat the fish and cause the bacteria to mutate again, so we need to warn the governments to let people know not to eat the fish or any carrion birds. We don't know how the bacteria will mutate.

"Sewage Effluent is still higher than normal in these waters, though in the lake it is still below safe limits. Silt emplacement and associate nutrients are evident closest to the dam thus far, and the dam is obviously keeping those from getting downriver to the delta area. Our lake ontogeny indicates that this lake is developing a very active and healthy oligotrophic stage.

"We were able to draw on studies begun in 1961 to determine the health of this particular lake. If pollution can be kept at bay it will provide a healthy source of water and life to thousands of mammals, birds, insects, arachnids, and fish. With a ready source of water like this we should be able to get a fairly accurate idea of how our endangered species are faring.

"Tomorrow we're going in close to shore on the Zambia side of the lake which means that crocodiles and hippos pose a very real threat. A team will need to go ashore to determine the effect of the lake on the land surrounding it, especially that land that is submerged during flood stages. Captain, I'll need extra men to guard my scientists for that trip," Alice looked at Jim as she said the last and he nodded in the affirmative, as she expected. She shared a smile with him.

"Two men to each scientist and lab technician," he replied after a moment of thought. "I'll have a four-man-team inland and at the water's edge for further protection."

"Thank you," Alice said, satisfied. "I'll send Dr. Lowe and Dr. Putnam with Lynn Ross and Stephanie Morris."

"He doesn't look like he needs protection!" That was Timothy Wallace, one of the family visitors. He was smiling at Dr. Putnam with whom he'd been having a conversation with earlier.

"No, he doesn't, as long as he can keep his attention on everything going on around him. But when he's busy gathering samples we'll watch his back," Jim explained.

The answer seemed to satisfy Mr. Wallace. Mike grinned at Jim, shaking his head slightly at the interchange. Jim grinned back. He understood. Mike was powerfully built, like many of his soldiers, and could indeed take care of himself. Jim was pleased to have such a man as part of his unit. Dr. Putnam had proved his metal many times over the past few years. His Australian accent and easy teaching manner coupled with his keen mind made him a popular teacher among the crew. He worked hard in training with the men and stood with them in skill and stamina.

"I will have to assign Delta to take care of Dr. Lowe," Jim announced with a grin as Dorf ducked through the door.

"Aye! I am a mighty hunter!" Dorf said, flexing his upper torso and pretending to tiptoe across the lab, sneaking up on something. Dr. Putnam growled and Dorf reacted by leaping behind Jim, holding his belt and pretending to weep in fear with his head against Jim's leg.

"Oh! Some mighty hunter!" Carol scoffed, laughing as Dorf peaked at her from behind Jim.

"I was just examining the captain's pants. The seam work is so terrible it made me cry!" he stood up and tried to look sheepish, which on him just looked comical. Everyone laughed again.

"My hero," Jim said dryly, folding his arms and shaking his head at his comical giant friend.

That evening Jim noted that Dorf and Carol won the Balderdash tournament, leaving those playing and those watching laughing hysterically at their definitions. He thought that perhaps there would be another wedding in his crew, and not for the first time thought that the time was fast approaching when he needed to turn the military operations over to another leader.

In the morning they found a place to beach all the riverboats, driving heavy metal spikes into the ground to hold them in place and expertly tying them off. On shore they gathered around Jim, Alice and John Dinsmore, and studied a topographical map of the area. Dr. Low, with Delta to protect her, set off northwest along a small tributary. Dr. Putnam, with Bulldog to protect him, set off east along the shore. Everyone else set off with Alice and John to count the number of species they could spot, heading inland and spreading out as far as they dared. No one lost sight of the people to his or her left or right.

Here one had to watch where one put his or her feet, keep an eye on the trees around them, and maintain an arch of vision in front. All of them had radios they could use to call for help, if necessary, and keep in contact.

Mark, taking point for his group, moved a little ahead of the rest, but not far enough to be out of sight. Dorf brought up the rear. There were crocodiles in the tributary, but only a few because the water was normally shallow. However, they were aggressive hunters, so the men used extreme caution. Watching the crocodiles warily, Carol was glad she had three armed men to protect her.

It was Dorf who noted the lion, standing seventy yards distance across a small clearing. The beast stood still, watching them, its tail flicking from side to side. A male, large and strong, the lion was amazing, but it was also intimidating. A low rumbling growl escaped its lips. Carefully Dorf raised his rifle, picked his spot, and fired, the bullet snapping bark off the tree closest to the lion.

His expectation was that the lion would be frightened away, but in the jungle, no one can guarantee what a wild animal will do. The beast's ears went flat against its head and its tail went straight up as it went from standing to full charge in two strides. Dorf kept his rifle up, aiming carefully, amazed at the sheer speed and ferocity of the huge cat as it charged him. Off to his left he heard Carol scream, but his eyes were on the charging lion. His second shot was true, taking the huge beast in the heart.

What he hadn't taken into consideration was the mass and speed of the animal, and though it was dying it crashed into him. Jaws closed on his shoulder and claws sunk into his side. He'd automatically braced for the impact, but that only made things worse, and he was hurled backwards, his own scream mixing with the death throes of the lion. Both crashed to the ground and the lion rolled over him and lay still. Dorf took a breath and felt the burning pain of his wounds.

"Thank You, Lord, for sparing my life!" he breathed as he sat up. He turned to look at the huge Lion and felt a pang of sadness. "I didn't want to kill you!" he snapped angrily, rising to his feet and straightening with some difficulty. Carol Lowe was there, her eyes red from crying, tears pouring down her cheeks and she hugged him tightly, bringing out a grunt of pain. She stepped back quickly.

"How badly are you hurt?" she asked, choking back more tears.

"He got his claws into my side and his teeth into my shoulder," Dorf looked at his wounded shoulder and realized that the bite wounds were deep. He quickly pulled out his medical kit and began to search for his Penicillin. There was a very real danger of infection from Pasteurella multocida bacteria. After giving himself a shot, he poured hydrogen peroxide into the deep wounds to help cleanse them until the doctors could take care of the rest. It was very painful, but he was aware of Carol watching and didn't want to alarm her, so he bore it as stoically as possible. Mark arrived at that moment, talking on his radio.

"We have an injury. Dorf decided to wrestle with a lion, and he got bit and clawed a little. He's standing, so I'm assuming we won't have to carry him back to the boats. Have the medical team ready. We'll take it slow getting him back," he reported calmly. He looked at Carol and winked. "Over," he finished. When he looked up at his huge friend his face was deadly serious. "Thought you were a goner!" he choked back tears, taking the bottle of peroxide and stuffing it back in Dorf's bag. "That happened so fast!"

"Tell me about it!" Driver said.

"That thing covered seventy-five yards in about four seconds!" Sparks commented, keeping his eyes moving around them. "I didn't even get my rifle up and sighted!"

"I didn't have a clear shot," Mark said. "I thought for sure I was watching my best friend die! I mean, it's bad enough losing him to a brain box, but this was too much!"

"Well, I figure if I date a really beautiful woman, she'll attract other beautiful women and we can find a short one for you to date," Dorf teased, resting a hand on Mark's shoulder.

"Hope she's not too picky about the men she hangs out with!" Sparks commented. Mark's rifle suddenly spun and caught Sparks behind the knee.

"Oops! Sorry!" Mark apologized insincerely as Sparks fell forward with a cry, hamming it up for all it was worth.

"I don't believe this!" Carol said, throwing up her hands. "My man is standing here leaking blood and you're joking about finding dates!"

"Who's joking?" Driver asked, looking at her with a straight face.

"I am kinda leaking blood here. Maybe we should get back to the boats," Dorf suggested with a grin at his friends. He set off, grimacing at the pain as he carefully placed his feet, once again watching for every danger. Carol followed him and Mark quickly hurried past, taking point again, while Sparks kept the rear watch this time. By the time they arrived at the boats the medical team was ready.

"We're going to have to flush these wounds to make sure we get all the dirt and bacteria out," Dr. Axlerod warned soberly, looking closely at the bite marks on the shoulder. "These are deep!" He began to inject the local anesthetic into the area and Dorf winced with each painful shot, feeling it as a burn with the pain, but made no other sound. He was just glad that he'd survived the encounter.

"He got his claws into you, didn't he?" Dr. Penny questioned, examining the wounds on his side.

"It hurt a little," Dorf said sarcastically. Donna appeared with the local anesthetic for his side and chuckled.

"This will hurt too!" she gave a maniacal laugh and Dorf ended up grinning, before he bellowed dramatically.

"Not two at once!" he complained. "I want a lollypop! A red lollypop!" he pouted.

"No sugar! It's bad for your teeth!" Carol said from the side of the examining room. She was almost laughing.

"Are you going to say that to our kids?" Dorf asked without thinking. He blushed a deep red.

"Are we going to have some?" Carol asked, playing with her hair coyly.

Dorf opened and closed his mouth, and she gave him an up from under look that had him forgetting all about his pain. Carol Lowe was a beautiful woman who could have graced any fashion magazine or silver screen, and Dorf often wondered that she didn't.

"Stop that!" Donna commanded sternly to Carol. "You're distracting my patient from the pain. I want him to feel the pain!" she was finished giving him shots, but Carol burst out laughing. Donna turned to Dorf. "Close your mouth. You look like a fish out of water!"

An hour later René patted his good shoulder after finishing the last bandage. She looked at Dorf seriously.

"We're going to keep you for observation. Many physicians underestimate the power of Pasteurella multocida bacteria. No one on this staff is going to make that mistake. However, judging by your health and vitality I'd say you have a pretty good chance of getting out of quarantine in three or four days," her head was turned toward Carol as she said the last and she winked at her friend. Carol kept her face straight.

"I guess I'll see you in three or four days then," she said to Dorf, standing up from leaning on the counter.

"Quarantine!" Dorf sputtered! "Quarantine?"

"Pureed lima beans mixed with fish oil will put him right in no time!" Donna said, entering the fun.

"Oh, Hell no!" Dorf croaked, standing up.

"Just don't lift anything for a few days, and no exercise until I clear you," Will said, coming into the room with a huge grin on his face.

"Aren't you supposed to make your patients feel safe?" Dorf asked Donna and René.

"Aren't you supposed to be a tough guy, able to take anything?" Donna asked sweetly.

"Nobody! I repeat! Nobody can take pureed lima beans mixed with fish oil!" Dorf retorted.

"Ha! We finally found something these louts fear!" Donna said with a triumphant laugh.

"I shall leave now with what little dignity I have left!" Dorf said, raising a hand with a finger pointing up. He walked out with his shoulders hunched, shuffling dramatically while the three women laughed. Carol shook her head, thinking that her boyfriend was a very special man.

"Are you okay?" Jim asked when Dorf appeared in the hall. Dorf looked at him sadly.

"They were really mean to me in there!" he whimpered dramatically. Carol came to his side and took his hand.

"Come on, wimp! I'll get you a red lollypop!" she said, shaking her head and leading him off toward their boat.

CHAPTER 26

Jim made the proper calls to the Zambian government regarding the shooting of the lion and was asked if he wanted to pay a fee to keep the lion as a trophy. He declined, stating that they left the beast where it died. He was not surprised to see a group of rangers collecting the carcass later that morning, and he welcomed them aboard to question the witnesses. It was sad to realize that a lion carcass was worth money, and these men had no reason to leave it lying there, as it should.

Every soldier had a camera on his helmet and Zeke had the footage of the attack from four different cameras to show the rangers. They agreed that Dorf had acted appropriately, trying to frighten the lion off first. His wounds, of course, had been carefully photographed by the medical staff and were offered as further evidence that he was defending his group and himself when he killed the lion.

Once more they offered the animal as a trophy and Dorf declined. "I don't hunt for trophies," he said evenly. "That's a magnificent creature, and the very last thing I wanted was to have to kill it!" he said sadly. "I think there's something morally wrong with people that hunt for trophies," he added. They could have the same thrill hunting with a camera as with a rifle, but they need to kill something. It's the kill that satisfies them. Afterwards they use the trophy to draw attention to what they've done, as if it makes them special. There is never anything special about killing!"

Jim could tell that the park rangers found Dorf's attitude different than the usual attitude of hunters in the region. He was rather proud of Dorf for expressing it so well, and saw that Carol was looking at him with renewed respect. Later that evening they gathered together to thank the Lord for protecting Dorf and his group. Everyone had seen the film. The speed of the attack had been frightening. Yet Dorf stood perfectly still, taking aim, waiting until the kill shot presented itself, at great risk to his own life. It made Jim very proud to lead such men.

Over the next several days it rained harder than ever, and much of the day, making it impossible to get out and about. Slowly the waters rose, flooding bringing stronger currents as the water crept over the land. Anchored as they were there was no danger to the boats, but the Wallace houseboat was no longer with them. Once again, they were alone and unencumbered.

No one chafed at the inactivity. Daily the science crew uncovered new information that would aid others in years to come studying the conditions of the lake. Weather patterns were carefully studied and a constant watch of the shore to measure the steady rise of the water level kept everyone interested. There were violent thunderstorms with the thunder so loud it literally shook the walls of the boats. Only the heat and constant moisture in the air dampened spirits.

Weapons were constantly checked against damage from the constant moisture, and oiled and protected against that threat. Only in the science lab and computer center was the moisture in the air controlled. Those who ventured beyond the mosquito netting reported insect swarms large enough to carry away a human. Those who did venture out wore netting around their pith helmets to keep the annoying insects from their faces.

Finally, they reached the rapids before Victoria Falls, an almost fifty mile stretch of water their boats could not navigate at this time of year, or any time of year for that matter. Jim considered that and went in search of Wade to find out if there were boats that could handle such waters. If anyone knew, it would be Wade, and his best friend did not disappoint him. They spent the better part of the morning talking about outfitting such boats for another trip Jim had planned.

Once again helicopters lifted the boats one-by-one and carried them to the upper Zambezi River, putting them down in the water at Livingstone. As before, mechanics, electricians, and security personnel checked the boats carefully before the teams once again took up residence. Visits to the falls occupied everyone for three days of photography and fun, and no one at Livingstone could complain about the company that came during the flood time and spent money buying supplies, eating in local restaurants, and touring the falls.

Once back on the boats they anchored between one of the smaller islands and the Zambia side of the upper Zambezi River, between the Falls Resort and The Royal Livingstone. Everyone toured the rain forest, Mosi-oa-tunya National Park, Victoria Falls National Park, and Zambezi National Park, spending nearly three weeks in that one spot. Work was accomplished, and well-earned recreational time simply enjoying the amazing beauty of the area. Jim and Cecilia often visited the falls, simply drinking in the beauty of sunset, or sunrise, through the haze of moisture in the air. Jim even ventured out at one place where one could lean out over the cliffs, safe from the swift water, and look below. It was, everyone agreed, a magical place.

This was a place of peaceful beauty, even with the roar of the falls in full flood. Yet behind the curtain of amazing beauty there was also danger, violence, and chaos. Disease and crime were more common than health and peace. Speaking to the missionaries of the area they learned much of the plight of the people of these South African countries, and the tale was dismal. Missionaries, Jim discovered through the years, were realists, not given to exaggeration, and he listened intently as they spoke.

Every morning during Bible Study discussions rose regarding the plight of people who lived outside of God's boundaries. Hardest of all was the realization that they could do little to ease the burden of the lost. Only God can change a heart, and only through His power can people change. It seemed hopeless, yet they knew that kind of thinking was the most dangerous of all.

Abe brought it all home one morning as he discussed II Timothy 2:15. Believers may not be able to change the world, but each person could do something positive toward that goal by following Paul's teaching to study, to be diligent, to be eager to present him or herself to God as someone who was working toward approval, striving toward the goal, because there was no shame. God didn't expect perfection and He gave approval far differently than man gives approval. It was the step-by-step diligence that won God's approval, not ultimate success. He'd taken care of that through Jesus Christ.

It was clear that every believer was at a different place in his or her life, unique, and therefore personally responsible for his or her own efforts toward being approved by God. None could judge another, for none could see into the heart of another. But Jim realized that he could judge himself if he could only remember to see himself through God's eyes. The embrace from his Lord that morning was sweet as he surrendered again to the care of his loving heavenly Father.

Soon however the time to depart this amazing place arrived and the boats began the trip upriver once more. Rain still fell heavily, and every morning the teams went out on maneuvers, practicing, training, getting ready to face Massoona and his small army. None of the men expected this to be an easy mission, because they were in enemy territory, and that always gave the enemy an edge. Training hard every day it wasn't long until Jim realized that they were once again where he wanted them all to be, riding the crest of that wave of perfection. Mind, body, and soul were in perfect tune, turning his team into a deadly enemy. They had to be deadly enemies to face the deadly enemies that waited ahead.

They stopped in at Kasane and Schuckmannsburg without mishap and finally dropped anchor at Sesheke, on the Zambia side of the river, across from Katima Mulilo. Flooding turned the river into a muddy mess with odd currents and eddies with which the bow thrusters on the riverboats often fought to keep the boats on course. Here the storms were spectacular, lightening flashing in the sky, striking water, trees, and rock with sharp cracks, thunder roaring overhead.

Massoona had spies in Sesheke, but Zeke already knew who they were, what type of radio they were using, and what towers were being used to relay the calls to base camp. Supplies were loaded onto the boats, food, fresh fruits, vegetables, frozen foods, medical supplies, and office supplies. It was a busy morning spent working hard to get everything accomplished in time to leave in the early afternoon. Zeke listened to the three radio calls that went out as they pulled away from the shore.

None of them dared follow on the river, and so their particular part of this job was over. Observe and report had been the orders, and they did this, giving details as directed. Payment had already exchanged hands and with their contract fulfilled they went back to their normal lives, never really knowing why they'd been hired and asked to perform such a task. Each one was allowed to keep his cell phone in the event that one or more should be needed for further reports. The money had been good. Job done each man returned to his life, never to know the full extent of the part he'd played in this drama.

Ten kilometers beyond the towns the riverboats pulled into a small tributary flooded enough to allow them entrance, tying off beneath overhanging trees. A full day passed as the boats were camouflaged with specially designed netting with cut leaves added to effectively hide them. That evening the crew gathered after dinner on the observation deck of River Venture Four. Jim stood when the last crewmember arrived, the men from the kitchens, and smiled at them as they took seats on the deck.

Dinner that evening had been prime rib, baked potatoes, mixed steamed vegetables, delicious rolls, and a salad and fruit bar. His men had eaten a delicious dinner, the last they would enjoy for some time, and he knew the kitchen crew had gone all out to make it the best they could. Patting his stomach, he grinned again.

"I'd like to thank the kitchen crew for that delicious meal. Like every meal they make for us, it was stunning!" he praised.

"Hear! Hear!" the men shouted in response. Abe and the crew waved in response.

When the noise died down, he spoke again. "Before Abe gives us another great Bible study, I'd like to go over the basics, one more time," he paused for the groans, smiling, knowing the men really appreciated the attention to every detail.

"Are we there yet?" FM asked as the noise died down.

"No, Mr. Miller." Jim said, grinning at his friend. "I want the Catalina to make reconnaissance runs twice every day. We are now eyes only. There are no satellites we can use at the moment, so we'll need that INTEL." Jim looked at Windy, Loony, and Ives as they nodded agreement.

"Inch and Wrench, I want you ready to use the AH-1 Super Cobra as our surprise weapon. We're facing superior numbers, but that bird will even the score and then some. Just be careful if you're flying during one of these storms!" Jim said, looking at those two men, who were sitting together with the other pilots. Several times they'd gone up during storms to get a feel of how the helicopter handled the weather. They were confident, he knew, as pilots become when they've mastered a particular skill. He turned to the kitchen crew.

"Those of you remaining behind have the defense of our boats, should they be discovered. I doubt if they will be, but we want to take every precaution. You go armed at all times." Each man who would remain behind was nodding in agreement. "Andrea is in command," Jim added, seeing the men smile and nod in agreement. There would have been a time when Finn would have argued against that, but he was a different man now. Jim smiled.

"We operate in 12 Teams. I have command of Team-2. John has command of Team-1. Tom has command of Team-3. Remember that I have our medical team in the center. We will know where everyone is at all times. Our first objective will be the transportation camp with the explosives and vehicles. We go in at night and we go in silent!" The men knew the plan and nodded. He looked around and saw that they were ready.

"Following that we hit the base camp. Any questions?" he asked. No one raised a hand. With a sigh he grinned once more.

"Let's bring everyone back," he pleaded. Nodding at Abe Jim sat down, wrapping his arm around Cecilia.

Abe stood and got the Bible study going, taking their minds from the battle to come and bringing them to focus on the Lord. Half an hour later four men led in prayer and Abe closed. An amazing sunset greeted them as they looked up from the prayer. Jim thought that this was how such missions should always begin. A time of focus on the Lord, prayer, and a reminder of the glory of the Lord to help them keep that focus.

He was especially tender and attentive to Cecilia that night, and their intimacy was especially rewarding to both. Not once did she ask him not to go or suggest that he take special care. Her faith was amazing, and it inspired him. She knew that the job they did was not only necessary, but also important. Both believed they were following God's call in their lives. That night Jim slept deeply and peacefully, rising at four in the morning, and kissing his still sleepy wife, his son, and then kissing Cecilia's swollen belly to say goodbye to their unborn child.

He took his time getting dressed, gathering, and checking his weapons, and then his pack. After he was satisfied, he checked those of his team, patting each man on the shoulder to let him know all was as it should be. None of the men ever complained about this part of the mission. Their Captain was a man of detail, and he cared about his men.

Silently the men filed off the boats onto the CH-53D Sea Stallion. Pen was at the controls, Wrench in the co-pilot seat, and Ives at Navigation and Communications, and when the last man was counted, and on the bird, Pen eased the cyclic back and the helicopter lifted off the surface of the water. From studying the transportation and storage camp they knew that no one stirred before seven o'clock, and they planned to be in place at 05:30. Two miles from the camp Pen hovered three feet above the ground while the troops leaped down and pulled away as Jim, the last man off, hit the dirt.

Anyone in camp who heard the chopper would not realize it had paused for a few seconds before moving on. In enemy territory now the men spread out, following hand signals from the three commanders and before the sound of the chopper faded, they were gone, moving into the jungle on silent feet, oblivious to the pouring rain, one with their surroundings. Jim listened and heard nothing and nodded to himself. His men were the very best.

It took them forty minutes to travel those last two miles and another ten to get into position around the camp. Even the guards were sleeping as dawn approached. Several men slipped into the camp and eliminated the guards, still making no sound, and alerting none. With their H&K MP's silenced, and set on three-round bursts, the teams moved through the camp, bringing death in the silence of the early morning.

One enemy rose to use the facilities, and everyone froze. FM, closest, rose out of the darkness and used his knife to silence the enemy, easing him to the ground. Quickly the men moved again, and within half an hour every enemy was accounted for and dead. Explosives were set to go off in two hours, just enough time to get to the ambush site. Once the explosives went off Massoona and his men would rush back to the transportation camp, and right through a deadly crossfire. At least, that was what Jim hoped he would do.

Mark took point, moving out ahead to scout the rough road that had been cut through the jungle to the base camp where Massoona planned his ambush of the boats. He would know they set off, and expect them sometime today, probably late in the afternoon. No one rushed or moved carelessly. On either side of the path, out of the mud, the men moved with exaggerated care, making as little noise as possible, eyes constantly moving, heads slowly swiveling, weapons ready. Here the jungle teamed with deadly enemies of man, much more fearsome than the human enemies ahead.

Sid Barrett saw the Viper at the same time he saw Sam Colt moving into range. He tapped Sam who moved away instantly. The snake struck, sinking its teeth into the bulletproof vest Sam was wearing, dropped to the ground and drew back to strike again. Both men leaped away, their knives flashing, both striking the serpent in its wide angular head, pinning it to the ground where it writhed for a few seconds before growing still.

Sam was sure the snake hadn't penetrated the vest, but he allowed Sid to check. When Sid was satisfied his friend was in no danger he nodded, and Sam quickly put his vest back on. When he was finished, he put a hand on Sid's shoulder and nodded once, his eyes saying "thank you" to his friend, who grinned and nodded in return. Carefully they removed their knives, cutting off the head and burying it, and then moved on.

A quarter of a mile from the base camp near the river the men faded into the jungle on either side of the road. Teams one and three took the west side, and Team two the east side of the road. While Team one and two set up for the ambush Tom led Team three further into the jungle and toward the river, planning to come in from behind in a flanking maneuver when the firefight began.

Less than ten minutes after everyone was in position the explosives went off in the storage facility, a shocking sound in the early morning light. Massoona leaped from his cot swearing profusely as he quickly dressed. If the *Bring It Up* expedition was close enough, they would hear that and be warned. Never dreaming his plans had been discovered he screamed at his men to hurry.

Soon they were marching noisily back toward the transportation camp, Massoona swearing that someone was going to pay for this, if the idiot was still alive. Coming in from behind the AH-1 Super Cobra was suddenly there, its mini-guns spitting death as it sped past. One of Massoona's men lifted a ground to air missile-launcher to fire at the speeding helicopter.

The spitting of silenced weapons surprised the men, and ten were down, including the one with the missile-launcher, before the others scattered to either side. Massoona still had forty of his sixty men alive, and screaming in rage, they began firing into the jungle, expending a great deal of ammunition. *Omega Force*, expecting this response, hunkered down and prayed that no stray bullets would find a target.

No screams of pain sounded in the eerie silence that settled over the jungle as Massoona's men began to reload. Still cursing Massoona quickly exchanged magazines. Somehow his secret plans had been leaked. He couldn't imagine they had been discovered any other way. The only thing he could think of was that Wikffels sold him out. The helicopter told him it was the men of *Bring It Up* in the jungle. That too infuriated him. It was he who should be exacting vengeance, and once again these men had interfered in his plans. How was a mystery. In the silence he raised his voice.

"I shall kill you, and then I will find your boats and rape and kill your women!" he shouted.

An arrow took Massoona's lieutenant in the neck, dropping him with a gurgling cry. That was Sam Colt, with his compound bow. He was already almost ten yards away when Massoona sprayed the area he'd occupied only seconds earlier with forty of rounds of ammunition.

From above, well hidden in the trees, *Omega Force* snipers accounted for ten more men in the space of ten seconds, while on the ground, other fire took down ten more. Massoona realized he was in grave danger and screamed out for his men to fall back to base camp where he had fortifications. Some of the men stepped out of the jungle onto the road and were met by fire from the direction of his camp.

Again, Massoona cursed. He'd seen some of his men go down, but he could see no enemies. He screamed his rage and turned in a complete circle, emptying the magazine of his AK-47, unaware that he had wounded two of his own men, and killed a third. As he drew out another magazine, cursing and screaming his vow to kill everyone on the *Bring It Up* expedition a knife touched his throat, and his threats were silenced. Fear mushroomed inside.

He turned his head to look into the eyes of Jim Shepherd, and in those eyes, he saw his death. Jim's knife thrust up through his chin and up into his brain, erupting from the skull at the top, and Massoona convulsed and died. As Jim removed his knife and wiped it clean on Massoona's uniform he snarled.

"That's a quicker death than you deserve!" he growled savagely.

An enemy soldier stepped out from behind a tree, ten yards away, and Jim dropped to his knee, bringing up his H&K Mark 23. The gun roared three times and the enemy's face disappeared in a spray of red as the body went down. Before the final shot echoed Jim was slipping back into the cover of the jungle.

More fire erupted as Massoona's troops shot wildly. Each time they fired they were exposed, and methodically brought down by snipers in the trees and enemies on the ground. Inevitably the wild firing found marks among Jim's men. MP screamed as a bullet ricocheted off a tree nearby and slammed home, just under the neck of his vest, entering high up on his back before it hit the spine of his scapula and stopped. DC took a bullet through the top of his foot, piercing his tarsus bone and exploding out of the bottom. Chance had one graze his cheek, thumping into the ground. He spun and brought up his weapon, firing a three-round burst that took the enemy center chest.

Hayseed called in Ox as he hovered over his friend, who was now gritting his teeth against the pain of his wound. Ox carefully removed the vest and looked at the wound. Carefully he treated the wound, and then immobilized MP's shoulder and gave him a shot to ease the pain. Moving cautiously Ox found DC, cut away his boot, treated the wound as best he could in the field, carefully wrapped it, and gave him a shot to ease the pain.

Slowly the firing died away as the last man died. Jim listened to his men report in and sighed. He had two seriously wounded, and four more with minor wounds. When the final tally was done, he called in the CH-53D to take the wounded back to the boats. None of the men with minor wounds went, and Ox stayed as well. MP and DC were strapped into seats and flown back to the boats where the doctors could treat them.

Bodies were lifted and carried to the six wheelers in the base camp, and then transported to the second camp inland. In the muddy crater left when the explosives went off all the bodies were dumped. FM started up one of the bulldozers and slowly filled the hole. He began by shoving felled trees into the hole, and then moving dirt, until the crater was filled. He worked for several hours until no one would be able to tell a crater had once been opened there.

While FM worked, Jim's men also worked with their captain, picking up all the shells from their own weapons, leaving no trace behind that they had ever been there. His men were thorough, and every shell was accounted for, bagged, and buried. Only the shells from Massoona's weapons remained.

"I can't wait to hear the stories about this!" Zeke said to Jim softly as they walked back to the transportation camp. Both of them were tired, dirty, and hot, but they ignored those things as only soldiers with a job to finish could. Jim shook his head.

"Judging by the superstitious nature of the people around here it will be a dark one!" he replied. Mark appeared ahead of them.

"Are there pigmies in this area?" Zeke asked with a grin. "And giants!" he added as Dorf stepped up behind Mark.

"I think the heat is getting to Uncle Zeke!" Mark said conversationally. "We need to hydrate him."

Dorf picked Zeke up and tossed him in the stream nearby. Zeke kicked and struggled, but to no avail, and as he pulled himself out of the water he scowled at Dorf, in mock anger, puffing out his chest and clenching his fists. "I was already well hydrated you overgrown lummox!" he said, pointing skyward. It was raining heavily.

"Oh! I didn't notice the rain!" Dorf lied. "It must not be as bad up here." Dorf was smiling as he said it. He was very tall, and Zeke had asked him many times what the weather was like at his altitude. With a good-natured grin Zeke walked back to the group.

"Don't drink that water by the way!" he said. "I think I peed in the pool. If I find a leach on me, you're in big trouble, mister!" he added, shaking his finger at Dorf.

CHAPTER 25

Jim knew from the bantering that his men were in a good place mentally. Once again, they faced an enemy force much larger than their own and came away victorious. This one had cost them, though. DC and MP, though both would fully recover, had been seriously wounded. The disregard for human life that Massoona and his men showed infuriated Jim. He'd seen the photos of the ships they'd taken as pirates, the bodies of the crews riddled with bullets. It did not surprise Jim that the vote to terminate Massoona and his men had been unanimous. Such men lived as if both God's and man's laws did not apply to them. In the end they would see the error of that thinking, but not until the very end, when they faced the ultimate Judge, and He pronounced their final judgment. Often Jim wished he could be there and watch that final confrontation.

For a few moments he stood and looked at the camp. Behind him four men were raking away their footprints from the road, though the rain would probably obliterate any sign of their presence. He nodded once at FM who was climbing off the bulldozer. FM grinned at him. As he joined the group, he looked at Jim seriously.

"Boneheads don't take care of their equipment!" he complained. "If the rest of these vehicles runs as badly as the bulldozer, they'll never make it out of the jungle!"

"We'll alert the Zambian government that we saw these vehicles when we flew over," Jim replied. "They'll probably come out to investigate, since it looks like a military operation. I hope they take all the vehicles."

"Better them than us!" FM snorted, shaking his head.

Jim praised the men for their efforts, and listened as they reported, making a few notes, asking the right questions, and when he was finished every man had a good idea of how the plan had worked, and what adaptations had been made to ensure that it was successful. Understanding the strategies was of utmost importance to soldiers. Leading the men in a prayer of thanksgiving Jim put away his notebook and nodded. Zeke made the call for the helicopter, and they made their way to the extraction location. It was near evening when they returned to the boats.

Jim embraced his wife and son, tears filling his eyes as he held them close, saying nothing, just grateful to have returned unharmed. Cecilia was holding him tightly and RJ was bouncing in Jim's embrace. It was a moment frozen in time, and Jim realized that God had changed him deeply. The tears in his eyes told him that much, and the depth of feeling he had in his heart said the rest. He sighed and lifted a prayer of thanksgiving.

Cecilia stayed close while he showered and dressed in a fresh uniform and walked with him to the sickbay. MP was sitting up with his arm in a sling and though he looked a little worn around the edges seemed in a good frame of mind. Jim came to his bedside, and they shook hands awkwardly, because MP's right arm was the one in the sling.

"That was close!" Jim said, gripping MP's hand tightly. "Glad I didn't lose you!" he added, hot tears filling his eyes. Wiping them away he turned to the two doctors who had joined them. "How bad was it?"

"The bullet lost most of its power on the tree, gouged through his skin and stopped when it hit bone. For a bullet wound it isn't deep, and it will heal without complications. He'll have full use of his shoulder and arm after the muscles that got ripped up have a chance to heal. Four weeks and he'll be ready to work those muscles and rebuild them!" Dr. Penny said. "Those strong shoulder muscles helped slow that bullet down so it didn't damage the bone at all."

"Four weeks!" MP said with frustration.

"You keep that arm in the sling and still for four weeks!" Doc Axlerod ordered sternly. "We'll let you out of here tomorrow, but you are on restricted duty until that heals! If I think you're doing more than you should, you'll end up right back here strapped to a bed!"

"You heard the doctor!" Jim said with a smile. He turned to DC.

"How are you doing?" he asked, grasping DC's hand and bumping shoulders with his friend. DC was still pale.

"This one was a bit more serious!" Will said, putting a hand on DC's wrist and checking his pulse. "The bullet went clear through his foot and did some serious damage. Leo did a heck of a job, and apart from a nasty scar on the top and bottom of his foot, DC should recover fully. His bone will close properly, and the wounds will also close properly. We didn't sew up the bottom. It's a neat hole, about two inches in diameter, and will slowly close. We'll have to keep that clean while it closes, so he'll have to stay in here for a few days before we release him. After that he'll have it cleaned twice a day until it completely closes. He should be up and around without crutches in four to six weeks."

"That sounds painful!" DC said grimly.

"Yes!" Donna said, appearing with a steel brush and chisel she'd obviously borrowed from the mechanical crew. "It will be painful!" she lifted a small sledgehammer she'd hidden behind her and mimicked tapping the chisel and scrubbing with the brush. Jim had to fight to keep from laughing outright.

"You weren't supposed to let him see that until it was time for the first cleaning!" Will said, laughing in spite of his efforts to keep a straight face.

"This medical plan is frightful!" DC said, covering his face. Everyone laughed. Jim grinned at Donna, and she winked at him.

"It must be the fever talking!" René said, laying a soft hand on

DC's forehead. "I'll give him a shot!" she smiled at him and produced a huge hypodermic needle.

"Okay! That's just unfair!" he said, but he laughed as he said it.

"I think you're in good hands," Jim said with a grin. DC grinned back.

"How about the other men?" Jim asked, turning back to the doctors.

"They're good to go. None of them received serious wounds. Chance will have a scar," Will admitted. Just then Chance appeared in the hallway and laughed.

"Hey! It worked for Harrison Ford!" he commented. His cut was held together with butterfly bandages to decrease the size of the scar.

"He was a white feller!" Lunch Box said.

"So?" Chance asked, his eyebrows raised.

"You're black, mate!" Lunch Box replied.

"What does that have to do with it?" Chance asked.

"You should have said Michael Williams, mate," Lunch Box replied. "He couldn't get a job acting until he got his scar! According to him it was a lucky thing he got it, because it added to his rough and ready character."

"Cool! I'm going to be a famous movie star!" Chance said, his eyes big. Then he drew his eyebrows together. "Who's Michael Williams?"

"Omar Little of the *Wire*," Lunch Box replied.

"Oh yeah! Cool character!" Chance replied. "My acting career is guaranteed!"

"Uh, don't you have to know how to act?" Lunch Box grinned.

"Nah!" Chance grinned. "Half the pelicans in the movies couldn't act!"

Jim traveled through the boats, checking on the men, especially those who had received minor wounds. Cecilia heard the comments, filing them away as she listened. How these men faced such danger and accepted the wounds they received without complaint was a mystery for which she still hadn't figured the answer. Her husband's bravery both thrilled and frightened her. Yet she admitted that she wouldn't change him one little bit. He had, she knew, once again taken out the leader of the enemies, exposing himself to danger yet again. Yet here he stood, unharmed, so physically powerful she could feel his strength even though she wasn't touching him.

Once more on the river, moving against the strong current, the boats made their way north toward Chavuma Falls. Jim allowed the pace to slow as they now traveled through one of the most beautiful parts of the journey, allowing his crew to recover properly from the battle near Sesheke.

Every single day produced amazing discoveries as they passed herds of elephants, pods of hippos, and life on the floodplains. Rain continued to fall, and life settled into a peaceful pattern that brought to the crew and soldiers a deep sense of satisfaction. It was, Jim decided, a perfect six weeks.

They celebrated Christmas just north of Mongu, anchored to the shore for Christmas Eve, and all of Christmas day. People moved from boat to boat, crossing on the observation deck bridges because of the presence of crocodiles, visiting and sharing cards and presents, and enjoying the fruit baskets the kitchen crew kept full on the front decks and dining areas. Jim, John, Andrea, and Wade all made sure the men of the kitchen crew knew their efforts were appreciated, as they wove through people carrying bowls and buckets of ice.

In the afternoon the games began in a Christmas tournament that lasted until nearly ten o'clock. Everyone was in the air-conditioned dining area of his or her boat, but the noise of roaring laughter often interrupted the noises of the night, causing a momentary stillness following that was eerie as all sound ceased around them. Those on guard duty, although they only had an hour at a time, noticed it most. They would hear the roar of laughter, and all sound outside would cease, beginning seconds later as the wary animals and insects responded to the strange interruption. Only the roar of a hunter silenced the jungle so.

Later that week, on a day when the rain simply poured out of the sky as if it would never stop, a family of gorilla moved through the foliage near the shoreline. People came to the observation decks as silently as possible to watch the family of gorilla come near the river.

Mothers held their smallest offspring carefully, and the tribe seemed intent on each other constantly. A huge silverback, obviously the alpha male, stood a little apart, his brown eyes constantly moving, his nostrils constantly testing the scents on the wind and rain. Bear got some great stills of the group and especially the alpha male.

"Hey Abe, I found somebody who can arm-wrestle with you!" Fagan quipped quietly in his com-link.

Abe looked at the huge gorilla and smiled, waving at Fagan in a boat ahead of his. "I think I'd lose," he admitted with a grin at his diminutive friend. "You should challenge him!" Abe added.

Fagan puffed out his chest, rubbed his hands, and looked consideringly at the huge animal. His shoulders slumped and he began to sing quietly. "I'm reviewing the situation!" Quiet laughter followed and Jim shook his head.

Further north a herd of elephants stood in the shallow water, watching them pass. It was obvious they were used to seeing people on boats for none of them showed any fear or even curiosity. Only the alpha male watched them pass with any sign of tension, though he didn't trumpet.

Expeditions of this nature are not all excitement. Every day there were chores and work to be done, and the crew continued to do everything necessary with the usual panache. Between Lukulu and Zambezi, Dr. Dundee went on shore to gather some samples, taking Team Sniper with him.

Africa is full of deadly enemies, and today it was Earl Duncan's turn to discover just how dangerous an expedition into the wild can be. It was a Puff Adder, hiding beneath a low branch that struck. Because Earl was wearing snake-proof boots, the snake did not sink its deadly fangs into his foot, but it was large enough, and strong enough, to cause him to stumble and fall, and in the fall, it struck his hand.

Norm Geissler's boot came down on the snake before it could strike again, pinning it to the ground. Donut leaped to his feet, holding his wrist while Rock opened his knife and quickly made two deep cuts where the bite occurred. Dr. Dundee was no less swift pulling the antidote from his pack, filling a syringe, and plunging it into Duncan's arm. All five men looked at one another, their faces sober, Duncan's screwed in pain.

"Close thing, bud!" Norm said, clapping Duncan on the shoulder gently. "If it bit you in the neck, you'd be a goner!" he still held the struggling snake down and pulling his knife he quickly removed the head, just visible beyond his boot. Even then the snake head continued to bite and struggle, as if still alive. Dr. Dundee had his pack together again in seconds and with Rock on one side and Counselor on the other Earl began the painful journey back to the boat.

Somewhere along the two-hundred-yard journey he passed out and Counselor hoisted him on his shoulders and began to run. Six days later he opened his eyes in sickbay. Standing around his bed were Norm, Lee, Lloyd, and Mike. Raising his right hand, he sketched a weak wave, and looked over to see Nurses Penny and Axlerod hanging another bag of fluid and looking at a monitor.

"Ah! You're finally awake!" Dr. Penny moved into his vision, checked his pulse, listened to his heart and then looked directly into his eyes. "How's your vision?" he asked.

"I don't know, doc! There're four ugly dudes just staring at me. I thought I'd rate at least one virgin, maybe not seventy-two, but at least one! Instead, I wake up to this! Two married dames, a grizzled old cowboy, and those four ugly dudes!"

Doc Penny choked back a laugh and patted his chest. "You'll do just fine. You're out of the woods now."

"I don't think he's doing fine!" Rock said. "He said we were ugly. Obviously, his eyesight is bad!"

"Every day you lay about in that bed we have to cover for your sorry butt, soldier!" Counselor said with a scowl. Donut could see the laughter in his eyes though. "Gettin' mighty tired of carrying your duties, soldier! You rested yet?"

"Good to see you awake and recovering, mate," Michael said. "Gave us a bit of a fright, you did! Don't you know you can't shake hands with an Adder?" he winked and grinned.

"Ow!" Donut exclaimed as Donna began to unwrap his hand.

"Sorry, sweetie. This is going to be painful for a while yet," her eyes were full of mercy as she continued to unwrap the bandage.

"Sorry!" he apologized. "I guess I'm still earth bound. I can feel pain."

"It was touch and go, young man. Mike got that antidote in you just in time, or you would not be feeling any pain right now," Doc Penny said seriously.

"Thanks, Doctor Dundee. And thanks, guys," Earl choked, his voice tight with pain. The bandage was off, and he looked at his hand, black and swollen, mottled colors running up his arm. The cuts Rock made were still open and leaking slightly. To him, it all looked quite horrible, and he wondered how much skin he would lose.

Just then Barbara and Mary Ann appeared in the doorway.

"Did I hear someone was looking for a beautiful virgin?" Barbara asked. She flowed into the room, bent down, and lightly kissed Earl on the lips. Mary Ann followed, and they stood looking at him. Finally, both of them crossed their arms and began to tap their feet. When he looked confused Barbara spoke.

"Well! Which one of us do you choose?"

"We kissed him!" Mary Ann said, her hand over her mouth as if surprised.

"Yes, so what?" Barbara said.

"Now we have to marry him!" Mary Ann said.

"Darling!" they both said in unison, bending down to smother his face with kisses. When they stood up his face was covered with lipstick marks.

"Let's go prepare for the wedding!" Barbara said breathlessly, pulling Mary Ann out of the room while she looked wistfully back at Donut.

"He's sick and weak! We should get the prenuptials done now!" she wailed.

"Our sweet virgin kisses will seal his heart to us, my dear!" Barbara said in the hallway.

"Why Mr. Duncan, you're blushing like a schoolgirl!" Donna said, holding a mirror so he could see his face, covered in lipstick.

"Struth!" he breathed. But the girls had succeeded. His hand was treated and rewrapped. Playing along Duncan waited until the two nurses, his four friends, and the doctor were leaving. Suddenly he leaned forward.

"They weren't serious about a wedding, were they?" he asked. His friends laughed and the Doctor smiled at him.

"He'll recover completely," he said as he left the room.

Jim stepped into the room with Leo Axlerod by his side. Watching his man carefully Jim noted the way Earl set his face, to hide the pain he was feeling. He was still pale, and his breathing was not back to normal yet. Gearhead checked vitals and studied the chart for a few moments. He took Duncan's blood pressure and listened to his lungs and heart.

"I'm glad you're still with us," Jim said sincerely, patting Duncan carefully on his good shoulder. Even then he saw the slight wince of pain in his eyes. "Doc says you'll recover, but this is going to be the hard part. That snake's poison is going to play havoc with your system for a while, so I want you to understand that I want a full recovery. Do what the doctors tell you, no matter how you feel! Okay?"

Duncan nodded and smiled wanly. "Thanks, Shep. I'll follow orders."

"See that you do!" Jim commanded with a smile.

"How bad was it?" Duncan asked Dr. Axlerod.

"Pretty bad. The antidote in time saved your life, but I'm afraid you're in for a bit of a struggle. You'll feel very ill for several days yet, and the pain is going to be the hardest to manage. I'm not giving you any pain meds yet. I'm sorry, but we have to wait another two days before administering any of that. Try not to move or hit your hand," Gearhead said, sitting carefully on the edge of the bed. "I've read everything I can find on treating this and all the experts agree that we should wait for the pain meds."

"Thanks for everything your team did to save my hide, doc," Donut said, his eyes suddenly full of tears of gratitude.

"Well, we would have done it, even for a friend," Gearhead said. It took a moment for Donut to get it, but he grinned.

"Thanks ever so much!" Donut snorted. Holding out his right fist he bumped fists with the doctor and with Jim.

Rachel Hague wandered into the room and smiled at Donut, her green eyes huge and full of concern as she looked at him. Jim watched her and realized that she must have feelings for his handsome friend. She bent down, her long hair falling around Donut's face as she kissed him lightly on the lips.

"If I'm gonna get kissed by all these beautiful women I need to brush my teeth and shave!" Donut said as she stood up. Rachel just smiled, found a box of wipes, and began to wipe the lipstick off his face. Jim saw the blush on her neck as she worked. She'd liked being called beautiful.

Duncan was good looking in the way Elvis Presley had been good looking, with a handsome face and dark naturally thick hair. It was longer than it normally would be, because he'd been in a coma for six days, and he had six days of beard and mustache growing. Some of the men, knowing he was a good-looking kid, had teased him about having a unibrow, his thick eyebrows almost meeting in the middle of his forehead. Jim grinned.

"Maybe Rachel can help you with some of that," Jim said easily. Rachel's smile broadened and she nodded. Jim turned and left the room, wondering what lay ahead for young Duncan.

For two weeks the patient struggled with fever and pain, but refused pain medications, knowing he would heal more quickly without it. Finally, after two weeks, the swelling in his hand began to subside, the pain to lessen, and the fever and illness lessen. He'd weighed in at two hundred and twelve pounds when they brought him into sickbay. When he finally was able to get out of bed and begin to move around, he'd lost twenty-two pounds, dropping to one ninety.

Another four weeks went by with him looking pale and gaunt until his color returned, his energy came back, and he felt the return of his strength. By then they were getting ready to make the final stage of their journey from Chavuma Falls. Jim had given permission to give the teams two weeks vacation at the falls to allow Duncan to fully recover.

Zeke and Bill Kline spent those two weeks in the company of René and Tiffany Milstein. Zeke and Tiffer had paired off and Bill seemed infatuated with René, whom everyone called Hot Lips. They were beautiful women and Jim was glad to see the relationship growing.

A big surprise was Frank Miller spending much of his time with Stephanie Morris. FM had finally fallen in love, and it seemed that Stephanie felt much the same way. It was inevitable, Jim knew, that a few of his crew would eventually pair off.

Dorf and Dr. Lowe seemed to be doing well as friends, and Jim suspected they would soon fall in love and perhaps marry. Right now, everyone was in the hand-holding stage, but Jim knew that would change in time. He noted that Rachel Hague had taken advantage of his suggestion she help Duncan, the two often together. Suspecting that relationship would also blossom he sighed. Things were changing, and he hoped for the better.

His own marriage had not hampered his abilities as a soldier. It had strengthened him in ways he never expected, and it softened him in ways he needed to soften. Above that, his relationship with his Lord and Savior had changed him the most.

CHAPTER 26

It was mid February when they set off in the Sea Stallion to make the trip from Chavuma Falls to the river's source. The range for the Sea Stallion was 540 nautical miles, and the trip there and back would cover over 400 nautical miles, leaving them plenty of fuel. As a precaution two 50-gallon drums of jet fuel accompanied them on the trip.

For this trip twelve of the science team were selected including Dr. Axlerod and Nurse Axlerod. Dr. Copeland, both Dinsmores, both Greggs, Dr. Lowe, Elizabeth Minor, Dr. Mirelle, Dr. Putnam, Lynn Ross, Dr. Rysdale, and Dr. Van Haaten filled that number.

Dorf and Mark were piloting the craft, John Smith was navigating, and News was the communications officer. Twelve-Team-One filled out the rest of the passengers for this trip. Driver and Sparks with Dorf and Mark of Delta, Zulu and Firefox teams were support. Zulu included John Shepherd, Wade Adams, C. G. Franklin, and Vince Hall. Bill Dodge, Sid Barrett, Roger Corrigan, and Sam Colt were Firefox.

Dorf and Mark followed the river, two hundred feet above the ground, moving at a speed of ninety knots, while scientists hovered at the rear door and side doors, taking still photographs and video.

After thirty minutes of flying, they set down on the river allowing the science team to take samples.

Here, where few people lived, the water was purest. Yet even here the presence of man on nature was obvious. They hovered over four dead elephant carcasses, taking photographs of the mutilated faces where trophy hunters had cut away the tusks. It was sad to see the wanton destruction of such a beautiful animal. Firefox had watch and kept their eyes on the jungle around the carcasses, just in case the hunters were nearby. They saw none.

Further north they watched a hyena, leopard, and small crocodile circle a dead water buffalo carcass in the water. The crocodile tried to drag the carcass deeper into the water, but it was too large to move, and the hyena and leopard growled and threatened each other and the crocodile.

Not much later, in a clearing not far from the river in the middle of a flood plain a lone figure staggered out of the jungle, looking up at the helicopter and weakly waving before collapsing on the ground. Dorf brought the chopper down near the fallen man while Zulu rushed out with a litter to rescue him.

A group of six Hyena's appeared, dodging back and forth in obvious dismay at loosing their prey. Sam Colt, stripped to the waist, leaped from the helicopter to the pontoon with his compound bow and six arrows. He notched an arrow, crouched, drew, and fired, taking down the biggest animal with a perfectly placed shot. The arrows were four feet long. His second and third shots brought down two more animals and the Hyenas turned and fled.

Where they were the helicopter would not drift, having settled in shallow water with the pontoons on solid ground. Dorf shut down the engines so that Dr. Axlerod could work on the victim. He watched as C.G. and Vince trotted toward the helicopter with the litter between them, the wounded man a dead weight, unconscious.

"He's burning up!" R&R said as she withdrew her hand from his forehead.

"I can't see any wounds, other than scratches and minor cuts,"

Leo said as he quickly examined the man. He got his stethoscope on the man's chest and his eyes grew concerned.

"Get me some Epinephrine, STAT!" he barked. His wife handed him the vial and a hypodermic needle. Leo measured out a large dose and administered the medicine. The stethoscope went back to his chest and after a few minutes he shook his head.

"This man is in a bad way. How long to the hospital at Kalene Hill?"

"Twelve minutes, once we're in the air," Mark answered.

"Then get us in the air, please!" Leo snapped, his attention all on the patient. The man suddenly gasped, opened his eyes and looked at the doctor and nurse hovering over him. He reached up and grasped the doctor weakly.

"In my pack. Small book. It's all there!" he fell back, still breathing, unconscious again.

Fifteen minutes later they were unloading the man at the hospital to a crew of missionary doctors and nurses that had been alerted by radio. Once Leo was convinced the man was in good hands, he rejoined *Bring It Up*, making preparations to visit the source of the river. In his right hand he carried a thick journal, held closed by a leather strap and small belt buckle, in a sealed plastic bag. He handed it to Dr. Gregg.

"He insisted I take it," Leo said, looking back at the hospital. "I don't think he's going to make it, and I think he knows that," Leo admitted sadly.

"You did the best you could, under the circumstances. Leave it in God's capable hands, my friend. Alistair said, taking the book and rubbing his hand over the book beneath the clear plastic. "We will see what he has to say after we've completed our tasks here. We all understand, Leo, it is difficult for any doctor to lose someone, no matter what the circumstances," Leo nodded, grateful for the words, but in his heart of hearts he still felt keenly the loss.

"I hate losing someone!" he said sadly.

"We know," Dr. Gregg replied. "Life is precious."

Most of the day they spent at the source, taking samples, photos, and recording everything they could. Despite the rain that still fell fitfully through the day the evidence they gathered would all go into a comprehensive study that would be used for generations to come.

After lunch Dr. Gregg, his wife, and Dr. Van Haaten went back to the hospital to find whatever historical evidence they could at Kalene Hill. Team Zulu accompanied them, despite the fact that they were quite safe at the mission hospital. Protocol was always followed. The nearby Democratic Republic of the Congo necessitated that protection.

Kalene hill is a low ridge of Karoo sandstone. It lies in Lunda territory and local tradition holds that a chief created it when he found his way was blocked by a huge swamp. Calling on his ancestral spirits, he dropped a magic powder along the route he wanted to take, and dry land broke up from the marsh and formed the long hill.

The DRC is to the north and Angola to the west. It rises to a height of 1,500 meters (5,000 feet) and the hilltop had been cooler than anywhere they'd been for some time. To the west the land falls away steeply to the headwaters of the Zambezi River, where there is the Zengamina hydroelectric power generation plant, providing power to the hospital.

In the 1880s Kalene Hill was an important slave trading center, where Ovimbundu slavers came to deal with Ndembu headmen. Frederick Stanley Arnot, a Plymouth Brethren missionary, traveled through the region in 1884, the first to identify the source of the Zambezi River. Deciding that Kalene Hill would be a particularly suitable place for a mission because the cooler breezes would keep it relatively free of malaria-carrying mosquitoes he reported back to his mission. In 1905 Walter Fisher, a medical missionary that accompanied Arnot on a later visit in 1889, established a hospital at Kalene Hill with a gift of just 50 pounds. Fisher was at that time in a well-established mission in Angola, and with his wife Anna founded the Kalene Hill station at the summit of the hill. Dr. Gregg found it fascinating that porters carried in the household and medical supplies from the coast, a trip lasting two-months! He wondered if any slaves died along the way.

The original hospital was built using the traditional Angolan method of making bricks from baked anthill. Still in existence, Dr. Gregg climbed over the ruins, noting in his journal that the good Doctor Fisher operated the hospital out of his home. Wise in dealing with the natives of the area the Fishers brought in ample supplies of cloth, beads, iron tools and utensils. In exchange for these they had no difficulty hiring labor and construction proceeded quickly.

Disaster struck one cold night during the dry season, when temperatures often dipped below the freezing point at night. A spark from the fire in the kitchen set the grass roof aflame, spreading quickly and destroying all of the Fishers' trade goods, medical supplies and personal possessions. When local Europeans quickly made good the damage and more help arrived from overseas, Fisher's prestige was enhanced in the eyes of the local people by the huge tribute that he received from distant parts.

After his death in 1935 the hospital was moved to its present location at the foot of the hill. Malaria is one of the main ailments treated there, with children and pregnant women most at risk. People have travelled long distances to the hospital for treatment, most of them making the journey on foot through hostile country.

In the 1950s the present hospital was built, an airy building with brick walls and a tin roof, with around 160 beds available. Thanks to Fisher and his family there are farms, schools, a nursing school facility on site, Sakeji primary school, and a flight service.

Having exhausted their studies of the texts, diaries, and journals on site they rejoined the other teams at the flight facility to make the return journey. As they exited the hospital, they saw one of the two planes at the flight center taxying onto the runway. It was the Piper and Alistair could see a pilot and copilot talking animatedly. The small plane bounced down the runway and into the air, turning west toward Angola. Missionary pilots constantly flew emergency patients to the hospital.

A dilapidated flatbed truck from the mid-sixties chugged into the compound, the bed loaded with a dozen soldiers, most of them children, all of them smoking cigarettes and looking tough. A delegation from the DRC was bringing a wounded soldier in for treatment. Other than a sad cursory glance Alistair's party paid no more attention to them.

At the Helicopter, Firefox watched the soldiers carefully, noting that four of them had broken off and were chasing after Alistair's party. Guessing they were interested in Heidi they trotted up, forming a barrier between the women and the helicopter, walking backwards, but showing no aggression. Alistair talked to them quietly as they walked.

Two of the soldiers looked angry at the interference and made threatening gestures but stopped their advance at a call from someone from their unit in the truck. Turning back, they ran and joined the other soldiers, while Alistair's group hurried onto the helicopter. Moments later they were airborne.

Once again, they followed the river, just above the treetops, running the cameras and taking notes. Twice they set down for more samples and in the middle of a sensational thunderstorm landed near the boats, still anchored at Zambezi. Dorf taxied to the shoreline and turned the chopper just right so that the back door could drop onto dry ground. Crewmembers were there to chain it off and keep it from moving out into the river.

That evening, as they ate together on the observation deck of *River Venture* 4, the scientists filled everyone in on their studies and showed the videos and some of the more spectacular still shots. Low conversations went on as the videos unfolded the beauty of the upper Zambezi River, right up to its source.

One of the stills that caught everyone's attention was perhaps a hundred natives in brightly colored clothing lined up under the shade of trees while a nurse saw them one at a time, assessed their needs and either treated them or moved them on to someone else. No one missed the look of desperation on the faces of many waiting for treatment, most of them mothers holding small children that were gravely ill. Jim waited for a few moments and then asked the question.

"Can they treat all those patients?" he asked.

"Most of them can be treated through outpatient services. They have around a hundred and sixty beds, and those are usually all full, especially during this time of the year. Malaria carrying mosquitoes are a serious problem on the flood plains," Leo supplied the answer.

"They have a dedicated staff, and that's good," Dr. Wonderland said emphatically. "Despite that, it is never going to be enough, is it?" her eyes were sad as she looked around the room. "Not until Jesus returns. We just have to soldier on and do the best we can!" she added.

"Well said, Alice," Jim agreed, nodding his head in agreement.

"We did run into something interesting on another frontier," Alistair said. "An unfortunate explorer and adventurer discovered proof of what happened to Stephanus Johannes Paulus Kruger's famous lost treasure!"

"The man that died at the hospital?" Jim asked.

"Yes, poor chap. In his diary, which he insisted we have, are two documents indicating there is merit to his story. One is a shipping receipt for 110 crates sent by rail to Beira, and the other a telegram to a ship's captain of a Portuguese freighter bound for his home port regarding the crates and their disposition. He took both of them from the oilskin packet in a leather valise on a skeleton he found in the jungle. Photo evidence of his find suggests that the bones belonged to an agent of Kruger fleeing for his life," he looked around at everyone for a moment, the two documents on the screen in front of them with the photos.

"Kruger fled to France, didn't he?" FM asked.

"You never cease to amaze me, young man!" Alistair expressed with a grin for his muscular friend. "Full marks! Marseille, to be precise, arriving November 22, 1900. Later he moved to Oranjelust, his home in Utrecht. The loss of his wife Gezina affected him greatly. I don't think he ever recovered from that, having loved her dearly."

"I don't see any marks," Zeke quipped, looking at FM as if to study him carefully. "With full marks, shouldn't he have welts or something?"

"Full marks means that I was correct, as if on a test. One day you might rise in intelligence to the level of my shoe size," FM smirked at Zeke.

"Huh?" Zeke grunted, as if confused. FM grabbed his head.

"Thinking through that sentence gave me a headache!" he whined. "I'm spending way too much time around you brain boxes!" he pointed at Stephanie and her friends. "Help me out here guys!" he pleaded.

On cue several of the men made grunting sounds and flexed their muscles, while others growled. FM began to make the same sounds, nodding his head.

"That's better! Thanks guys!" he heaved a sigh. Jim threw his head back and laughed at the antics of his men, joining with most of the rest of the crew.

Lynn Ross began to sing the popular song from South Pacific, *I'm gonna wash that man right out of my hair!* Naturally, she knew the song well, as did some of her friends, who joined her. When they were finished, Sam Hammer lifted her hair and studied it.

"No men there! Must have worked," he observed. "Girl! You need to try my conditioner!" he said, holding one lock of her hair. "You have split ends!" his voice had changed, and he sounded quite feminine.

Sam's head was shaved, and everyone laughed again as he sat down. Lynn hugged his arm and put her head on his shoulder as she laughed with the rest. Jim was glad to see his crew had developed such trust and friendship.

"If I may?" Alistair snapped as the laughter died down. He was smiling at everyone, having enjoyed the comedy.

"Please doctor. If I laugh any harder, I'm going to pee my pants!" Barbara said with a sigh, holding her sides. Near the railing Roger Corrigan poured some of his water into the river, sounding very much like someone was peeing. "Stop that!" Barbara snapped. Corrigan, with his handsome smile and high forehead grinned wolfishly at her.

"So sorry!" he pretended to be contrite. "There was a thirsty crocodile down there," Roger added. Grinning at her wolfishly he continued. "You know they can't drink the water of the river! All that water! Doesn't it make you thirsty too?"

"Stop talking about water!" Barbara snapped, getting up quickly and heading down to the bathroom while she pointed her finger at Corrigan. "You, I will take great pleasure in punishing! Doctor, please continue!" she added as her head disappeared beneath the steps.

"I believe we can find this treasure!" Alistair said with some excitement, shaking his head at his assistant's bold threat. "The ship was lost off the cape during a storm. According to some reports the entire crew was intoxicated at the time, leading to the disaster. There were no survivors, so we won't know that until we actually locate the ship and see if any bones are still with her at the bottom of the ocean!"

"One hundred and ten crates of Kruger Rands!" Smitty breathed with excitement. "That's a lot of gold!"

"We would have to melt it down. Kruger Rands are not legal in many places," Neff reported, rubbing his hands. "We could make a museum display with a few pieces and pictures of the find to commemorate the historical event," he nodded at Dr. Gregg.

"And while we search, we can measure the red algae growth in this part of the ocean. It will give us a better idea of how fast it's growing and give me a chance to see how my nanobots affect the bacteria," Dr. Putnam said. He was obviously excited about the prospect and smiled at Dr. Gregg encouragingly, who was nodding agreement. Others were thinking along the same lines.

Jim stood, looking over the side of the boat at the river and glancing once at the shore. Turning to face everyone he spoke.

"This is going to take some hard work, folks, but we're used to that. We're going to invite representatives from the World Bank, WHO, Science representatives from neighboring countries to Victoria Falls, all expenses paid so we'll know they will come. Alice actually wrote the grant to cover some of that expense. At Victoria Falls we'll release all of our findings.

"Zeke, keep your eye on Zimbabwe. They've given us the most trouble, and the government is in chaos. I think we can expect trouble from them, especially as the results of our studies are released. Also keep an eye on our coalmining corporations. They'll fight us every step of the way. We know how they've worked in America. It will be worse here.

"Science Team! You now have four assignments, all of equal importance. Finish our study, convince the world leaders of the danger, testing our nanobot technology, and designing a search grid for the treasure hunt.

"Everyone has maintained discipline and training and I'm proud of all of you. Omega Force stay vigilant! We need to protect our science team and our boats against all threats. Let's get to work and finish this expedition with our usual panache. JR, would you please lead us in prayer," Jim finished.

John stood up and everyone grew quiet. He cleared his throat and began.

"Father, I never really understood the joy of calling You that until I had JAS. I absolutely love when he calls me Daddy. You've permitted us, Your beloved children, to speak to You this way! As omniscient, omnipresent, and omnipotent God, none can stand before You. You are holy, and still, You permit us to call You Father! We bow in awe of Your holiness, and every name You've given us in Scripture displays that holiness in unique ways. Humbly we come before You with this simple request. Help us do Your will. We can't accomplish Your will without Your power in our lives. So, we thank You in advance for the ministry of Your Holy Spirit in empowering us to accomplish Your will.

"None of us asks for safety. Your will may take us into danger, and even through the valley of the shadow of death. Since You rose from the dead, Lord Jesus, that's all of death that remains, a shadow. Instead, we ask for courage to follow You, strength to accomplish Your perfect will, and wisdom to discern the path set before us. Broken and contrite hearts seek obedience, not safety.

"Give us eyes to see Your provision in our lives to increase our trust. Let us see Your mighty power at work in our lives as our enemy seeks to destroy Your godly line, to thwart Your purpose. He will ultimately fail, for the last enemy is defeated! Please purify our hearts in Your refining fire. We can't love You yet, as You deserve, but each day You increase our love! Who are we that You should regard us in this way? I stand in awe of You, Father. I love You. Help all of us to model this life so that everyone who sees what we do, sees You at work in us. Amen."

Jim smiled as just about everyone echoed that final word. It didn't surprise him to see John wiping tears from his eyes. His own were moist. The two brothers bumped fists, confident now that God would answer.

CHAPTER 27

From Chavuma Falls to Ngonye Falls the trip down river was delightful. The rains stopped except for the occasional thunderstorm, and the vistas along the river were amazing. Here they found larger pods of hippos, some nearly two hundred in number, and along the places where the river overflowed the banks life seemed to thrive. Raider took two nights to photograph some of the larger predators, coming away with amazing photographs that would add to Bear's fame as a wildlife photographer. Some of his photographs of butterflies also won notice in the field of photography, appearing in nature magazines around the world.

At the conference in Victoria Falls the full weight of the scientific findings stunned the world. The Dinsmores, knowing how bleak the situation was, were careful to remind the ecological groups and scientists that alternatives were available. Dr. Dundee's nanobot technology had proven that the threat could be neutralized. But neutralizing the threat was not enough. Action needed to be taken to save both the water, and the wetland ecosystems.

Hypertrophication paleolimnology studies indicated just how the reduction of wetland ecosystems was affecting wildlife. They also provided much needed information about the lakes that had been formed from the dams. Perhaps the most revealing study showed how the massive reduction in emplacement of silt and associate nutrients had depleted those wetlands of life-sustaining necessities.

There was an idea presented, by the science team, to dredge the silt built up at each dam and allow the floodwaters to carry it downriver. Many thought the idea had merit, but others thought the cost of the equipment and manpower too much. Jim thought that perhaps their foundation could cover some of those costs. Only time would tell.

Sewage effluent was another sore subject, especially with governments that resisted spending money on such facilities. But the World Health Organization was adamant that changes needed to be made. It was here that Wade, and his group of engineers shown. He was able to provide plans for sewage treatment facilities that would withstand floods and quickly turn the tide against this growing threat. His ideas on funding these projects, he knew would meet with opposition from both governments and the coalmining organizations, because they would bear the brunt of financing them. Including in his presentation creative ways to finance the projects and fast track their construction got everyone's attention, some interested, some realizing their companies would bear the brunt of financing the new facilities.

Once again, the crew was made aware how wicked their world had become. False gods like money and power were cruel gods that left those that worshipped them empty and broken. Yet those who worshipped such gods were blinded to this truth.

Zeke, listening in on the chatter from the government of Zimbabwe uncovered a nefarious plot to bring the study to a full stop and discredit the expedition. Gilles Ramanantsoa was behind the plot, so it was both well conceived and wicked. The boats would be seized and evidence that the tests had been falsified planted, then discovered, discrediting the expedition. Skewed test results would demonstrate how the science team had manipulated the information to show what they wanted to show.

When he had all the information, and all the players, Zeke made his report and then prepared to give it to Jim. With a sigh he rose from his computer center and walked out to find the captain. Everyone was on board the research boats and he knew the captain was probably still on the observation deck with his wife and son. He found them there with John, Pippi and the boys. At the moment they were all watching some monkeys screaming in the trees near the water. Both boys were clapping and laughing at the antics of the simians.

"From the look on your face there is trouble brewing," Jim predicted with a grin, as Zeke handed him the file folder. "Synopsis, please, Lieutenant," Jim added, with a friendly nod at an empty chair. Zeke sat.

"Gilles Ramanantsoa has hatched a plan that actually might have worked had we not been aware of it," Zeke reported after a moment of thought. "Zimbabwe is ready to go along with it. I'll call a general meeting for after dinner tonight. Two things stand out. One, Martin Marius Wikffels will own or control ninety-nine percent of the blue diamonds on the market in about a month. Ramanantsoa is furious that he has to use his own special forces, since Massoona Maximiliano has disappeared. The Zhanzhu Triad hired a Somalian based mercenary group to take Ramanantsoa down, steal the diamonds and the laser. They outnumber Ramanantsoa's elite forces four to one and are on about the same par when it comes to skills in the field, so the battle should be long and bloody, but superior numbers will probably win, though Ramanantsoa will be on his own ground. That advantage may just even the odds. However, Ke Yi Zhanzhu and his uncle Tao are sending in Chinese operatives to clean up the mess and secure the diamonds and laser."

"That will be one insane blood bath!" John whispered, reading the report with Jim. "Do we know what assets the Chinese have?"

"Two assault boats and two small all terrain assault vehicles on the ground. They look like armored Toyota Land Cruisers with .50 caliber machine guns mounted on top. The assault boats are from the Viet Nam era!" Zeke replied. "It's all in the report."

"Good work, Zeke. Set up the meeting and we'll all talk this over then," Jim commanded, smiling at his lieutenant. Zeke grinned back.

"Uncle Zeke is watching," Zeke said as he rose and left them.

"Thoughts, ladies?" John asked, looking at Pen and Cecilia.

"Have the boats transported by night to just below Cahora Bassa Dam. The Zimbabwe government will spend days looking for us, and by the time they figure out we bypassed them, there will be nothing they can do," Pen suggested, after a few moments of thought.

"Apply some pressure and have economic sanctions promised if they do not comply with the pollution reduction plans. By the time they figure out what happened, they'll have enough problems dealing with that," Cecilia added. "We do have the attention of WHO and they are ready to apply pressure."

John swallowed dramatically and looked at Jim with a face framed in alarm. "We married these women!" he choked. Then he turned to JAS. "Son, don't ever mess with your mamma!"

Pen lashed out with her foot, knocking his chair down and John came up grinning. "See what I mean?" he said to JAS, who was giggling.

Later that night they all met together on the observation deck. Each observation deck had its own projector and a white screen, which Zeke used to show what intelligence he'd gathered. Discussion followed, some on the dangers from Zimbabwe and Ramanantsoa, some on how to handle the upcoming three-way slaughter, the blue diamonds and laser prototype, and what to do after a successful mission on both counts.

When Jim had fleshed out the plan, he gave it to Zeke. This was one time when the plan did not get flashed on the screen, because someone on land might see it. Instead, Zeke promised to send the plan to everyone on the team to study in the privacy of their rooms on their laptops. After a word of prayer, they separated and went to bed.

In the morning Zeke began to make the plans to move the boats under the cover of darkness. A British company provided the helicopters to lift the boats. The *Bring It Up* crew flew down in their own helicopters and PBY. It all happened two nights later, with utmost secrecy. Since helicopters often brought equipment, few even noticed the noise or number of choppers that arrived to move the boats. Zeke helped the charade by setting up a projector to project all six boats docked in 3-D holographic images. Under cover of darkness the boats moved to the far side of the river to be picked up.

Looking out his window during the evening the one person reporting to the Zimbabwe government troops saw the boats at dock. When he heard the choppers, he looked out, but the boats were still in place. Not until morning when he rose, later than usual, because he was up far into the night drinking, did he realize that the boats were gone. Frantically he dialed the number and reported that they were on their way through the lake toward the Kariba Dam.

By that time however, they were nearing Tete, where they would visit the mission hospital once more before heading further south to release the nanobots into the waters to study how they dealt with the red algae. The Wozniacs welcomed them joyfully and were able to report that Jim's message had gotten through. No one had tried to steal any of the mission's medical supplies. Difficulties with infant mortality and high death rates from lung diseases had not changed. Nor had the alarming rise in HIV cases. Cecilia noted that the Wozniacs looked worn and tired, as did all of the staff at the clinic.

"Aunt Millie, you look tired. So does Doc," she said with concern one evening when the Wozniacs joined them for dinner on the boats.

"Oh, we are!" Millie admitted with a tired smile. "We had a dozen children hovering on the edge of death, ranging in ages from three to seven. For the past seven days we've practically worked around the clock to save them. Yesterday we got the last one stabilized, but we've been watching them carefully, because they're not out of the woods yet."

"What was the diagnosis, what kind of viral infection are we talking about?" Cowboy asked.

"They contracted a respiratory syncytial virus infection," Doc answered after sipping from a glass of white wine. "This is really good!" he said, looking at the bottle. "Orvieto Vineyard!" he looked at Andrea. "Well done, sir!" looking back at Doc he grinned.

"The virus attacked lungs already weakened from coal dust inhalation. I didn't think the kids were going to make it, but we pumped them full of antibiotics and fluids, and drained the lungs. In the end we had to put in a shunt to drain the fluid into the abdomen." He smiled happily. "That turned the tide."

"Poor kids," D.J. spoke up, shaking her head. "You don't always win the battle, do you?" she said to Millie with deep sadness in her eyes.

"No. The mortality rate is high, especially among children. Tears filled her eyes, and she took a deep breath, wiping them away. "We do what we can."

"I'm glad these people have people like you and your team here to care for them," Jim said, putting his hand over Millie's hand gently and giving her a tender squeeze. "God will give you the strength you need. But don't forget to rest between the challenges!"

"You have truly grown, young man!" Millie said with a smile.

"You had a hand in that," Jim admitted with a smile.

After a delicious dinner the Wozniacs stayed for games and the Bible study before heading back to their clinic housing. Jim, John, Wade, and Andrea accompanied them, making sure they arrived without mishap and after saying their goodbyes the men left and returned to the boats.

Not far away Giles Ramanantsoa watched Martin Wikffels sputter in rage as his men removed all the blue diamonds from his storage facility safe. Blood soaked his golden shirt and pants. Torture had revealed every place where the diamonds were stored. Weak from loss of blood Wikffels still sputtered in rage, not fear.

"I will kill you!" he finally ground out at Ramanantsoa. "There's no place you can hide from me."

Giles smiled at Wikffels and calmly shot him in the abdomen, aiming his bullet so that it would do maximum damage and cause maximum pain. Wikffels staggered back, hit the wall, and slid to a sitting position, and then began to pant as the pain mounted.

His men paused at the shot, and then continued to work. Wikffels slowly bled out and died in agonizing pain. Ramanantsoa studied him as he went through the stages, his smile never slipping, his eyes seemingly curious. Some of his men shivered when they looked into his eyes. Screams faded to moans, which finally ceased as life left Martin Wikffels body.

Zeke, ever watchful, picked up the boats leaving the area at high speed. He accessed a satellite and studied the photos. Ramanantsoa had the blue diamonds and was running. He hit his COM.

"Jim, Ramanantsoa is running," he said tersely.

"Roger that. Get men ready and the Stallion and White Knight ready to rumble!" Jim replied.

They had a very small window of opportunity to take Ramanantsoa. He would head up the shire and would have to dock his boats, making his way toward Blantyre on shore. On the road to Blantyre, they would take them down.

Once more Omega Force set out in full battle gear. Through the darkness the two choppers flew directly to where they knew the trucks were waiting. Lazy guards, waiting the arrival of Ramanantsoa and his men shook in fear as thirty-six men appeared out of the darkness without a sound. They were bound and gagged and moved to a storage shed far from the trucks, while the mechanics worked on the engines. When they were finished, they vanished, and later the sound of helicopters could be heard as the two birds once more took to the sky.

Giles stood some distance from the trucks as they were started, fearful that the absence of his guards meant the trucks had been wired to blow up when started. The engines turned over and the trucks started, and nothing happened. He scowled for a moment. It appeared the guards had simply left without permission.

"When we find those guards, they are to die," he said softly. His lieutenant nodded in agreement.

With the men loaded on the two stake-bed trucks, and Giles in his own Range Rover, they headed out, still wary, watching ahead and to the sides. But for ten miles there was nothing and the men began to relax. That was when the engines suddenly began belching smoke and steam and came to a stop.

Dawn was still an hour away when the ominous sound of helicopters could be heard. From front and rear two guns laid down a frightening display of fire, covering every square inch of ground on either side of the vehicles, as well as front and rear. The guns stopped.

"Take off all of your clothing, leave all your weapons on the trucks with your clothing, and move into the jungle on either side of the trucks. You have ten seconds to comply." A voice said over a loudspeaker. Ramanantsoa listened to the clipped British accent and cursed. One of his men fired a single burst at the rear helicopter but his shots never reached the bird. A bullet took him in the head, and he toppled over, wounding two of his fellow soldiers as he died.

With curses the men began to remove their clothing until they were naked. The spotlights lit up the trucks like daylight. Finally, they began to jump down and move slowly into the jungle. Twelve men appeared out of the trees, fully armed, and when the men were all in the jungle, they moved to form a line facing away from the trucks. Slowly the CH-53D landed and men leaped from the bird to carry the cases of blue diamonds to the chopper. They worked in absolute silence.

Ramanantsoa cursed as the rear of his Range Roger was opened and the prototype laser was carefully removed. He had not dared leave it where any could take it, and he kept it with him for this final phase. He listened as two men talked excitedly in a foreign language. It sounded like German! Further down the line he heard two men conversing in French as the last of the blue diamonds was loaded.

As the laser was loaded onto the chopper the Super Cobra fired rounds down both sides of the road again. Giles watched the men with guns facing him and his men. They did not flinch, nor did they move for cover. He understood the warning. Anyone who left the jungle would be mowed down. Those mini guns were more than frightening.

Finally, the men all moved to the CH-53D helicopter. Giles noted the camouflage exterior. He remembered that the *Bring It Up* CH-53D was the same colors as the ship. So too was the Super Cobra, and this Super Cobra was also camouflaged. The different languages suggested NATO forces. Once the two helicopters moved away, he and his men returned to the trucks, dressed, and faced a long walk to Blantyre.

Giles did not send out scouts, and so his men walked into another ambush. For twenty long minutes a pitched battle raged about him until his last man went down with a cry. His men had made a good stand, and many of the cursed Chinese soldiers lay dead or dying. Giles raised his hands, letting his gun drop to the ground. Two Chinese men approached cautiously, one kicking the gun away, the other keeping him covered. A third appeared. Studying them as they moved, Giles weighed his chances of killing at least one before he died.

"You are Giles Ramanantsoa?" the third man to appear asked. "You will now turn over the laser and the diamonds."

"I can't," Ramanantsoa smirked. "An international group of soldiers, probably NATO, hit us ten miles from the river and took them."

The soldier questioning him watched him carefully, turned and in Mandarin shot off some orders. A small Eurocopter AS332 Super Puma lifted off the ground a few minutes later and sped down the road from which Ramanantsoa came.

"What makes you think they were NATO forces?" the officer said, turning back to Ramanantsoa.

"I heard at least two different languages. One, I think, was German, the other French, which I speak. One of the Frenchmen spoke of Angola."

"You recognized none of the soldiers. Was it the men from *Bring It Up*?

"No," Ramanantsoa said suddenly. "They have some very large men. I did not see those men." He had no way of knowing that Dorf was in the CH-53D with Bear to help load the crates. Tom Patterson and Bob Hinkle took their places, both men proud to be asked, and so well trained they were actually part of the unit.

"You are sure?" the man asked.

"Yes. Of this I am sure," he answered.

There was a silence of about seven minutes after that, during which his hands were zip-tied behind him and he was searched for weapons. They used simple zip-ties, not restraint ties. Also, they left his feet free, and he smiled. He would at least kill the man questioning him before they shot him down. After seven long minutes the report from the helicopter came in.

"You did not mention helicopters," the man doing the questioning said.

"There were two," Ramanantsoa said. "An amphibious and a Super Cobra, both without markings and both camouflaged."

As the officer turned to give the order to kill Ramanantsoa he lashed out with his foot, feeling his heel crush the windpipe of the questioner. Three bullets ripped into his chest, and he was hurled back, but he was already dead when his body hit the ground. So too was the officer that questioned him. Giles Ramanantsoa died with a smile of satisfaction on his face. One of the two men watching Ramanantsoa also spoke English. He barked out orders in Mandarin.

"Find *Bring It Up*, and then find their aircraft!" he snapped. "Someone has those diamonds and that laser. Let's make sure it is not them!"

It took them a day to track down the research boats, between Tete and Sena. All three aircraft were at Quelimane, and none were camouflaged. They were simply sitting there at the airport.

At ten o'clock the following day four patrol boats roared down the river, slowed, and took up positions around the *Bring It Up* river craft, at the moment moored to the shore. Armed Chinese soldiers covered the boats, but there was no one with a weapon. Jim appeared on the stern of his boat.

"What do you want?" he asked in Mandarin.

"We will search your boats," the leader replied.

"This is a scientific expedition. We are not armed and will offer no resistance," Jim replied.

"You give me permission to search your boats?" the leader asked, perplexed.

"You are armed, and obviously looking for something or someone. The safety of my crew is of utmost importance. I guarantee no one will offer resistance of any kind. Again, we are a scientific expedition. Please keep that in mind."

As Jim finished speaking a news helicopter from Zambia, and another from Port Elizabeth appeared. Knowing the Chinese would come, Jim had taken the precaution of inviting them to the scene. The leader looked up at the helicopters in surprise. When he discovered who they were he swore.

"You will search the boats carefully, but do not threaten or touch any of the crew!" he snapped at the officer in charge of the search. Turning to his communications officer he issued another order. "Find out what is happening that has news crews so close!"

The answer did not please him. Rio Tinto had taken over the mine in Tete that belonged to Ramanantsoa and Wikffels. Not only had they shut down all operations temporarily, but they were actively involved in moving local natives to new and better dwellings away from the harmful coal dust. That worthy company was also bringing the mine up to American standards to protect both the people and environment, to the best of their ability. Worse, it seemed that Rio Tinto was in possession of the blue diamonds, and the company had already sold many of them at auctions all over the country! How that was possible was a mystery.

The Zhanzhu Triad had no way of knowing that Jim used the diamonds as a bargaining chip in convincing Rio Tinto to take over the coal mine and lead the way in cleaning up operations. World Bank eagerly loaned funds to the company to help in these endeavors, also a deciding factor.

The search took three long hours, and when his men returned the officer on the boat realized that *Bring It Up* could not have been the force that took the diamonds and laser. There were no military weapons on board the boat, no uniforms, and none on the choppers or PBY. He'd also had the ship searched, and there were none on the ship. In Mandarin he spoke to Jim.

"We are sorry for the inconvenience we have caused you. Obviously false information was given to us. Please continue your worthy endeavor in science," Jim saw in his eyes no apology, and he had not really expected one. Once again Omega Force had proven to be an invisible force for good in the world.

Jim translated what the officer said to the news helicopters, and they moved off, following the Chinese boats as far as the Shire River. Later that day the Zhanzhu Triad learned that the laser was being studied by both British and American scientists, and that it resided in London. Receiving the report from the captain of their forces in Africa they ordered him to get his troops out of the country as quickly as possible.

Tao Ling Zhanzhu looked at his nephew Ke Yi and Mae Hao. "What do you think?" he asked.

"Vasovitch disappeared, and is probably dead, and most likely at the hands of someone on that crew," Mae Hao finally said. "There is no trace. No one knows what happened to him or how he died. I do not think we will ever be able to prove that one of them had something to do with it. Is it not interesting that Calvin Weston is part of that crew?"

"We did look into that," her brother interjected. "His cousin never contacted him by phone or email. He never contacted any family members. Also, we watched, and we did not witness any representatives of MI6 making contact with *Bring It Up*."

"Thrice now they have been in a location where things have gone badly for us," Mae continued when her brother had finished speaking. "It is not coincidence, I think. Twice, perhaps, but not three times, and not with such success! My guess is that they are spies and that the military unit that responds to their information is a NATO force of some kind."

"I have seen no evidence of that, other than them being on location three times. Yet I agree. They bear watching. Twice we know they have appeared in uniform and with weapons, and twice shown they are an elite force of fighting men and women. Where those uniforms and weapons came from is still a mystery. One report says they were borrowed for the occasion. We will not underestimate them," Tao said.

"Perhaps the pirates will discover something," Mae suggested quietly.

"We shall see!" her brother agreed, nodding.

Zeke soon had a transcript of that meeting. He smiled and nodded once.

CHAPTER 28

"It's working!" Alice Dinsmore crowed with delight. "We are seeing a significant decrease of red algae in the water!" She looked at the room full of scientists, suddenly still and looking back at her, and smiled. "We've done something significant!" she breathed. "Just look at those nanobots work. As soon as they move to another organism, the one they worked on begins destroying every similar organism around it!"

"Is there any sign of mutation?" Dr. Putnam asked quickly, coming to stand beside her. She motioned to the microscope, and he leaned down and looked.

He stood up and looked over at Iris Copeland. "Your theory proves correct. We can mutate the bacteria so that it eats itself!" he walked over and hugged her.

"Your nanobots, Dr. Copeland's idea, and our research made it happen!" John Dinsmore laughed. He pressed his transmitter.

"We are pleased to announce that our theory proves correct. The bacteria strain can be mutated so that it eats itself. In a period of time the red algae that presently inhabits these waters will cease to exist!" he crowed.

"Nulli Secundum!" sounded in his ears, with cries of *"Bring It Up!"*

mixed in. People began pouring onto the riverboat to congratulate the science team. Jim was one of the first.

He surprised everyone by hugging his science team, one at a time in a fierce hug and telling them how excited he was at their success. That night they held a celebration feast and ceremony and Jim presented them all with newly designed ribbons and awards. These he had Omega Force design for the scientists, a ribbon of green, gold, and burgundy. On the burgundy stripe at the bottom were the words "Zambezi River Expedition Scientific Merit Award. Two equal green sections with a gold section in the middle, held images. In the first green section was the image of a microscope and red algae. In the center gold section was the image of a beautiful blue Zambezi River section. On the right green section was the image of a red algae and the image for genetics.

He was not surprised when the entire science team appeared in uniform at breakfast sporting their newest ribbon in the rows of ribbons already displayed. Dress uniforms were not often worn, and after breakfast they removed them to keep them neat and clean, hanging them carefully in their closets and dressing for another day of work. After certifying their findings that day the news went out. Scientists across the globe took note of the new technology and genetic response to red algae and the science team of *Bring It Up* once more went into the annals of history.

Eighteen days later the Riverboats arrived in Quelimane. Finally, after a long and arduous expedition, the intrepid explorers climbed aboard their ship. Calvin Beardsley met Jim as he climbed down to the deck. There were twelve British Navy personnel behind Beardsley's men and Jim looked them over. Noticing his look Calvin smiled.

"Sir Angus Merril sent these twelve men to keep this ship in pristine condition for you so that I could concentrate on my work. The lads have done a marvelous job, I must say. They were a bit priggish at first but warmed up to my winning ways after about a week of tongue-lashings," Beardsley smiled. The navy men behind him remained at attention.

"At ease, men," Jim said, and the men stood at ease. It was obvious they were not fresh recruits, but men who were proud to have special duties assigned. He looked around the deck and noted that not a speck of rust or dirt was visible. "Let's inspect your work and get to know you a little better," he invited, waving them to follow him.

His inspection was thorough, and for the first time he'd left his ship, he felt that very little had to be done to bring it up to his standards. Praising the men for their great work brought smiles. He called Sir Angus and praised their work while they listened.

"Good men, those twelve," Sir Angus replied. "I sent them to help Calvin. You're paying them, of course," Sir Angus added. "There's a British destroyer coming by tomorrow. They will transfer to that ship. Please don't ask," he finally said.

"Thank you, sir," Jim smiled as he said it. "Thanks for the trust, and the loan. You can send them to do this any time."

"Do you mean that?" Sir Angus asked, surprised.

"I do," Jim replied.

"Admiral Runion said you would. Working with you blokes takes a bit of getting used to, what?" he laughed.

After hanging up Jim looked at the men for a few minutes and saw what Sir Angus liked about them. Nodding to himself he led them down to his office. Ives was already at his desk, typing away at his computer keyboard.

"Mr. Ives, would you please pay each of these worthy seamen six thousand dollars cash," he looked at the men and saw raised eyebrows. Knowing it was twice what they might earn in the Navy he smiled. They, he was sure, expected less than usual pay rates.

"No taxes, gentlemen. A gift for the excellent work you did. I will not report that I've paid you. Tell me, were you suspended from service for thirty days without pay?"

"How did you know, sir?" one of the men asked.

"The navy can sometimes be very short-sighted. I'm sure you are used to that. You stayed the thirty days, so your careers will probably survive this little mishap. How many left?" Jim answered.

"Twenty, sir," another man answered. "The navy is my life. My mates and I decided to stick it out, and Sir Angus came to our rescue. Do you know why, sir?"

"What's your name?" Jim asked the man.

"Derrick Andrews," he replied.

"Derrick, please call me Jim. Sir Angus has his reasons, and he didn't share them with me. I trust him, and I trust his judgment. My guess is that he knew you were good men the navy could ill afford to lose. Don't betray that trust, my friend," Jim said solemnly.

"I won't, sir, er, I mean, Jim," Andrews smiled crookedly. Jim grinned, knowing how awkward it was for the man to break with tradition.

"Hey Shep, are these guys staying for dinner?" Winky asked, pausing by the office door.

"They are, Winky. Please let Abe know. Thanks," Jim replied, and Winky headed away.

Ives came away from the safe with twelve stacks of bills for the men, and Jim watched as most of them checked to be sure the cash was real.

"Blimey, Jim. Can I work for you?" one of them asked.

"Maybe someday," Jim replied with a smile. "You did a fine job working for me the past month, and I thank you," he turned to Ives.

"Please extend an invitation to Beardsley and his band of thieves to join us for dinner, will you?" he asked.

"On it, Shep," Ives replied, picking up his phone. Jim nodded at the men and went to his stateroom to discover that changes had taken place there.

His stateroom was like a luxury stateroom on a cruise ship, and for that he was grateful. Cecilia deserved a beautiful home to call her own, and the stateroom and adjoining cabin for the babies was all of that. He found her standing in the nursery, turning around and around with a happy smile. And well she might, for everything had changed.

"This is perfect!" She said, throwing her arms around his neck and kissing him.

Like all ships, space was limited, and Calvin Beardsley had

become an expert in maximizing space, especially for storage. All the wood was mahogany with cedar inside the drawers, and the hardwood floors that had been installed shown beautifully, making the room look larger than it actually was. Even the stateroom had been altered and Jim had to admit, it was great.

A loft had been added, their bed above a desk with two spaces and two chairs with laptops sitting ready for use. On each end of the desk was a ladder up to the bed and once in that space Jim realized he could sit up in bed and read, as he often did, his head an inch from the polished wooden ceiling. There was even a curtain that could be pulled around the bed for privacy.

Bookshelves for their favorite books lined the wall next to the bed and on both ends track lights could be used for reading. Jim hoisted RJ up onto the bed and the little tike giggled and crawled about.

At dinner that evening, when everything had been stowed away properly and the ship readied to leave in the morning, people came into the dining room with happy smiles. Each cabin had been redone in wood, instead of metal and plastic, and everyone loved the changes. When one lived on a ship for long periods of time it was nice to have a special spot where one could relax and feel comfortable, at home. It seemed that Beardsley and his crew had done wonders with the women's cabins, making space for shoes that had not been there before and secret hideaways difficult to discover. They were ecstatic.

After a sumptuous dinner of prime rib, grilled scallops, cold and grilled shrimp, and all the fixings the crew met in the library and began to discuss the next part of their adventure in this part of the world. They were going after Paul Kruger's treasure. Once again, they were preparing for the unknown, for risks yet to be discovered, and Jim listened to the chatter and ideas with mounting excitement.

"*Sea Serpent,* a Portuguese freighter, is reported to have taken on a large shipment of crates at Beira. It then set sail for Lisbon, where the crates were to be loaded onto another freighter bound for Bilbao," Dr. Gregg said when he had the floor. The freighter put in at Port Elizabeth, restocking and heading for Cape Town. Between those two cities it disappeared without a trace.

"Two months later a large amount of money was expended trying to find the ship. In those days nearly four hundred pounds sterling was expended to no avail. That suggests that the crates were indeed filled with gold coin. Between April and August of 1901, the search lasted with no results and after that the family made no further search.

"The Kruger Rand, as you know, is synonymous with prejudice, slavery, and ethnic cleansing of the most despicable kind. It was minted with pure gold and therein lies its only value.

"However!" he paused dramatically, before continuing. "Several treasure hunters have attempted to find the ship since that time. None have succeeded. I've asked my experts to detail every known weather report around the disappearance of *Sea Serpent*. Mr. Smith and Mr. Neff have some pertinent information for us. Gentlemen, if you would take the floor, please," he gestured grandly to the two men.

"Is there a raise that comes with that promotion?" Smitty asked as he stood up and gathered his laptop and papers.

"I'm sorry, I don't understand," Dr. Gregg replied.

"You called me Mister and a gentleman," Smitty said seriously, never cracking a smile. "Is my dad here?" he looked around as though trying to spot his father. Most of the science crew chuckled at this exchange and the other soldiers laughed at Smitty.

"Ah yes! The proverbial clowning about when serious things are afoot," Dr. Gregg said, scowling at Smitty. Smitty looked at his feet. Sturdy was sitting close to him, and he pointed to his shoes.

"Those are serious things afoot!" Smitty grinned. He put his foot next to Sturdy's and looked around.

"Just get up here and tell us what you've learned, you pernicious miscreant!" Dr. Gregg snapped with a grin.

"He must be talking about you," Smitty said to Neff. In an uncharacteristic gesture Neff slapped the back of Smitty's head, propelling him forward.

"Let's get to work, miscreant!" he ordered.

"Hey!" Smitty complained. Looney shot up.

"No-no-no-no! You gotsa bow to da white man, an' say stuff like yes massa, I gets to work right now, massa, sir. Yes massa! That's all da white man wants is your respect!" Looney slapped the back of Smitty's head. He stood there, as if expecting something.

"I can't say that to you!" Smitty whined.

"An' why not, boy?" Looney asked.

"You're black!" Smitty said. Looney put his hands to his face with a mock look of horror.

"I am?" he asked. He looked around and spotted Paul Jennings. "You show him how it's done, then!" he said.

Paul didn't miss a beat. He shook his head. "I'm black too," he said.

"That's what's wrong this this crew!" Looney said, raising a hand. "There is only supposed to be one token Nigger!"

"Looney!" Dr. Gregg said with shock. "That's a horrible word!"

"Token?" Looney asked, his face a comical mask of confusion.

"Stop it!" Lynn Ross cried. "I'm going to pee my pants if I laugh any harder."

Chance raised his hand. "I believe that I'm the token black feller on this crew," he said.

"That would be me," Lee Roy Brown claimed.

"No, it must be me!" Hammer sputtered. "I'm sure it is I."

"Look at dat!" Looney exclaimed. "You gets one black man in the crew and they breeds like rabbits, now we got six! Tomorrow there will be more, I just know it!"

The Milstein twins grabbed Looney and dragged him to his seat. Jim was roaring with laughter. Looney's seat was next to Sturdy, and he looked up at the giant. For a moment he looked startled, shook his head, opened and closed his eyes and mouth and looked again.

"See! This white boy tryin' to be black, being tall and all. Brotha! You gots it all wrong. Tall black men play basketball. You look like somebody put a uniform on a Mack Truck! You gotsa look like da brotha!"

Sturdy crossed his arms and flexed his muscles and Looney swallowed dramatically. "Okay big brotha! I shuts up now," he whimpered as if terrified, ducking his head and holding his mouth with both hands.

When quiet settled over the room Jim stood, and everyone focused on him.

"I think it is sad that we live in a world that judges people based on the color of their skin, or what job they have, or how much money. Looney made us all laugh, but I get the point. We're good enough friends, and comfortable enough with each other, to joke like this. But the prejudice is still out there. It is still real. Kruger proved that, and our trip through this part of Africa proved that. Slavery is still very real and active in this country, but on this ship, and with this crew, every man and woman stands proud, confident that he or she is accepted for who he or she is. When money is more important than people, things get really bad. Thanks for the lesson, and the laughter. Now, if you please, let's get on with our meeting!" Jim nodded and sat down.

Smitty and Neff, smiling as everyone returned their attention to them, explained how a storm had probably blown the freighter far off course, but not in the way everyone thought. If the ship was damaged in the storm they would try to make for land, and they believed that the ship was probably somewhere closer to shore, than further out.

Smitty put the search grid up for everyone to see and there were groans as the grid pattern was studied. Sometimes months passed by while searching a grid pattern like this, and even then, they were not sure they would find the treasure. One could almost feel the change in the atmosphere in the library. Jim knew what it was. Resolve. Each man and woman was resolute to see the job through. He sighed with pleasure.

Four days later they entered the first grid, and the HROVs were employed as the ship began to slowly move through the water. For the pilot this was a task more of vigilance than difficult work. His job was to be sure that the ship was on course. Captain Rob, the automatic pilot helped with that, as did the computer programming, but human eyes were still the trusted checks to the system. One man in the bridge kept a constant watch for floating debris ahead, while the pilot glanced at the instruments and out to sea to be sure they were on course. There was no relaxation, reading a book, or watching something on the laptop that lay ready at hand. For four hours the pilot kept constant vigilance.

On the rest of the ship, those not involved in the actual manipulation of the HROVs were busy keeping the ship maintained. There were cables to oil against corrosion, decks and windows to clean, and a host of other jobs going on. On the maintenance deck men were busy fixing small motors and other gadgets used constantly on a ship.

Jim walked through the galley area and found the kitchen crew hard at work preparing lunch. He grabbed a piece of celery from a relish tray that was being put together by Winky, nodded his thanks, and continued his inspection. Crunching on the delicious vegetable Jim enjoyed what he was seeing. He could tell that the crew was happy to be back on the ship. The galley on the riverboats had been cramped and tiny. This one had room for everyone.

At three in the afternoon the call for all-stop was made and the ship slowed and stopped. Jim listened to the science crew.

"We have a heavy gold deposit at a depth of eighty-six feet. There's a ridge on the ocean floor here. There are also deposits of iron, suggesting old cannon and chain. Dive team, prepare to have a look, please," Dr. Flush said calmly.

Jim hurried down to the aft moon pool to get into his diving gear. Omega 1 and Zulu had dive duty. Grinning at John as he began to shed his uniform Jim looked around to be sure everyone was present. John, Wade, C.G., and Vince from Zulu were all there. Zeke, FM, and Smitty were also getting ready. Using the buddy system, they checked each other's gear carefully before stepping into the water and heading down.

FM was Jim's partner for the dive and the two men paced each other carefully as they headed for the marker that had been dropped by one of the HROVs. The water was remarkably clear, and Jim could see the other six divers around he and FM as they moved together toward the marker. There were great white sharks in these waters, and other sharks that could be aggressive, so the divers were on full alert. None came near them as they continued down towards the bottom.

"Dr. Dinsmore to *Bring It Up 1*," John Dinsmore's voice sounded tinny in Jim's ear.

"Go ahead, doctor," Jim replied. The new dive masks were working properly, and visibility remained clear. These didn't fog up like the last ones had occasionally.

"You are ten yards from target," John indicated.

"Roger that. We can see a Portuguese carrack!" Jim said, identifying the ship quickly by its unique lines and three masts. Only parts of the mast stood upwards, the others having broken. "It's not the ship we were looking for, but it is in pretty good condition."

"Yes, we can see," Alice mentioned. "Let us know what you find," she added.

Jim signaled John to take Zulu on the port side, and he took Omega 1 on the starboard side to examine the ship. Cameras on their dive masks recorded everything they saw, and Zeke was busy uploading the digital images. When the two teams met at the back, they talked to each other.

"I didn't see any damage on the port side," Wade commented.

"I didn't see any on the starboard side either," Jim reported.

"What do you suppose sank it?" John asked.

"Could be a rogue wave, or a vicious storm. She went down whole, but the way the masts are snapped I'd say a wave took her under," Smitty offered.

"Okay divers. Bow and stern, meet in the middle," Jim instructed. "Zulu take the stern; we'll take the bow." John nodded and he and his divers moved up over the deck to find a way into the ship.

At the bow Jim entered through a broken door, hanging askew and saw immediately that the ship's death had been sudden and violent. Carefully the men made their way through the ship, looking into quarters and storage rooms and marking things they wanted to raise to the surface. In the main hold they found four large wooden chests filled with gold *reals*, or *reais*. Jim lifted one of the coins for the camera to study, holding it so that both sides could be studied.

"That's a 500 *reais* gold coin issued during the reign of King

Sebastian!" Alistair's voice sounded excited. "He reigned from 1557 to 1578!"

"Yeah! Well, there are two chests full of these gold coins, and they still look pretty good," Jim grinned at the other men around him. Once again, they'd discovered an ancient lost treasure.

"What's in the other chests?" Dr. Gregg asked.

"You're not going to believe this!" John said, lifting out a flower centerpiece made of porcelain overlaid in gold. It was beautiful, a rare and beautiful design. Turning it upside down he discovered that it came from Bilbao, Spain. There were porcelain vases, also embossed or overlaid in gold, gold goblets, and ornate gold decorations, most of them molded into the shapes of various African wildlife. Every one of them was precious and worth far more than the gold!

"Sandbox on the ocean floor, to the starboard side," Goody's voice came over the mask earpieces.

"Roger that. First load coming out and divers returning to the surface. Delta and Firefox, start heading down to finish loading what we've tagged." John ordered.

Two chests were loaded into the sandbox and the divers followed the cable to the surface, stopping when necessary, passing Dorf and Viper and their teams at the mid-way point. Dorf pointed at his shark stick and up, signaling that there were sharks near the surface. All the divers nodded as they headed toward the ship.

Near the surface FM spotted the sharks. Four of the great whites circled the ship, and several bull sharks were present as well. One of the latter darted toward the divers and then darted away. They arrived at the shark cage that had been lowered in the moon pool, and John opened the trap door at the bottom so the divers could swim in, waiting with Wade, watching with shark sticks ready as a huge great white glided by, just beneath the surface.

"Wow!" FM said when his mask was off. "That big boy has to be eighteen feet long!"

"They're really quite beautiful in the water," C.G. commented, watching the huge shark as it glided away. "Too bad they're also so unpredictable." He added. John closed the trap door, last to enter and broke the surface, climbing onto dive platform with a huge grin.

"Did you see the teeth on that guy?" he asked.

"Have another look. He's trying to decide if he missed a meal!" Jim said, pointing at the shark as it glided past the cage.

"She. The shark is female," Dr. Dinsmore said over the speaker.

"Somebody tell Sturdy his date is here," FM quipped.

After the men changed into work uniforms, they headed topside. Having finished their hours of duty they had free time. All eight decided to wait for the sandbox to come up. Jim, knowing it would be at least two hours, went to the office to sign the necessary papers for salvaging the cargo of the *Lady Celeste*, and to see if anyone had tracked down the port from which she sailed.

Ives handed him the papers as he walked through the door.

"She sailed from Lisbon," he said as he gave the papers to Jim. "She was a merchant ship."

"Her last business seems to have been quite profitable," Jim replied, nodding his thanks. "Thanks, Ives."

After signing the papers that gave his company exclusive rights to the treasures discovered he brought them back to Ives, telling him he was headed up to the CIC. Ives nodded in return.

"Sharky." he said, nodding to Finn. Finn sketched a wave.

"Afternoon, Shep," he replied easily. Jim chuckled as he left the office. Finn had finally come into the fold, and he was an integral part of the crew. He rarely criticized or chastised anyone, and when he did, it usually had to do with written reports and paperwork that hadn't been filled out properly.

CHAPTER 29

Jim pressed his COMLINK button. "Are we secure out here?" he asked.

"Roger that, Shep. No ships in the vicinity. We're keeping an extra sharp eye out for pirates," Kagan replied. "I'm on the observation deck and Fingers is on the stern," he added.

"Thanks guys," Jim replied. With a smile of satisfaction, he headed up toward the deck, thinking about the piracy threat. The Zhanzhu Triad was going to use pirates. They would probably be local and most likely vicious. His team's plan for the pirates was complex but would probably ensure that none would dare try to hit his ship in the future. Zeke, he was certain, was already overseeing the setting up of all the holographic units that would be used.

On deck excitement ran high as the crane began bringing up the four chests. Jim stepped up beside his stepfather and mother.

"I always thought I would miss my museum and my studies there," Alistair said without looking at Jim. "This is truly far better than anything I imagined. What an adventurous life we lead chasing after lost treasures!"

"Every ship we find at the bottom of the ocean is a treasure, Dad," Jim said quietly, putting an arm around his stepfather's shoulders.

"Yes. We are seeing pieces of history that have been lost. Just the photos alone of the carrack have given me enough material to write an entire treatise on commercial trade in that era. I'm seeing things I never would have witnessed in the museum, or on my digs. On a dig it was all about discovery, as it is here, but digging in the ground is much easier than recovering history from beneath the ocean! And that map you photographed! What a find!" Alistair was crackling with energy and Jim smiled across him at his mother.

Finally, the sandbox rose to the surface, with the eight divers who had risen with it to avoid a confrontation with the sharks swimming about the ship. Majestically shedding water that formed a rainbow the platform rose above the deck and the crane turned, setting it down gently. Bulldog appeared with hoses and began to spray the chests and the sandbox, washing the saline and sand away quickly.

Carrying their fins, the divers headed below to change, appearing twenty minutes later to help dismantle the sandbox, store it properly, and clean the deck. In companionable quiet the men worked together, making the job go much faster, as Dr. Gregg, Dr. Mirelle, and Dr. Van Haaten cataloged everything. That quiet business said volumes about the crew and their dedication to detail. Jim swelled with pride.

It took four men to move each chest. In pirate movies the chests were always huge, making Jim laugh when he thought about the weight of filling such a space with gold. These chests might have been eighteen inches square, and none had the typical rounded tops. Made of iron, much of it rusted away, each chest was now inside an aluminum alloy chest to protect it from coming apart.

Once the deck was clear and passed inspection the ship began to move again, still following the grid pattern, looking for *Lady Celeste*. Over the next several days they uncovered a World War II Panzer tank that had obviously broken away and gone over the side, two cargo planes from the 1930s era, two British PT boats, a German destroyer from World War I, and a steamer from the late 1800s.

Each of these vessels gave them artifacts that could be offered at auction, and deeper insights into the history of those times. One of the cargo planes carried fine china from various parts of the world, most of which was broken in the crash. Only a few pieces remained unbroken, two of them worth thousands of dollars. The instruments that could be salvaged were carefully cleaned and prepared, and if necessary repaired, ready for museum display.

On the twenty-second day of their search the HROVs picked up another heavy gold deposit. Jim watched from the CIC as Sniper and Nightfall dove to one hundred and six feet to discover *Lady Celeste*. Looking at the pictures on the computer screens Jim could see why the ship never made land.

Her one funnel had been sheared off, the lifeboats aft smashed flat, the canopy over the rear deck torn away and the mast in the bow gone. Damage like this was done when a huge wave came down on a ship. Burning around the bridge roof was evidence that they had somehow gotten the engine going again and headed for shore. But the ship had burst seams and slowly sank before they ever reached safety. It looked as though she'd gone down in heavy weather. There had been no survivors.

It took them four days to cut through to the hold in which the boxes of Kruger Rands were stored. The Rands had been encased in hardwood cases, which were still intact. Two days later the winch lifted the last cases to the deck. Each case was emptied, the nearly petrified wood dropped back into the ocean, and the gold pieces melted and poured into the *Bring It Up* brick molds Neff made earlier. Each gold ingot was stamped with the company logo.

Steve was in his element, purifying the gold to the highest standards, and when he was done each brick was cooled and then stored in the safe in the secret war room. Later that evening the crew gathered for dinner and when everyone had made good headway into the delicious food Jim stood up. Silence settled quickly.

"Dr. Dinsmore proposed an idea earlier this afternoon. I'd like to share it with you. John suggested that we use a portion of this gold to finance the efforts to clean up the Zambezi River. The funds would be managed by the three mission organizations we visited during our trip up and down the river. He suggested twenty-five percent. I'll open the floor for suggestions," he waited.

Wade stood up first. "I think it is a good start, but I also think we can add some more unexpected capital to the project. Ramanantsoa's properties are significant, and we found the deeds to all of his properties in his Range Rover. I don't think he even knew we'd found them. Also, Massoona Maximiliano's compound could be seized by the Madagascar government, consequently auctioned, and the funds used to help clean up the red algae. Those properties will add a substantial amount to the cleanup efforts," Wade looked around as everyone began to clap.

"Great idea!" Jim said when quiet settled again. "The World Bank should be able to pressure the government of Madagascar to do just that with Massoona's property. If we have the deeds to Ramanantsoa's properties, we should turn them over to the proper authorities with the same suggestion. Did Gilles have any children?" Jim looked at Cecilia.

"No. He had no family and he never married," Cecilia replied. "Most of his properties were in Madagascar, so the government should fall in with our suggestion on using the money from the sale. Offer the government twenty percent of the sale as a reasonable fee for the service," she suggested.

"Any other suggestions?" Jim asked after a moment of silence. "Okay. All in favor signify by saying 'I', please." When the words died out, he looked around. "Those not in favor signify by like sign." No one spoke. Jim smiled.

"You have no idea how proud it makes John and me to lead a crew such as this. Nulli Secundum!" he snapped the last two words loudly.

"Nulli Secundum!" thundered in the dining room.

"Now!" he said when quiet settled. "Let's finish this exquisite meal and then enjoy the evening. At twenty-one hundred hours we will meet in the library to discuss the pirate threat. We're going to be in the Mozambique Channel in a few days and I'm sure that pirates will hit us," he sat down as conversations sprang up around him, most about the clean up efforts.

"I say, boys," Alistair said, leaning in so that both Jim and John drew closer. "Prepare for a mission that will necessitate us to go to Egypt, following the Nile and other bodies of water into Sudan, and perhaps even central Africa. Southern Sudan, Congo, Ethiopia, even Kenya."

"What have you discovered, Dad?" John asked, punching Alistair lightly on the shoulder.

"Remember that wooden map you found in the carrack?" he asked, winking at both of them before putting a finger up beside his nose. "There are three cities on that map that don't exist! Two are supposedly vast diamond mines, one of them belonging to Solomon, and another by Tutmose II and his wife, Hatshepsut. Both cities were lost less than fifty years after being founded, and no one, to this point, knows why! The third city is reported to be an emerald mine founded by Menelik during the Solomonic dynasty of Ethiopia. By the time of Negus, the city was lost, and rumor has it that great pains were taken to find it. No one has. Not yet!"

"What makes you think those are the cities you're talking about?" John asked, interested. Jim nodded, having the same question.

"Because the cities are not named! Two are marked with a tiny diamond chip, and an emerald chip marks the third! The map itself is from 300 **A.D.** I think that captain was looking for those cities! I think he found that map and was on his way to try to discover the cities for his king. That explains the huge amount of gold and wonderful pieces we found!" Alistair beamed at both of them, nodding his head vigorously. "One of the artifacts you brought up is from Thebes. He couldn't take his ship up the Nile, so he was trying another way!"

"The sale of the gold from that carrack would certainly finance an expedition," Jim said quietly, his eyes alight with excitement.

"Oh no!" Cecilia said suddenly, noticing her husband's eyes. "What are the three of you planning now?"

Jim leaned over and kissed her. "I'll tell you later, love of my life," he whispered in her ear. Cecilia's neck grew red with the blush of pleasure and Jim kissed her again. Whatever it was, she knew he would indeed fill her in on all the details. Sighing with pleasure she snuggled into him. He continued touching her gently while he and John talked excitedly.

After dinner they went together to their cabin and spent the time with RJ, playing and laughing as they prepared him for bed. When they were sure he was asleep they left the cabin quietly. Any crying or noise he made would be heard by both of them. RJ usually slept quite soundly.

In the library the plans for the pirate raid were carefully laid out. Many of the crew laughed at the whole plan, but the soldiers didn't join. Pirates were deadly enemies. By the time they boarded *Sea Venture* the crew would be safely tucked away in the war room, and *Omega Force* would be in their teams of four to take the pirates down deep in the ship itself.

Zeke showed Jim the ghostly images of the crew that would appear at just the right moment when a pirate or two could be taken down without discovery. Jim had to admit that the specters were indeed ghostly in appearance. Many even spoke.

Their words were whispered and echoed in the corridors of the ship, enabled by a host of hidden speakers. Messages were simple. "Die. Dead men tell no tales. Death comes!" The voice saying: "Dead men tell no tales" was the most spectral of all the voices and quite impressive.

"If this doesn't work you can always get a job at Universal Studios or Disney World," Wade said, clapping Zeke on the shoulder.

"It was fun putting it all together," News and Zeke said in unison, and then laughed at each other. "It might be fun to do this on a ship of some smarmy admiral we run into in the future," Zeke added.

Returning to the Mozambique Channel seemed somewhat anticlimactic, though they did weather a particularly ugly storm that gathered quickly and formed deadly waves. *Sea Venture* weathered the storm without mishap and was called upon to rescue a cruise ship and tow it to Maputo. The sorry state of the cruise ship angered Jim, but he kept his opinions of the company that ran such cruises private.

Excitement mounted as the scientists took samples and discovered that the red algae count was vastly reduced. *Sea Venture's* science team had already stunned the scientific world by making its findings public. *Bring It Up* already owned the patent on the nanobots, but none of the other information was patented or copyrighted. They did warn the scientists of the world that red algae was capable of mutating, and would in the future, pose future threats to the oxygen in the ocean's waters, and danger to all aquatic sea life.

CHAPTER 30

When the pirates attacked it was, as usual, in broad daylight. A warning klaxon sounded, the automatic pilot was set, the CIC locked down, and everyone deployed. Once the teams were suited up and armed the crew got into the war room and watched the walls close. They were all safe. *Omega Force* disappeared in the bowls of the ship, shadows among the shadows. The power to these sections was cut, plunging them into darkness. The computers controlled the systems and no matter how hard the pirates tried, they would be unable to break into the bridge, the CIC, or the engine room.

Slowly the ship came to a stop, the bow thrusters keeping it pointed forward, the engines working at keeping the ship in that position. The pirates scrambled on board, expecting to be fired upon, only to discover that the deck was empty.

Forming up, their captain split them in three groups, sending them off in those groups to search the ship for the crew. He took his men up to the bridge, and after shooting at the locking mechanism and using a sledgehammer to try to break the glass he stormed aft toward the CIC. It too proved to be empty, but also impenetrable. His men seeking the engine room reported the same. The captain cursed.

"Find them!" he snarled into his radio. "Find the gold!"

Two men, their rifles forward and ready to fire, moved cautiously down a corridor not far from the engine room. Suddenly a ghostly apparition appeared in the corridor before them, hanging in space, and a spectral voice whispered, "die."

Shaking in fear the pirate in the rear did not hear FM slip up behind him, nor did his partner hear him as FM lowered him to the deck. When he did not answer his partner turned and looked for him, finding him on the floor, his throat slit. Another apparition appeared behind his fallen partner. "Death comes," it whispered.

He fired his rifle, the sound loud in the silence and the ghost suddenly had glowing red eyes. In fear he tried to cry out, but Jim was behind him, and his cry was never uttered. He too was lowered quietly to the deck, his throat slit.

"You deserved a slower death!" Jim whispered as he disappeared into the darkness again.

Delta met another pair with similar results, Jack Boswell and Mark Drumheiser dispatching the pirates with quiet deadliness. On the upper deck the captain listened to the fear in the voices of his men as they encountered ghosts and died. By the time Zulu, Firefox, Knife, Raider, Sniper, and Nightfall were finished he and his three men were the only ones left.

They went together, moving cautiously, deeper, and deeper into the ship, finding their fallen comrades one by one, all with throats slit, all with horror on their faces. All four of them saw the apparition at the same time, and they recognized it as Captain Shepherd. He floated in the air above the floor, his body visible from the knees up, his face covered in blood, his eyes filled with threat.

"Dead men tell no tales." A spectral voice echoed, as if coming from far away. Real hands grabbed their ankles, and they were jerked to the catwalk upon which they stood, dying just as silently as all the rest of the men.

"That's it," Zeke said quietly, wiping his knife on the shirt of the pirate he'd just killed. He lifted his radio.

"System subset zero, zero, one, zero, one," he commanded. Jim heard the engines power up and the lights came on in the corridors. He smiled grimly.

"Work on your video and get it out there on the net. We'll clean everything up," Zeke nodded and headed topside.

Every crewmember knew what to do, and the bodies were soon committed to the deep, weighted and wrapped for a burial at sea, sent below through the moon pools. Blood was carefully wiped away and everything cleaned so that no forensic evidence remained of the pirates. The bags from the vacuum cleaners were carefully emptied and tossed into the solar incinerator that burned so hot it left no residue. By the time they were boarded by the Madagascar Coast Guard everyone was back at work.

"You were boarded by pirates," the captain of the vessel said as he stepped down onto the deck and met Jim.

"Yes," Jim said quietly. "They are all dead."

"You killed them?" the man was obviously surprised, and immediately suspicious. But this crew was world famous, and it had done his country a great service. He thought he was boarding a ship in the hands of the pirates, and his men had been armed and ready. They stood now confused. He too was momentarily confused.

"I will need to search your ship. You understand, yes?" he asked, watching Jim carefully. Jim smiled a genuine smile.

"Please feel free to look anywhere. We will cooperate and stay out of your way."

"You do not insist on shadowing my men as they search?" the captain asked, his eyebrows climbing his forehead.

"I do not," Jim replied. "Please carry out your search," he was polite, nodding to the officer in an encouraging way.

"And the bodies?" the captain asked.

"That we don't know," Jim replied. "I have a man checking the camera feeds from our security cameras."

The captain and his men took several hours to search the ship. No evidence of the pirates was discovered, no traces of blood, nothing. Everywhere the Captain traveled he found a ship in pristine condition, a model crew, and busy hands. Even in the science labs they were busy with their study of the red algae, one of the reasons they were so well known. The threat was fading, much to his relief.

Finally, he found Jim on the compass deck, plotting a course with Smitty. The two were leaning over the chart, talking easily but they stood up straight as the captain walked over.

"There is no sign of struggle," the captain said carefully.

"Come, Captain. You must have seen the damage from the bullets from the Pirate's guns on the third and fourth levels!" Jim said with an easy smile.

"So, you retreated from them, luring them down where you had the advantage?" the captain asked after a few moments of thought.

"They were not shooting at any of us," Jim replied.

"They did not find you?" the captain was obviously perplexed.

"On a ship with two moon pools one does not need to hide in the ship," Jim laughed. "Surely you saw all the scuba and diving gear."

"Then who killed the pirates?" the captain finally snapped.

"After an hour there were no pirates on the ship. We searched, but we found no trace of them. Their boats were still attached to our ship, but not one of them could be found.

"Yes. We saw your men looking over the side. That was just after your ship began moving again."

"Odd, wouldn't you say?" Jim asked, spreading his arms. "They just weren't there."

"Where will you go now?" the captain asked after a long silence.

"Mahajanga," Jim replied. "Some of our crew will fly to Antananarivo to speak with your government, and representatives from other parts of the world," as Jim finished speaking Zeke appeared.

"Hey Shep! I have footage of the pirates on board our ship!" he said eagerly. "Our security cameras caught it all!"

"Do you know what happened to them?" Jim asked.

"I know what the security cameras saw. I'm not saying any more!" Zeke replied mysteriously, crossing himself as he spoke.

"May I view these images?" the captain asked.

"Please. Follow me," Jim said, leading the way to the CIC.

Even though Jim knew what was going to be on the tape it still gave him chills. Zeke's cameras were not the usual grainy images, but clear sharp images of every part of the ship. The entire crew could be seen going below and nearly half an hour passed before the first pirate leaped to the deck and turned, his assault rifle ready. The camera showed the surprise on his face when he found no enemies to face him. Another camera showed the last of the crew members stepping into the water in the moon pool, video Zeke shot earlier for that purpose.

As the ship stopped several of the corridors were plunged into darkness. The captain drew in his breath as he watched the first ghost appear. Behind the pirate in the rear a spectral figure rose, claws extended, and the pirate died as the creature seemed to follow his body down in slow motion, its jaws clamped around the throat of the victim, and then the figure simply vanished. The other pirate finally realized his partner was not responding and turned to see yet another spectral figure hanging in the air. Another beast appeared behind that pirate, and he too died, making not one sound. This time the creature backed away on all fours, its jaws dripping blood, red eyes glowing in the glow of a flashlight that lay on the floor.

"What is that?" the captain cried.

"I don't know," Jim replied in a tense voice, playing his part perfectly, crossing himself.

"Your ship is haunted!" the captain said. He continued to watch as other ghosts appeared on other cameras and other pirates died horribly. Finally, the pirate captain and his three men appeared, and beasts rose from beneath them, the apparitions actually appearing to come out of the floor, to bring them down and kill them. Suddenly it seemed as if an entire pack of the beasts was there, growling horribly and crunching bones as they appeared to eat the pirates. When they finished licking the floor they moved on, and two by two the other bodies were devoured, until none remained. Finally, the beasts themselves became bright lights that hovered for a moment, and then rose through the ship toward the skies.

The captain was shaken. He looked at Jim for a long time. "I saw those beings leave your ship!" he breathed finally. "So also did several of my men. We could not explain it. Thirty-six lights that simply faded and were gone as they rose!" he crossed himself this time. "I humbly ask permission to leave your ship now," he requested in a quavery voice.

Jim walked with him to the gangplank and a gray and shaking man left his ship. When he returned to the CIC he finally let go of his laughter.

"Did you see his face!" Zeke asked, laughing with Jim. "I thought he was going to wet himself!"

"He was thinking of all that time he spent below," Jim roared.

Word spread, as it does, and the reputation of *Bring It Up* increased. In some circles it was a reputation of fear. Many saw the video, and when the video was finally released it was released with the official report of the Coast Guard Captain. Those who were superstitious would fear going below. Others would laugh at the video for what it was, good entertainment, and would know that somehow the forces on the ship overpowered the pirates. That was good.

As fall approached *Sea Venture* finally put in at Seagirt Marine Terminal in Baltimore harbor. Everyone would be on vacation until the twelfth of January when they would return to the ship and prepare for another adventure at sea. After a week at Live Oak Retreat, Andrea flew to Italy to join Rosa. They would return at Christmas together. Jim, John, Wade, Alistair, and their wives stayed together, with several of the crew, at Live Oak Retreat, while others headed home to visit family. For now, it was good to rest.